MIXED BUSINESS

MIXED BUSINESS

ALAN WEARNE

PUNCHER & WATTMANN

First published in 2024
Published by Puncher & Wattmann
PO Box 279
Waratah NSW 2024

http://www.puncherandwattmann.com
puncherandwattmann@bigpond.com

NATIONAL
LIBRARY
OF AUSTRALIA

A cataloguing entry is available from the National Library of Australia.

ISBN   9781922186553

Cover design by Joe Scerri based on original artwork 'Chase, 2010' by Bevan Honey

Printed by Lightning Source International

Mixed Business is dedicated to my brothers Bruce and David.

Contents

I In Our Four Dominions

for Louise Byrne

In 1913 a young English journalist visits Australia for the first time.

Pride

'Proud? Most certainly we're proud!
In this land we've a first of everything!'
And Mayor Moriarty, seed merchant,
escorted me up, through, down and around
his suburb's first Town Hall.
        And if, as I were to find, his womenfolk
checked him, just one side of humbug,
still this silly man seemed to prefer them
schooled and daunting.
                Jean surely was.
    'We've a surprise,' the Mayor seemed pleased.
'My most brilliant girl has volunteered
to enlighten you on what our younger set believes,
and if our younger set means Jean,
and Jean believes what Jean believes,
I'm sure you will be charmed and thus adjust.'
        I had to. For outside his Mayoral chambers,
with a pixie-slight demeanour I sensed would prove
disarmingly robust, there she was.
And chaperoned by their municipal chauffeur
we headed to the Boat House where in its Palm Court,
to an overlay of tea dance numbers
flirtatious chat commenced.
        'Though I've been introduced as Jean,
you may refer to me as Minx, father does:
His Worship being something out of Mr Arnold Bennett,
I'm something out of Mr H G Wells.
Welcome to that kind of place where women,
in case you weren't aware,
possess the vote, and our last PM before the last
was Affable Alf.'
           That kind of place and
these kinds of women, with Jean forever to remain

this small and bustling girl with eyebrows raised
and quizzing sidelong glances.

    Attempting one better to top her catalogue
seemed my only option.

        'Recall the attribution,'
she was asked, *from our Colonial Correspondent?*
Well Miss Moriarty, I am he!'

        'Colonial…'
and the sidelong glance returned, 'elsewhere may think themselves
in such a fashion, Australians though are a Commonwealth now,
up-to-date as can be allowed and when we aren't…
let's make it up!'

    Little 'side' then in this most pragmatic
of Dominions, merely an insisting cheek that I,
this visiting London journalist *Should try us out!*

    The very reason I was there.

Dominions

    My uncle, an outward-looking man,
also was my editor. And believing I wasn't yet a drab,
and trusting I wrote both wittily and well,
made this proposal.

        'On balance then,' he stated
(since he loved to state) 'what quarter of our globe
seems better blest than where we British truly reign
yet fairly rule? Reasonable?' he asked.

    'Very,' I replied as he arose and pointed
to his map.

        'India,' he announced, 'our jewel…
Africa, our mission…whilst for a spread of sheer diversity:
Middle and Far East, the South Seas and the Caribbean. But…'
he paused (since he also loved to pause)
'what of those partners-in-empire, our Dominions?
Having learnt so well from us (and aren't they us?)
what indeed might we learn from them?'

    Knowing who they were,
he and Britain wished to know who and what
they *truly* were. And such would be my brief:
(with backing from certain chaps of clout
and six months touring our Dominions) to discover

who indeed and what indeed they were.

Somewhere my uncle had his list:
those he knew, those he'd met and those his correspondents:
chaps of clout in Cape Town and Melbourne,
Sydney and Auckland, Vancouver and Toronto.

And though he planned I'd meet them Uncle warned:
'In ten or twenty years they may or will
be heading fogey. So as an extra brief seek out
those men of your age, chaps of the future,
for both articles and an eventual book.'

Moriartys

'And such if you like, Miss Moriarty,'
(how we enjoyed such fake formalities!)
'are the reasons I am here.'

'Chaps of clout?' quizzed and answered Jean.
'Chaps of the future? Seed merchant mayors or
seed merchant mayors-in-training?'

Though this Sunday
might I be free to visit all the family at their Bella Vista?

If Father may have seemed the Minister,
Mother it was who ran the Ministry.

'Book us into your calendar,'
he might say.

'Now,' she'd fine-tune, since someone
must employ that side of the initiative,
'let's arrange those dates…'

She allowed him though
his MC role: 'May we present, starting with our eldest,
Heléna, Jean (you've met) Edward (Ted)
Stella and Vera our own Gemini.'

Yes, let's meet
the Moriartys: first up their medium pacer,
middle order, all-rounder of a son who,
beyond even that, was a wag confessing:
'Surrounded by such girls-and-girls they'll say
he's spoilt, spoilt with all a lightweight's faults,
excepting you can trust him:
for if and when a stoush arrives he'll be there,
he'll have to be.'

And doubtless believing
After saying things like that, one does things like this
Ted stroked his trim moustache.
        'And how did you find us Moriartys?'
Mother asked.
                I had an uncle taking pride
in just how many men he knew throughout
the Empire, her husband being a friend of
one of these.
                'I think we can agree,'
Ted offered, 'that's how our Empire's run.
One sends a cable knowing it'll be read,
correct?'
        And more than opinions
he seemed to offer his very self as a small, yet necessary
anchor of Empire: you commenced with Ted,
then his father, his father's friend, my uncle and next to him
the Colonial Office, the India Office, the Foreign Office and
who-knew-what beyond.
        'We're so glad to know,' Jean humoured him,
'your place in the great-Imperial-chain-of-being.'
        'Do you play charades?' a Gemini enquired.
        I had been known to.
                        'Then please return,
return and play!' her twin kept urging.
        'And this is Heléna,' Father intervened,
'with an accent on her second e, now don't forget,
the Empire's only one. She invented that when she
was twelve.' (For he was a man well proud
of all he was connected to.)
        'And may I book you in?' Heléna asked.
'I've heaps to be informed upon.'
        The twins re-intervened:
might we make a picnic and watch Teddy play?
And did I play?
        (Always out first ball, alas.)
        We embarked for dinner, we disembarked
from dinner. Soon, I was told, the chauffeur
would arrive, taking me to the Windsor.
        'See our guest out will you Jean?'
See me out? Oh yes Jean would!
Was her mother thinking that somehow

I might be a man to give an extra meaning to
this daughter's life?

                    Though what extra meaning
might she need if the family supplied enough?

        'I love my little brother,' Jean confessed,
'I always have.' But then: 'So he's in college?
So he's attending university and wishes to become
Sir Edward Moriarty KC, so?' And then:
'I think all snobs are sad and that Heléna is
the saddest snob of all with not the remotest brain.
She never went to varsity whilst I did.
I studied French and wish one day to use it.
I only read French nowadays, I've very few
to speak it with…might you?

                    'Alas,' I let her know,
'my languages being purely classical, I've missed out
on all this modern stuff!'

                  With her look announcing
I can and will both understand and even enjoy this man
yes Jean liked that!

         And yet
enough of that! She'd to make it known
what kind of friend I would be getting.

        'History…' (was this some lecture?) 'still informs me,
although I'm well beyond mere Whig.
You sir see a Roundhead. But what can I,
what will I do about it? Don't suggest school mistress,
the very thought of being one and what I was
at school makes me right glad for all those girls
I'll never teach. And never please suggest the wife
of any famous man. Throughout the municipality
His Worship's constantly famous for being
His Worship, and what does that get Mother?
An avalanche of mere good works
with all their attendant tut-tut-tut.
Just give me works; but what?'

        The chauffeur had arrived, I too had works:
seeking out those with their clout who'd tell me where
we British stood, this corner of the Empire;
to meet their sons, the future, those I'd recommend to be
the kind of chaps Britain might rely upon;
and finally to interview four of the men who ran

this Commonwealth of theirs: the affable Mr Deakin,
the combative Mr Hughes, the gentlemanly Mr Fisher,
the rather plodding Mr Cook; nor could I forgo the luncheons,
dinners and smoke nights, though I sensed where I'd be
welcomed most, those weeks in Melbourne.

      ('Liberty Hall young man!' the Mayor,
her father offered, putting forth his *side*,
if his special, unaffected brand of *side*.)

      When I was younger, though hardly that much younger,
night after night entranced by some light opera soubrette,
I would return to gaze on her alone, and mouth
milady's lines.

      Unlike the stage though,
each Moriarty evening was a premiere,
and I'd make my return just to re-discover
what Jean (and even I) might be saying next.

      Name a soubrette who could announce:
'From hereafter, year-upon-year,
you men will need us more and yet still more,
need us and our vote. In those countries where we've
got the vote!'

      And later:
'You'll notice if you haven't yet,
how my older sister acts like she's some Maharani?'
(Aspects were noted if hardly that descriptive.)
'And you think *I'm* unmarried...' (Well I hadn't.)
'Poor woman's set on forgetting just how old she is
and will become. But can't. She knows she's twenty-six
and still hasn't seen England her England.
That's why His Worship's set she'll go, and go they will
in 1915, '16 or '17, to find herself this England
or a husband. For me your country may as well
be Mars.'

      Though at times we talked
of little else.

      'Even if,' she proposed, 'we're British,
as many think we are, and this is a British world,
it's far more yours than ours, yours to accept,
interpret and amend, in particular amend.
Yet this is a world which cannot last,
you've doubtless heard
On dune and headland sinks the fire,

15

and stuck on its less-than-certain edges
we're the dunes and we're the headlands.
Not so?'

        That currently was part of what
I'd set myself to find.

                  Here though was the start
of my credentials: those interviews arranged and held
with Messrs Deakin, Hughes, Fisher and Cook.
Smiling I lounged back just a touch and watched.
        'Well done,' she cheered, 'well done!
An Englishman who understands there's something
far beyond mere England in its tepid, three-week
summer!'

               Why spoil this game reminding Jean
she'd no more been there than Heléna had?
It simply underscored all I enjoyed about her,
as the Colonial Correspondent returned
(most late afternoons now) seeking to discover
what this Australian bluestocking truly thought.
        'Since,' I asked, 'women in this country vote,
what do you suppose they might want next?'
        And fearing he had made himself her foil,
Jean's latest innocent mug, their dinner table paused.
        'Why birth control!'

                     'And that's our Minx!'
With embarrassed pride her father beamed, spluttered,
then continued beaming, egging on Jean,
so that she might rise and further rising
rile her mother.

            Part comic, part preposterous,
was this some kind of game certain Dominion
families played? Well the Moriartys did
and an idea bloomed, oh how it bloomed
Jean's saying what her father wishes he could say
except his wife won't let him...
as yes the wife was riled, riled and recoiling:
'Oh must you Jean!'

            And being twenty-four yes,
yes Jean must she must.

        As being twenty-six Heléna mustn't
so she squirmed.

           Seeming as tall as Jean was tiny,

Heléna had those kinds of hands on those kinds of arms
made for sweeping, know-it-all dismissals;
though she lacked her sister's sense to check,
bemused, who or what was right before her.
　　　　　'One really tries,'
Jean had to explain, '*not* to consider
one's parent's conjugal relations.
But with the sheer variety of the Maharani, me,
Teddy and our twins, something somehow
must've happened. And she's known, Heléna's known
since birth, that if an impression's to be made
she will be the first to make it.'
　　　　　　　　　　　Which Jean didn't?
Well not with all that throaty bombast gushing
from her older sister.
　　　　　　　　'Shall we pity her?' I'd ask myself.
'Though why? How often does Heléna get her chance
to seize on any British accent, matching it with her own
refined attempts?'
　　　　　　　　Yes pity would've been considered,
except Heléna hardly understood her prattling,
nor would she ever.
　　　　　　'Yours is a land,'
I tried, 'that uses space so well:
its broad streets and roads are near to boulevards.
How old is your city? Less than eighty years,
so even better everything is new!'
　　　　　　　　　Did she flinch?
Heléna didn't need it *new*, whilst any praise for
this Dominion proved, like her father's pride
(Jean's too) in how they were forging their traditions,
foreign and perverse.
　　　　　　　　'Ah yes,' Heléna itemised,
'traditions: heat, dust, flies and boors: mutton breeding,
mutton digesting, mutton-chop whiskered boors…'
which hardly equated with those I'd met,
the trim-bearded Affable Alf for one,
who could have strolled straight into the Asquith Ministry.
　　　　　　'Out of date by forty years, Heléna!'
Jean seeing an opening had pounced.
'Those squatters are either shaved and civilised by now,
or dead.'

Thinking I'd understand what she understood
Heléna in reply was tragic:
'My sister and her most Australian twang,
I know you've heard it, I do every day.
What man will respect her if she talks like *that*?'
            I wouldn't bite the bait.
Some men might enjoy this twang if indeed
there was one; some other men, I include myself,
would near-love her, twang or no.
                        I was so pleased
I'd met a world that wasn't an unending reproduction
of certain men with whom I had attended school,
or their sisters. Rather it seemed I had been bred
to tour the Four Dominions and even more befriend
Jean Moriarty.
            If not Heléna.
For now we were to talk on what she *really* knew.
How about my club, wasn't I the member of a club?
(Once it had been proposed I be proposed.)
Did I by chance know a duke, an earl?
A marquis, baron, baronet?
I never got a chance to answer since
I must have.
                For now *her* catalogue commenced:
highwaymen and their saucy wenches,
Hearts of Oak and *Drake's Drum*,
the honest toil of simple folk and what The Bard
had given the world, yes yes, she admitted,
almost all ephemera but, but, surely it wasn't about
mere knowing one's place for no, no, it was about order,
an order seeing to it *all* flourished, was she not correct?
        Then, as we caught Jean's eye-rolling and finger-drumming
Heléna pursed a smile's preliminaries,
pleased she might show a certain toleration
towards a younger sister.
                        'So might you,'
I was asked, 'have one of these?'
as a hand was lightly flapped in Jean's direction.
        Did she mean (she did) that I had sisters?
        'Well I have two...'
                    Though none like Jean,
ushering me down the steps into Bella Vista's garden,

who bemused yet seething asked:
'You see the Maharani, hunkered there on our veranda,
taking up the white woman's burden,
staring down the hordes amassing at the gate?
Of course she's tried Theosophy, says it calms her,
but other than ghosts there's very little prospects.
Teddy will marry, Stella shall and Vera,
whilst I am certain to remain bluestocking me.
But Heléna? She's betrothed you know, beyond betrothed
to Old Father Thames and Mother England.
I'd call it comic but the comedy's too tragic,
call it tragic but the tragedy's too comic.
Though be the outcome sobs or giggles
I'm sure we'll need each other, one day!'

Bluestocking

Oh no Jean didn't!
Already seeing herself as some middle-aged companion to
that vapid sister, what sort of bluestocking was this?
To rescue her from such a future the Colonial Correspondent
would fix that!
                    And very soon,
one hot afternoon, striding back to the Boat House
she's hearing this unedited tumble of words concluding:
'Haven't you potential, Jean? Why stymie that potential?
Come with me and see the Dominions, the Dominions
and beyond…' for more than any Colonial Correspondent,
Jean, this is your suitor announcing:
'After we wed let's head to the nearest liner!'
Not exactly the silliest thing he'd ever said,
though he'd never be as young as when he was
proposing *that*.
                    'Liner?' he hears. 'Ocean liner?
Ah no we won't.' Since she will never marry.
'I don't know why and even more don't think
I'll ever know although…what a scandal,
what a superb scandal we would make.'
No sidelong glancing now, Jean raising her head
looks her straightest at him:
'I like you more than any man I've met…'

which seems the sort of phrase needing to end in
but... except Jean (who's sensing diplomacy's time
is now) knows any qualifying *but...* would hurt,
and never adds it. That's how much she likes him.

      'So this,' I'm hearing,
'I'll respond like this: you remain here.
With Melbourne always needing your chaps of clout
we'll get you introduced; and if our ladies rarely
seem viragos, still I foresee that kind of girl
you may require. Who isn't me. Stay and I will be the one
reporting on our four Dominions.'

      We knew that wasn't viable.
For it was safe, still safe at Bella Vista,
where you were cultivated as a very clever girl,
the family Roundhead. It would take much more than
this suitor-in-transit to make her what she wanted to become
(which then neither of us knew).

      Though Jean had commenced understanding something:
'I'm just starting out. Even if he didn't wish to
any man would stifle me. Better this way isn't it,
Colonial Correspondent? We may never agree,
but I believe you understand me. Not so?'

                   Very much not so
although, after laying such a temperate siege to Jean,
Milady of Clout, Milady of the Future,
any girl I might require in this modern, adequate city
would seem passé.

Scared

         I hardly felt inclined to woo
their faux Home Counties Maharani,
and wouldn't wait around for either of the Gemini.

      Teddy at least may have become a younger friend
(if ever he arrived in London)
but for all the spins in his motor, not quite.
He hadn't decided 'What I'll actually do...
Law of course...' whilst what occupied him seemed to be
'...some filly-over-the-river.'
Who needed any girl if you had one of *them*?

      In their *Buck up old sport* mode

Jean, Teddy and the Mayor farewelled me,
for with its branches of both clout and future,
plus certain Moriarty cousins, I'd Sydney to inspect,
thence to my third and fourth Dominions,
home in time for a kind of paramount summer
made for hours of writing in the garden.
        Six days I'd labour (though it wasn't labour)
whilst on the seventh friends would motor down
for a lazy Sunday at my family's cottage.
                        War was declared,
In Our Four Dominions paused; war continued,
my book ceased; I joined the war.
Then with the too-hideous speed of it I was on leave,
Teddy was on leave. We met.
        And if possessing that kind of commission
young lawyers usually obtain, this officer
still seemed a boy, though no more scared than I
or any fighting man in Europe,
so he was scared.
             From her Commonwealth
Jean never would upbraid me,
though I was to understand this: the more the war,
the more women, women such as her demanded peace.
So she wrote: 'I'm doing what I can not to support the war.
I've joined these other women, not mere viragos let me add…'
though I was warned '…they're opening our mail by now.
It's obvious I'm no fan of the Boche,
but my country's scared, scared of what women such as us
are thinking.'
              Once liberal comfort itself was life,
life for a seed merchant's daughter.
Now with Roundhead turning Jacobin
(and who turns better than a favourite?)
His Worship, rallying for war bonds,
was quietly infuriated, even if he always knew
that's how Jean was.
              'Bluestockings against bloodshed?
Yes,' she supposed 'that's a way to put it.'
Though the women, the diversity of women,
she had met at meetings became that education
varsity never could have given her:
'We wouldn't have met but for what unites us:

trying to stop this useless war.'
And sensing I might understand 'It's down to dunes
and headlands now, the Empire's going bung,
and if I'm one of that ten per cent agin it,
I never have felt less alone.'

   Heléna was doing nothing much about the war
except to follow it. 'When we meet,
which we both try to avoid, one of us
finishes in tears. It may be big but Bella Vista's
never been that big. Why won't she just get married?'
Then to remind me Jean remained a Moriarty
'One day when it's over I'll be needed.'

   'How did you live through *that*?'
it seemed like the World would ask, the rest of our lives,
if you lived, which Teddy didn't.

   Though Captain Edward Moriarty wasn't merely killed,
we had to understand his body like so many bodies
had evaporated, along with his promise, the promise any future
Civic Leader may have had.

   For Jean it wasn't merely sad, this act of death
was hateful: 'If he wasn't sent to France even to merely die
then what? It's worse than murder, this uncomprehending,
mythic waste. Except for its slaughter
there's little great in that Great War:
just chaps of clout needing to sacrifice their
chaps of the future.'

      'For many months and into years.'
she later wrote 'we've walked out of one room, into a next
and onto another, to end at the first. All fine thoughts,
all decent ambitions that here, our country
would be somehow different, finished right when
Teddy finished. I'm much more Bolshie than they think,
and so I sit about reading, knowing I want it altered,
all unbelievably altered and know it never will be.'

Between Wars

Then though came an alteration.
'You wouldn't know this, but Teddy left a child.'
Where, I wondered, when? Melbourne whilst in college,
France or London whilst on leave? But who?

The filly-over-the-river, or any filly over
any river? ('Might take you to meet her,' offered Teddy,
though he never would.)
                                 'It was a son.
His Worship told me and, since Mother or my sisters
needn't know, he thought I'd be the one best to appreciate
what lawyers and their clients kept murmuring
behind closed doors.' At one level much had been negotiated,
but at another a woman's touch seemed paramount.
'I'm still the person my father wished to be,
but being a man, a merchant and a Mayor
he wasn't. So would I visit her?'
                                 Part mousey, part flinty,
Doreen lived in some suburb Jean had never known.
And though they hardly warmed to one another,
and any crying they'd both shared on Teddy
had been spent, Jean believed the girl,
arranging that from such *Moriarty millions* this Doreen,
her boy and mother weren't to be ignored.
                    'It was,' she wrote,
'another part but more than just another part
of what war is: throughout the world
a host of missing Teddys and their children.'
                    Alterations continued:
Jean moving to an apartment heading chic
from which she would emerge each weekday as
Miss Moriarty, Ladies College mistress;
and if I were to find her inconsistent now,
she knew she was, but living with her parents
was turning her right placid...
and not so inconsistent that I'd not find her
'...still hopefully a real red ragger,
well I would be if I had the time.
These then are my adventures
(Heléna sits at home and sews.)
And yours?'
                    Mine?
                                 When you were through with flappers
nearing half your age, you got engaged to Ida,
our new proprietor's great niece,
that's what you did.
                                 And as with the War,

23

the Empire and indeed the world, my uncle tried
to understand. 'Ours was a universal effort:
Papists, Non-conformists, Jews, your friends
the Australians…and as to this matter of Ida,
it mightn't be quite what your parents had in mind,
but if falling for a Jew lass works…'
and uncle, who tried so hard yet loved to veer,
veered. 'I once knew this amusing sodomite
who told me straight: "It may be unnatural to you
but it sure feels natural to me…" and do you know
I laughed and near believed him.'
After the Great War,
after the stillborn *In Our Four Dominions*
I'd neither be a chap of clout, nor one of the future.
Rather I hoped one of sense, sense on my terms mind:
who could marry my Ida for love;
who kept on corresponding with my friend,
the Australian bluestocking; whose six books, I hoped
were witty, useful books, continuing where my late uncle left:
how are we meant to appraise the world,
judge what this world was becoming,
when in a time of flags, a time of hunger,
very quickly a word might turn completely unacceptable,
appeasement for one.
Some way past forty (now with a chance
to finally reconcile their Englands)
Minx and Maharani would visit us,
two well-off Melbourne spinsters who had both,
at one time, 'Taken, well let's call that chosen suitors,
lovers if you must…' Jean seeming happy
enjoying the sheer idea of it
'…almost to see what they were like. But no…'
and in true virago style she qualified:
'less chosen more rejected.'
Though right now they'd come to see
what all the Empire fought for, and not so strange
it didn't seem Australia or Australian to Jean.
Her sister's vision headed somewhere else,
and if Ida's brother's in-law's country seat
was hardly Cliveden, for Heléna it had
overwhelmed enough: 'Truly have I ventured home!'
Which was, as she confided, news yet hardly news

to Jean.

      From a terrace I saw my lean, tall wife in slacks,
and tiny beside her, Miss Jean Moriarty,
wandering through the house party, scattered about
the grounds.

         'After His Worship died,' Ida was told,
'she won't journey anywhere without me.'
And, 'Hang the Kaiser one minute, appeasement the next,
that's Heléna.' And again,
'I'd dump her here of course except…
like you in your country we are stuck in ours now,
always will be. And it's not that she's too old
(over-ripe brigadiers might rate her passions highly)
it's just she bungs on things oh so very wrong.
"The Bugles of England –and how could I stay?"
How couldn't she, except she can't!
Then I'm informing "Teddy was destroyed by England…"
or else "I'm going out to find myself some Modern Art…"
which leaves her miffed and sobbing half a day.'

      Though Ida was entertained, and understood
why I remained the Colonial Correspondent,
this tirade had bewildered her.

               'Might this be,'
she asked, 'the way Dominions are?'

      'No,' I assured, 'only the Moriartys.'

      And had their Roundhead-Jacobin-Bolshevik daughter
become more cruel? If your sister was an appeaser, maybe.
Was this then an only way Jean knew to protect herself?
Yes, but unintentionally cruel, entertainingly cruel.
And I thought of that eucalyptus-tart, true–brickfielder
of a day when, chancing myself I told her what I had already
told two other gels: how I'd marry 'em;
though none like her and none in such a place:
walking to the Boat House, smothered in one of Melbourne's
ruthless Northerlies.

               'Oh…' she sighed,
part flattered, part annoyed, in need of diversions,
any diversions now, and 'Oh,' she asked,
'that would spoil things, so why spoil things?
Please never spoil things my Colonial Correspondent.'

Empire

The family had believed in Teddy and his promise,
the world believed in all its Teddys, all their promise.
     'Doreen and the son?' Jean once asked herself
on my behalf. 'It hasn't worked.'
     Then there was no need ever to describe
that afternoon on leave when I saw, heard and grasped
the amount of guileless swagger her brother
had been shedding (the more of a boy he became,
the more of a man he doubtless was).
     Stella and Vera married young.
'Much too young…' Jean told me, 'as if their brother's death
urged them to seize upon two of our town's more eligible
chaps who've survived, whose future had arrived.
With a former Mayor and civil benefactor
for a father-in-law, there'll always be money in seeds…
or a seeds' estate.'
     That though had been two decades back:
by now the only child at home would be Heléna
(minding, tending if hardly nursing their mother)
still wanting to see the Kaiser hanged, still trusting that
appeasement worked and when it didn't
still lecturing her sisters on how we all should
hammer the Hun.
          'I'm Ed,' a young man phoned,
'Ed Russel, Stella's son, here in the RAF…'
and another young man, fresh from the Dominions
(guileless still if hardly swaggering)
would meet that-chap-you-must-look-up,
Aunt Jean's friend.
          We talked of Heléna who,
with incensed bafflement that Russia was our ally now,
had collapsed, a briefest prelude to her stroke.
     If not Heléna the current Edward would survive,
we and all the Dominions would survive,
though to survive, commencing with appeasement,
concluding after Suez, and trusting that our world survived,
more than enough stupidity was courted,
enough at least for me to discover
Plenty of these men may be my men, but plenty of these men
are fools!

'What,' Jean asked me,
soon after that even Greater War, 'what gives you most pride?'
　　It was one of those small important things
with which you make your life. And if it cost me certain friends,
it offered me many more: trying to make appeasers unacceptable.

The Kangaroo Route

　　Yes, let's see this widower, some sixty-six year old
manner o' fool, clamber up and into a BOAC Constellation Starbird,
observing how he's losing count of how many days and nights
it will take until arriving in an Australian winter,
he re-discovers what a strange woman Jean Moriarty is
and how, after adjusting, he knows she never can be 'strange'.
　　　'Come a-courting have you?'
And if he thinks a-courting might remain an option,
he's second guessed: 'At your age no, nor mine.
Not whilst each year I'm set to do my school and I
yet another Melba. Back at the Windsor, are we?'
　　And if, after near four decades little had altered
at the Windsor, elsewhere Young Ed, wife and child
were proud to show us, there were certain changes:
here Bella Vista conjured into a nursing home,
there the Municipal Chambers' Moriarty Room.
　　　'We've Seed Emporiums throughout Victoria now…'
and this pleased Ed.
　　　　　　　'Meanwhile, if tea-dancing's finished
at the Boat House,' Jean expanded,
'at the Town Hall every Saturday night, the foxtrot alternates
with jitterbugging. Would you like to try?'

The Correspondents

　　I'd phone my sons most weeks,
most days see some friends, or simply tell myself:
'Nasser's holding all the trumps,
the Americans won't play banker, vale clout,
any future's set to become a different future.'
　　And as if she'd planned it
(with Nasser or with Eden planned it)

Jean arrived in time for Suez.

                'C'est moi!' I knew that voice.
'We've been in Paris. And trying our Antipodean French
upon the French, Vera and I have been deported.
But very apolitical Vera is (and this weekend
what could be less political than a bus tour
of cathedrals?) which is why with something set
for Sunday in Trafalgar Square, I want you with me.
Come on,' she urged, 'come on. The worst can only be
that you'll get spotted.'

                Exactly and I was:
by someone I loved to argue with,
someone not quite Red but Red enough,
who stared, adjusted his stare and smiled:
'You're hardly the kind of chap to attend an event like this…
well are you?'

            And I would have replied
'Curiosity old sport, curiosity…' but as I knew my Ida would appreciate
the old saw 'I haven't changed but circumstances have…'
I stalled, simply stalled for Jean to reply
'He's escorting me, since I'm his Anti-colonial Correspondent.'

          Then arrived the bolt upon bolt upon bolt
of Mr Bevan's oratory, thundering at its climax
'Get out, get out, get out!'

            And an Empire it seemed was over.
As if twenty-four again Jean was entranced:
'Now here's a Britain I can understand and sad Heléna
never could. Alas I know she was my sister,
but please accept: there's too many Helénas
in Australia or anywhere, getting it all so wrong.'

Dream

      Sometime in those years before she died Jean wrote:
'Crankier, I am getting crankier,
not with you although I'd hardly wish anyone to hear me,
some days, days I hardly wish to hear or understand myself…
you though are remaining famous:
Great Aunt Jean's Englishman-beau, who visited briefly,
twice, who sends her and us Christmas cards and birthday cards…
But was it that romantic, that very strange?

These youngsters think we gave each other up for war,
some Great War. Not quite. Though they can't be told
we never had each other to give up…
"Then how did he…" they're searching for a word and ask
"accommodate your views?" By showing he understood
I was correct (or thought I was or thought I thought I was).
"He is," I tell them, "that kind of Englishman who looks out,
sees beyond, tries understanding. Any other sort of Englishman,
or anyone, must be avoided." So thanks for understanding
when you did. But though you might excel in understanding,
what dear man whom I've liked more than (you know the rest)
whatever were you thinking?'
                              'Dear Jean' I wished to write
'I hardly recall what I was thinking and how it was said,
except that by this Boat House our elopement was proposed
(recall the liner?) and how this offer rightly was refused.
I near-thought you would. Plus detachment helped me
as it always has.'
                    Jean was deserving of better,
and for the only time I phoned her, phoned to tell
'Yes, call-it-detachment is bred into me.'
              'Like me and whoever I am? Yes,'
she responded, 'one may call that breeding,
Heléna would. The rest of us Australians rarely fall
for breeding. Remember how my big and silly sister
tried to impress you with her bunged-on ardour,
all her chat of Home? And you were hardly touring
the Four Dominions for that.'
                              'Dear Best-of-Menfolk,'
near to a postscript her final letter was a postcard.
'Was there any need for me to be that scared?
Truly I was timid and as we know the timid often show
the most bravado. So with her better intentions
young Jean got in first, she with her bluestocking motto:
Virago ever harpy never.
Really how could I, how could you, Colonial Correspondent,
regret that you knew *that*?'
                        And I couldn't.
                              The night after she died,
after the telegram, after a phone call, this dream arrived.
And finally, we were on that liner, strolling the deck,
in opposite directions so that we met each other

Port and Starboard on such perambulations.
If the dream had more, that more has not remained.
But as I awoke I was recalling what my uncle
told me: 'This Moriarty mightn't be quite our chap of clout,
though he is some kind of suburban Mayor
with four daughters and a rather clever son…' and then,
how an hour or so before I met Jean
I phoned her father, His Worship the seed merchant,
who asked: 'At the Windsor are we?
Hold fire, I'll send the chauffeur round.'

II The Gumsuckers

Melbourne August 1960. For the first time in four decades Jock, an expatriate composer, returns.

Most of my music is Australian. Not the bush or the deserts, but the brashness of the cities. The sort of brashness that makes Australians go through life pushing doors marked pull.

Malcolm Williamson

Booked In

Enid and that husband are at the aerodrome. And if
'...a little sister can't enjoy her fuss, who can?'
so famous brother's enjoying passing for elderly:
trim silver beard, long scarf and ludicrous wide black hat.
Though he can still flirt, this time with a perky reporteress:
'What's on your hit parade young lady? Not me!'
Whoever supplies tickets must send her one
so she can watch our passing fogey who's not been
'In the vicinity these forty years...' wave his arms and produce
The Queen, his *Antipodean Variations*,
the *K466* (meine frau Birgitta Hoff as soloist)
interval, Honorary Doctorate, and that sour, not-meant-to-be-
particularly-pleasing *Second Symphony* (encores as required).
       'Oh I recall *your* Town Hall...'
(for over ninety seconds now there's only been us two)
'we'll rug up won't we?'
       Name a better place than this broad, flat city
with matching skies to own the word 'overcast',
as ten-by-ten-by-ten layered shades of grey push east,
long shoals of the stuff. 'Our sun,' Douglas my brother-in-law
informs, 'is up there, some place.' (Which may've been a joke.)
'Booked in at the Windsor?' He knows we are.
       Yes booked, like every dignitary, from the fully fledged
to any passing would-be. And where to place Birgitta and myself
on such a scale? I know where I would place Birgitta,
first rank of those European lady pianists,
near-to-born with an intuitive love of Mozart.
       And where to place my sister? Even at fifty-nine
there she is, more than passably attractive

and making sure of it, Enid, who once confessed to rather enjoying
the sounds that prominent dance bands make,

still wishes me to know where my opus rates with her:
'Well, some of what you've written, those marches *The Dominions*
and of course plenty of the film scores…' as for the rest
on balance she was flummoxed, '…though we snap any of your offerings
through the Record Club.' And she'll adore the Mozart.
        'First time in town?' Enid asks Birgitta.
'I'll show you around unless you have to practise…'
        She's thanked '…maybe after the scheduled concerts,
or whilst Jock gives his lecture at the Con.'
        With Enid set on understanding what women
gauge in other women, 'Right now I guess
you must be tired?' she asks, she's guessed correct.
        So after we've been driven back
and booked-in for her lie-down, elsewhere in the city
Douglas will escort me to his office,
it's where he's telling me about his ABC:
'It's rather like your Beeb except…' he pauses,
hoping I'll imagine, urging me to intuit. I do neither.
'Of course,' he lets me know, 'it wasn't around
when you departed…' (radio hardly was)
whilst today, verging on retirement, he seems employed
commissioning chats, talks and discussions,
lectures plus an occasional Address to the Nation,
telling me: 'For fifteen minutes, Sunday, you'll be made our
Guest of Honour.' And here he has a tape of last week's
contribution: 'Nothing will show it better…'
                                        I guess it won't,
prefaced by the opening bars to *Song of Australia*
that stirring dirge which, I recall to Douglas,
being played much more than once by our school's
brass band.
        'Your school,' he wants to reinforce, 'not mine…'
but then attempting diplomacy:
'Surely you must notice differences, so go on Jock,
name some, name some…'
        How many hours since our arrival and he wants a verdict?
        'Well hasn't the town said to have expanded, somewhat?
Not that I'll venture much outside your Golden Mile.

No, what's already given me delight, Douglas,
is hearing words pronounced *that* way, my way,
the way I recall, the way I trust I sound, still sound…'
  As you do not. Next question please.
  'You landed first in Sydney, how did you find Sydney?'
  'Where we spent ten days and may I say…'
(may I toy with you, you dunderhead)
'if ever we return to live, that's where we will.'
  As I see him blanch, accounting for my taste.
  So be it: after dinner or over the wireless
they're wanting me to chat, are they?
Either way, this'll get them digesting:
'Good evening…' (you must know those kinds of low key crass,
expatriate put downs, so low key you nearly miss the crass)
'Good evening. This night I'd like to say
a few brief words about what it's like
being an Australian and please believe me
I still remain one…' Better not blather-on about that,
not when you've spent over a dozen years
trying to make up your mind whether
to decide if one day you'll return and you don't
until you do. Or should I tell them how
three, four, five times during those years
a film might arrive in London and I started knowing again
those trees, those plants, those kinds of houses,
some of the words and how they sound; except
what I was seeing and what I was hearing
were being conjured through British or American
eyes and ears, and I'd stamp into and out of the foyer
with my mock demands: 'Please understand there is a way
for that country, that country there where I was born,
to be seen and heard! Not as yet another novelty land:
a form of Albania with amusing English,
an approximate Uruguay with odder fauna…'
  'Easy does it old chap…' and since their concerns
folded as they always had into condescension,
how could you tell the difference?

With Wendy, With Kitty

        In the Windsor foyer I recognize and are recognized
to the delight of both, for she's the reporteress!
I needn't itemise the times and personnel
for I've been interviewed by worse,
why though have they sent you?
So needing to be plain if diplomatic she's asked,
and I'm informed those more senior were 'indisposed'
and Wendy, that's her name, is set to seize the moment:
'Will I ever get a second chance once I ignore
the first?' A motto I appreciate.
        And if, for an upcoming profile
in their 'Saturday Supplement' she latches on,
how can I mind a touch of latching? Besides,
if I'm to be so 'made' in Melbourne, might I aid her
in the making?
                This is how she's to see it:
'Drop by for tomorrow's rehearsal,
I'll demand they let you in,
and you'll see sides of me audiences never shall.
Then later nab me Wendy, and up Collins Street
we'll stroll for High Tea and my profile...
no no, nab us both, Jock and Birgitta,
you shall have the team!'
        This might've become a remarkable afternoon,
what with Wendy's reappearance in the foyer;
and as for Enid bringing back *The Dominions*.
She aside, who recalls that potboiler march suite,
one in which it was *de rigueur* there'd be
an understated clip throughout, until that is
some nancy boy 'musical director', him with his
If we must we must disposed all four
(or were there five?) in down-the-home-straight
record time.
        'Well done?' they asked.
        'Oh yes,' I replied, 'like beef, barbecued beef.'
And my joke went the way of the music.
        Besides, these were the times I'd rather think on girls
(very pretty girls like Wendy, though that day
one arrived from tennis on a bicycle)
girls to give a man such improbable/possible/probable

34

longings, whilst his clumsy heart clangs
like the J Arthur Rank gong,
girls all set to loll about a den in latticed,
late-afternoon sunlight, and how ten minutes earlier
this impish being who'll become my very first wife
came pedalling up her cousin's gravel driveway:
'So, aren't you our Australian?'
           Well, I'd be your Australian, Kitty,
 if you were after one.
           And speaking (weren't we?) of record time,
isn't it rumoured how very soon after Walton
met his future bride she was informed:
'I am going to marry you, oh yes I am I am…'
which never quite occurred with us except,
mark this, her aunt being away where her weekends
should be spent, there we were that afternoon
in Lady Milly Moderne's over-deco'd apartment,
thrashing about on some big, white, woolly rug,
first saying, but then much better hearing
all our ridiculous thoughts.
                         Later this reward results,
Kitty telephones her brother, turning the day's highlight
into something near to a nursery rhyme:
'Binky, Binky, please be the first to know,
Jock's asked me to marry him!'
           Oh yes I'd asked, we'd both asked,
asked plus a damn sight more.
           Who knows what occupies some men
after all of *that*? Here's how I was occupied:
we see him stumbling out for a breather,
head filled with five of the craziest chords,
striding like he's on parade, around, around, around,
with whatever nerves remain to conjure,
near complete, ten minutes of his thrashing, roguish
Fantasy Overture: Hornpipe.
                   'Where'd *that* originate?'
they asked.
         'Ma femme,' I counteracted.
'That one, that only one, ma femme!'
(What Englishman could get away with what
I got away?). 'Surely you must hear *that girl*
that girl inside my head?'

I still can,
for there she is announcing 'Come, silly chump,
can't you see my very lap's awaiting?'
                                        Or later,
'Let's find something to do, Jock, let's open a boutique.'
            'Let's get me the odd commission, Kitty,
or if I must, a teaching position, since now
I'm old enough.'
                        Or weeks, months later, here's my wife
(if very much still my bride) sighing:
'Your island continent at the ends of the earth…
so fabulous!'
                        To which you could only reply
'It's a promise Kitty, one day you'll see
where I came from.' (She never would.)
            At seven or eight my parents took me
visiting relatives (Tasmanians on my mother's side)
and I must have seen their villages, being told
'It wasn't always like this…' if for them
it may as well have been, this 'old family'
of just three generations attempting to pretend
they'd been there at least five hundred years.
            Coming from such 'stock', you'd either trust yourself
to emulate 'the pastoral', its dells and dales and downs,
or you would not, and I chose not.
            I'd seen this other Britain,
that jaunty-sour insistence of men on parade;
or later trying to understand the strikers
and the hunger-marcher's sombre trek and tread;
to appreciate the whole potential in such bitterness
I never knew I had until,
when Kitty left her life, my life, all life,
what the yellowest of the yellow press proclaimed
BRIGHT YOUNG THING DIES IN CHILD BIRTH
merely multiplied the worst of it;
and believing this as a total violation (nothing more)
I, who celebrated Kitty with our *Hornpipe*
fought back the only way I could.
            And if some may term my *String Quartet* 'Horror Music',
how couldn't they? I still do,
hoping for one of those portmanteau German words:
music-never-to-be-enjoyed.

These were the days when not merely hoping for enemies
you'd see me seek them out, hardly my most stable reaction;
though given that death what reaction would be?
       And as 'Mr Heseltine?' is quizzed,
a brow gets raised and aren't I shot a glowing stare
for 'I am Warlock,' is intoned, 'Peter Warlock.'
Simpleton, please attend seems his desire
to just how magnetic I'm becoming.
                                 Oh yes,
afternoons, evenings and nights of the magnetic,
excepting that such proclamations of 'Warlock'
aren't up to you, surely they're for your acolytes.
       Three villages away, still there wasn't space enough
between me and all his Black Mass rum-tee-tum.
And if there's found that two-bit swagger
someplace in my *First*, reducing itself to Fraud! Fraud!
it's my Warlock being blown up, being blown away.
Not that he ever knew it was.
       Which I know remains the problem:
you love, you hate, you make your bit of art,
as I made him much more fascinating than
he ever was.
             But as a loved one dies,
and the child she's carrying dies, so it's taken out
on Warlocks.
                Kitty was the final movement,
more than anything I'd written this one
finished in silence or, as I guess now,
what silence could be.
                And then...
if only I could tell it this way:
as if I'm talking to someone Australian,
but stupidly Australian, hearing a bloated
'Jock old sport, surely in recent times
as a single man again, haven't you indulged
and played the lad?'
                 'And if by that,' I puncture him,
'matey, cove, bloke, cobber, coot,
you mean a right spot of rooting, well after my Kitty died,
you might or mightn't understand, I put an end to that
for certain years. Some widowers can,
some widowers cannot.'

With Norma, Without Norma

To realise the talkies would need music,
at times plenty of music, if often music you'd barely notice,
with a few years set on making a living whilst making art
on the side, did I hawk myself merely to entertain?
No more, let's suppose than at eighteen
amusing friends with ragtime syncopations.
        Name it the flicks, movies, cinema, motion picture industry,
that's the world where I met her, forthright, streamlined Norma,
Norma Buchanan who, if she wanted to be loved by you
no woman seemed less boop-oop-a-doop,
who married me because behind that manufactured sheen
that comes with stage and screen,
Norma could produce a certain pity,
though she would require pity in return.
        There was no confession, she just itemised the facts:
'If you must know (you'll need to I assume)
at times not now not now, I possessed the morals of...'
leaving me guessing such occasions.
'Unlike your profession, Jock, mine is one where,
for nigh three hundred years they require their women *so*.
And if some of us get that way and some of us do not,
all are made to thrive on hints, promises, intimacy
(for some) and gossip...' naming a suite of actors,
directors and producers, many one day to be knighted.
'Really, it's like acting. You just turn off the self
that's you and perform your role.'
        And it helped I wasn't mainstream, part of that cabal.
        Yet in Britain Norma had to chance it still,
with one decent film twice (at the most) a year,
and West End bit parts she recoiled from,
either them or being carted round the provinces
in *Cavalcade*, 'Let's do it Jock,' she urged me,
urged herself, 'let's go international.
We're worth more than any Quota Quickie.'
        And near two decades back there we'd be
in Southern California, myself and Norma,
made, we like to think it, for the movies.
Well she was for a time. As for my skills,
'Whatever you need,' I replied to the appropriate personnel,
'it's all mine to deliver...' and for eighteen months

produced such tunesmith foolery, which paid the rent,
or some of it, for our truly cultivated bungalow existence.
Equally see me almost make it *in* those movies,
as, whilst the stars, co-stars and extras
continue their foxtrotting, there he goes,
that man in the sleekest of tuxedos, waving his arms,
playing the band-leader, caught for a five second profile
with, courtesy of some designer-chap's constant demands,
a Melvyn Douglas moustache, my *Oh come now!* moment.

      Of course I thrived on moments,
like this one: having produced some phrase,
or kind of phrase, there they'd be, certain locals, pondering
'Say it…oh say it again!' followed hardly by questions,
rather this series of nods, after which they stated
'Well you're not exactly *English* are you…'
and I'd be proud, bunging-it-on proud:
'Australian, Australian as a certain Mr Errol Flynn,
you've doubtless heard of him?'

      I love admitting to Australia,
it helps to catch those needing to be caught off-guard
quite off-guard.

          And by now Norma's being noticed,
when, for her second role (a heroine's stoic sister
in some weepie) she's nominated
Best Supporting Actress and it's been assessed
where this will land her.

          No mere co-star now,
she's been cast as star in what will feature,
I've been told, my breakthrough soundtrack.
For after *Captain Blood* and *Robin Hood*
we're to have a trilogy, I heard correct,
with our Errol set to play *Don Juan*
with Norma set to be the spitfire lass
who tames the Don (or so it's hoped).

      'Like you,' I'm asked. 'he's from some place…'
(They love a certain ambiguity, don't they?)

      'Oh yes,' I reinforce, 'there's plenty us Australians
who not only think they can play the Don,
we also know he's one of us!'

          So see me, hear me
prepare the score for Hollywood and Errol,
Hollywood and my Norma: large wondrous surges,

near to out-surge any latest Korngold.

      But what's occurring at their Juan project?
With two directors down, certain stars being indisposed,
all is over, it never happens, never will.
And, if I'm paid off, just as bad if worse
here's Norma confessing she believes he's given her
the clap.

        'Who has?'

                    'Your countryman of course.'

      And if I'm thinking *Not on the set?*
First she has to talk about it, I've to ask about it,
with this for the asking: 'Well was it forced?'

      Well it was yet it was not.

      What then to do with Norma?
Separation now, divorce one day? It's that or pen myself
a *Handbook for Cuckholds* song-cycle.

      Yet even here in Southern California
there's pockets of discretion, places to go where you
might ask: 'Please solve this one...'

      So both of us line-up at Beverly Hills
resident clap-doctor, to find whatever Norma has
is not the clap and yes is curable.

      Meanwhile is this curable, what's left of
my *Don Juan* music? Well, it's there to be used and,
being my pragmatic self, see me soon enough
enter with a *Sinfonietta*. And what's that word evoke:
all fiddle-dee-dee, trotting out oh so nicely-nicely?
Not this one, at twenty minutes wouldn't it be
wham, slam, thank you Errol and when required
no surges, just my exercises in the pure raucous.

      If ever there was near-to-silent pandemonium
that's what occurred, much of the Hollywood Bowl stunned,
even if this reception was punctuated by an odd 'Bravo!'

      Bravo! though never was enough.
I still barely knew where I might belong
or better if I had to. Return to Britain, visit Australia?
And I might have, had I not quit California,
achieving with Norma a form of semi-amicable divorce,
giving me that biggest break America allowed:
my brief Manhattan phase, dabbling in the Urban Ballet world:
Rush Hour distilling most that Hollywood taught me,
and the adaptation of the adaptation of *Grand Hotel*.

Then with the aid of friends, well-connected, rich-enough
theatre friends, I find that for an upcoming World's Fair
one of their foundations is commissioning
my *Double Piano Concerto*. America rather liked it,
particularly many tunesmith elements,
returning to what I'd acquired and polished
at those Melbourne soirees, twenty-five years before,
topped by a brace of Ragtime syncopations *there!*
in its Rondo Finale.

My Bit

      Was it appeasement and its coming aftermath
headed me to Britain? As widower and then divorcee,
plus what some folk term as middle-aged,
I could have proven myself, now I suppose,
something of a man, the toy of certain, wealthy
New York matrons, except that exile in me
still wouldn't decide, and though a well-bred, Upstate
college beckoned me back to teaching, I stayed two terms.
      Or was it still my Melbourne side,
the one desiring to be defined on my terms,
reminding the world it better guess correct?
      Doing my bit, against appeasement and beyond,
whatever that bit was, whenever that bit was called for,
I still like thinking that as my choice was sailing East
that late Spring, a few that I recall (no names)
had chosen to sail West.
                   Fanfares for the forces,
fanfares for various occupations,
after *The Dominions* though, I'd done with marches,
declining that I conjure something brisk and jolly
for the Home Guard; then balancing wartime film scores
upon wartime film scores with sonatas
(to be one day heard by a few, a very happy few, if when?)
trios and quintets, never quartets, my *Horror Music*
deemed it one enough.
                Now please consider 'none enough':
all those works plenty have tried composing
and then ceased. My contribution to that genre?
An opera (untitled, incomplete) centred on a Mezzo

so approximating Norma and her love-life
it had to be a two-edged case of
Oh Jock you shouldn't have!
The first librettist was a prude, we parted;
the second guessed where it came from,
quitting with threats. But never to waste a note
much of the score got re-used in costume dramas.

        Post-war I did try opera once more,
see Aldeburgh commissioning *Vanity Fair*,
less a plot, more a series of forgettable tableaux,
one critic in every ten approving.
Alas there was no riot, just everybody trying hard,
too hard to be polite.

                There'd been a brief,
wartime, third wife, as I her brief fourth husband;
and since our lives have mutual indices
each may be listed. And some might be unkind
terming her The Heiress as if I had been purchased
which I wasn't. How'd we meet the other,
let alone live together?
We'll say that life's a hotel corridor,
all you need do is excuse yourself:
'Sorry, I knocked on the wrong door,
though if you've a moment...'

            As for Birgitta,
after my *Double Concerto* was revisited for a Prom
that's when I truly wished to know her
(this phrase to be interpreted as required).
A year before she and Noel her nancy-wonderboy
had done the Poulenc: a work to annoy
just about everyone bar conductor, soloists, orchestra
and audience. And 'Teutonic?' I thought.
'Hardly with such light-fingered pizzaz...'
and as for *him*, with all his repartee demanding
a mutual tease, we needn't worry about this one
for a rival.

          'Coo-ee!' he'd cry.
'Isn't that how Australians hail each other?'
        'Yes Noel, if you're drunk.'

Answers

How to ask her, this Wendy something truly simple:
'Surprise us, even annoy us, catch me as I'm sure you can,
but with one proviso: never make me bland…'
how to tell her that, how to urge upon her these examples:
Married four times, Jock, tell me about them?
The wives or the marriages?
What's taken you this long returning home,
if indeed you think that here's your home?
No, not my home. Australian though,
I cannot be anything but.
Among your compositions do you have favourites?
                    And if the question's *that*,
often I prefer to seemingly ill-serve myself
announcing: 'All those other works I'd wish I'd written?
Let's start with *The Rite*, then onto *Les Biches*,
Walton's *First*, *Appalachian Spring*, even *Peter Grimes*;
and as for a 'standard', since my movie time taught me
there was much to learn from them,
one of the better 'standards', 'Stardust'.'
And if you throw that morsel to your mob
it's just to get them asking 'He doesn't mean it?'
Indeed he does and why not, he has to.
Already with each new piece I'm feeling yet again
I'm being introduced, or since plenty think
I've yet to start and never will, who knows where
I might be placed? Given a century there'll be more than
merely dozens of us, just awaiting rediscovery, if ever.
If in 1960, with all these future Wendys wishing to know
how I came by 'composition', I'll set out these examples
as a legacy.
                    1913. Studying at the Con,
never daring to go public with my not exactly Opus One:
'Variations on a Popular Song (Dolly Gray)';
whilst at my old friend Teddy's family soirees
I'd moonlight it with plenty of keyboard quicksteps
and cakewalks, seeing delight in three of his sisters
as he placed another Ragtime he'd acquired
onto their family phonograph;
and as the remaining sister recoiled,
'Must you call that music?'

'What am, Honey Lamb…' her brother improvised.
Then, as if apologizing, we'd sweep into one almighty,
overdone 'Come into the Garden Maud',
Teddy as tenor-fiend set on ravishing Maud.
        Late 1914. Mayor Moriarty, seed merchant,
Teddy's father, reminds us how, although our nation's Australia,
this war means we're remaining British;
hoping it will end by Christmas his wife would like to do
what's right; which isn't enough for their first daughter,
whose reasons seem centred on this catalogue,
placing in order God, King, Empire, Country,
your mother, your sisters. The second sister, a true bluestocking
urges her brother and I desist, there seems to be a better future
she wishes that we join. And you mightn't guess it but,
unlike this Moriarty clan my family is quiet,
though Enid wants to understand my place in the war
and I attempt an explanation.
Early 1915.
By now the patriotic coo-ees, let alone the bugle calls
appear so natural, Teddy and I desire to enlist
in what we think is set to be a Ragtime War,
our cakewalk chance to view the world.
Enid wants to see my departure, our parents forbid it.
        1916. Somewhere behind the lines,
if not too well behind, just find Jock 'n' Teddy
an undamaged Upright and mark how they entertain
with Ragtime medleys and Coon-show adaptations;
all this we know being but a respite, merely that.
        1917. If I receive a Military Medal, Teddy Moriarty
is evaporated.
        1918. And I'm hearing fate,
like some chirpy batman: 'Come, come, sir,
you attended one of Melbourne's leading schools,
you should get through this.'
1919.
With every second British cenotaph unveiled to yet
one more brass band a-wailing *The Nimrod*
I head home to find by 1920 how
every second Mayor expected I'll be giving
a rousing set of patriotic speeches,
something, I'm informed, Teddy would've desired.
I cannot speak for him and thus ship out,

on a bursary heading to the RCM.

      1921. And, for the first time I'm hearing *The Rite*,
with this most wonderful thing about *The Rite*,
it never demands: 'You shall compose *thus*.'
better it advises: 'You can compose whatever way you wish,
in whatever way you like.' Thanks *Rite*:
which rules to keep, which to break, which re-made,
which abolished.
                    These would become the years when
the best of artists adored to play that game,
and damn us didn't we mean *play*!
Yes, yes, head a decade before to find
how Ragtime syncopations were fine enough for would be
Ragtime syncopators, and see us loving that idea!
Now though we had the license to be annoying,
truly annoying for those who'll be truly annoyed:
'You call that music, sir?' 'Yes I call that music, sir!'
those who, forty years on wouldn't be around
to listen (as if they ever had).
      And though after the final bars I prefer applause,
wouldn't you rather opt for a riot than silence?
I'm sure that Melbourne (hardly some riot town)
still retains adherence to such silence.
And if I'm hardly on their bill of fare
they're lucky that Birgitta and the Mozart *Twenty-Three*
can soothe them. At the Interval they can leave.

High Tea

      Now, after staring down the Town Hall, its staff
and middling acoustics, *meine frau* shall follow us
up Collinsstrasse for High Tea with our Wendy,
who's being asked: 'You've heard of *off the record…*'
which she has, 'well it might surprise you, maybe not,
just how bad some of us can be abroad:
that benchmark toadying that emanates from Australia House,
let alone Victoria House with its latest pipsqueak Agent-General…
and to reward them one of London's finer, second-order clubs
stands always in reserve. If you were born in 1910
or better before, which Wendy you were not,
you'd doubtless understand my bemused despair,

how supposedly we've come that far…
or this far: because I left town to succeed and did,
here I am set for another bout of fawning,
oh yes it is.'

       Though Wendy doesn't fawn, she's like me,
at High Tea to be entertained, and though I'm tempted
to suggest: 'Go on, tell us about yourself…'
I'm sure she'll baulk and so propose,
'Wendy you're receiving six free tickets, that's right six…'
      (And can't I view her entourage:
two Old Girl chums, that earnest young tunesmith
of their acquaintance, and a duo of right nancy boys,
confirmed-bachelors-in-training.)
                  '…the weather Wendy,
may be brisk, but even if you've not been over there,
you'll understand today's much like an English summer.
So even if it is August I'm back as much re-visiting
the climate, the vegetation, those words and ways they still
might sound, plus those sad enough, pretentious fawnings.
And to reward them I'm to get a decent sound
out of the local band, who I know are trying hard
not to displease me, so that as you've heard,
I can inform the boy tympanist, after he rounded off the Adagio,
I liked that, that was very good.…

      And there's little, there is no use in some apologetic
I hardly intended remaining abroad this long…
for so much simply isn't intended: after the Great War
that's what we survivors understood,
for I still cringe every time I hear
He saw a lot of fighting… when such *fighting* was
the one and final thing plenty ever saw…'
      Which is where I'll bring in Teddy,
and whether he becomes hero or scoundrel, legend or wag,
here's Teddy receiving a letter from his 'filly',
informing him he's set to be a father,
and there he was telling me how
(counting backwards on his fingers)
unless it wasn't his…no no it would be his,
this child who now is someone middle-aged
with no more than a legend for a father.
      He's there, Teddy, somewhere in my *Second*,
my near-to-requiem, not that I'd ever use that term

for yes it's sour, yes discordant, and yes I'd love to pause
let's say at the end of that opening Adagio,
turn and announce:
I know much of you have never seen fighting, correct?
I'm trusting now that all of you will hear it…
then enter with, what one clever-dick critic derided as
'Jock's schizophrenic Scherzo'.
                                             As it should be
the Windsor's quiet, save for Jock ruminating to Wendy
who, after thirty minutes plus surely has heard enough,
both waiting for Birgitta.
                                  And here she comes, my wife,
raising high the banner of her art. Wendy though is primed,
having read all the record sleeves and more,
knowing yes yes it's well well known
Birgitta's prizes from the Mozarteum,
the very early DGG contract,
her stellar presence at the Proms
and of course her marriage, after a plethora of suitors
to that Australian.
                           'We met…when was it Jock?'
        'The night,' I know she knows, 'the night
that you and Noel demolished the Poulenc,
mind you in a manner he'd approve, as one year on
you demolished me.'
        ('Our Four Doubles', she and Noel call them,
the Mozart, the Mendelssohn, the Poulenc and mine,
just give them time and they'll set up a double DGG LP.)
        Birgitta began unfolding how she viewed herself:
'Even at the Mozarteum this I understood,
you have to look demure Wendy, not fashion-tart demure
and certainly not prim. Never though draw too many eyes
towards, shall it be said, your body shape?
Coloraturas might need such attractions
or distractions, women pianists do not.
For when an audience is lulled to think
My, what a sweet sweet lady
you can shock them with, what Jock's been known to say,
pizzaz. Though never quote me even in the Mozart,
surely not the Mozart, unless of course it's Poulenc's
or my husband's pieces, isn't that correct Jock?'
        That was how we met, my soul mate,

oh, oh, aren't you so well-planned.
She's done such interviews before and yet
she's making this girl feel that what is being said
is just for Wendy, just indeed for Melbourne:
'I'm certain that tonight, tomorrow night,
will be worth our efforts, and of course
the efforts of your orchestra. The Town Hall is…fine,
the musicians I am sure know how to impress,
as does my husband's music.
And no one knows more than I how it entertains.
Even in his sombre moments simply pay attention.
As for the Mozart, I always trust we can do him justice.'

At the Con

The Dean is even worse than Douglas
(who at least possessed a certain bumptiousness):
'Here at the Con we pride ourselves…'
(fawn on Dean) 'as you do too,
in what your Alma Mater has produced.'
        As if I were the Dean not him, I give him time
to settle in, so that my reply might resonate.
But then I hear him say my name, after which applause.
        'Teaching composition,' the students are informed,
'always requires someone to respond *to*,
or if you have those skills I barely had when young *against*.'
        Even if he doesn't agree I see the Dean is nodding
in a *good point!* manner.
                        And for him at least
here are more *good points*! 'What propelled me?
My love for friends and loved ones, the death
of friends and loved ones. Or to balance that
what I learnt, as indeed I did, in Hollywood:
a desire to entertain.' (I dare not glance towards the Dean.)
'For remember this, not too many in one's audience
can read music or write it. What's on our pages
is quite beyond mere language…'
                        I trust I understand
what I am saying, though barely will recall the way I spent
the ongoing hour, except in how my lecture finishes:
'And do you know the sincerest compliment I've received

and probably my finest? *I want to thank you Jock,*
confessed a student. *Having done your course, I realise
I am no composer.'*

      The entertainment over the Dean indulges thus:
'A bright young Honours candidate
would love to interview you for *Farrago*.
He's penned scores for quite a few undergrad revues
that brim with satire to bewilder those
who barely know they're being satirised…'
(Indeed, I wonder who?) I catch this student's name
and then forgetting it shall term him Tunesmith.

      'Of course,' implores the Dean, 'your option
can be no.'

            Whatever my return to Melbourne
has brought on it isn't silence, so never 'no',
with this proviso: 'Formalities will cease
and he'll call me Jock…' with this acknowledged by
a somewhat Deanish grin. 'There's a Staff Club?'
he gets asked. 'Let's take him to that staff club.
And if it's not allowed let it be allowed.'

      With mumble and blush Tunesmith confesses
how he's working on a musical,
and, as one who's close to a decade penning and conducting
movie scores, 'In art,' I ask him, 'aren't we near related?'
For now he's offered something that I rarely offer,
an exposition of my latest project.

      'When I heard that Errol Flynn had died
and how he died, do you understand his lover-child
(fifteen?) was with him? For me the only art
accommodating such excess must be opera, *my* opera
underway which I am naming *Errol*.'

      Uncertain if he must approve of these ideas
this young man smiles a nervy smile.

      'Now,' he's asked, 'how detestably diseased
might the man be made and how to make it?
In music mind, in music. By him knowing
something's sure to happen and with required dissonance
all control he possesses surges into infinity?
Or else with graceless, buccaneering swagger
some two hour patter-songfest for a life
cuckolded totally by booze and the clap?
I'm opting to choose both.' (I gather Tunesmith's

not quite 'innocent', he rather likes this.)
'And with my first self-penned libretto
I just might give the man a countertenor's squeaks,
though unlike Flynn I've too much regard
for countertenors. Like Australians
it's hardly their fault, whatever they've been given.'
(If Tunesmith's looking puzzled I barely care
how I arrived at that comparison.)
'Did Flynn believe he was Australian?
As one of the *Now you come to mention it* variety
well yes and yes with Melba gone was none of us
more famous?'
                    'Yourself aside,' Tunesmith adds,
'there's always Grainger.'
                              Which makes way for my take
on Grainger, how he taught it form, true form,
to bung on the larrikin, and didn't he just look
the well-bred larrikin!
          'Do you know his *Gumsuckers' March*?'
(Tunesmith believes he does.) 'When I was growing up
that word still prevailed for natives of Victoria.
Then some wag chose to say it with a lisp
and it was dropped. For my encore I should play
the march, as if to say
Thanks Gumsuckers. I just might be one of you!
          As for Australia, I appreciate the distance
it has given me, even after forty years away
enjoying that *they* know (whoever they are,
wherever they are) I'm not exactly, never have been
one of them. You know I can conduct,
and probably conduct quite well?
But given I acquired most of what I know
in Hollywood, call me please *Something of a conductor*;
as you can call me, I'll quite admit it
Something of an Australian.'

Up Collins Street

          After the second concert we have to farewell Wendy
(she and her contingent, I have demanded,
will see the program twice and free)

and here she is and these are her five friends,
two of whom, am I not correct! are nancy boys,
one proclaiming: 'Oh Madam Hoff you were magical!'
Will he meet her or her like again? You bet he will,
next time, well the first time he's in Salzburg
won't he be looking her up, or trying to.

      Us two performers would love some local snack,
partnered by a sip of something but past Ten pm
how restrained truly is this town?

      'Very,' Wendy tells me she's been told,
'though we know a dive or two…' and recommends
a folky-jazzy place in Armadale, which at this hour
might be open and certainly on weekends.

      Rather than the ABC chauffeur, whom I've dismissed
with thanks, we have the six of them escorting us
up Collins Street: three will quiz Birgitta on the Mozarteum,
while I'll inform the other three how tomorrow
a further interview is planned,
this time for some glossy quarterly, *Melbourne Style*;
one girl squeals, one chuckles, whilst nancy boy mark two
just moans. *Melbourne Style* shall drive us to some mansion
('Yes,' I'm told 'it *must* be Como!') for glamour shots
of this composer, of whom I'm sure they hadn't heard
a month ago, and his famous wife, both talented and European:
she'll be the glamour, I'm there for the shots.

      Birgitta of course suffers such with grace,
but this will be as starch, Wendy after all was High Tea
and *Melbourne Style* will not be hearing things
Birgitta's been informing her.

                  I ask my cohort:
'How pretentious is it, *Melbourne Style*?'

      Oh yes very very but, the three pause for a chorus,
'Everybody buys it!'

      Which doubtless atones for a city closing down
by Ten, which in its dour way seems more pretentious.

      And as we leave them I'm telling my reporteress:
'I've been made, made and remade, that's me, done.
So Wendy may our article contribute to *your* making.'

Jean

        Dear Jock, given the whole town knows
you're staying at the Windsor, I'm trusting
this will reach you.
                 Earlier in the week
among our mail this caught my attention.
I'm Jean she wrote *one of Teddy's sisters,*
and if this Melbourne visit recalls other visits
to our Bella Vista *I'd think it wonderful*
if you and your wife might spare some time
for us to meet…
        She gave a number and giving the concierge
his kind of appreciated task
(the conductor and his famous pianist wife
have these Melbourne friends!)
I ask him to phone Jean, suggesting that it be
a Friday evening dinner, requesting that he recommend
some place with decent alcohol and food.
        And his response sees near to adoration:
'It's nearby as indeed sir, at the Windsor
we have an arrangement…'
                    'Jean's brother,'
I inform my wife, 'was a school chum,
both of us enlisted, he did not return…'
        I may have mentioned him before,
though lacked much desire for elaboration.
Throughout the world similar refrains still replicate,
and given Birgitta's brother's fate at Stalingrad,
I'd never seek to share too much of mine
or any war. Being lucky I've put it into music.
War? At my age, which one day some decades on
will be Birgitta's age, please let's ignore it.
        I hadn't meant to cut the Moriartys,
but when I was repatriated, I'd seen the Mayor,
by now the former Mayor, who then turned briefly
into a teary, aging man. No, I never meant to cut them,
and you could hardly blame the War and yet why not,
what with certain brands of Melbourne blowhards
urging me: 'Speak up, speak up,
you were made an officer, weren't you?'
        Now though I wasn't one and once more

was London bound, trusting to the music that
I hoped to write.
        Of Teddy's sisters which was Jean?
Hardly the one who never cared for Ragtime
and flounced off to her room.
                    And when we meet
I see she is and was the tiny one, enjoying my attempts
at syncopation; though all I can do
after near to fifty years is ask:
'Weren't we to regard you as the Moriarty bluestocking?'
        Again she was and is, although the term
Jean likes to think, now seems a trifle dated:
'Try saying it to girls of twenty,
they'll probably just stare. Still I await for what
they must adapt to, there shall be something.'
        Birgitta enters, and after introductions
the three of us chatting for the quarter hour,
my wife requests she be excused,
a forthcoming festival recital demands she study up
the *Dvorak Opus 81* plus *the Dumky*.
Please never think her rude.
                  Jean understood:
'A woman does what a woman must…at least she should.'
        It's early and at the restaurant we are it seems
the youngest of their current guests, seeing five couples
who I'm sure (and unlike us) truly recall times when Australia
wasn't a Commonwealth, but rather colonies, British colonies.
The diners must be graziers, with of course their wives
and probably retired, staying like me where as our hotel boasts:
'The PM resides when he's in town.'
And these remnants, attempting what our Italian hosts
are offering, surely are original Gumsuckers.
        Then listening to this slightly older woman
from my youth, I'm recalling how, when she interrupted Teddy
and Teddy interrupted her: 'Agh,' he'd taunt,
'we gave you the vote, don't women have it good!'
           'We?' I'd thought. 'Was he set to be a politician?'
        And how her mother tutted, how her older sister
headed to the veranda, how her father counselled
her brother (hardly with success):
'She has arguments Teddy, meanwhile you recoil…'
           'Those *Bella Vista* afternoons and evenings,

I am reminded, 'Teddy in charge of the phonograph,
you and your syncopations, though by now
you're known for more. Is that where it started?'
(I mention that it helped.) 'My younger sisters…
yes they're twins, our parents indulging somewhat, somehow…'
and the older sister 'Who,' as Jean describes,
'later so reacted and reacted, becoming near to a female
Colonel Blimp; then after Russia joined us in the last war
had two strokes and died. We'll put the blame on Ragtime.'

      I'm not set to mention Teddy's child
but Jean seemed eager, investigative-eager,
since I might supply some clues to ponder over.
She certainly recalled his 'filly', even met her
three times, four, once had seen the child.
Lawyers put a Trust in place, with only her father
and Jean negotiating. After Teddy's death
his mother had no desire, and she had been
the family negotiator. Whilst with ongoing spinsterhood
and early marriages, the sisters had their own agendas.

      Though what followed from the 'filly' was merely
Thanks. Goodbye. 'True she was honest,
yes Teddy was the father, but hers was a class,'
and Jean would term it class, 'my family and I
had hardly dealt with; even if my father and I
thought we could and tried. I never asked her how
she met him. Teddy once hinted to a friend, my friend,
this man I know about some girl, although this friend
was circumspect, never asked and only told me
decades later. Who else did Teddy tell, anyone,
not even you?'

        Only when fatherhood arrived, and then…
      As for my visit '…why not call it a tour?'
she suggests. 'You mustn't stay away a further
forty years.'
        Jean and a niece had attended a performance
and the Mozart was: 'So well past *as it should be…*
but how,' I know the question that will arrive,
'how does your Birgitta do it?'
It is Jock's to ponder every day.
As to the symphony: 'Cath my niece has noted,
if so much of the work comes from thirty years ago,
the Great War with all that moral legacy preceding

and succeeding it, since Teddy isn't buried where
so many of his fellow fallen are,
maybe he lies somewhere in your *Second*?'
     'Sometimes it takes…' I'll try to find
a way I might reply, 'a family to recognize.
However one might cavil against much of Melbourne
I'm more than glad they asked me to play it.'
     I ask her and she tells me how
after she'd taught, she travelled, corresponded,
trying to remain forefront of what she thought correct.
Too old for television though, she would ignore it.
Music, well it was more than mere background,
if rarely going to concerts: 'We just wished to see
somebody I recall in action, and of course,
more than of course, to listen to his wife.'
As for her own *in action*: 'I'm aiming for
another ten, if I am lucky fifteen years…'
Such phrases as I'd never hoped to say,
though with a wife much younger and still not
at her peak, they resonate.
     Being my brother-in-law's *Guest of Honour*
amuses Jean and she's told how I've tried to fit
into my spiel, even after forty years,
what this country offers, where we're different,
saying that if many of our cities qualified as brash
it was a creative brash, though (and this would never
make the speech) I'd seen small evidence of this.
     Before we left Jean informed that she
would pay her way tonight, since she always offered
or more simply did. (Douglas would have stared astounded;
Wendy would approve as yes 'Going Dutch'
was something some girls some days did attempt,
though always with the right man.)
     We glance towards what graziers remain,
her eyebrows slowly rise, she shakes her head,
as if we both know where they'd got it wrong
and doubtless still. Yes I understood her:
unlike them we at least are living *now*
though why not for the future? Why not? Thank you.

Saturday

And Enid wants to entertain,
giving us a *Bon Voyage*, dinner for eight at Seven:
'The other four are simply Melbourne's finest…'
Though finest what we've simply not to ask,
besides how could I quiz Enid when she phones
with news that's more important:
'In this morning's paper, the broadsheet not the tabloid,
Aubrey has done you and Birgitta proud Jock proud!'
      Aubrey? Or am I hearing Audrey?
No, her name is Wendy.
           But when we get the broadsheet,
under the name Aubrey, here's presented all we told her,
all that Wendy's skill is making us,
quoting most answers, the best of every anecdote.
Then why is it me who wishes to apologize,
and on behalf of who, my generation,
as if I, not Aub, this purloiner Aub,
was the one who did it?
          On a Saturday
there's little use attempting to solve all this,
to phone the paper's switchboard and demand,
as if she were my girlfriend:
'I want to speak to Wendy!' For even if
the switchboard's operating, isn't it certain
I'll be hearing: 'Wendy? Wendy who?'
      I could ask for Aubrey, requesting of him:
'Well, who did the work?' But Aub will hedge:
'What's your trouble, what's the fuss? The work?
I may as well have done it!'
      Did I go to school with Aub?
There's one or two in every class, every clique
and claque, getting right away with what he has.
      I might of course phone Enid for the sympathy,
or Douglas who may know him,
and ask if he's invited to their dinner.
      'Who?' they'll ask.
             'This Aubrey,' I'll reply,
enjoying the sound his silly name is making;
and if he's not invited suggest he should be,
for that's where, to make him more than indisposed,

I'll thank him for the article:
'So glad we meet once more, Aub…'
pile on what's required in piling-on,
then see him glance towards his watch,
mumbling something fatuous and leave.
            But I'm stymied and cannot wait 'til Monday,
for tomorrow we'll be heading off to Edinburgh
or Salzburg, or any latest Summer Festival.
            After such a stale morning until Enid's dinner
what's left of Saturday? Explore the town,
though much will close at Noon; see a Continental Film
we've been warned the censors cut; visit the Gallery
and its adjunct the Museum; view another
open-to-the-public colonial mansion;
take a return train trip to the hills?
Douglas has informed me how, this time of year
there's always football games, six of them,
or if you prefer the races, races.
            And it isn't that such options verge on
melancholia, but it's better that we both stay Windsor-bound,
Birgitta to study her Dvorak as I return,
or try to return to *Errol*.
            Later as we're dressing-up for Enid,
dressing-up for Douglas, 'How do you rate,'
Birgitta asks, 'our time here…quite successful?'
            In one more medium-sized English-speaking city,
with yet another middle to upper-middle class
of audience, let's qualify it with *yes quite*,
for even if most never quite appreciated what I wrote,
you can never mind evenings saved by Mozart.
But no, let's leave the audience on hold, saying
yes unqualified to the youngsters:
Wendy and Wendy's friends, those nancy boys
thought us both a hit, whilst Tunesmith liked the way
I treated him as near-equal, and of course my jokes.
Though a success?
                        'Our Mozart surely was.'

III Post-War or My First Husband

Cath recalls the years leading to 1960 when her husband Lew made headlines as an industrial lawyer with political ambitions whilst she taught at an outer-suburban high school.

Bella Vista

Whatever it's become Melbourne was a town,
large if still a town, with us the middling-refined
at the edges of its core, encircled by a solid wave
of shabby-gentility with, we thought no better,
the makeshift and the motley scattered through what else remained
(of whom I'd barely know until years later).

    Grandfather Moriarty, seed merchant and one time
suburban Mayor, was a man determined never to be pompous,
though many in the robes, gowns and chains were famed
in having run the risk.

    Whilst Grandmother, Jean my aunt informed,
always ran proceedings.

    Commencing in the previous century
they had five children: Heléna, who aped the British
more than the British ever could,
Jean the spitfire bluestocking, Teddy who vanished
(name a simpler word) on the Western Front,
Vera my mother and Stella her twin.

    Like the tribes they are, families can possess
their coded cache of words and phrases,
near for some a language, and plenty of these I inherited from Jean,
whatever she said and the way she said it:
'After the bunfight turnout any hoop-dee-doo
proved a complete ho-hum. Whilst for the beaux,
it's all show and no go.'

    And if in each generation,
when someone's bound to be the family radical,
that applied to her.

    Though when my brothers,
Keith and Ross, thought that was my tradition,
the girl who knew where some things have to stop
and as important where they have to start,
those boys never had attended that less-than-encouraging

Eureka Youth League summer camp,
Anna, a girlfriend at the time, thought was made for us.
      'Which,' concluded Jean,
'sounds like a truest bunfight,
bet they were the kind demanding "Pay attention now…"
And was attention paid?' Jean knowing what she would support
and, unbeholden to any latest fad, what she wouldn't.
As for Heléna, most knew her not as the semi-invalid recluse
that she became, more the hare-brain on the family porch
wailing for the Empire, railing against the Reds, those Reds
set on storming the family's *Bella Vista*.
Yet to the thought of any others goose-stepping up
the driveway she offered an appeaser's ho-hum,
until another war arrived and all the ho-hum died.
Though you could barely demand she leave the porch,
leave and do what plenty of women now were allowed to do.
Heléna, alas a lady, was stranded in her other wartime,
the one where Teddy, off to give the Kaiser a thrashing,
vanished. And with the Moriartys, as with many families,
she was the one living out that tragi-comic myth:
why there he'd be plain strolling in for Sunday roast.
Then towards the final days of that sequel war,
after Heléna's strokes arrived,
she gagged on nothing left to say and died.
      Aware that they were 'catches',
in the way their sisters weren't, my mother and her twin
had married early, Moriartys at last making the Society Pages,
where if he'd returned Teddy would have been paraded.
      Could anyone replace him? There were hopes,
for here were the twins bringing two professional men
into the Bella Vista fold, heirs at a remove
to that still-substantial shadow they'd never met,
though my Dad recalled maybe it was Teddy he'd seen.
once as a kid, fielding at Deep Mid-on.
      No one knew where the body lay,
or if there was any body now,
only that what remained was of the country's
sixty thousand dead. And if at ten, fifteen, twenty,
I attempted to make certain sense of it,
I knew of my three choices: ignore the lot,
be one of the melancholy-exultant like Heléna,
or one of Jean's more-than-mere-annoyed.

'These are my opinions,' she'd announce,
'but I'm sure you know that they are.
Need they be followed?' Jean asked if never answered.
For then she'd divert herself into another,
much-less-gruelling subject…men:
'I've had suitors, I trust I always shall,
and that's what they'll remain, my suitors.'

      Apart from an Englishman who, on a visit
tried proposing, then became her loyal correspondent
('Yes, he's my legend…') most of her beaux, it was assumed,
verged on Bohemian, a prof or two or (you know their sort)
the actor types. Teaching French,
excepting for an Alliance turnout there'd be few places
Jean truly spoke it. If only there had been a French suitor…*non?*

      The family was tolerant or thought it was,
though did they fear a strain of 'Where does she get it from?'
might well infect me?

      Dad being paid to administer other people's funds,
Mum unpaid looking after ours,
they were the quietest of the *Bella Vista* clan,
who grew still quieter as the sons enlisted.
And when for Stella the living became too quiet
she had me moved to Jean's, weeks at a time.

      And you might have thought of Vera the twin,
excepting she was somewhat removed,
there in her provincial hub, as the CWA's very busy
Two-I-C, an exemplar of that Moriarty motto:
At least do something!

                  Neither injured, neither captured,
Keith and Ross returned to do their something;
Ross to choose his somewhere and someone semi-rural,
it remained for Keith to think he'd be my (on occasions)
chaperone: 'It's hardly how you've grown,
rather those ideas you believe you have…'

                               Was it meant?
From an emerging businessman-about-town, why not?
To take it seriously you had to try, and trying fail to pretend it did,
since on campus (that is at The Shop)
it helped to be discreet (though not too discreet)
when most young ladies were aping their parents' views
how many rebels would I know or join?
You could admit to attempting the Eureka Youth League…

then what? Besides, wasn't I moving quite some way from 'youth',
finishing an Honours degree, soon being qualified, somehow,
to teach?
      As for men, my next turnout,
the one I'd be naming, courtesy of Jean, Operation Bunfight,
plenty considered it was my time surely. Not I,
who was expecting yet again the hoop-dee-doo of yet another
ho-hum beau, with little show and certainly no go.

At the Jazz Band Ball

Had I though the need for any beau?
   'Well why not try a few for starters…'
suggested Keith, taking me to a Jazz Convention,
telling me how I had to meet this Saturday afternoon
pickup band who'd just achieved their breakthrough:
'They may not possess finesse,' he warned, 'crikey though
the energy!'
      And at the piano of his Ding-Dong Daddies
(how had that name ever been permitted?)
Keith's schoolfriend Will was recognized,
late of the Air Force, whose brand of Dixieland,
be it overdone or underdone made no difference.
Worse than either laughed or booed off stage
came half-hearted sighs with meagre clapping,
enough to signal: 'By kind indulgence of the management,
Ding-Dongs, you've had your thirty minutes worth and,
whoever you are or were…it's over.'
   'I don't think,' Will gave his verdict,
'we truly made it. Who likes to think we ever had a chance?'
      Their only chance had been to appear on stage,
look around and marvel: 'Seems like we've arrived this far…'
But little need in being so abashed since you could listen to
much better acts kidding yourself
'If we tried we might learn from this lot…'
                One day perhaps
but that afternoon saw the agenda change. Did Will recall,
Keith asked, '…this one here, my young sister?'
   Yes I was and more than mere recalled
by him with all the polish of film star looks,
let's say British film star looks;

with Keith seeming proud enough to enthuse my
'…finishing up her studies at The Shop…Honours.'
            I'd heard of the legend, Will's legend,
how when an adolescent pianist enamoured with
the idea of rebellion, though one of a kind, his kind,
he emerged more a piano-player, by Chopin out of Boogie-Woogie,
hardly that concert virtuoso his mother wished for.
Redemption arrives when he joins the Air Force.
            'His family,' Keith would enjoy informing,
'since the first of them arrived a century back,
are loaded, do not dispute it loaded.
Old money? Very few are older.
Nowadays all they need to do is sit on boards,
businessmen of course, never 'in trade',
unlike our Grandad the seed merchant,
even if he made it as a Mayor and entertained at *Bella Vista*.
And beyond business what might remain for them?
Just politics. So when Will nominates one day and runs
I'll vote for him, as I'm sure you won't.'
            I wouldn't, which would make no difference
since he'd be elected, how more blue-ribbon need he be?
And with solid opinions of what he'd offer he'd be fair,
too fair at times, and so devoid of vanity you'd be near-pleased
for him and his ambition.
                        There'd be Will,
always trying to see your 'other side',
yet forever returning to promote their self-proclaimed
Party of the Individual, for of course he had to.
Leaving the RAAF he'd received a much delayed, gilt-edged
J B Were share portfolio, though years on when by accident
this windfall was admitted, one saw him blush.
            Now though he didn't have to blush,
not with this proposal: did Will ever have to worry?
Well if you looked into his background, no,
he could afford not to; so let him worry then on your behalf,
since that's what the better politicians did
(all parties, all beliefs)
and even if he'd yet to join that breed he understood:
how fine it was to serve, as one day it was hoped
he would.
            And if my upbringing verges on well-heeled,
it's hardly Will's well-heeled-well-heeled,

one that in kidding you kid's himself:
'If my family's rich we've rarely been *that* rich.'
           A naïve man, an honest man,
but not the template for my kind of beau.
So what was his mate Lew?
I'll put the blame on Will who that evening,
at what we'd later term The Jazz Band Ball,
during a bout of what all called 'imbibing',
introduced his Ding Dong Daddies:
the man from the bookshop, the man from the Weather Bureau,
the man set to become a dentist,
'...and now our vocalist...' being promoted hard,
this solid male crowned by his brush-back sweep of hair,
who, like Will '...would love to be a barrister...
get over such ambitions,' I was informed,
'plus some of his weird ideas (unless you too agree with them)
this lad's a catch and recommended.'
           He'd first met Lew debating at a RAAF base,
waiting for their time to be welcomed back, into studies,
into the workforce.
                      'What are your plans when this is over?'
With all that confidence certain junior officers possess
came Will's advice: 'We'll be back to ground level,
and with the nation set on rebuilding itself
be like me Lew, try out for the Law.
Sometimes all you might require is coaching,
someone to advance you beyond your witty asides,
for even when you entertain us
there might be more?'
                      Well yes there was.
If to many it would seem Will was more the driven,
Lew simply took on those asides
(easy for starters, more a hobby) until, until
Hang on, hang on a bit! all ease had ceased,
those asides were growing into arguments,
ones soon forming one solid forensic club,
enough to bludgeon both you and your ideas.
           'Debating eh?' asked Lew.
'Well mate, we're fighting in the same war,
though afterwards I guess that's how it will be.'
           Both only sons each was for each
that brother you liked the thought of,

with this proviso helping:
you didn't have to barrack for the same team.
Pre-war there'd just been Lew and his widowed mother
back in their Northcote weatherboard, living on…
what had they lived on? A small inheritance? Some pension?
A boarder supplying just above a pittance?
Just how political Lew might evolve he'd not be taking
Will's direction, loving the idea of government,
a government that truly governed, as in war-time
why not in peace? Name him an alternative?
Whingers really, those who, unless they sought to scare you
were men of so little passion, though like his friend there
at the keyboard, rumbling out his quasi-Dixieland,
there had to be exceptions, the man we'd blame
for making us a couple.

      And let's believe that for some decades
I helped to run Lew's life, since he'd be waiting
(although he'd never admit to waiting)
for I or any girl I'm sure, to offer in her code
I don't know about you, but don't our times demand it?
      Yes these were our times, although at first
I wasn't set to fall for any beau, wasn't set to ponder
Shall any time ever be the right time?
      Though for him it was,
making this for a near-enough proposal:
'You're a good sport Cath, believe me when I say…'
Name the occasion and if required
he'd sound more like some swoony vocalist,
this time turning his form of courtship
into one of those Big Band standards I discovered
Lew was good at, as our times demanded.
      'Mind if I pinch him, boys?' As family legend states
that's what the dance promoter asked.
'All Lew has to do is toss away his silly banjo
and won't Melbourne flock to hear him!'
      Well plenty did, to all those fifty-fifty turnouts
held in my late grandfather's 'very own' Town Hall,
where my husband crooned his serenades,
though if an audience required up-tempo
they received it.
      A hobby earning whilst you study,
what better way to spend a Saturday night,

with each performance see me in attendance,
right up to the week when Rod was born.

Will

Around those years Lew turned weekend vocalist
that's when, for Will, ambition, patronage, the ever-arching
Red Scare and even Jazz collided. And you weren't warned-off,
merely warned, pleasantly enough:
'Didn't think of this one, did you Will?
Well, you're needed, thinking.'
So imagine it, the young Air Force veteran,
whom plenty might pass for a blue blood
(not that he believed in 'blue blood')
being counselled by some patron-in-the-know:
how to get on with your career and, whilst you're about it,
son, how to contain the ever-sprawling Soviet menace.
Yes imagine what some might call advice,
and others call the Party of the Individual telling people
what they should or shouldn't do.
'For,' came such advice,
'you may not know it Will but you are vulnerable,
since Jazz, it's documented, even in its entertaining way
is yet another point-of-entry; they work it well and work it hard
this entry. Your fellow Jazz fiends, son,
none we believe are Communists but are, you need informing,
quite naïve. Sure, when you head home pound-out that
Boogie-Woogie, but show some independence, son,
and if you attend any of their Jazz Conventions
watch who might appear and who you might appear with.
Surely you know that quite delightful Russian turn-of-phrase
useful idiots? Australia is full of them!'
Then, after hearing this
and plenty more than this, Will informed a further patron,
one though who just kept smiling:
'Well some of us are like that...' if with more advice:
'Remain cautious, remain patient, do the minimum.'
He didn't sulk he just retreated,
somehow he had to.
Was Will seen less?
Well, after our marriage and with a career to cultivate

quite understandable, except…
                          'See the way they do it?'
Lew chuckled at his friend's predicament
and much preferred his own, reminding himself
'We're in our party because we're in our party:
Labor, mateship to a fault.'
                          Not quite, I wondered.
For if I'd vote for them, maybe campaign with them,
I'd hardly join them. Come off it comrades, brothers,
gentlemen (however I'm to style you)
maybe a little less mateship, a little more,
dare we say, equality?
                          Of course with Will
you'd hardly call it mateship,
merely this understanding reached through patience
and patron-approval that a young man's hour
had finally arrived.
                    So one Saturday over breakfast
Lew reads out the news: Will's pre-selection
'Out of a field of ten…'
                    'Ten what?' I asked.
        Six lawyers, an accountant, a GP,
an engineer (how did he sneak in?)
and do we detect a housewife?
        Lew phoned him:
'Can't you hear them, Will,' he teased, 'I sure can:
"After we win the next election the PM's sure to pick you
for a Ministry…"'
                    For whatever he was becoming
(and the crowd he was becoming it with) the man who used to
'Play at Jazz', that suspect *useful idiot* of old,
deserved congratulations.
                          'Play at Jazz…'
as he would later term their efforts,
'we never had to kid ourselves that it was Jazz,
but let's admit we tried, or something like it.
Though if our attempts turned anybody Commo,
the Reds were welcome to them.'

The Future (i)

                    Some lunch hours
Lew would meet with an older colleague,
someone with a deceptive arrogance
wealth-upon-wealth acquires, one whose work
seemed next to a hobby, though a man that Lew
found easy and adapted to:
'If Popinjay QC didn't entertain I'd say
he talked too much…'
                    This was a man who told him:
'Aren't you too broad-minded for the crowd
you find you're part of?
You should get somewhere with them,
you may get further without.
Conservative or radical you could become
more than you ever thought you would be.
I did and I revel in it.' His life now challenging himself
Popinjay asked: 'Why should tolerance be easy?
You've heard of antibodies? We vaccinate our civil liberties
by tolerating bigots. I let 'em blossom since I believe
they'll die. Today's future I still trust lies not with them,
whilst for tomorrow's… this is tomorrow's:
if you've the time and knowing where your sympathies
might be, you'll enjoy this action.
I'm briefed to defend a Red, the show's not political per se,
let's assume it's rather worse.'
                    Though plenty in the Cold War years ran risks
Communists often assumed all risks were theirs,
and when the time arrived for front-line martyrdom
who would ever fault them?
                    You hardly wished for paranoia, but
it was possible maybe heading probable,
that Menzies or ASIO or a cabal of Groupers
had used a charge of child molesting to ensnare
this leading party figure, an austere hardliner,
credentialed as a family man, so ideal for either side,
since if a Commo's to be nabbed
well why not *him*? And guilty or not,
hadn't there been messages to send?
When he's arrested it makes the news,
when he's acquitted it barely does.

'Imagine you're a Commo,' reckoned Lew,
'setting-up some kid of twelve and she's
a Grouper's daughter, see any sense in *that*?
It's just too pat, too grimy, too inane.'
         And here's what was required,
an objective man, dispassionate enough
who knew a system most of these martyrs
never wished to know, a code so much removed
from all their theory, hectoring and slogans.
         'Here,' their lawyer smiled, 'is what I am:
a worker they've employed to do a task.'
         Given the case all arrogance lay subdued,
with sympathy as a watchword seeking that
this witness, this child might guess and even understand:
'If you are being used it's not by us.'
         First comes the jumbled recitation
of all that's been rehearsed,
next finds her admitting all she wasn't meant to.
And the case is closed, with the magistrate
most reckoned, trying not to smile
seeing the Grouper edifice collapse.
         Later Lew was told:
'Although my client will be seen by many as
some narrow-minded Marxist prig,
holier than not just thou but all of us,
I'm certain he was framed.'
And would the Commos pull a similar stunt?
'Some would like to, but in this country no.
Only they'd believe it. Would you? I wouldn't.
Meanwhile they'll have to accept that
what they keep rejecting as bourgeois Australian justice,
got him off.'

                          *

         First in solidarity and later celebration
Darky Nolan and his comrades each took
a one-day sickie, so that by three pm,
at a local bar brimming with vindication,
was where and how Lew first encountered Darky.
         Each with his well-meaning brand of
what the future held, how could Lew
disapprove of Darky, wasn't he that kind of mate
who'd tell you what the average Commo

had in mind? Perhaps, though Darky-in-the-ranks
hardly had that much in mind,
and if he held appointed roles
(heckler-in-chief at the Yarra Bank for one)
there were also 'errors', ones to be corrected,
excessive 'errors' on occasions, as when.
yet again, one of his less-than-practical jokes
backfired, embarrassing the leadership;
which had to be 'adventurism', or whatever term
they'd chosen.
              Such would be the tales that one day
Darky shared with Lew, his mate who brought
a needed sympathy to all those activism strictures
Darky had signed up to live by.
              Someone would arrive at Darky's place,
and being made to sit in silence,
like the delayed juvenile delinquent
they believed he was, Darky got admonished.
              'When we attend the Yarra Bank,'
came one demand, 'your job is to heckle,
not to light a brace of double-bungers.
We're tolerant, Darky, we permit you to attend
those fifty-fifty dances most would find
too openly bourgeois. Your errors though
stretch such tolerance. Here's what's to be done:
tomorrow night we're painting SACK BOB
over an underpass, and you're assisting. Be there.
The Working Class and History demand it!'

Housewives' Choice

              Once in Ascot Vale there was a mansion
which became a rooming house,
as later, when we'd acquired it, this former mansion
(four bedrooms and a bungalow).
Given its location my late grandparent's *Bella Vista*
could buy up three of these at least,
as post one war then post another the area slid well past
shabby-genteel into the plain run-down;
though as this decade closed immigrants arrived
who may as well have announced

'If you Australians don't require such properties
we surely do.' Lew and I could hardly blame them,
me because of what I'd inherited via Jean,
he because there was a class he barracked for,
and who by now he was representing.
       Lew's mother had taught him gratitude
and this would help when I returned to teaching.
For understanding how I'd backed him
Lew gave support, his kind of support:
with the worker's advocate, indeed and orator
attempting to show his feelings…to his wife,
a touch embarrassed that he meant it,
no other options though, he had to. Given those times
I'd heard all that was igniting him,
those evenings that he mimicked the responses
of the supposed well-meaning:
'When work that ladies undertake proves to be of equal worth
then in theory let us say this might, just might
be mirrored in their pay…mind you in practice…'
And who, demanded Lew, plain commandeered the practice?
       For me there was another kind of practice,
certain in-laws or those met at reunions
who asked me in undisguised bewilderment:
'With a husband doing what your husband does
where's the need for *work*?' Or else,
given the side of town we'd chosen,
where and who would I exactly teach?
Then maybe as a form of misplaced joke:
'You mightn't admit per se to be a housewife,
but aren't we all?'
       Housewife days, mod-con days,
and days when you only encountered on *Blue Hills*
that disappearing brand of housekeeper/cook/nurse/
governess, well hardly governess,
though from his rural bailiwick my brother Ross
proposed his niece as a form of governess:
his brother-in-law the Shire President's daughter
to live with us and study as we all had at The Shop;
who if she'd mind our children
(did we call it 'child support' in those days?)
Grace staying with us would save her family something.
       She was that kind of 'Give-us-a-cuddle' country girl

born to be pleasing, doing 'Arts, Arts of course…' and studying
'Well you know, a few things…' bringing back one night for dinner
her Third Year Med student boyfriend,
a kind of shy young man you'd meet in any caf.
We tried to get him talking so he smiled a bit.
      'Mmm.' Later Lew went 'Mmm.
I fear they'll never vote the way we vote.'

The Drive

    I guessed my brothers,
the city businessman, the rural entrepreneur,
often asked themselves: 'What's he want to be
when he grows up? A Collingwood full-forward?'
      Yet Lew's naivety was more than mere show,
it was a good show; when he announced
'I just like helping folks…' he meant it,
and when he kept insisting 'It's in the numbers, brother…'
he really meant it.
            'There's just so much any bloke can do
and Cath,' he'd catch me looking up, 'I never want to know
just what my so much is.'
      You knew it was an act and yet it wasn't.
      Will would recall how he'd dropped by
a Lew performance, hearing in those plain-speech theatrics
some smarter version of his dance band patter:
'Thank you, and for our next number…'
which plenty of those bosses he was lining-up
just fell for.
        Though some of the family saw this as incongruous:
the one-time Town Hall vocalist/would be politician
for my husband; oh and he'd been known to practise Law;
though with his rather dated crooner's charm
Lew bemused my parents, even my brothers
who later would admit: 'The unions love him
and it seems to work…for them. His reputation's growing,
it's said he is ambitious.'
                Jean though stayed guarded,
accepting charm, though never till delivery ambitions:
'I've seen, I've heard (mostly from men)
too much self-promotion, since what they're saying

tells me little, excepting that they've said it.'
        Yet with Lew's reply 'Oh come now Jean…'
she knew that he was entertained and being entertained
he listened.
            'It helps to do a lot of that,'
she was reminded. 'There's some real characters about…'
(or charmers we were to understand, like him).
'I need to know what might be on offer…' And this too helped,
no one, he'd admit had ever bored him. All those bosses, Lew?
Yes indeed those bosses.
                So you require delivery Jean?
Trust him. Soon she would receive delivery.
        Sundays we'd drive over to his mother,
a woman who fussed as much as I did not,
I tolerating her fuss, she my lack of it,
both tolerating for the benefit of Lew.
With her grandkids she'd be taken driving,
though with this catalogue of zoo, hills, gallery and beach
what else remained?
           Once we landed at the Yarra Bank,
hoping to catch Lew's mate Darky leading some Commo
heckle squad…no Darky that day,
maybe he was with some comrades interstate,
doubtless organizing… for isn't that what Commos did?
        The afternoon proved most perverse to Rod,
yes he was intrigued, but speakers shouting,
being shouted at, saw what results?
You called that politics? He'd rather be an auctioneer.
        Then came that later Sunday drive.
        An aging sitting member soon to be farewelled,
his were voters Lew the ever positive
knew he could represent, for hadn't he heard hints
from someone, and no mere 'someone'
of numbers lining up?
            And yes, you might know
where those numbers are but how about the voters?
        'At least,' I proposed, 'drive out and see the place.'
        Paddocks, former paddocks, gravel streets
with preparatory gutters; tired looking homes
no matter how recently completed, in fibro, weatherboard
and brick; a poultry farm, a disused market garden
waiting for both purchase and development;

a new church, a second new church; a Catholic church with
Catholic school; a state, a high, a tech; a row of shops
with flats above them, surely the suburb's only flats;
whilst further out empty blocks that alternated with
a smattering of houses; and heading off or returning
a mother pushing a pram; in what might be parkland,
one day, boys with an inevitable football;
a car unloading visitors in Sunday best;
and over all this a quiet that announced
'This is where we've landed and what we're making of it...'
which, Lew would like to think, was inviting
someone like *him* to represent *them* and truly help,
once he got the numbers.

Trixie and The Boss

    Small matter how professional we were
ours remained a one-car economy:
I'd be driving, Lew would need to tram it;
and that Sunday heading out to where we'd driven
months before and where I'd work the next week
we saw the school: graders, ditches, gravel,
some uncompleted wall, and other still emerging sections
requiring me to ask *They hack such pioneer stuff out here,
can you?*
        That Monday, in the doorway of
the designated library, greeting everyone entering,
there stood our man-in-charge,
after which would come his adept, expansive welcome.
Too adept? My look may have indicated.
Rather too expansive? Since here was a man
who started every joke by laughing:
'Come now, this is not the army.
There's volunteers out there, I know,
and those that offer...' as we all would
'will be thanked.'
            'Don't ask,' my neighbour muttered.
'I've been here since we started and know as much
as you do: three forms in three years,
makeshift from the start.'
                She was Trixie who,

back at our desks elaborated:
'Every day he gets his way, The Boss,
or what he believes it is. There's one hierarchy
outside this place and he's enamoured with it,
the Minister, the Director-General, the Inspectorate.
"Yes yes…" you'd almost hear him, "I do believe I have their ear."
With what results? He's in charge enough.
Never though enough to make a difference,
defers all details to our Senior Master.'

   She was convenor of her self-proclaimed
Fast Set, one I sensed I'd opt to be
an honorary member, with Magda of
the Middle-European purr and Monica
who saw no need for commentary:
'Let's raise our brows and roll our eyes,
leave Trixie to the mayhem.'

   And if I saw The Set as at the remove,
indeed as somewhat younger which they were,
Trixie at twenty-eight hardly required protection.
She'd say: 'You name it, we short and buxom ladies
have it plenty, cop it plenty, brazen if required
though school is not the place…'
as later she'd unfold items from her catalogue
of the forbidden: a friend who had to see
a Collins Street abortionist (and please it was a friend
not her) or the two banned books
Trixie and her husband owned,
which more than anything seemed trite.

   In this though she was adamant:
'You may think it but I'm no red-ragger,'
Back from teaching in The Bush she'd not expected much
but three years on, same gravel, same ditches,
same graders, same Headmaster on parade…
and adamant again: 'If he's termed The Boss
the name's a parody for he's a parody.
But yes the man seems very fond of it, The Boss.'

Plans

With snap-to-it gait, arms swinging and officer's moustache
The Boss was on parade, inspecting buildings and grounds,
staff and students, so that quite soon you'd see us spy
certain Form Three mimics marching, swinging,
and we could hardly blame them.

He had plans, he said he had (certainly had ambitions)
informing staff how 'As with the pioneers of old, we're building our school
ground up…' which meant what? For there was in him
that comic vanity you'd see in certain British movies,
believing him and his good points were most unique.
I'd known of plenty as unique and, given a more comfortable
side of town, there they were, one for every street at least,
raised to be ambitious, striding forth.

Why, we'd be informed, given his position on
the Headmasters Association, he'd speak if necessary
to the Minister, the Minister himself.
And given such a concept he would laugh along
with all his staff.

Yet you'd to understand
not everyone can found and build a school, so perhaps
such gentleman-in-charge bonhomie was required;
though not where Trixie placed him:
'He'd hardly know it, but he's that kind of man who,
sixty years ago, didn't want us women voting.
"Ladies, ladies…" I hear him announce
"You don't need to vote…we can do it for you!"
He may have his plans, his Five Year Plans,
but how many Five Year Plans are needed?
Maybe he is the-man-for-the-job, hardly though
the job he has.'

For this was the year when finally,
month-upon-month all operations stalled,
when for a term the graders so planted themselves
you feared they'd start to sprout,
when with ongoing rain all the proposed grounds
turned more off-limits; when lunchtime was at most
half an hour.

We had to understand how still we were
post-war, yes it was a time of building,
yes, we heard of plenty much worse off

and such could be accepted,
if there weren't those blithe and hearty nostrums,
that incongruous pomp: school crest with Latin motto
displayed outside his office, 'Colonel Bogey' or similar
each Monday morning as our students (plenty of Maltese,
Yugoslavs and Greeks) headed to their classes.
We were teaching in weatherboard country where,
if there was a style it was a *Western Suburban Style*
no *Melbourne Style* could comprehend.

      Whilst to the beat of the latest hammering
there arrived not mere paternal but grand-paternal
put-downs and pretensions. 'We'll be letting this one ride?'
we once more accommodated. 'They shall be as we have all others.'

      Not quite Trixie, Trixie speaking up and out at meetings,
who saw to it he justified all she required justified:
'May I ask this?'

              Making him the more polite,
the more annoyed: 'Yes please go ahead.'

      And if this was some Five Year Plan,
might such plans be still pragmatic?
If only pragmatism hadn't copped this mayhem, yes:
a wall is built, the wall collapses, a drain is dug,
nothing fills the drain. And there they remained
into this next half year when once again
the hammering continued, the graders graded.

      'I'm very pleased,' his school was told,
'that soon both wall and drain…' so with this sop
our *Fast Set* eased themselves into their observation time,
viewing for a different round of entertainment
these other of our colleagues:
Mr B in his stove-pipe slacks, white socks and brushback;
that very thin and nervy Catholic school ma'am; the laconic boffin;
and Alison that younger woman set on going out with her man,
her man from the Colombo Plan; and, if some might consider asking
'Are you sure you know what you are doing?'
she certainly knew something;
unlike that other younger woman, the one who, innocent or not,
somehow seeking out schoolboys in the yard,
needed to be informed and re-informed:
'They'll never see you as some kind of playmate,
they'll see alas a rather tiresome flirt…or worse.'
      We had this rumoured Communist.

Quiet and conscientious he held back
doubtless as instructed, so we imagined he and his comrades,
required no *Fast Set* antics: there might come an hour
to complain, and when that hour arrived
he'd be informed, patience and obedience was how
their world was run.
              As if ours didn't.
I can't recall who or what I was trying to teach,
except outside two graders had returned
to do whatever they'd been doing, off and on
for the past two years.
             'Let's hold someone responsible…'
I'd love to tell my students, were they to hear me,
'someone who's not us and we know who…'
        Yet even after three years plus of slush and gravel
that someone was immune, for there he'd be
off at his military clip to greet his doting Mothers Club.
Had the man ever been criticised?
Not once we supposed.
            'Now, now ladies…'
he finger-wagged Trixie, myself, our set,
'don't get any funny ideas…'
              No, he had the funny ideas:
informing Assembly how, when young he'd captained
the Glen Eira Grammar Rifle Team, hadn't he?
Just what this or any school required, a rifle team
(ours never happened).
        Assemblies though were fodder for the inane:
a Bible presentation from the Gideons;
the yo-yo demonstrator; an Englishman who,
upon visiting 'home', sought to tell his children's school
about their Mother Country; that local councillor
set on his civic pep-talk, if scattered with what he hoped
were gags: 'Now here's a joke I'm sure you'll get…'
        But beyond all these the Boss awaited
with his plans. In these work-in-progress days, in these
makeshift parts of town, it must ease a load
to know there'd be such plans, so long as any *Fast Set*
never challenged you.
          'That man would love to see us moved.
'Well,' Trixie announced, 'I'm pregnant so I'm moving first.
How's that for plans. I see our Commo's set to stay,

poor thing. But everywhere he goes they'll be informed
I'd watch out for him if I were you.'

History

    In classroom, schoolyard, where many of the great domestic sagas
have been conceived, born and raised, what I was observing never evolved
into what was hoped nor what was feared.
    These were the kind of children I'd not have met,
many near-set for the immediate workforce, some even at their age
poised for marriage, with a minority making Matriculation.
    And whilst The Boss measured up his grounds,
conferred with foremen, waved-on the graders,
glad-handed any civic personnel, presided over assemblies
and their march-pasts, co-chaired the Headmasters Association…
others tried to run the place.
                         'Could you,' I'd been asked
'take History?' since the thinking seemed that unlike Algebra or French,
but like Geography or Needlecraft (probably not Needlecraft)
anybody could, and better yet, you didn't have to teach it
you just took it.
              'Yes,' they'd been informed,
'plus I'm qualified.'
                Though my despondency was minimal,
for I had the luxury of two all-girl classes: 1C, 1D,
and asking first-up for their favourite times in History
recall these two replies: Greek gods and the Roaring Twenties,
which doubtless were enough.
        'Hey!' a colleague cried. 'In need of boys?
Plenty of boys at the Tech, Cath.'
    Two years before students had proclaimed him Mr B
and the staff concurred. Yet he also taught,
swinging his way through what an English syllabus demanded,
though you'd to wonder, would he remain to teach after such pizzazz
evaporated?
        'You'd hear a 'Hey!' and there stood Mr B.
Did anyone recall his name?
                  'Bartok?' offered Magda.
    'Brubeck!' Monica seemed certain.
    And if 'Hey!' was his hip call-sign
here came the tut-tut-tutting of Miss Malone,

younger than I was, yet well into the early days
of her Catholic school ma'am spinsterhood.
        As for the quiet one, our Communist,
if not quite letting-on, though with flyers promoting Peace,
a certain brand of Peace, stacked neat to one side of his desk,
whatever the questions you knew the answers would verge on equivocal
as I suppose they had to, it suited the times
when for many a certain care had to be maintained
with what you said and who you said it to.
        These were still the days when even to imagine
some possible end to White Australia
seemed more like the to-and-fro of a very glib debating club.
        Though here came less-than-worldly Alison
being courted, as we were told, by Cedric,
her man from the Colombo Plan. Had he, I'm sure somewhere
it was being asked, had he intended on remaining here;
and as a couple mightn't they become an issue, a target even,
certainly a situation that required study
Due to the risks involved…for their own good really.
        But it would be History, not merely 'taking' us
but teaching us how late it was and getting later,
when Alison, more worldly than we'd ever guessed
became engaged.
                'This is us…' she passed around
some photographs, 'and these are my future in-laws…'
        And where were her fiancé's family from?
Or were we supposed to ask that?

Melbourne Style

        With his Ealing Studios looks and demeanour
Will seemed made for monochrome,
a neat-neat man with big shaggy Lew as
friend and foil, each devoted to their
new worlds and all the possibilities,
two only children neither threatening
the other. Or to quote Fred Daly:
'Son, those opposite are your opponents,
the enemy sits behind you.'
                        'Let me expand,'
Lew liked to tell, 'upon the hidden Will.

When your name's put down at birth for Scotch
and the MCC (LLB, RACV, MHR,
just love those initials!) when your name's put down
so nothing is unplanned, then something's sure to urge
Haven't you been too patient Will?
So watch how he rebels…'

                                The boy's eighteen:
prefect-perfect, near enough to dux,
with more than an adequate talent as a pianist,
which is how his mother wants him.

           One Sunday afternoon the family
and the family friends assemble, it's to be a recital.
Will walks in, they clap, he bows, sits,
adjusts what needs adjusting, pauses with the silence,
they're all expecting Chopin, it must be Chopin…
so he breaks into Boogie-Woogie, briefly but enough.
When required Will knows how to treat them;
how they'll be treating him!

           A prominent young barrister
he's into his early thirties now, primed to escort
out of St George's that year's luckiest bride,
whoever she'll be, Lew for best man,
all ripe for the Women's Pages, as indeed
was near-to-promised, until the telegram
JUST MARRIED SHALL EXPLAIN POST HONEYMOON
WILL.

           Explain? Later when Lew's look announced
Come on mate, you can tell me
all he received was an edgy, rather coy
'Well you know how it is…'
though we would never know the how or even what
'it' was, and just how enigmatic was our friend.

           Like Lew, Will had just a mother, now, unlike Lew
he had inherited (some would say been rewarded with)
a Malvern mansion far too big for two,
let alone for one.

                    But soon he married,
and all that we were later told was Dotty sketched.
Some days, were it fine, she'd amble into Central Park
and sketch, returning to that room designated as
her studio, this shy, thin woman with her spray of curls
most adept at hinting at what she required:

'If I possess no time for you, please I beg ensure
the same to me.'
      'Didn't you,' she asked,
one of the few times Dorothy asked me anything,
'didn't you marry as your parents wished you?
To some it might appear Will and I were deemed…'
    'By whom?' we wondered. 'Her mother, his mother,
Mr Menzies?' A bewildered Lew termed her Potty Dotty,
and I agreed.
     Her father once had been an aide-de-camp,
now he sat on Boards, plenty of Boards;
though if hers were the 'right' folk wouldn't you be
happier with the 'wrong'?
    Will as he always did adapted,
though had our boogie-woogie man married as career move,
one that had him striding towards that gilt-edged
pre-selection, let alone election?
You asked yourself yet knew such must be fiction,
for if his crowd might do many things (as might all crowds)
though hardly so clumsy, ruthless and clumsy again.
To act like that made them sound like Commos
(well certain Commos).
     Then the invitation arrived,
Will's day to meet the mansion, meet the bride,
for men (with wives) from his Air Force days,
his jazz band days, Will's other days; to meet
his study, her studio, his piano, their twenty-one-inch set,
the paintings bought more we hoped as art than
mere investment; whilst on a lowboy a pile of
Melbourne Style.
    Dotty flushed, embarrassed:
'My mother never buys it, she subscribes.
Dumps them when she's finished.'
   And on the cover of the latest *Melbourne Style*,
that quality quarterly aimed at the Top Five Thousand,
plus further would-bes jostling in the queue,
there on the cover with swept-up coiffure
and elegant neck, Margot Lightfoot beckoned
in all her cool-jazz cool, with enough restraint to set-up:
'Watch out, this one's capable of plenty…'
she being a Civic Leader's model wife
(all knew that) one of those foremost *Style* faces

famed for their deportment and charity work:
Margot Lightfoot, Poppy Brasch, Annabelle Eggleston
and Cherry, just the singular Cherry
(which many thought seemed rather daring).
            Emerging in time for the first Royal Visit
and fading-out as the PM strode into the Portsea surf,
Melbourne Style lasted longer than plenty thought it could
or should: this guide of where to eat, what to wear,
who to know, what to read, watch, listen to.
            And if like me you considered such a publication
and its clientele provincial, it still possessed
that perverse attraction which betrayed my origins.
If being published for those like me, well aware of *that world*,
was it bought just to be rejected? Never,
but to imagine this certain kind of voice being aired:
'Oh, I read about it in *Style*…' for it entertained me
scarcely in that way *Melbourne Style* wished
to entertain.
            Someone had conjured its testimonials:
'You must admit it's most well done and, like us,
anything but crass.' Anything but what? Or else
'Sydney may have her Harbour Bridge but we've got Melbourne Style.'
I'd check with Sydney first; though who would want to when,
through the unfolding of each season
a cover lady arrived: good-sport Cherry, wistful Annabelle,
beaming Poppy and the regal Margot, *Style* Incorporated.
            It was when I coined the line:
'When I'm dumped don't dump me for a model…'
not that Lew would dump, but 1960 seemed a year
for plenty like it: Will dumped, if hardly for a model;
a Civic Leader soon to be dumped by his model wife
and all she stood for; Lew dumped by the Cement-Heads;
Will dumped once more, this time by his Party,
            Each *Melbourne Style* saw an Artworks Supplement,
all selections headed by a portrait:
the prominent headmistress or the Governor's wife,
one of that year's leading debutantes or Dotty,
yes indeed Dotty, conjured by an equally strange
young woman into angles: yellow, red, orange and brown angles,
becoming a modish talking point to those who,
staring at the artwork announced:
'I do believe, yes, I can make her out, can't you?'

And you had to think
'If anyone can make her out, he'd be Will the husband,
but when she as ever never appeared
he shrugged in return, shrugged and pleaded:
'Well you know Dotty…'
    There was no time for scandal,
only for a hushed agenda settling over these,
the middling-refined: 'But haven't you heard,
Dotty's vanished, seems she lives some place past Eltham,
sharing a mudbrick with that painter girl,
don't you know the one…'
And living on what? Inherited investments,
certain talents, and a current reputation which those,
assuming to be in-the-know would term a 'rest cure'.
For it wasn't quite their Melbourne nor their style,
and if two artiste-types were 'What exactly?'
that portrait it was decided, spoke for many.
    Melbourne Style was too high-toned for gossip,
gossip just decayed to natter, and natter never was
the style of *Style*. As for those insinuating pithy pars
in *Truth*, that was men-folk stuff: 'Topical Taps',
footy and the form guide.
                Now once a week
here came Dotty, returning to collect more things
and more things, clearing out what remained
of marriage, heading to the waiting taxi,
her round trip back past Eltham.
                Will needing to recover
that's how we joined the Telethon.
    Good Friday: name no better day or night
for any Telethon, no better place in town than where
a man might get free grog.
Meanwhile, all that I could do was bristle at
what we'd have to watch: variety acts
so low-key they verged on no-key,
waiting for the man I'd married, the one who'd
never dump me for a model, to do what he had
once done well and croon, gratis: for friends,
a hospital, its children, the general well-being.
      'Will's needing a diversion, Cath,
he's on their Board, they've asked me for a spot…'
and yes I would accept Lew's explanation: 'I know, I know,

but it isn't quite the Amateur Hour, more the Semi-Professional…'
and, if he'd to give them some standards, how about
'Moonlight in Vermont', 'Perfidia' and that latest hit
so well beyond mere standard now 'Volare'.

   And Lew might've supplied the sound track,
supplying it well, but when the night and history unfolded
year upon year upon year, *his* was not the story.

   Throughout Good Friday it was deemed
donations would be acknowledged thus:
to pair-up boy-with-girl, as in that hour a *Style* model
with some prominent man: Cherry with a pleasant
Labor lightweight, Poppy with an exuberant tennis champ,
Annabelle with that philanthropic hardware king,
and in the belief how great they looked together
Margot with Will, acknowledging families they would
never know, from suburbs they had barely heard of:
the Perrys of Heathmont, the Van Der Zees of Jacana,
the Rushings of Hughesdale and in memory of her late husband
Mrs O'Malley of Kingsville South, their pounds, shillings and pence.

   And it was that Easter,
with Potty Dotty off on her unending rest cure,
that Will Fairburn MHR met a very prominent
Civic Leader's wife, and you'd barely know it then but here
became the essence of *Melbourne Style*,
high grade *All for Love* on a Telethon,
since if there were to be a Telethon why not make it that,
that and 'Volare'.

     I for one would love to think so,
although this Telethon didn't seem the best place
to announce: 'I saw you and knew there'd be no other…'
Will's finest boogie-woogie moment;
rather it was the more prosaic: 'Pleased to meet you,
I'm your local member, I live by Central Park…' and
'Really? I often stroll in Central Park…'

   Good Friday, Will meets Margot;
Lew arrives home more than rather drunk.

The Occasion

Then in the months following the Telethon
came Lew's true occasion.
                              For my true occasion,
and one day I deserved to have one,
please file under *Women must wait*.
                              But for now
it's 1960 and here he is announcing 'Without you Cath,
you and the kids, how could I have done it?'
something he loved to say and probably believed,
as each evening he'd be reporting-in,
how his opponents with all their sloppy melodrama
were sinking into even sloppier farce.
        It didn't start that way.
With all the benefits of headlines proclaiming *Union Greed*,
plus reportage with all their hints of unending kickbacks,
unspecified thuggery and subterranean passages
terminating at the Kremlin, we saw a cabal:
these emerging Civic Leaders, the young old-money
and their upstart newer-money mates,
campaigning against the Red and every other menace,
to be rewarded with a Royal Commission
into such perfidy and how they'd suffered...
see justice take its course!
                        And briefed by an appropriate firm
who would represent such Moscow-centred harbingers
of unending greed? Why Lew of course and who,
though never let his clients know this,
for opinions and better yet advice,
spent some hours with the avuncular Popinjay QC,
who saw some opportunities for Lew
tempered with this proviso:
'Given the mess your red-ragger mates can cause
this crusade might break you. Proceed Lewis,
but proceed with calm, your kind of chatty,
well-modulated calm, and this could prove your case
and no one else's.
                        It proved no one else's.
        To ambush rising Civic Leaders
isn't how some Royal Commission's meant to act
and surely never this one.

It was assumed that Lew was briefed to hedge,
to stonewall and above all plead,
for if his clients still protested they were hardly Communist
it was assumed they may as well be.
And Lew was facing men who since their birth
were nurtured by assumptions.

   'He near-to-spoke their lingo…'
Parliament in recess Will dropped by,
becoming more than mere bemused,
the man was captivated. 'Nothing remotely pompous,
he merely knows and speaks their very words…'
were how his friend's abilities were itemised.
You saw Lew chatting, simply chatting with these
young-men-on-the-make, in club-talk,
or what they thought was their elders' club-talk,
though often with vestiges of a supposed plebian…
and there they'd be in near-confessing mode:
'If, mate, I tell you in near confidence
you won't be saying anything…will you…mate?'

   Excepting matey-mate,
all confidences are over, any secret's out,
for as of now we're set to headline every station,
channel and above all front page. Guess why?
We've just given them one perfect story,
that you're a total, first-rank, greedy crook,
or may as well be.

   As the Civic Leaders sighed
their Civic Fathers groaned,
was their Royal Commission meant to finish thus:
becoming the finest day for a Northcote widow's
only boy, and no mere day but the start of weeks
then into months, that saw him making headlines,
as much as any Civic Leader.

   And of all of them,
Civic and beyond, Lightfoot it was
misjudging Lew the worst, who took the greatest tumble.

   Coming from a rather minor grammar school
and near enough self-made, here he was
the once-outsider transformed into the keystone
(Premier one day or merely Party President?).
Shorter than many, with waves of hair curling from his forehead,
bursting forth with a required charm,

with Margot the model wife (or any model) on his arm,
set to become the ultimate *One of us*,
even heading the Board that oversaw the Telethon…
      If plenty wished to do without him
it was believed they couldn't;
so it took not *One of us* but *One of them*,
our easy-going legal vocalist
and somewhat champion of the working man
to act (although he'd never guess) on their behalf.
And if his mates the union clients enjoyed the act,
certain bosses made it known they loved it,
seeing this Lightfoot and his style prove so unwitting,
so compromised, as a tepid 'What you must appreciate…'
veered into 'What I really mean is…'
to finish with a rousing 'Now that is hardly fair!'
      Lew had to believe it: 'We've done it Cath,
seems the whole town knows me.'
      Even these mannequins, yes mannequins,
posing for fashion shots on the Treasury Building steps,
as he strolled by they knew him, true!
      Or here he is with Darky at the footy,
who's telling Lew some Commos liked to think
Lew was one of them.
                  'Hang on comrade,'
Darky was kidded, although Lew meant it,
'I'd hardly be that daft. One side *them* are crooks,
one side *us* are not. That's how it's been handled.'
      And wasn't he correct. Few it seemed
cared little what propelled the Royal Commission.
Forget 'class struggle', forget 'free enterprise',
ideology was out, theatre in,
for characters were what this town required:
these dour, beetle-browed union heavies,
these fine-tuned but ever overreaching Civic Leaders,
and that counsel, Lew the deceptively laconic,
or those opposite, more measured true yet quite
as ruthless.
            No one went to trial,
Lightfoot with his Lightfoot mates,
and this, for their reward, neither did Lew's clients,
Darky proclaiming him Melbourne's Perry Mason,
since there he'd be, Darky, back at his Commo's

boarding house, watching the latest episode,
trying to guess like most of us
who *really* did it.

                Who? Lightfoot of course.
        Or Lew of course, with his special look:
'Has all this Cath, Mum, Rod, Helen
truly happened to me? Oh yes it has!'
        And though he'd aspire again and yet again
his life would never hold a grander highlight.

Dinner with Darky

        I hardly was that brand of housewife
up for feeding all my husband's mates
(or even with their wives-of-mates).
But then there was that Saturday when
after the footy Darky came for dinner,
Lew's 'Commo mate', still on his latest 'bad trot',
still needing an amount of 'looking after'.
That was Lew's promotion with urgings that
I'd understand, trust and maybe find in Darky
the 'truest innocent'.

                      *

        They'd meet at games half a dozen times
a season, except that afternoon
since they were playing Melbourne
Lew invited Will, with a phone call that brought out
all of his excesses:
'At the Magpie's nest my sons of honest toil
are up against your exploiter class…'
and the clichés didn't merely roll by now,
they were cascading: 'It might be rough
not seated in the Members, okay standing in
the Outer, Will?'
                'Been there often, Lew…'
and pleased with his answer commenced to itemise
the where and when of all the other Outers.
        Which Lew had to stop:

'There'll be you, there'll be me and there'll be Darky
who's my Magpie comrade and I'm warning you
a Commo. Sure my watchword's Peaceful Coexistence
(who wouldn't love to see another Summit Conference?)
but, and it's an even more important but,
are you allowed to meet them?'
        Though if anything was allowed
mightn't it be the Honourable Member's poise:
'Commos Lew? Meet 'em every day.
But can your Communist meet *me*?'
        Easy, Lew had planned ahead
and Darky wouldn't know: 'There's little need to
shock him. Being a Commo's mighty hard for some
and right now my mate's suspect:
not enough *correct line*. Commo or not
something that most of us can understand.'
        'There were times,' Will mused,
'it's been known to happen. Better make me
just another lawyer.'

                              *

        Those times he met with Darky
they talked footy, briefly skirting politics,
(not quite as he did with Will).
        Now, near the ground,
assembling in a public bar, to a cry of Darky's
'Comrade I've arrived!' Lew entered his response:
'And this here's Will, other than the crowd
he barracks for this man's okay:
let him tell you he's just one more battling lawyer.'
        Then came a mutual sizing-up,
with Lew imagining: 'So how's a Commo meant to look, Will?'
Well the one in front of him was lean, sharp-nosed
and darting forth shook with a decent hand.
Then after another round they wandered off
to watch the Second's final quarter,
Lew setting up his near-to-schoolboy skit
the one commencing: 'A Liberal, a Labor and a Commo
go to the footy, let's put the three together
and see what happens…' But little happened.

Melbourne ran out, Collingwood ran out
and 'Fellas, this is it,' once again Lew became excessive,
'class war beyond the merely miniature!'
        'That's one to remember,' Will responded.
'Are you often like this?'
                                Rain all week,
drainage problems, next day Lew presented his report:
'You must know that kind of game, Cath.'
(I believe he believed I did.)
'Grinding through wet weather mud…'
        And, if not polite exactly
(why should they ever be polite?)
Will and Darky knowing the game, knowing the conditions,
by half-time turned somewhat even mates,
mates to set up Lew.
        'His politics?' answered Darky.
'Let's just say he tries.' ('Sure does,' said Will.)
'I know of a mob who, if only he'd just understand
would snap him up.'
                        'Sounds familiar, Darky.
What do you reckon he believes in?
Something like the fair go?'
        'Well something like it, yeah.'

                                    *

        When Collingwood won even for the victors
it was dull, whilst as the loser Will tried hard
to make amends, tried harder meaning it:
'Next time in the Melbourne Members you're my guests…'
as he headed off: dumped husband, by now spare man,
to yet another Malvern dinner party,
pledging he'd never forget the afternoon,
that exercise in something not quite memorable:
'The day I met your apparatchik, Darky.'
        Like Lew (like Darky doubtless)
he'd never be that total politician,
not when he meant to mean every uttered word,
telling me years later that somehow (somehow!)
he *trusted* football, even in defeat
(his that day not theirs)

the game made as the truest leveller;
or even better, though this he'd not admit,
that evening's truest headlines
Demons Drowning In The Vic Park Wet.

*

        As for the much-promoted Darky,
Lew had me prepared:
'To the comrades my mate's made some errors,
and needing to atone he's been quarantined,
from what he's not allowed to say.
But Darky needs his mates and not just
Commo mates.'
                And would there be a Mrs Darky?
There wouldn't. 'That church…' as Darky told it,
had gotten to her; she'd cleared off with the kiddies
to whatever Gippsland town she'd come from.
Divorce? He was getting there, or trying to.
          In from the game, no hat, no tie,
but in this well-worn purple suit, at Lew's introduction
Darky became that man who, you were certain
believed his every word:
the 'Nice place you've got here…'
and 'Gee, aren't your nippers pleasant…'
and 'What's your team, son?'
                     Amusing himself
Rod offered that he'd never had a team
and 'No team eh?' without prompting
Darky turned protective: 'Just watch out,
that's the stuff spooks out there will file away.'
          Rod did not relent: 'And you do what?'
        'Linesman for the PMG that's me…'
whilst for a hobby, yes let's call it that,
Vice-President of the Bulgarian Friendship League,
and he might get there on a tour one day,
we indeed would be most welcome.
Then, with a magnifying glass of Rod's
lying on the mantelpiece, Darky picked it up
and peering at our son announced:
'You're looking at the eye of a worker!'

I moved them into dinner.

      'You Commos seem always out of favour,
especially with yourselves, so Darky,'
offered Lew as if for the defence,
'you're with friends and, if you'd like to,
tell us please what happened.'

                'Y'see…'
(should he be telling, should we be hearing this?)
'Like most of us I'm being trailed by spooks,
so with one parked out the front all flamin' night
in the morning feeling sorry, though I shouldn't,
I bring him out some brekkie. Great tale isn't it?
Some comrades but didn't think it that great
so, y'see, when an error's found and needs correcting
the Committee sends her out, Marj,
Marj if you like, keeping us in check.'

      'Right,' Lew nodded, 'right.'

      'Want my opinion?' I had to ask.
'Wouldn't call it mateship, Darky.
Mateship is the enemy of the bosses, and this Marj
sounds like she's the boss.'

              Ahh no. No.
'Marj deep down is somewhat of a decent sort,
not that she allows herself to show it.'

                'Right.'
I guessed the coming answer but I had to ask:
'Masons, someone told me, have their Ladies Nights.
Do Commos have *their* Ladies Nights?'

      'Every day and every night. Women?'
Darky asked for both of us,
'Centre of the vanguard, sister. Unlike with
you silvertails…' he winked my way.

      'Son,' Lew became the big kid, even if
he hardly was, 'son, I'm Northcote bred.'

      Since my flirtation with the Eureka Youth League
was Darky the first Communist I'd met?
Of course, were you to accept the rumours
and kept watch, you'd meet them every day,
or those who may as well be.
That quiet man at school, hadn't our resident
nervy Catholic seen *some pamphlets* on his desk?

      'Ask him,' Trixie urged, 'would he ever lie?'

But in those days with so much summed-up by
'What's it to ya?' I'd no need to hear
'Who wants to know?' Who? All who wanted to
and they were plenty! I understood it was understood
how yes, they can be pests, if more so to themselves,
and imagined our guest Darky being quizzed about
the evening: needing to attach required labels
to our house, family and even dinner.

        But no, dinner with Darky hardly supplied
such tensions, only the occasional look suggesting:
'I'm no disaster, am I? Haven't I been brought up fine
with table manners?'

                  Of course.
Why shouldn't that be true? But come on Darky,
must you see in your mate's wife or doubtless any wife,
some version of this avenging Marj?

        I saw to the kids, leaving the men to drink,
talk, drink and re-talk footy.

                Lew was set
to drive him to some Commo-friendly boarding house
where Darky prepared for what tomorrow held:
to heckle or be heckled on the Yarra Bank,
or later, since wasn't there television, try watching
what was on.

           But Darky gathered what I'd gathered:
'Lew, you've drunk too much again.'

          'No need for that lift you've offered
I'll be tramming it.' And beyond their win
Darky had approved the day's encounter:
'Your mate took his drubbing rather well,
he seems okay, one more lawyer eh?
When you don't deliver reckon we'll be hiring him.'

          'Alas,' sighed Lew enjoying this, all this,
'he's working for the bosses.'

        With 'Right…' Darky returned the sigh, 'right.'

Cement-Heads and Rah-Rah Boys

There were days when Lew just revelled in
his progress, and no one blamed him:
raised in Northcote by a widowed mum,

local schools, into the RAAF and out,
gets his education, gets qualified, sings,
sings in Town Halls and with a wife, boy and girl
buys into Ascot Vale and does, he likes telling folk,
'All that the missus demands!' (I'm glad he thought so.)
          But Lew for all his vocalist's ease
knew Law, his Industrial Law,
and would rarely niggle, rarely demand,
setting up such a routine of chat and banter
many were to admit plenty that they weren't
supposed to.
                  Then after a near-decade of success
would come his Party man's reward:
that put-your-money-on-it certainty of pre-selection.
          Though not that other certainty as when
this cabal, the Cement-Heads, dump you.
          'I'm not what Labor needs,'
Lew in excuse insisted to himself,
when dumped by those three, four, five, six,
make that a dozen stooges.
                  And couldn't you hear them:
well yes on occasions they had hired him,
and yes he'd done the tasks they'd set,
done them well enough, but that undid him, see?
For unlike those Cement-Heads (how Lew loved the term!)
he knew the system, how to work the system
and was successful at it.
Besides and even worse, hadn't he been
much too lightweight, an all-things-to-all-men man?
Okay, Lew had Commo mates but, and the Cement-Heads bridled,
he had even Liberal mates, and who knew,
if they dug deeper, Grouper mates,
'Who aren't,' the stooge-in-chief confirmed,
'what we call mates. Nah nah, let's be simple brother,
where's the consistency? Mates have their place,
but what we need right now is hate.'
          (As if these weren't the men
Lew had the spine to hate, if only he could spare
the energy.)
                These were the times then?
Why ask? Name any belief, any personnel,
any times, look hard or not so hard

and there they lurk, Cement-Heads.
          How unlike his friend:
you joined Will's crowd like some debating club,
then enjoying what you had to say
they slapped you on the back, young fella,
so in you strolled. And it had to be imagined thus,
since parading themselves as pragmatic-plus
there were more subtleties than we might ever guess,
if indeed we guessed.
                    'I'm in,' he emphasised,
'of course I'm in but there are those who
were it possible to have me in their sights
would see me in their sights. We have our Cement-Heads,
I call them the Rah-Rah Boys, the Empire's finest,
men who hardly can accept a Commonwealth
and what it might become. There is for one
an undercover, if still effective South Africa lobby,
and those recoiling if it is suggested that one day, one day
any White Australia may not be as viable. I'm in,'
he repeated, 'and I'm safe: right time, right place, right party,
lead by a most successful man who accepts, no who believes
in our broad church…'
          'Pretty damn broad,' came Lew's reply.
'That's pragmatism.'

Matinees

          A Saturday, a matinee, I'm with Jean and Helen
at Her Majesty's: *My Fair Lady*, my second time, their first.
          'Who'd not appreciate the songs?' asked Jean.
'Though what they've done isn't exactly Shavian.' For she was Shavian,
thinking the show a tranquilised *Pygmalion*.
          Then during the interval, as the crowds shift,
they shift enough to set my daughter asking:
'Is that Uncle Will, is she his invisible wife?'
          And just as in the movies you glance across
to see them: Will with Margot Lightfoot,
Helen's commentary heading to its climax:
'She looks more like a model than an artist.'
          Well yes though to a girl of your age
let's say a friend.

Jean knowing faces
recognized him: Lew's Air Force comrade, jazz band mate,
ideological combatant and though she'd never vote his way
her local member. Whilst with him sat one of our nation's
premier models (even Jean glanced through *Melbourne Style*):
'Who's, married to that very pushy…what's the latest term…
Civic Leader? Yes Civic Leader, Lew's recent chum.'

      With my aunt there was no wish
to brand this couple as 'together', but now,
as I felt completely 'in the movies', if certain kinds of movies,
indeed they were together which set me telling *sotto voce*
'I've no idea re her, but Lew tells me he's quite divorced.'

      Yes it was final and yes selections of his party hierarchy
were informed if few others; those being told headed sympathetic,
believing in his version (what else need be known?)
for when a man who never blunders
blunders into some ridiculous arrangement,
in this case his marriage…except that there he was,
besotted with that model he'd met on the Telethon,
set once again to blunder. Should he try to find her
and if succeeding how exactly with discretion might they meet?

      The answer arrived: near to schoolboy stuff,
with Lew-the-mate to volunteer:
'I'll phone *Melbourne Style*, where else?'

      Indeed where else since he was told:
'Why Margot's just arrived,'

      Lew passed the phone and left the room
to guess what followed, the man announcing where, soon, one day
this week or next he would be lunching,
and if the woman might drop by…or something like it.

      Yes it would become this, their *Brief Encounter*,
or not so brief, progressing some weeks later as
the *My Fair Lady* couple, doubtless murmuring to the other:
'Do you feel the same as I do?' (which would become to Lew and I
our near-paragon of romance).

               Mind you,
most of the matinee wouldn't have noticed,
let alone known who they were seeing,
and if a few might have observed and guessed
there'd be no need for paparazzi snaps,
or insinuating pithy pars,
not when we were living in some wowser's *Dolce Vita*

just ripe for one-on-one gossip, after tennis, during golf,
after church, whilst the Ladies Auxiliary assembled.
      But that day, if she'd been noticed,
Margot flaunted little, though were she in pyjamas
or a sloppy-joe her composure would remain.
      And here I was imagining those who saw
and understood could only sigh:
'Would you believe it...' but mind, they'd then attempt
to rationalise, 'what with that direction his former wife
had taken...see though how they've just snuck in,
Melbourne's next-up glamour/scandal couple...'
Bedrooms, the ladies would admit, might do very well
if such things could remain there.
      But here they were in public,
public to the very tune of 'Show me'!
Eliza Doolittle demanding 'Show me'! As '...very soon,'
Will and Margot might respond, 'we'll show you!'
      For they'd have to, if not yet.
      A few weeks on it was arranged for Will
to bring her over, our side of town, a second matinee.
      Were they by then living together?
      'Well,' Lew had been informed,
'after running back to her mother, briefly,
Margot's staying at my place now.'
      But didn't they know where such a stay lay centred?
Not merely the shortest stroll from Central Park,
but in their big city/small town where,
if the place tried hard enough accommodating
certain peccadillos, it was a very limited accommodation:
for though one may forgive, why should forgiveness be required?
      But that Sunday we'd just been introduced,
so I could hardly counsel:
'The marriages you've both emerged from failed;
there's plenty that have failed much worse
yet still continue. You're lucky, please stay lucky....'
(Though it only dawned a few days on that in meeting Lew
she would've met the man who'd engineered
the Lightfoot downfall.)
      Some women talk about their husbands
and some too much; Margot was neither,
only later indicating how necessary for their careers
(necessary but rarely fun) their marriage was,

confessing that at twenty-eight '…with one hubby down…'
she was '…getting on a bit…' which got me verged on warning
'Just don't tell *Melbourne Style*.'

    Could we be more than just acquaintances?

    With 'Will set on quietly thawing her…'
would come Lew's verdict, 'all the girl requires are just a few
to laugh along with, which may be us.'

    That afternoon I discovered what she knew about me.
Or rather, having attended the same, well-credentialed
Girls Grammar, who I'd been and who I was,
courtesy of an ambivalent Old Girls profile,
being the one who somehow disappeared to Ascot Vale,
the wife, came rumours, of a very radical man
employed by certain unions.

    Our one time Town Hall crooner *radical*?
If only he was…and as for *somewhat disappeared*?

    Margot required a gentlest education
in life beyond her Inner South-East enclave:
'This is a suburb where, until we moved here,
unless you were heading to the aerodrome or at a pinch
the Show or Races, I'd rarely seen.
Now I prefer remaining disappeared, telling her I was teaching,
though she wouldn't know the school, few would.
'Totally new, all girls and boys who give no trouble
at least to me; the staff are fine, I've made a friend or two;
mind you the gentleman who runs the place
ensures that it's a shambles. I'm not a one for shambles.'

    Nor was Margot, for that word had resounded.
Here was a couple who'd be more than stepping out…
and into what?

        'We're planning,' I was informed.
'All this just has to work.'

        Out in our backyard
Lew and Will discussed their fates:
one stymied, one about to be.

Guest of Honour

    Well before retirement Jean's world seemed centred thus:
her visitors, those trips abroad, her correspondents.
Call it a spinster life? Then let's have a spinster life!

When Rod was two, or thereabouts,
we'd met Jean's English friend and one time suitor,
from those days when women still had suitors,
since it would verge on an aesthetic outrage
suggesting they had 'dated'.
                              A widower by now
he hadn't come a-courting,
just wishing to visit a country once enjoyed,
and because he thought my aunt 'most admirable',
knew the truth of what she'd reinforce:
'There was a one time family legend that
but for the Great War we would've married…
well, the legend's wrong.' Legends added to any war
were wrong.
                    'Indeed,' stressed the Englishman.
'Was I damaged? Who wasn't?' If never admitting
what his damage was but '…nothing fatal.'
          Whilst later, arranging that she raid the family trust,
saw her six months in Paris, Paris and beyond.
Whatever the French for bunfight, hoop-dee-doo and ho-hum,
her portfolio found further phrases.

                                    *

          Then Jock arrived
(though he had been too young to be a suitor)
family friend and soiree regular,
Teddy's chum with whom he had enlisted,
Jock it was believed had been lost to all that remained
of *Bella Vista* life, until this year and his return.
          Composer, conductor and let's say famed enough,
he'd been based where most of us still rarely visited:
London, Hollywood, New York, London again and now…
was it Salzburg?
                    Back in Sydney, Melbourne,
for Town Hall concerts, plus an honorary degree,
the publicity, once located, centred on his successful film scores,
and the precise yet sensitive skills of his pianist wife,
the Mozart specialist and concert drawcard.
          We would attend the first of their performances
and Jean would attempt to contact.

Would Jock be pleased or even would reply?
Yes he was and yes he did.

*

After the second movement of the Mozart
I heard a woman behind me sigh,
with a man beside her murmuring
'Cripes, this is good.'
                              Throughout her encore
Rondo alla turca Jock with his well-crafted, silver beard
couldn't stop smiling towards his wife,
though after the Interval as Conductor
the man was girded, here also was a Composer
offering for the first time in his hometown
a work which most had never heard before:
sombre, angry, then with possibly a redemptive closure,
you might imagine it being written in my uncle's memory,
except there were those many millions other war dead,
for the music said, at least to me:
'If post-war means anything this still is wartime,
still containing so much of what it was
and far too much of what's to follow.'

*

For the Friday evening Jean had arranged
the three of them would meet,
and though the wife was pleasant
she excused herself. Jean understood? She understood.
    Since near five decades since the *Bella Vista* entertainments
Jock had no regrets. What though was this country,
was it his? Even if he barely knew it now,
the one he understood it had become,
he still liked the idea of certain things remaining,
though much had altered.
                          'If not enough for some of us,'
thought Jean.
            Not pompous through that dinner, no,
and not exactly shallow (facile perhaps?)

100

Jean was pleased he was not profound,
since that must come, surely, with his music.
        Or with this Sunday evening session the ABC
had snared him for, being deemed for fifteen minutes worth
their *Guest of Honour*. Recorded some days earlier
here was this somewhat prominent Australian
(if prominent more abroad than here)
giving not so much a chat, less thankfully than a speech
(being a touch facile helps at times)
listing an eclectic range of Australiana he'd missed,
being right glad of his reacquaintance…yet more,
trusting how he felt we'd be the future, yes the future,
just when we discovered who we were.
        Listening to Jock, knowing what we knew
of young Jock, no one's actual beau,
though no mere *Bella Vista* remnant,
more somebody Jean recalled there at the Moriarty Upright,
giving them all the latest rags and cakewalks,
till he and Teddy enlisted, he survived,
survived enough to think he might return, though didn't until now,
now saying in his quarter of an hour:
'Well who exactly are we…I'd love to know…'
attempting we supposed to remain Australian.
        Even after forty years away we would allow it:
'He's still one of us. Perhaps like Melba it's where he'll retire.'
        Though had he remained in Melbourne,
progressing through it had been rumoured
some three or four marriages, plus doubtless more liaisons,
that may have proved contentious even within
our Bohemia which, unlike Sydney's, rather enjoyed
remaining semi-hidden, knowing such lassitude,
yes we'll call it that, barely was encouraged.
Which is how I saw it then, itemising these latter-day examples:
our one time suspect Jazz Convention Jazz
we'd lost touch with; Trixie and her banned books;
finger-snapping Mr B on yard duty in dark glasses;
Potty Dotty and her artiste friend;
and life as I assumed was lived in Darky's Commo boarding house;
all that seemed hardly Jock the *Guest of Honour* asking
'Who exactly are we?'
        For Lew it seemed more a case of
'Who exactly don't we want to be?'

He could accommodate the Silvertails:
'I must. Although they run this place, I'm here to help make sure
they never run it too much…' No, for him it was the Wowsers,
the Wowsers and their Grouper mates, their Cement-Head mates
'Who one day I'd truly love to throttle,
yet know I mustn't…'
                    Correct, Lew,
it's been your biggest year, too big perhaps,
but calm it down, shush and listen,
on this Sunday evening listen to this one:
how a talented musician with an even more talented wife,
revisits his past, tries to accommodate the present,
has certain fantasies about the future. Yes, yes… but,
if some nostalgia holds him and she may even have enjoyed
the novelty, you'll hardly see them emigrating.

Lightfoot

        If I never knew him I knew the Lightfoot type,
recoiling but with a bemused recoil
from that certain quizmaster patter
a friend of my father's brought to our house,
the one seeking to convince a girl
not only was she a primed contestant, better yet
she would scoop the jackpot.
Well that's how I saw whatever I saw,
to observe such men much as I observed *Melbourne Style*
not for the question *Is this for real?* rather its reply
You know it is, you always have.
        So, as a husband, how had Lightfoot
sought to be treated?
                    'My Margot,' as *Melbourne Style*
quoted him, 'never sees herself as mere prop.
In her occupation few rarely are as good as Margot,
which in my position helps to see how far a man can go,
we both can go.'
                For he wished the world,
or Melbourne at any rate to know
where such glamour and ambition might be taking him.
When you're this rising Civic Leader with a wife
much more than mere appropriate,

please never call it overreaching,
few, only a few could fill these roles,
it was near-demanded of them.

       Until Will, Lew and that Royal Commission.

       'If Lightfoot goes,' the City doubtless asked,
'will we profit more or less without him?'

       'Better still,' one smart-arse proposed,
'great man brought low, or mediocre man
made more mediocre?'

                Whatever the answers
this was 1960 and this was his brief:
to get you amazed then have you ask
'How many setbacks can this man accommodate?'

       'In some years dozens,' he loved admitting,
though his were no worse setbacks than for any
rising one-of-us with requisite know-how.

       True, but money magnifies and magnified
you're not just caught, you get caught out,
thinking you could more than mix it with some one time
Town Hall vocalist, but to push it truly push it.
Well who emerged the pusher who the pushed,
since when you fall for legal slapstick
name the straight man, name the clown.

       Yet little seemed to block the man,
whatever Lightfoot was he'd be relentless,
so that when Will somehow acquired Margot
(that's how it was termed) giving her spouse
strong causes for revenge, you merely indicated
I still have friends and plenty of them.
(And the same applied with Lew.)

       'I'm returning Margot to her mother…'
that was the gossiped boast,
although she owned a truer one,
having returned herself, if very briefly.

       'There he goes,' the muttering would come,
'the Comeback King, what's on offer now?'

       For starters his trademark resilience:
still employing a succession of Charity Queens,
still striding into this Ball or the next,
somebody at his arm, with Poppy, Annabelle, Cherry
and their gentlemen in attendance.

                For she'd quit,

Margot was no longer at his arm,
and who needs to know the co-respondent
when gossip's out, spreading itself:
it's that prominent (you said it…now, one more time…)
rising Civic Leader who's been diddled!

      With barely time for revenge per se,
all he had to do was let his hopes unfold:
'No more warbling on my Telethons…' for Lew,
whilst with Will he'd opt for more refinement,
making sure these words would be suggested:
'Yes there are rules but today they are these rules:
We've more on you than you'll ever have on us.
Therefore, invent a good reason and retire, Will.
Then you can't be dis-endorsed, humiliated.
Oh do it please for your sake, Margot's and the Party's.
Order! Order! The Honourable Member's time has expired!

      It's rumoured that when Lightfoot had the time
he chatted with his vicar: the Margot business
making them both bewildered men.
Though even any sympathy would cut him
as he told himself: 'Here it is mate,
what we've to do: wave tat-taa to the kudos
of church-going, the power of charity,
we'll let others prop their charities,
attend their churches, browse their latest *Melbourne Style*.'

      More now than any Comeback King
he's a middle-aged man in a hurry,
knowing when it was best to quit, quit town,
relocate to the Gold Coast. And if up there
what they had was still quite infantile,
through him they'd be growing-up,
with expertise plus energy on tap to run each two-bit Telethon,
expanding the portfolios of his fortunes, their fortunes,
to emerge once more the rising Civic Leader,
this time marrying a meter maid.

Procedures

      After Margot phoned me hoping we might meet up,
and meeting in some city tearoom told me
she was pregnant, there was no melodrama,

just her confused if wistful questions, answers,
questions and answers.
        I wouldn't ask why I was made her choice:
the wife of a friend of her friend/boyfriend/lover/father of her child.
How that morning was I to describe Will?
And how to reconcile Margot, premier face of *Melbourne Style*
with this befuddled woman in lowkey blouse, slacks
and cardigan I barely knew; or myself with some
older sister role, one I was never needed to perform.
        'It's Will of course, I'd hardly tell you
if it wasn't. This helps though,' she explained,
'having a friend (you don't mind me calling you a friend?)
from elsewhere in my life.' And emphasising yet again
'Yes it's him.'
                Precautions had been used of course,
but all she could announce was 'Haven't we been clumsy…'
with Will replying 'Sure looks like it.'
        And her marriage yes, her marriage?
Lightfoot had, as he always had, his latest Charity Queen
for company. Say a word against him?
Margot had been poised for years except that now,
with her current problem that was cancelled.
Lightfoot didn't know, maybe he never would,
and she recalled he had been fun at times,
if boring fun, which excused whatever that excused.
        But if things might need 'adjusting',
such made Margot shiver: 'Should this child…'
as she tried to find the word, a word, any word;
but this resulted: 'Last month I left my husband,
today I'm propping pregnant at my lover's and asking
like some adolescent: *What's a girl to do?*
        Would she inform her friends, Poppy, Annabelle,
the other one? Not yet, best keep the models well away.
They were professional colleagues and yes admired,
but people she had no need to be close to,
not now. If she took one choice they'd never know,
taking the other would make it obvious.
And there was Will, wondering she supposed
what he'd prefer, the procedure or the child?
        She wanted to ask, who though could she ask?
        So I would ask: in me she had a friend
who had a friend who had a friend…

sometimes such patterns must succeed and I phoned Trixie,
employing the now quite hackneyed 'You'll understand,
it's not for me...' And seeing two days on, a specialist,
one known for 'women's problems',
not merely, I was assured, this problem.

*

      Possibly too sleek, professional as he must be,
now was the time to ask him 'What's required?'
and hear what was on offer: '...which is simple,
certain women need my services.'
      I wouldn't be his patient though: 'We're asking,'
I confessed, attempting at discretion,
'we're asking for a friend.'
               He answered with a question:
'Does your friend know that you're asking?'
      Yes, we had discussed it.
      And since there was a father did he know?
      The situation yes, but not that I am here.
      'And are there any others?'
                   There are what?
I had to pause, a pause which answered all.
'My friend,' I didn't wish to snap but snapped,
'my friend is married, the gentleman is divorced.'
      Was he too calm? But given how often
similar conversations could occur, such calm
to some might appear acceptable.
                  'Please inform me,'
I was asked, 'of your friend's well-being,
let's say her state of mind. Please understand...'
      There was quiet, for me there had to be,
but reasoning I told him: 'She's stoic if confused...'
then listened to his catalogue of terms and phrases
you merely read in certain books,
thankful he would not resort to euphemisms.
And as he itemised I jotted down the what, where, when
and cost of *What's a girl to do?*
              Then came his proviso:
'Even more than any of our patients
we require discretion. In case your friend is unaware

106

our procedure is illegal.'
                              Margot was aware.
          I'd no need to 'enjoy' our conversation,
though I was surely fascinated, the way he trusted me,
the way he mentioned: 'After seeing half a dozen cases
botched then going wrong, decidedly wrong,
that cured me.'
                         A quiet man
for a quiet task few would speak about;
don't make him some crusader though,
he also was a Collins St professional.
          It can be imagined can't it: his wife the churchgoer,
not him; weekends centred on his hobbies,
first editions or vintage cars, wood-carving or
the *World Record Club*; a pipe-smoker if only in his den;
or this one could be conjured:
rounds of golf with men whose daughters, sisters, wives
and even lovers he may have assisted,
men who might've guessed yet didn't wish, want or need
to know such things that required discussion,
except it seemed with women like myself.
          And did this specialist understand for whom
I deputised? We'd not meet again,
so even if there were an answer that was doubtful,
only three others were aware such actions, such concerns
were being contemplated: Margot, Trixie and myself.
          Will of course told Lew his situation:
they mulled, drank a bit (Will in moderation)
then mulled some more. A politician with pregnant
mistress/lover/girlfriend, he wouldn't be the first.

                              *

          Then, and Will would never know it, Margot baulked.
Hardly due to any illegality, she told me
though still asked: 'Is this how I'm meant to live my life?
Except,' she answered, 'I'm out of adolescence Cath, well out...'
With much she'd have to quit or quit quite soon:
Lightfoot and that Lightfoot life, *Style*, its kind of Melbourne,
to finish with her Will. 'My man,' she told me,
'is definitely the right one.'

'That was my clumsiest time,' he would admit,
'though I am rarely clumsy…'
                                        And if recalling his first attempt
at marriage, we let him think so. With an expectant,
less-than-official spouse in residence (even with her sister
and a daily help nearby) Will negotiated with his party
for some form of leave, we never asked an explanation,
he would inform us what he wished informed,
allowing us to observe adjustments, readjustments,
for Margot now was set she told me,
and if a model's working life was finite, what would she
be doing next? Starting some deportment school?
You put that in the *As if!* category.
                                        How set she'd be
Margot understood, was when the photographers
arranging the Racing Carnival promotion,
indicated how she, the serious, elegant one just beamed,
as Poppy, Annabelle and Cherry all conceded.
Within weeks they would discover the reason,
make it the only one for the beaming:
'Not that Civic Leader? No, that Politician!'
                                        And if some might see our couple starring in
some wide-screen weepie, I trusted something more discreet,
British perhaps, surely in black-and-white:
two vulnerable adults from a certain town's well-heeled section,
this town priding itself it lived without pretentions,
though there were plenty: petty, temperate, quite hidden,
with gossip seeing to it there was no scandal (first off)
just a rumour trail commencing:
'Don't want to mention it but I may as well…'
urging-on an appropriate *frisson* (how the term was loved!)
to vibrate through the core which was considered *Style*.
Since hadn't Margot seemed the very face of Modern Melbourne,
even before her marriage being one half of the city's Golden Couple:
rising Civic Leader with attendant model,
if becoming much too modern now, a woman for whom
a man might sacrifice a whole career, as he would,
that career at least. 'Go ahead,' he'd be advised.
'Might the UK be suggested? Aren't you as well connected there
as you are here?'

Lightfoot had been known for vengeance,
if never towards Margot. Was she paid off? Perhaps.
When it came to the rest of her, she'd be ignored.
His only target was (it's heard he put it this way)
'The man who has acquired her.'
With an amount of Melbourne heft if hardly style
there'd be enough to suggest their party not dispose per se
of Will, but with another young, ambitious man
anxious for a Federal Seat, some avuncular windbag
might suggest that though 'The Party's proud of what you've done…'
and other clichés, Will might dispose himself.

'And even with that crowd,' came Lew's reminder,
'it's in the numbers, brother.'

Blunders

No passengers, just him heading home
from yet another Party function,
the night that Lew ran off the road
and tipped into a gutter. There should've been a bend
except the road, like nearly most of Melbourne's roads
required no bend.
                                    Those were the years
plenty ran off the road, and with the night parade
of ambulance, tow-trucks and police
some were rescued, some were not; also the years
a nearby GP might advise (what some might term advise)
'Nothing too much wrong…cut back a bit…
just teach yourself to stop…' Near fatuous as Lew's
'Been unlucky Cath…'
                                    And lucky for you, for us,
Cath was on holidays and, as in the opening lines
of some gag: 'A sheila walks into a panel-beaters, see…'
that's what she did.
                                    But even with a lack of injury,
though with its skewed attendant optimism,
these were as Margot had reminded me still crazy times,
such times to carry Lew's admission
'Been misbehaving, Will.'
                                    He needn't have asked.
Will would contact whoever he knew

and if there were to be a file that file might be mislaid.
　　　　　Or there'd be checks, there had to be,
about the papers, keeping it out of the papers,
though with the continuation of the Road Toll
one more car tipped sideways into some gutter
hardly rated news.
　　　　　　　　　'If unlucky,' he was told,
'you might make *Truth*, but Lew it's sure to be
just one more pithy par in their Topical Taps.
What else? You're not that famous…yet.'

*

　　　　　Some days I would accept:
'Yes you're married to an amiable, talented man…'
yet other days I had to understand
'He's still a foolish one who may again
tip into a gutter. He likes to think how much
he backs our marriage, but what does Lew believe in?
Winning of course, in his deceptive, easy-natured style;
family life, after his fashion; his mother after his fashion;
and good men for mates like Will, indeed like Darky.
"You guessed correct," I can imagine his response,
"having a decent time of it." Sure Lew, in a gutter.'

*

　　　　　After those holidays when I attended first to Margot
then to Lew, then to our car, the first week back
I finished wrecked, at least wrecked enough
to have me yelling (and I'm never known to yell)
at children I believe I liked:
'Please don't push me…accept that I'll not be pushed!'
Whatever those words meant to be they meant to me
where did *that* come from, and where indeed
would it be heading?
　　　　　　　　　It headed to this other outburst,
when, on a Friday, late afternoon, I'm discovered crying
at my desk, hardly bawling though why not,
everyone had left, and rating my tears six on a scale of ten

110

I felt safe.
        But the door opens and in strolls Mr B,
who might say 'Oops!' though 'Oops!' just barely says it,
instead he's using his well-developed 'Hey-y-y-y…'
but stops, for is a man supposed to see this,
and if he is how must he react?
        Who was the more embarrassed?
He may have blundered-in but who's the blunderer?
This member of the self-proclaimed *Fast Set* in tears,
tears which now increase,
which rather tests the style of Mr B who,
giving no thought to any of his supposed cool
tries to assist: 'I'd help if I knew how…'
and if the situation seems banal, let's make it more so:
'Do you,' he pleads 'need a glass of water?'
        She'll have a glass of anything,
confessing how, not so many days ago
'My husband ran off…ran off…'
and as Mr B stares near-to-horrified
he sees her adjust: 'Not with another woman,
off the road! You won't know who he is…or will you…
and yes it's drink, drink which keeps him amiable,
so amiable, our car, my car finishes on its side
in a gutter.' But if she tries to emphasise
'Car, driver, and even marriage all are fine today…'
that he's to understand also applies to her.
        'So,' asks Mr B, 'can you drive home?'
        And I'm thinking: 'Who do you take advantage of
if in fact you do? And given you're the first one out the gate
what's kept you back tonight?'
        If such answers never will arrive here's the consolation:
an unspoken assumption he won't be telling anyone.
Yes Mr B I am recovering. And thanks, I'm driving home,
home to find a husband not drinking much tonight,
how's that for a pithy par?

*

        Whilst to reward him for a tact
few knew Mr B possessed, over the remaining months
I'd listen to this voluble boy (we'll call him that)

111

and as if *Please hear me out someone has to be told*
I got to know him.
        'Even if all teaching seems an act,
it isn't just-an-act, you merely act yourself.'
And if Mr B had done this for all his bonded years
it wasn't to become his working life.
'Headmaster material?' he asked to assure us both.
'Very doubtful.'
            As for the current one,
bête noirs require an energy Mr B decided to forgo,
indeed a near-to-pity almost rose.
Except *that man* might be The Boss for most,
instead he was for Mr B plain Bossman,
and in a ramped-up reverie here came riffs upon his fate
for Bossman: 'I'd love to know how someone
truly riles him, so we can see him lose it though he won't.
Bland is the very word except it never will be bland enough,
for there he'll stand, four square centre of the schoolyard,
holding his latest sheaf of plans,
discussing with an appropriate foreman
where a grader might be grading next,
then waving on that grader. We've seen three years of this.
Hey Bossman,' Mr B was primed, 'it's 1960!'

Truth

       'He may be loyal but Darky's made some errors,'
Lew informed. 'Whatever they are that Bulgarian tour
of his has been postponed. Perhaps he'll get back with
his Mrs Darky, move bush, put up with her church,
see his kids again if she lets him, if they let him,
if anybody lets him.'
            Were the Commos permitted
to leave town? Whatever the comrade's errors
and their penances, Darky's we compared with Will's:
'Bye-bye co-respondent, you've a future somewhere but
let's ease you out. Do it please, for Margot and the Party.'
        And what of Labor's errors?
Always in the numbers brother, always the numbers.
       Lew had been phoned, Darky's morale was down,
for Marj had been around, avenger Marj:

'No Bulgaria this year, comrade, you've brought it
on yourself…' whatever he had done.
        And Lew with his code of *What a mate's
supposed to do* headed to that pub where,
afternoons after he'd knocked off early,
Darky did his drinking.
                    Though that day saw
an even more bewildered Darky:
'You pulled a swiftie mate, a real one nothing realer.
Was I set up to meet this Will, this Honourable Member
and, I can't believe it, at the footy?
Whilst today I find, not only is he in the Ruling Class
he's getting it off with some high-grade model!'
        This needed answers:
the grandeur of the Will and Margot passion
transformed into a Commo's paranoia,
if only Lew could find the questions.
Darky though obliged.
        Though the scandal may have been suppressed
by all who wanted it suppressed,
they hadn't figured it being found in *Truth*,
and if for Darky the essential *Truth* was footy
and the form guide, right here he's reading on page three,
how the Civic Leader's model wife has run off with her
MP lover, all three featured with these glamour shots.
        And Darky's telling himself, if no one else:
'I know that cove I know that cove I know that cove,
Lew's lawyer mate I met at the footy!'
        'Look here look here,' he waved page three
'how could you Lew…' he sounded near-to-jilted.
'How could you?'
              Then came the only explanation,
that true Aussie one: 'He's a mate like you are Darky.'
        Which didn't settle Darky:
'He knows who I am so what does he suspect?'
        Lew tried again: 'Commo or not
aren't all us Magpies suspect?'
And, as if that was understood,
Lew commenced to improvise: '*Truth* eh?
They've tried hard keeping it a secret since, y'see,
my mate Will's in love and so is she,
and love's been known to happen.'

Darky though seemed less romantic:
'Tell us,' he asked, 'you know that mob,
what's worse, rootin' some Civic Leader's missus
or being at the footy with a Commo?'
      Though Lew was no expert on that mob:
'I reckon we better say the latter.
And if your comrades found out you were at the footy
with a leading member of the Ruling Class?'
      That would prove yet another error,
time again to send round Marj.

Leaving

      What do you do when crying at your desk
there enters Mr B?
              What does he do?
      Months earlier I improvised for our *Fast Set*:
'Being a decade older, Mr B, let's offer some career advice.
Disc Jockey, that's today's term isn't it?
Imagine you've become one and after your evening time-spot,
in the wake of your *Melbourne Style* profile,
you're scooting to some South Yarra pad of Annabelle's
or Cherry's.'
         We barely knew him,
thought we understood just what he was,
then I discovered him to be less, no make that more:
a youth quite vulnerable at times not of his choosing,
still finding out what yesterday has taught today,
what today might teach tomorrow.
      By Third Term he had had enough, and be it cool
or be it hot, like something *Mad* magazine had conjured,
parody was taking over and he was set to leave
and leaving be adored: 'Oh Mr B, how could you go?'
      That improvising wasn't so far off,
the school was made for improvising, and ever since
Lew had rolled our car I'd possessed too much of the makeshift.
Though the *Fast Set* knew this wasn't improvised:
'My mistake girls, I loved being committed,
and thinking that I might adapt this much
isn't quite inverted snobbery, but when our year is up
I might need to walk away…'

Since now there was Grace,
'our governess…' in Rod's estimation, dull, consistent Grace
until she wasn't.

'He's asked me,' she informed.
He's asked you what and who is *he*?
'You mightn't understand, who does, but I think…
Grace paused, 'I *know* we're getting married.
How can I wait?'

I can still recall him, him the medical student,
if not his name. And Grace? A bush girl really,
and more a marrying kind than I had been when her age.

Babies delighted her: 'One day soon, yes please!'
But they'd be living where and how on what?
Oh there'd be plans, he had them.
Sure that student did (he better have) and I'm thinking
'No one should do it quite like this, but plenty do…'
knowing I hadn't grasped on that idea as much as some,
maybe finishing like Jean, amused by a longish trail of suitors;
though meeting Lew I'd avoided that.

Lew had sensed his career was fine,
quite necessary, though in life there must be a plan.
Well like Grace's boyfriend I possessed it
and what we'd be requiring now was someone
less of a 'governess', but quite pleased to
when possible assist.

The plan came swift:
let's persuade Lew's mother to sell Northcote
and that our backyard bungalow (renovated)
would be acceptable: she'd live with us but
it would be private.

I liked to think this would suit a woman
fated to whinge in moderation:
'I know I wasn't the only widowed mum living through
the Depression but…' and though tempted
I gave no response, knowing what levels of overreach
to avoid.

Styling this sleep-out 'My gunyah',
she headed to her sister's most weekends.

Some, though I've never met them,
might suggest she was being used, terming me ruthless.
True, but only through necessity, for us, the children
and for her; not the only mother such was occurring to

(if never mine).

        Jean's age, well let's say
born the same year, Gladys 'Lived for Lewis…'
that's how she framed it, when re-referencing the Depression,
never seeking suitors, even to reject.
So please, never talk to me of Mother's Day,
every year being Mother's year with, in 1960,
Trixie, Margot and their gentlemen setting the tone;
for if Trixie continued teaching, slowly or not so slowly
it turned obvious.

        This too was obvious:
even with the *Fast Set*, Lew's defeat of Lightfoot,
meeting Margot (meeting Darky!)
I'd had a no more compromising year.

        My Old Girl life and style had been avoided
until the night that somehow I was phoned
and succumbed to meet with Anna, fellow survivor
of our Eureka Youth League days.

        'Wasn't it all a folly? So,' she emphasised,
'if you find you're set to mention it to anyone bar me,
I beg please not.'

        If hardly radical by now,
Anna at least liked proving she was up-to-date,
teaching in a manner considered most progressive:
'At our Alma Mater, some of the girls I'm sure are set
to have careers…'

        And I was doing what?
Then after she was informed Anna stared and smiled
to ask: 'Indeed, what are you doing *there*?'

        Like being in the Eureka Youth League,
wanting to do good, which I assumed I had been,
all our staff had been, but then I listed
certain incongruities: 'Though the suburb's very new
and very basic, we're headed by a man who thinks
he's running Melbourne Grammar,
for if we have, as all schools have, our houses,
they're named after Homeric heroes,
our annual magazine is called *Olympus*,
and to guide our new and basic students
where they are from and where they should be heading
behold, our Latin motto! Whilst behind this Classical façade
it's shambles, more than merely shambles,

which staff and students never should deserve.'
        I mentioned the graders,
and all of her response was 'Graders?'
Yes there'd been three years of them, whilst this year
I'd shambles of my own: and our resident hipster had
discovered me in tears.
             Anna was amazed:
'Cath it sounds bewildering…' Surely it was correct
to have me found. And given her position where she worked
(the Deputy certainly had her ear)
she now proposed for 1961: Form Six British History,
Form Five English and coordinator of the magazine,
part-time yes, but near enough the salary
I'd been used to.
           'It'll be your world,'
Anna emphasised, 'we've plenty there like us…'
as if she were in fact announcing:
'Even if it means you've to cross the Yarra,
returning as an Old Girl by default,
do it Cath, do it for your own sake, back to where
the houses are named after Nineteenth Century benefactors,
the magazine is Helicon and it's natural, quite natural
to have a Latin motto.'
           Yes I wished to be employed,
yes I'd grab at anything to suit,
and if it were said much was falling into place,
hopefully without an emphasis on falling.

Quitting

     If I was leaving he wasn't merely leaving
Mr B was quitting.
        'These buildings, grounds,' came his confession,
'that's where my limit lies. Name us a teacher here or anywhere
who at times hasn't felt out of place. No?'
        I wasn't to get him wrong mind,
plenty were made for such a life and liked it;
some even enjoyed it, if hardly him.
Although with his five final days this still held:
2A had to be his favourite class,
thirteen-year-olds with all their 'Hey hey hey Mr B…'

like he was their own, much-too-cool DJ,
which gave his self-esteem little to do but smirk at me
admitting '…and don't I play along with that one…
telling them when a break's required "Take five, baby…"
knowing that they'll never get the reference.
Oh I understand, that's how I was at their age,
the more 'grown up' those boys sound,
the less they are. After Form Two I'd put 'em in
cold storage, bring 'em out, if they've survived,
in Matric.'
      Whilst for the girls,
some lunchtimes I'd see *Mr B Is Fab!*
scrawled across a blackboard, if underscored by
Mr B Loves Mr B, doubtless penned by a boy.
      And how did 2A come to love their fab Mr B?
Simple: all this term on Friday afternoons
he's read them Damon Runyon, with teacher as showman
they'd revel in his wise-guy accents.
Though Bossman finding out (from who and how?)
requested a toning down,
not that there'd ever been complaints, except there might be:
'So let's not have anything too subversive, shall we?
We do a good job here as you will too,
I'm sure.'
      This edict was ignored:
'What we're to read, what we're not to read,
doesn't that sound familiar?
Primed to almost dare him have me ambushed
it's like this: you have to think you'll make it.
And in this caper I cannot. I know this isn't meant
to be a mug's game, by 1970 though it will be.'
      When he'd commenced it had been all novelty,
next year though all novelty would evaporate,
and even if we designated Mr B as 'hip'
he loved confessing to 'A touch of the right bastard…
not 2A not now, but the moment some of them
get any older there I'll be, staring them down,
right down as required.'
      Whatever his future teaching wasn't it,
yes he had qualified, worked off his bond,
gained with certain skills a form of meal-ticket,
but at twenty-four and 'Single enough',

he still could ask: 'What exactly are you doing here?'
to answer: 'This isn't where you're meant to finish,
finish before you've even started.'

    Throughout the year he'd considered a life in music,
its promotion, its production. The risks?
He only knew of one, staying here to lead the life
of Mr B.

      'Television?' And, as if I'd asked it he replied,
'My parents tried suggesting that one,
for it still seems new, well isn't it? Too new?
Hardly new enough.' He'd only to catch
local content variety shows to know of this tradition
being set-up: songbirds and gagmen, gagmen and songbirds,
who liked to imagine how adept they were at improvising,
when improvising, this he'd learnt from Jazz,
must be an art. All else was makeshift.

    And as he flicked the word my way I flicked it back:
hadn't we seen more than a touch round here,
making-it-up from one attempt to the next,
in schools like this and shows like those
shouldn't there be something better?

    With friends he'd started up a High St coffee lounge,
and Friday evenings plus weekends
he helped to run it, music of course, mainly folk
for those who like that stuff, but on Sundays, Jazz:
the latest, mentioning names and alluding to styles
I don't think that Lew or Will or I had ever heard of,
imagining Lew's response:
'For anyone like me born to sing the standards
that might be somewhat interesting…perhaps.'

    'Jazz,' Mr B informed, 'it's neither cold nor warm,
it must be cool or hot. Can you imagine it,' he asked,
'warm Jazz? Exactly.' And here I am
thinking of all that Jazz Convention Jazz
from back when you were doubtless in Form 2.

    Now though with five days left as Mr B
it's this that matters: to spend the time remaining
reading Damon Runyon with 2A:
'Which if some might think subversive let 'em!
It's more an education than any platitudes
Bossman conjures at assembly,
this would-be, very would-be improvisor,

who loves to think we think he runs this show,
applauding himself for a first rank gagman.'

The Future (ii)

When Rod was seven some relatives considered:
'Those things he comes up with...' bewildering,
and with all the damage they entailed
verging on preposterous. Santa Claus and God for him
were interchangeable. But shutting him down?
Whether adults enjoyed what you had to say or not
weren't opinions made to be performed?
His world was heading that way.
    One Saturday the year he was ten,
Rod got to see a local auction,
and Saturdays over the next few years
he'd seek out any within the area,
so that by lunchtime there he'd be once more performing
what had been observed:
auctioneers at full throttle, inserting asides
approximating wit, which if we understood them
might be found amusing.
'Til he was turning one of *those* adolescents:
a boy crouching over a microscope,
a girl with a subscription to the ballet,
a boy at the wireless poised to catch a race-caller,
and Rod watching and listening to these auctioneers
whose confidence and swagger got him knowing
who they were, what they did and why,
and then propose, one day soon enough:
'I just might do it.' People, he had us understand,
were helped, people were even entertained,
and more important weren't you the one in charge?
    Was this the adult he might become:
a man whose grin of edgy affability told plenty:
'Maybe I am a bit of a rogue, but given I'm consistent,
a rogue you'll trust.' Though there'd be another Rod
he wanted known: 'If you're important you're no more
important than I am.'
    Yes he was clever though at what?
And seemed I guessed that kind of student

teachers either admired or dreaded,
for if a comment was required he'd give it,
if a comment wasn't, even better,
something at times Lew found difficult.
Each with his wary accommodation of the other
was his father scared? Let's say he didn't need
to seem embarrassed as, a few years further on
(Rod getting wiser by the day)
those times Lew tried not to appear too drunk
which meant of course the old man had been drinking.

  Or I'd be quizzed on what exactly
his father did, and if you explained:
'He's an Industrial Lawyer, he represents the unions,
speaks for the working man…'
this became like Santa Claus or God, fodder for his opinions,
adept at playing the grown-ups when required.

  One Sunday afternoon here's Will being asked
does he know any auctioneers (a few were known)
and if the auctioneers were working men
and were they in a union?

  Which leads Rod knows into another of those
adult mock-debates, his father being told:
'There's a lot more classes out there than
your monolithic working class,
there's classes within classes.' Will could name at least
a dozen.

    'And doubtless from those heights
you occupy,' was Lew's rejoinder,
'you might peruse these patterns in some vast terrain,
hardly though where I am operating: ground level.'

  What better way was Rod to learn,
as if, like those auctioneers, this routine
was played out for the boy's amusement, and how
he might surmise, he'd make his system operate.

  Lew as a man could promise much,
but as a father he delivered less, much less.
So any explanation that commenced
'Y'see, son…' stood little chance.

      Or later,
not much later, I'd be the one caught out,
caught out employing that double-edged demand
on which adults love to believe adolescence pivots:

'Think for yourself and do what you're told.'
      'Really Mum,' came Rod's slow smile,
'glad you've told me that one.'
                              And smiling back
I rehearsed: 'Just give up, Lew, you've lost him.
Our boy the auctioneer will hardly turn out working class,
never join any kind of union.'

                              *

      There would arrive those years when,
three times a week, if often with a mildest let down,
I returned old-girl-as-teacher to that Alma Mater
and in answer to where I'd taught
mention a suburb few may have heard of
and most hadn't.
                  'So,' I'd be quizzed,
with that brand of sympathy some women have been
bred to impart, 'so how bad was it?
                        No, it wasn't bad,
my colleagues all tried to be professional,
if likable the children hardly extended one,
and if I tried The Boss remained forgettable.
'Of course there were the graders…'
      Whatever they thought these graders were
they never asked so I never answered:
'As we have grounds staff, they have graders.'

                  *

      Who was to know that Lew, I and our marriage
had fifteen remaining years together,
call it together. Yes he'd become a politician and yes
a minister but, with this being more beyond mere guess,
most glory had preceded him.
Sure there'd been occasions, (if sometimes only moments)
when Lew exceeded Lew; sober Lew of course,
the singalong family man on Sunday drives,
or that much too dutiful son, though he had to be;
and then there was that less-than-sober Lew,

though still the friend to Will, the mate of Darky's;
or earlier our easy-pleasing featured vocalist;
or high-achieving Lew as advocate and defender,
of which a pressman once enthused:
'Few can so combine the forensic with the affable,
for such a finely-tuned routine commencing hardly as
some cross-examination, rather as a getting-to-know-each-other
always concluding: "Well thanks for the confession comrade,
why did it take so long?"'

*

            As a father Lew had tried,
or tried to try, yet setting those examples merely meant
Rod convinced himself 'I'm sure not finishing like *that*...'
and many times I barely blamed him.
Qualifying well beyond his auctioneering dreams
our son moved North, met up with sections of
Lightfoot's White Shoe Crew, developing an estate
on which he lived with, as I was told,
'Rochelle my Queensland missus,
and the family, Mum, never forget our family...
Brissie,' he proclaimed, 'isn't the slow-motion town
of Southern rumour, not any longer...' even if it possessed
'Good drinking weather...' and no, he wasn't set to down
half a dozen schooners for lunch, though for deals
Rod may have sought out those who did.
He saw and knew that game, so it amused him,
being more observer than participant.

*

        Some thirty years back, whatever grade she was in,
Helen too observed, observed and kept on asking,
the year that Sharpeville helped some imagine
'At least we're not like that...well are we...'
the year of 50 Kiloton blasts making plenty to believe
little was left to accomplish...except, except that
in Australia we'd been given a summer's worth of cricket,
that Calypso Cavalcade and other clichés,

123

the sort of cricket to get us accepting
'Colour doesn't matter that much, at least for now…'
and also, beyond all these the year of a certain election.
'Were I an American,' came Will's verdict,
'Kennedy would get my vote, if only for the glamour.'
   But closer to Ascot Vale
it may have been the year both Lew and Will skewered
the Lightfoot glamour, it also was the year of the Cement-Heads
plus the one when our car was rolled,
the one that found me visiting an abortionist (if for a friend)
the year that Rod discovered Property and its game,
the year that the Honourable Member fell *All for Love*,
giving-up so much for the attendant glamour (and it was)
of Margot and their sacrifice.
   Yet it's not that so much was done to be marvelled at
or cringed at, rather at times I seemed possessed by an off-hand
'Yes this occurred and this occurred yes yes…'
   Helen's sympathies are well beyond
those of her contemporaries who, question hard
'How did you ever put up with it?'
Although if the reply comes 'Many more put up with worse…'
that rarely assists.
     She never worshipped Lew,
I'd be horrified if she had, but she understood him
and where necessary forgave, in ways her mother
and her brother never grasped.
But then as Lew's own mother said,
certain it was being overheard,
'He's been a grand one for the ladies…'
if hardly Lew the grand seducer, more likely Lew
the less-than-grand seduced.
   Later, after those years Helen pursued then married
her lecturer (far too young was my opinion,
though I'm admitting now it wasn't) she and Kurt tried living
a kind of life offered by that form of anonymity
where Vermont South discovers itself as much a soapie
as a suburb.
    'Well,' Helen would inform,
'it didn't *not work*…' though then they had moved further out,
taking on a very mudbrick option.

*

Will never blamed those Rah-Rah Boys for his departure,
although he should have and we did. After their son was born
and Margot was divorced (yes they finally married)
after enough of let's term it intrigue,
that kind which *Melbourne Style* would leave unsaid,
after…after…after…the three of them flew out,
becoming this well-connected Australian family
in Chiswick. Jobs, employment, even plain career,
Will never need apply, our friend was always offered:
advisor to certain emerging nations (if requested)
spokesman for countless civil rights campaigns,
and an apolitical panel member, like he was becoming
Britain's most impeccable man,
and therefore, to a seething set of Empire diehards
a Socialist!
       'Oh hardly…' he was caught to sigh,
wheeling forth that well-rehearsed part maxim/
part excuse: he hadn't changed the world had,
and better yet he possessed the evidence.
       Will might return at times, Margot never.
We flew to meet them twice, once in our Summer
to endure their Winter, and once when we stretched
a few small parliamentary perks, ignoring protocols
that Lew's opponents, a twenty-three-year-old
crumbling government never sought to implement.

       *

       Then Lew's side, our side won, and after he became
a Minister we separated. Though soon, post our divorce
(too soon?) Lew phoned since someone needed telling:
'Can't think of anybody better, Cath…Darky's married Marj.'
       I'd meet with Trixie who, since motherhood
so she told me, was 'Growing bolshier and bolshier…'
Mind you she'd never join the Bolsheviks or any party.
       And as for Mr B…

My First Husband

Both of my marriages were hardly bland
and one day reasons might occur
to tell of my second spouse; not now though,
since what I've given accounts for much of my post-war years,
years with plenty of the Lew-stories,
though stories which one day would have to cease.

      For if I found myself admitting
'Yes, he's a good man…' there finally arrived the how and why
his being such a good man wasn't quite enough
and my patience stopped.

                What should be my response
(and here's but a minor example) to Lew near-reminiscing:
'Gee Cath, I'll never forget the time I almost rolled the car…'

      Almost, Lew? And would you ever take
an *almost* brief to court, an *almost* set of policies
to the voters?

          Well certain politicians like Lew, like Will
(and Darky had he been one) did,
being in the best and worst sense amateurs,

    'Why, Lewis,' asked Popinjay QC,
'why would you ever enter Parliament,
and for a side like yours? You want to serve 'em?
Serve 'em in the courts.'

          Which Lew did until he turned
into an Honourable Member, by now a sucker for anybody
primed to ask: 'Tell us, mate, what's been your finest hour?'

      And his answer, rolling out so easy
you had to believe his sentiments:
'Every hour spent with Cath has been my finest…'

      Even if you were his wife.

      Still, to audition Lew's most resonating 'finest hours',
and see how they might extend his modesty,
many ticked the Telethon, the Royal Commission,
and that afternoon when, sponsored by *Melbourne Style*,
he became unstoppable in sending-up the very world of *Style*.

      'It was 1960…' years on he'd be light about it,
'no, early '61, so let me put the blame on cricket.
I was caught up, as so many were in all that
great Australian mayhem, and as it closed I was asked to sing,
and so I sang…' He liked to put it that way.

I'm no sportswoman, the details shall remain with others,
but even we, who hardly cared about the game,
were most aroused by the way the country was infected,
when, after summers hosting the English,
headed by men with impeccable Oxbridge credentials,
and many of us thought themselves as
'White folk, just like them…' or even 'British',
enter the West Indians with a brand of cricket
set to challenge us, to prove we might be different.
How different though?

                    And reading, hearing, viewing
South Africa's contribution to that euphemism
Race Relations, 'Were we ever like that?' asked Will.
'It's possible though not now, not now.'

        'I'd say,' mused Lew, 'we better ask the Abos,
though few think about them, not where we come from…
yet here in our land of White Wowsers and White Silvertails,
White Cement-Heads and White Rah-Rah Boys,
we're welcoming black men, not just to play
but be enchanted by. May as well put the blame on cricket.'

        He went of course,
one day as Will's guest in the Members,
the next with Rod and Darky in the Outer,
wondering, although he never asked, where cricket would land
among those ever-evolving Marxist labels.

        And here is how that Melbourne Summer finished:
for the cricketers a motorcade and Town Hall reception,
after which a somewhat private celebration
brought to you by *Melbourne Style*.

        Best call it History: that moment some just plain forgot
(did it barely matter?) we mightn't be that dominant,
that different.

        'Our small contribution to the Winds of Change…'
Lew offered, whilst Jean proposed the Empire was dissolving
via sport, suggesting though we best step back and view the sham
this Summer might have been or yet become:
'Will Australia ever welcome as fine as it farewells?
Though for once, this once, it's not all novelty, all sham.'

        Will had a theory on Democracy,
applying it to this and other issues:
the population is divided into four:
the enthusiasts in favour, those who'll one day play along,

those who'll probably reject but then give up,
and that five, ten, fifteen percent who'll reject forever.
He put himself and us among the first of these
and through connections (yes plenty being still maintained)
he had us join the *Melbourne Style* shindig,
and given how much History would be present
Jean too would be welcome.

      Though Will's presence had this proviso,
the cricketers having their own Calypso outfit,
after which with Will at the keyboard Lew would croon
a set of standards, maybe not quite a set,
one that they'd been working on would see to that.

      'Out there in that certain wave of suburbs.'
Lew conspired, '*Melbourne Style* is no mere magazine,
it's family, theirs not mine, one where everyone
is well aware who is doing what with whom,
adding *Please, just don't parade it* for their watchword.'

      Yet parading's what they had done,
Will and Margot, parading past a civic cabal who,
despite some pretence at Old Boy refinement,
delivered power in ways that any Cement-Head
could but imagine: 'It's in the numbers, gentlemen.'

      What was left but making fun of it,
and there'd be Lew, that amiable legal scourge
as even more amiable entertainer
informing every Wowser and Mrs Wowser,
every Silvertail and Mrs Silvertail: 'If you want subtle
I won't be giving subtle, if you want unsubtle
you'll be getting subtle…' though despite this message
few were barely getting it, and most being present
to be entertained, Lew was acclaimed.

      'Subtle or unsubtle,' Will would enthuse,
'this has been a memorable season.
For in today's black-and-white accommodation
aren't we somehow mirroring the other?'
And he entered into almost reverie:
'Deferring just how very white we've been,
if only for a summer, yes here's a way the world
should run. True, give me time and I might itemise
the knowledge and those values that we've given them,
cricket for one…'

        'Funny,' Lew contributed,

'we gave them cricket, they gave us Jazz.
Reckon their cricket far exceeds our Jazz,
so I'm admiring *that*.'
          Did the nation actually pause, pause to announce:
'If there's an effort to be made let's make that effort…'
as when our *Fast Set* admired the courage
(though it was even more than that)
of Alison and her Subcontinental fiancé,
if that's how he'd be termed and yes, how would you?
For some of us it became near a sport
discovering and adjusting, or to overhear,
after the reception as we proceeded to the party,
the Deputy Town Clerk ask Will:
'You know these men, correct?
How might we describe them?
I'm certain they won't take offence, shouldn't though
we get things, how might it be said, in place?'
          Will as diplomat was quietly adamant:
'Let's name them the Tourists, our friends
the Caribbean Tourists. Aren't we besides all part of
the Commonwealth of Nations?'
          Lew though was primed for mischief:
'Whatever we are at least we're not South Africans,
well are we? Imagine South Africans doing this,
any of this? Mind you,' he turned my way,
'don't see any Abos here…' and to amuse himself
surveyed the party, 'funny that.'
          I surveyed my husband:
'You're not about to say that publicly, well are you?'
And his look had this moment of
'Let's show 'em something truly daring for once…'
but Lew deferred.
                          'Some day I might but now
they wouldn't get it. Let's see a future though
when they might have to. We're on board besides
to entertain them, entertain ourselves.'
          Centre of the Reception Hall,
they'd wheeled-in a Concert Grand, just right for Will,
the Honourable Member for Boogie-Woogie
to pound-out his farewell to Melbourne and its *Style*,
set to quit his Federal Seat, his fifteen percent swing,
all for his pregnant mistress, accompanied by his mate,

sometime worker's hero and Town Hall crooner
who in ways Leading Citizens were unable to,
performed that memorable duet with Lightfoot.
They were still delighted: 'Did us one right service
our guest vocalist…though does he know it?'

Now, on this late-afternoon,
fuelled by canapes, bubbly and laid-on best behaviour,
all framed by the sponsorship of *Melbourne Style*,
a city's élite would hail as friends these Caribbean Tourists
as none had ever been hailed before.

I recognized some of our Civic Fathers
then guessed their sons the ever-rising Civic Leaders,
each escorting his Charity Queen they gathered round
Will's presumed replacement, a no-hard-feelings type except
the man was in and Will was not. 'Hard feelings? None at all…'

'Our Silvertails are still in town,' Lew muttered.
'Melbourne remains their bailiwick, they'll never leave.
I'm off to find some cricketers…' and primed
away he ambled.

Whilst over there, Margot informed,
were Poppy, Annabelle and Cherry, and as she waved
they returned her wave.

'Shall I introduce you?'
But 'Hey Cath hey!'
And being more announced than named
I turned to face an exuberant Mr B, to find myself replying
'Life after teaching, eh?'

Yes life well after it. Last week,
whilst his High Street coffee lounge was being profiled,
Melbourne Style knowing talent right away
plain snapped him up: 'You can't get any place without PR,
it's where I've landed. If Bossman saw me now…but hey,
explain yourself!'

'What brings me here? My husband, Mr B,
is set to sing. Shall he be introduced?'
I summoned Lew.
'Sing?' asked Mr B. 'Sing what?'
Why standards old, standards new, plus truly emerging standards.
'Volare' for one.

Mr B put all his Rat Pack mode on hold to stare,
fearing I'm sure 'Hey!' to sound a touch excessive.
'If not today,' Lew reassured him. 'Our cricketer friends

130

have persuaded Will and I to join in some of their Caribbean standards,
the kind of numbers all Aussies need to know since...'
I knew Lew's in-excess enjoyment,
'since aren't we in the Commonwealth of Nations?'
                                                        'Hey!'
            We welcomed over several of the Tourists,
and as polite and doubtless as bemused as us were introduced to
the singer's wife, her sprightly aunt, to a somewhat pregnant
younger woman 'A friend of ours...'
and to an energetic younger man speaking an English
one might have thought he'd gathered at the movies: 'Love your game,
mine's PR, hope your music's equally percussive.'
            And it was, with bongos making many a Melbourne dignitary
all probity suspended, commence a-nodding and a-tapping
since with such a novelty well, wouldn't you?
            Popinjay QC would neither nod nor tap,
the spectacle of his supposed confreres
losing what had passed for sense gave the man his cynic's smirk,
which smirk increased as Will approached the keyboard.
            And it is like he's eighteen again,
facing what passes for Society, expected to perform Chopin
or Schubert, beginning though with thirty seconds of
Meade 'Lux' Lewis; except today he's a divorced man,
somewhere in middle-age, set on exile, confessing to us
'Negro music, name a better mode of rebellion!'
            And after he had pounded out his boogie-woogie
(those who applauded certainly did applaud)
'Jean,' muttered Lew, 'let's offer you an even truer bunfight.'
            'Yes let's,' came her agreement, 'yes let's indeed.'
            'With our cricket mates,' Lew announced,
'Will and I have been adapting an old Calypso standard,
this time,' he bunged it on, 'into a dinky-di
Australian one.' And though it mightn't be exactly *Style*
Lew was granted both the sound and sense of dinky-di.
Now very much on his terms the bunging-on increased.
'And we're playing this for you our Civic Fathers,
our Civic Mothers (ladies!) their sons our Civic Leaders,
Silvertails and Rah-Rah Boys, Wowsers and Cement-Heads,
old boys, old girls and pre-selected candidates,
Melbourne Style, may we present for your great democratic family...'
then bowing to his pianist, 'Maestro...

In Melbourne town there lived a high-toned gent
whose career path finished-up in Parliament,
and though he's well known we won't mention his name
for it's too much connected with scandal and shame,
since there's no better place for an imbroglio
than his blue-ribbon seat with all voters in tow.

Woe is me,
shame and scandal in democracy,
woe is me,
there must be standards in democracy.

He'd a grim former marriage but past his divorce
guessed being single was a mighty resource.
For one woman would give him the time of his life,
excepting this lass was a businessman's wife.
But they started parading as belle and as beau
in his blue-ribbon seat with all voters in tow.

Woe is me,
when it's this version of democracy,
woe is me,
this rather challenges democracy.

For our young politician living in sin
the numbers went out and the numbers came in,
with this party elder set on speaking his mind,
he'd a ruthless demeanour though he tried to be kind:
'Your status is buggered when the status is quo
in a blue-ribbon seat with all voters in tow.

Woe is me,
so sorry mate but that's democracy,
woe is me,
cave in for us and for democracy.

For now it's on notice you've been sowing your field
and here comes the harvest that the sowing will yield,
if you start to nibble another man's fruit
he'll organize that you'll be given the boot
the order's been issued, the order says go
from your blue-ribbon seat with all voters in tow.

Woe is me,
please do your duty to democracy,
woe is me,
my, what a credit to democracy!'

Giggling through the performance came Margot
(had she ever been known to giggle?)
'You reckon it's shame, you call this a scandal?'
Well yes there'd been some scandal if no shame,
hardly with the man she loved,
and she knew that Poppy, Annabelle and Cherry
just wanted to stride in catwalk mode across the room
and embrace her for 'Oh, those exquisite risks you've run!'
neither shame nor scandal to them but a lovers' triumph.
Now it's becoming that kind of song
doesn't this town deserve, and if Lew seems excessive
isn't the afternoon deserving of excess:
'One more time the chorus, please!'
Then whilst the Civic Fathers and their Civic Leader sons
bellow forth the chorus Lew's demanding,
with certain flummoxed clergymen and matrons
heading to the exit, and Charity Queens a-squealing
'What shame, what scandal, woe is me indeed!'
Mr B makes sure he owns the bunfights
by letting forth his greatest ever 'Hey!'
At home Lew will perform it
over the next few months, trying to embarrass Rod
who'll understand, and Helen who won't appear to;
but on this day Lew bows and savouring that it's his show,
his show and total go, sees to it both pianist and band
shall be acknowledged. But isn't set to stop:
'Now for our next number…any requests?'
Might it even be 'Volare'?

IV Breakfast with Darky

A middle-aged high school teacher, Melbourne, the late 1970s.

Often parking when I visit Kim
I recall this other car:
the one that returned to prop outside
our place, Marj and mine, in Ascot Vale.
          'Don't tell me,' I forgive myself,
'I'm starting to feel just like those spooks
of twenty years ago…the ones
(not dim-witted, not even thuggish)
I tried to write about in
'Just Doing My Job'
the flagship story of my first, my finest,
make that my one collection.

                    *

At the appropriate committee
the chairman felt I'd been too kind.
          'Without the working class,' he fantasized,
'that lot would slit our throats.
Of course you have to wonder what's
inside a rapist's mind, a priest's, a spook's…
you do it well though…' and,
as his mind changed gears, 'Well I suppose
they're victims too…' (well they weren't) and,
before he could be halted,
headed into closing mode:
'Now what was it that Lenin said…?'

                    *

I've never been a spook of course
and these days, catching me parking
outside Kim's, am just a father
visiting his daughter.

Early one school year Mick,
a young newcomer, sought me out:
saying my name then saying my name again:
'Does anyone round here know who you are,
who you really are?'
        Macho, bustling with it,
he had a loud, a very loud
matey integrity. His job, I was advised,
was making sure the kids he taught
both read and wrote. I liked him
and he (he used the word) 'Adored'
Just Doing My Job: Stories from the Struggle.
Hadn't the Special Branch
'Those pale, pinched men in gabardine…'
been buried by my sheer humanity?
        Mick was so sincere, so fragile with it,
I couldn't bother to advise:
'In the end I only wrote what the Party
wanted. Quitting that much of my life
required…how much heroics?
Just one. One on a day I would not
be labelled. Simple? Yes simple.'
        Though I might've told him next time:
'Bugger the form guide. Every smoko
didn't Darky Nolan reach for the very latest
in realist writing, just as they were doing
in Bulgaria?'
        But Mick never fawned.
And he if anyone might still enjoy
Breakfast with Darky and other stories
typed neat in their manila folder,
waiting in a drawer, our very special
'What's the use tell me what's the flamin' use?'
Australian samizdat.

     *

       Outside Darky's
like outside ours, there often parked

a spook. So one morning, feeling for the man,
he trolleys out fruit, cereal, toast and tea
with 'How'd we like our eggs today,
eh comrade?' Poor spook, poor so poker-
faced, with all that golden rule rammed
right up him, spook.

     The struggle too had spooks.
   'Yes yes,' the committee would concede
(and Marj served on this committee)
'yes yes a fine adventurist game,
yes yes might make a brilliant skit on
Sunnyside Up…' But no no,
didn't Comrade Nolan truly understand
we're at war and our warning is:
'Don't serve spooks, serve the only class
that matters!'
     Would we'd all been warned
just how much game (and not just Darky's)
life had become: their spooks, our spooks,
and every committee: all game.
    Which is what my story said.

         *

   Marj shook her head:
'I always knew you were…' and giving out
her weak, wan smile, 'a capitalist roader!'
   If it arrives from no matter where
(managing directors, elected representatives,
the foreman, your spouse, history itself)
there are some, the truly lucky few who,
first time they hear it, already know:
'Friends, we're listening to a cliché!'
And more for any 'class that matters'
I wrote for that small few.

         *

      In Ascot Vale,
on kero-heater nights, just made

for the very coldest war, I'd worked
at what's required to be
a whiz-kid, vanguard, realist writer.
Succeeded. Stopped.
                              So that later,
years later, Mick could tell me: 'Those days
bred near-giants: Hardy mate, Waten, Morrison
sure…but you, you were writing
the history of our future. What happened, mate?'
           And if I wished I could've asked
'You are meaning what?'
but liking the man only had the wistful
energy to answer: 'Mick, the future had arrived.
'Breakfast with Darky': who'd publish that?
Quadrant? For the wrong reasons,
and even if they were the right ones
I still believe in self-respect…'

                              *

           I had to.
Imagine having a wife, a comrade,
who not just left you but
went to try and redeem Darky Nolan,
wean him off the neddies,
turn him from proletarian court jester
to indispensable leadership-group cog.
           What is a game if not that?
           Well this: a half-life as elected rep,
from one staffroom to the next,
accommodating all who would've once passed
as 'enemy': the insisting principal who has
'Not haha immodest claims…';
his deputy whose only interactions
all seem to end in 'No seriously folks…';
some lady coordinator whose faith proclaims
'There's lots to admire in today's Top Forty…'

                              *

Or this game: with some try hard
Jazz band merging in their fashion
'The Internationale' with 'Oh, Didn't He Ramble',
and a waterfront heavyweight
part bellowing/part blubbering 'On yer Darkeee!'
and me biting my tongue knowing
that goose down there in his purple suit
with overdone lapels, that mega-goose
was chosen (no other word)
to be the second (more appropriate)
Mr Marj.

    (Ahh Marj, ever loving, evermore
correct line, fully indignant, spook-hating Marj:
when we turn into a People's Australia
you'll head our Secret Police!)

    With the deceased
hardly the type for eulogies the afternoon
would give us tales, Darky tales:
heckling in 'a robust if predictable
Marxist vernacular';
on the Bulgarian Friendship delegation
and getting lost (thirty-six hours mind!)
in Plovdiv; Darky hardly coping but
really trying with Women's Lib;
Darky as stepdad well yes as stepdad;
Darky, the spook and that legendary breakfast.

    And walking from the wake Kim got told:
'Well Darky always meant it!'

        Not so.
'He was a fuckwit, Dad. You ever seen him
in that suit at some trash 'n' treasure?
And going on how everyone was proud I went
to Uni High. And pleading things like
"Show your father gratitude."
What do the bosses do with all their Darkys, Dad?'

       *

    From the community centre
the songs that Darky sang spread
into the late spring evening.

(If you didn't know them word-
by-word you might've sworn them
to be vaudeville.)
      'What do the bosses do
with all their Darkys? Parliament, Kim.'

V Moonlight in Vermont South
or
Also Starring Bob Hawke as Himself

Helen's father was a member of the Whitlam Government (1972-75).
The Melbourne suburb is pronounced Ver-mont.

I d-d-don't care who's got the n-n-numbers brother, so long as I get to c-c-count the
v-v-votes.

Pat Kennelly

Dramatis Personae

Long after we had moved from Vermont South
(and our boys were up the bush, interstate or overseas)
Kurt and I would find ourselves as dinner party special guests,
this pair of aging raconteurs telling and re-telling younger friends
our repertoire: how never had we viewed such tragi-comic
farce-disasters than from our twenties into our early thirties.
        And, as kids at story time, both from the hosts
and their other guests this cry arose for more:
'Tell us again, about Lew's finest moment…'
and there we'd be that lunch hour in the city where
(mid-November 1975) desperate, but loving every minute of
his desperation, my father, clambering onto the tray of a Ute,
breaking every rule of oratory he could,
gives forth his wonderous harangue,
the one which (as second item on the evening news)
made him near-to-famous.
                        And speaking of fame,
how about my mother Cath who, of course,
should have become the politician, and who,
after their divorce remade herself,
and as a columnist of great repute,
so attuned to what so many women thought
that when she wrote her memoir, Germaine Greer
(you heard correct!) was first in line to pen
a blurb-quote!
                'Was that enough?'
we'd ask the table.
                'No no, it never is enough,

we still have to hear about (you know) that couple,
tell us once again about the Curnows…'
and what it was like when Ingrid, our candidate,
and her sniggering Des, tried turning all Karinya Crescent
and beyond into some rumpus room,
who acted like they had, or might have had,
or tried to have had (or hoped that everyone
would think they truly had)
a swinging, Vermont South style, open marriage.
Except it seemed that starting well before
the night Bob Hawke came by for drinks
certain things were turning not-so-gently
into the Curnow's dopey-soapy, 'adult' sitcom.
          And that's when, I'd confess,
whilst observing what had to be observed
in Vermont South, how I enjoyed tending to
my inner-bitch, that one who thought: 'Oh Ingrid,
you should've stuck with the Glen Iris Young Liberals
woo-hoo!'
          Then Kurt would ready himself,
side-tracking us with Rod, my bemusing bane
of a brother who, as master of perversity,
finished up working for and living on some
Queensland country club estate,
and who loved telling us how yes,
he might vote for Dad and all his has-been mob…
but only just.
          Then, while Kurt was on
the topic of perversity, how about the truly non-perverse,
the most boring man he had ever known:
Ewan Adcock, bank official, glum Labor stalwart,
he of the world's most masterful groans,
and Marlene Adcock, grand sleuth of marital and
not-so-marital peccadillos, forever
'On the case…'
          More tales and still more tales,
of Lew, Will and the Ding Dong Daddies;
of Margot the model, Poppy the model and Dee
the Go-to Girl; of Gib the Glib;
of Phil Baxter, Ingrid's paramour and his invisible spouse;
yet returning almost by default to Lew, Lew Johnson:
dance-band crooner and barrister,

scourge of both the shonk and stooge,
set to bloom briefly as one of the better loved
Well he wasn't the worst! members of the Whitlam Government,
my Dad on that Ute.

That Hero, That Fool

When he was sacked (when they all were sacked)
it turned out the best of times for those like Lew,
him in all his kamikaze honesty to demand:
'If someone's set to make himself a fool,
comrades, let him be me!'
                                        So they let him,
the Minister for Something Once,
a beefy man laughing on the back of a Ute,
trying to woo White-collar-land, one lunchtime in
the Melbourne CBD.
                                        Then, when the sneering comes up with
'Factions, you lot were nothing but factions!'
how does Lew reply?
                                        'Some call 'em factions, brother,
I prefer mateship!'
                                        'Boom. Boom.'
Later that evening my even-more-deflated Kurt went
'Boom bloody boom. They've caught him, Helen,
caught him saying things like *that.*'
                                        Yes, except
when a campaign's ten-out-of-ten doomed,
why not that luxury landslides never permit:
the truth? Since if a rout's to have its heroes
wasn't Lew that kind of hero?
                                        In seven years he'll be reduced, 'Jeez Bob...'
to not much more than Boy Scout babble:
'Sure I'm no Patrol Leader, but hey,
mightn't I still make a decent Second?'

Why are We in Vermont South?

Soon after the defeat,
when Ingrid joined our Labor branch, Kurt and I
at first agreed our young-married-land required
what this Ingrid Curnow might supply,
whilst Ewan Adcock and Marlene
(our Mr and Mrs Vermont South)
thought near enough the same.

      And hoping that the suburb (indeed Australia)
would realign with justice, sense and us,
our local branch still convened, so that
one February evening, before proceedings started,
as I was seated by Marlene,
girl-chatter started to consume us:
'I'm new to Vermont South,
so what's our local beer-barn called…the Bur-vale?'

      I looked up to see a woman's head
shaking in slow if mock despair, or not so mock.

      'How could you find yourself in a place
with a name like that…the Bur-vale?
Let's have some standards please, which is why
I'd love it if *you* (the ALP) would turn out *we*
(that's me and the ALP). Oh I'm Ingrid Curnow,
during the election I was at a rally
and the speaker, bit of an oldie sure but he was both
adorable and brilliant, possessed that kind of passion
I didn't know politics still had.
Want to know my history? Where'd you two go to school?
At Korowa (where I, the former Ingrid Frame wanted to be captain,
but was too much the loudmouth)
you could only dance with private schoolboys,
hand upon clammy hand. So I was taken on a date,
believe this one, to the Glen Iris Young Liberals woo-hoo!
Will this go against my application?'

                       It didn't.

      I told Kurt: 'We just met this amazing woman,
though why she's finished up in Vermont South
defeats me.'

      Then came his correction:
'And why have we? Might be starting here,
sure won't finish here…'

Vermont South:
great place to raise those kiddies, sure,
depending, we sensed, on what those other kiddies
proved to be, them or their folks.
Great place as well never to be a snob,
with Korowa Old Girl Ingrid Curnow neé Frame, trying hard
never to be a prefect nor a snob,
adjusting as required to all those Aussie-tucker, BBQ,
Vermont South essentials: *Testing her testing her,*
testing one two three…
                                    Meanwhile in Box Hill,
Forest Hill, Blackburn and Ringwood, Mitcham and
most surely at the Bur-vale, see us arriving for fund-raisers:
funds raised to stare him down:
embodiment of Labor loathing, mediocre local legend
Gilbert Bland MHR, him with his Fifties' slick-back,
his Seventies' side-burns and
'You'll never amount to anything will you, Bland?'
            No no no, he would not say that,
he was a man with a record, one *Damn good* record yes,
with *Damn good* Aussie-tucker ladies and gents,
who knew he knew he wasn't wrong.
                                    Still Ewan, our Ewan,
election after election gave his glum, bank officer's
best shot at being Bland's opponent, though last time,
this time, next time, please try more smiling Ewan,
please?
            Yet how could he when
each Sunday morning saw *Bland's Your Man*
in any number of his electorate's churches,
worshipping; when Bland not only knew the words to
'My Home Among the Gum Trees', deep down in Bellbird Corner
he *lived* among those gum trees; and if an occasion
so demanded he be Anti-Commo well he was:
a big big Anti-Commo, three-sixty-five times
any election year. You name any *it*,
check if he was *it* and behold Bland was!
He even owned a wok and look, look at him now
in chef's hat 'n' apron cooking *Damn good* with his wok.
In those years when 'Your local member more than ever counts!'
Ewan rarely got to smile and, even more rarely,
rated.

On Faith

And, as the branch year headed beyond Autumn
the party's only hope, if we ever had a hope,
seemed to rest on old Horrie Mason's belief
that few accepted: 'Next time this other mob
will be a pushover…'
                'Pushover, eh?'
And now came Ingrid's turn.
'Please tell us how?' She gave him little time.
'This is a mob never to be pushed-over.
And since I was a P.A. in the corporate sector
(one big lousy multinational) trust me please,
I know what can and can't be pushed.
I've had days, all women have these days
when you get up and howl "This is friggin' it!"
knowing how they'll pat your bum then plead
you have to understand, to understand,
for this is them appealing to their haha better selves.
Well pat 'em back I say, hard-word 'em
in reply and watch 'em shrivel. Whilst our opponents,
like what's-his-face this Bland,
are just their deadshit younger brothers!'
        And a murmur breezed the room, which gusted
into a squall, with the squall announcing
'She's right! This Curnow woman's right!'
      'But she's saying *what*?'
Kurt didn't wish to be bewildered but
'Surely,' he muttered, 'there's more to her
than pantsuits and some Charlie's Angels hairdo?'
      'Jane Fonda,' old Horrie sighed,
as he and his Beryl quit for a calmer branch,
'Jane Fonda isn't what we need.'
              'Old goat.'
Ingrid delighted being riled. 'Aren't we this broad church?
Am I *that* bad?'
        Of course she wasn't (yet)
and for months it seemed we would attend our meetings
just to hear her speak. Thus stage one.
      Very soon stage two: she corners Kurt and Ewan:
'You and yours must come around for drinks
chez me and mine, 23 Karinya Crescent…'

where we met 'My greying eminence and father to
our sons…' her tubby, beaming Des.
      Then Ingrid asked herself on our behalf:
'How did I become a Curnow? Well back when Monash
seemed just another husband farm, I met this man:
Psych 1, and did I last? No me and my maiden name
and maidenhead did not. Which is why we marry
don't we? And wasn't it great Des, wasn't it great,
P.A.-ing to some CEO I learnt so much about
the multinationals: how sex became two dickhead root-rats
caught by blundering me…in a broom cupboard!
Well that was great yet wasn't great I mean,
the idea of two like that, there, certainly gave
the place and me one mighty frisson
(even if she did get sacked). I scooted home
right to our flat and blabbed just blabbed, had to
didn't I? Then who could blame us, retiring
in our way to kids and this…' as from her patio
her hand swept Vermont South:
'us in Karinya Crescent, you Pet in your Winmallee Drive,
the Adcocks in their Yarralea Close,
our imperfect paradise.'
                Stage three:
Branch President within a year and
'Comrades you've been warned, serenity ain't
my middle name…woo-hoo!'
      One fund-raising buffet at the Burvale
did Marlene and I want to know what Ingrid thought?
(And if we didn't?)
                    'Well Women's Lib was okay, okay?
But little in politics beats that pinch of raunch…'
So how about she and me and Marlene
tart ourselves up as Kings Cross hookers,
with Des and Kurt and Ewan for the pimps
and work the friggin' Bur-vale floor for funds.
An Aussie first? You bet it would be World!
      And Marlene, three cab-sav glasses in,
was whooping at the thought: knowing how Ewan
wouldn't get the joke. (It was a joke?)
      Then, with us heading to the Curnow's
our hostess continued:
'In your vibrant mid-thirties hustle, you know the one

that comes when as a girl,' she let us know,
'you've sussed them out, the ways those ways:
power love sex men and kids of course,
a woman said,' said Ingrid, 'a Simone, a Germaine,
that other one or another one, anyway call it politics
but it's both the personal (obviously) and this…'
We were on their patio once more and, from right to left
to right she raised a sweeping hand, 'all this!'

      Staffrooms having one at least of these
I had been schooled in how to play the side-kick:
you shook your head, slapped your thigh and
'Ya gotta love this gal…what's coming next?'

      This is what: 'As for menopause…' Kurt and Ewan
turned to stare, 'baby, here we come!'

                        'Do you think,'
Marlene later asked, 'and tell nobody please,
that Des and Ingrid have what's termed an open marriage?'
She's read of them in *Cleo*, was on the case… and
please don't tell, mark two, the thought just wouldn't leave her.

      Pulling my search-me-face I filed the idea under
Marlene's wishful thinking. Though who of us knew
how an open marriage worked? Or if it didn't?
Or any marriage?

With the Ding-Dongs

      In the Air Force
one of the smarter lads from Northcote High
meets one of the smarter lads from Scotch,
and if that was 1942 what was 1945?
Young men eager to return home,
find some lass to fall for, after which
becoming two young barristers, hearing,
if hardly listening to the other.

      'When your crowd, Will,
jabbers on about the individual
they mean of course the boss.'

      'When your mob, Lew,
hammers away about the workers,
you'd have us think no one else had ever worked.'

      'Who owns this country?' each demanded,

with each replying as the other's conscience,
'Yes indeed, who does?'
                                    Uncle Will would say:
'For Lew of course it was always Labor,
for me of course it never was at all.
Besides, we couldn't think of a livelier disputation than
where the group stops and the individual starts,
which if we suppose is politics it's also Jazz,
and Lew and I joined forces over Jazz.
There was that post-war delight in being amateur,
to be still young enough and amateur once more:
five young ex-servicemen finishing their degrees,
hoping to play Jazz and see the post-war world,
or failing that, the world of post-war dance-halls:
Lew on banjo and vocals, myself on piano,
with a poor man's Johnny Dodds, a poorer man's
'Baby' Dodds and a cornettist capable of hitting
some of the not quite better notes:
Lew Johnson and his Ding-Dong Daddies.
Sharing a few dozen, very loud Saturday afternoons,
each man improvising beyond billy-o,
which could've been exciting or a mess, but
in the History of Jazz no act was messier,
we weren't even mediocre!
                    Knowing someone from the Jazz Convention
I conned him (name no better verb)
sight unseen and sound unheard except
ours was no sound, it was noise, that special kind
of noise to make a smartarse Emcee go:
"Let's hear it for those Ding-Dong Daddies…
well let's not…" and who could blame him?
                    Though Lew of course possessed his certain
baritone something, and putting that banjo down
your Dad was fine. Indeed somebody thought
that here was a right voice and soothing tone
for his chain of fifty-fifty Town Hall dances,
which was hardly Jazz, then or ever.
Yet we headed (me, my fellow Ding-Dongs, your mother,
all the girlfriends) to watch our Lew hamming it
and loving it: calling the bandleader Maestro,
crooning all those smoochy serenades,
making a nice little interim career of it,

148

all his way to an LLB.'
     First as vocalist,
then lawyer, politician, this became Lew's pattern:
he'd hike to some plateau, arriving to find plenty
of his mates resting up and, with Jazz in the air,
grog on tap, sheilas to mutually entertain
he sure liked it there.
      Cath though would arrive,
and with Lew's easy-does-it tenacity, thinking a touch
better of it, they'd hike again,
this time to where Mum said he, no make that we,
are headed.
     'And yet,' she told me,
'he could've done so much bloody better!'
    In that post-war bohemian austerity
they met at this Jazz Convention, Lew falling for
Cath's improbable hyperbole:
'Either I sat home and sewed to Donald Peers or
Mario Lanza, or else I'd foot it off to hear
those Ding-Dong Daddies at their mythic worst.'
    And once Lew entered the Student Prince
hardly stood a chance, with the one-time
Girls Grammar School debating captain, BA (Hons)
who knew there must be more, much more,
quitting all that old gels' hoop-dee-doo,
to that big house in Ascot Vale, where she raised us.
    Few of the old gels visited,
though Will, Will Fairburn MHR, our Uncle Will would,
if rarely with his strange, sad wife.
    Decades on all this emerged as part of
Cath's early opinion pieces. How '…in those years
after our messy amateurs trudged off stage,
this town became a wowser's paradise,
the clergyman was king or king enough,
everyone evangelising, everyone needing that side to take,
all in opposition: Groupers needing Commos,
Commos needing Groupers, whilst funny (or not so funny)
little men, you would never know, minded your business.'
    Yet there they were,
Lew and Will and Cath actually agreeing,
remove a pinch or two of politics
then see them agree on just about the lot.

(But what a time for Will to enter politics,
to try and make sure everything was reasonable,
that no one would be hurt.)

Group Portrait with Telethon

'Oh for the love of Mike!' my mother sighed,
as mothers might in those days.'
                                                'Big news
Cath and kids!' my Dad cried out,
'I've been asked to sing on television.'
        'Whatever happened to you, Lew?' he'd been asked.
'Like to quit retirement just-this-once, for charity?'
        Charity? And Cath sussed out that import:
flip Wowserville and the town became its prurient,
forever-ogling twin, with an ongoing parade of
Sportsmen's Nights and Pleasant Sunday Mornings
(one more smutty funnyman, yet another
exotic dancer) which each Good Friday
the telethon disinfected, those twenty-four hours when
not much occurred but feeling bi-partisan benign
about those poor sick kiddies, all clubs represented,
Melbourne personalities manning the phones:
why there was Uncle Will, a well-known model beside him,
which stood for a single highlight as,
captive to the shoddiness, a mother, son and daughter
stared down those kinds of variety interludes
we'd never be allowed to countenance:
squeaky ventriloquists, juggling unicyclists,
that line of dancers not getting too much incorrect,
all awaiting one-time townhall balladeer
Lew Johnson and his medley of big band standards.
        After which, as we paused for a message from
the Premier, Mum shut off the show.
        But no use to rail against ogling do-gooders,
this was charity and charity made it
irreproachable.
                        'So? I'll give you charity,' she snapped.
'Any Good Friday it's the only place in town where they
can grab themselves a free wassailing grog.'
        What better way to con their softest touch, her husband,

150

the man who could've done better than that but didn't,
who (one more dumb drunk) got home by two,
just avoiding the road toll.
                            And I wonder if prefect-rebel
Ingrid Frame, a decade or so my senior, had that Good Friday
sat through all we'd sat through,
her parents over at some neighbours, a Glen Iris Young Liberal
disconnecting her bra…

Melbourne Style (ii)

        And then some unions hire Dad for that Kickback Case
which makes him. This Collins Street boss-of-bosses
struts into court with his posse of silks,
and under Lew's truth-induced duress slinks out
through a small side door.
                        Not yet forty,
and plenty are in awe of such forensic folksiness:
'Let's go over this again plain bloke-to-bloke,
shall we?' And the word goes out to clients:
'If you're ever faced with Johnson never fall for it,
you'll end admitting all.'
And of course they would and did.
            A few though couldn't hide their admiration.
'We love it,' came the gushing, 'all of it:
pro bonos for your queue of little chaps,
taking on the shonks and doing what we could hardly do,
doing us a service too…'
            Since after this, Business would learn, learn to right itself,
and then with Business and the Party of Business scrubbed clean,
see them set for an eternity of rule!
                            Hardly Lew's desire,
nor how he saw himself: he wasn't that brilliant,
no way that powerful. 'It's just,' he tried to kid the town,
'those bastards there were crooks.'
            'I know a party that'll snap you up,'
said Will, 'and it isn't yours.
Keep your ideals, just trim the expectations.
For you are loved, yes loved, by leading figures in
my crowd.'
            And sure Lew played it admirable-folksy

to certain 'leading figures', except to others,
others who may have mattered more,
his scrubbing had been plenty rough,
skewering those who lead Melbourne to be generous
once a year, the men who love their Telethons.

      Never invited back, '…must've looked awkward…'
Lew wanted to sound rational,
'I mean I'm not our only vocalist…Cath?'
bleating for her approval.

          'Yet again naïve…'
Mum called him, certain what she deemed as
'Their betrayal…' entered family lore.

      Then came his next 'reward':
he needn't be after safe or even winnable seats,
but to be bypassed by Cement-Heads,
one pre-selection to the next and to the next,
snapping but once, the time he baited
someone-of-true-importance with:
'Look at him, at him this Stalinist stooge,
in his big, wide hat and big, thick coat
straight from the top of Lenin's tomb…'

      This copped a stuttering response,
something about Lew as 'bosses bum-boy…'
which didn't work, he stayed this calm:
'I don't like frauds, I don't like thugs, I don't like
hypocrites. And I cannot stomach much of these
each time I visit Bossland.'

      A backtrack might commence:
'Okay, he's a hired gun, we pay for his results
but but but…' and here arrived their skewed payoff:
Lew was suspect because Lew was successful,
winning through the system just delayed
historical necessities, see?

      And when that couldn't nail him
here as ever came that final catch-all
term of abuse: bourgeois as in
'His missus teaches at some bourgeois school.'

      Those days they said such things
and even worse believed them.

      Make this then Lew's true reward,
how he became a Melbourne personality,
with this to gauge the measure of his fame.

On one of Winter's grey and misty afternoons,
coming to or from whatever appointment
brought him out of his chambers,
he saw them up the top of Collins Street:
four women in pillbox and other hats,
aligned for a photographer on the Treasury Building
steps: Margot, Poppy, Antoinette and Cherry.
And into style, all this mid-season's Melbourne style
he ambles: scourge of bad-mannered business
and workingman's staunchest ally, the famous Lew.

    'I'm getting to be known a bit around town…'
If Dad were up for writing songs, we reckoned
one would feature that refrain. 'There's that famous Lew…'
we liked to think he heard them say.

    'They knew me,' he reported to his family,
'I reckon they knew me.'

                    'Well one did,'
sighed his spouse. 'Will's Margot from that Telethon,
correct? Who were the rest?' She shuddered.
'Spare us, models!'

              Once it had been Will
(whose invalid wife they rarely saw)
now it would be Will-and-Margot-from-the-Telethon,
with her estranged marriage and too, too prominent
husband.

          Did *all Melbourne* know? No *all Melbourne*
didn't know, just that three/four/five percent
who thought they had the right to know,
since wasn't it theirs, this world,
the world of Will, the world of Margot,
a couple marking time whilst Will's career went bung,
in need of friends, that kind of few supportive friends
who, Lew thought, live in Ascot Vale.

      And how he loved it, looking down from Ascot Vale
cheering them on: more victims of that class of hypocrites,
the kind that booted you off Telethons,
the kind who in their little corner of a corner of
the world (let alone Melbourne)
sustained their days to that ludicrous hum of
Will and Margot, Will and Margot, Will and Margot.

        'There's bored…' well beyond any ho-hum touch
Mum drummed her fingers, 'and then there is

bored-housewife bored…' She'd glanced at
the Women's Pages, she'd seen shots in *Melbourne Style*
of Margot Lightfoot, Poppy Brasch, all their model chums.

    'Margot,' Dad tried to explain,
'attended Mum's old school.'

                      'Can't say,'
said Mum, 'that any Margots get recalled.'

    Margot though remembered her most well:
the 'What'll she say next…' of Cath Campbell's
debating team glamour.

              Next?
This is what she said next:
'And when we're out upon our foursome,
will she and I have to convene some Ladies Auxiliary,
whilst you two Ding-Dongs reminisce and wassail?'

    Never mind the wassail:
the evening turned into an old gels hoop-dee-doo
Cath thought she had disposed of,
as the big kid debating captain captivated her new,
young friend.

           'Debating…' for she was the one now
reminiscing, 'if you were lucky they'd let you say
what the hell you wanted to,
never an adult intervening, *that's* what I loved
about debating.'

    Yet behind their Malvern privet hedge
it was supposed Will still had a wife far far beyond
bored-housewife bored, refusing to like anybody much,
with Will a rising Party man expecting they would sire
some kiddies, which wasn't set to happen.

    You *could* leave your wife of course,
leave her, even, for someone else's wife
(who hadn't known of that?)
but when that someone else is Margot Lightfoot's husband
(chief patron of telethons, head shonk Lew Johnson
is pursuing) a man of entitlement fighting for and
well beyond what he deserves, that's when,
rising Party man, your career heads bung.

                 Mum years on
would tell me of the Margot saga:
'She loved Will, she wasn't very happy;
she needed friends and I admired her.'

Out in Ascot Vale the Ding-Dongs held
their last reunion: the weatherman, the dentist,
the bookseller, the ex-MP and their host
the industrial lawyer proposing: 'To Will and Margot!'
who soon quit Melbourne.
                                    No matter how legendary
any *All for Love* bravado proved, you did that then:
quit town for London and never returned.

Often my parents clipped items from *The Age* and
for a small cost airmailed them;
and two or three times Lew and Cath flew together there,
with Will and Margot more than well aware
of their friend's career: the by-election, the Ministry,
the sacking and all his Ute glory.

Volare!

Don't tell them they were staring down
the barrel of victory! With the factions realigning
those stooges of old '…aren't merely routed,' Dad exclaimed,
'they're rooted!' With his mates the newer power-brokers
ensuring that, when one of those time-serving stooges
serves his time by dropping dead, Melbourne personality
Lew Johnson is found announcing:
'A by-election, eh, that should do us wonders…'
                        'So you ready, Lew?' they ask.
                                    'Have been comrades,'
he replies, 'these twenty years.'
                                    Though mightn't it be
a tiny bit too late to turn you into a politician,
ever thought of *that* Lew?
                        'Never son, I'm in my prime
and younger by the hour.'
                        'Singing something for the voters,
Lew?'
        'Stardust', 'Perfidia', 'Moonlight in Vermont' and
for all our Italian friends…don't even guess…it's
'Volare'!
        And on the wings of such standards,
with a stratospheric swing, right into and well beyond the blue,
my father entered Parliament.

　　　　　　　　　　'Does being an MP,'
this was Rod's opinion, 'turn our old man
into anything new? I still recognize the silly bugger.'
　　　　Then two years on, after they'd truly won,
Lew became a Minister, that kind of okey-dokey Minister
still getting the job done, except the job was being done
on him and on the lot of them.
　　　　　　　　　　　　　'The trouble now,'
and it was Rod again, 'all this'll wipe their marriage out…'
I sensing but he knowing how for Cath,
all this playing Mrs Johnson, the Minister's wife,
proved not merely ho-hum, it was no hum, no hum at all.
　　　　So Lew moved onto a couch,
then off that couch and into some apartment.
After which he was sacked, they all were sacked.
　　　　And when some union mates, it still was useful knowing,
found themselves a Ute and handed Lew a megaphone,
he cast aside that megaphone, which is how Australia heard
and saw him, a man on the evening news,
somehow enjoying himself.

All His Ute Glory

　　　　When I was twenty it seems I spent my days
in targeting a beanie-wearing tutor,
five years my senior, endearingly opinionated.
　　　　'Telethons,' Kurt held forth,
'when this town makes itself the total fool…'
　　　　Fine it must've been for him, his folks and brothers
out in their Hurstbridge mudbrick;
where I came from, even if you never watched
Melbourne's 'entertainment', in all its shabby-genteel tedium,
you felt you had.
　　　　　　　　For circa half-an-hour
Kurt had seen a Telethon, how it captured:
'All that greatness in us, our Aussie Feelgood Fascism,
with just a patina of charity.'
　　　　　　　　Cath would love that
(and I'd tell her) but first Kurt had to know how,
after the Kickback Case, somebody decreed:
'No more Telethons for Lew!'

'Which went,' Kurt knew,
'with the paranoia of those times:
there must be a Commo living in our street…who is it?'
        Cath liked him,
Lew liked him, and brother Rod would shake his head,
liking Kurt as much as anyone he liked…enough.
        'How radical am I?' Lew would ask and answer:
'How radical would you like me, Kurt? Being more
a Melbourne personality than a socialist,
guess what got me pre-selection?
You know of the Establishment I reckon?
I say let's form our own Establishment,
that's looking like as far as I can go.
Know the one thing your New Left has taught me?
How it was okay to grow my hair…'
        And though that rather undermined much
of Kurt's New Left, Lew was correct. Face these facts:
he *looked* like a Whitlam Minister,
whose broad optimist's face and plenty of middle-aged hair
had once proclaimed: 'Join us for a heap of fun!'
All of which continues till that lunch hour in
the Melbourne CBD.
                        But, as the rally closes
and Lew is getting mobbed, 'You may not remember me,'
one of the mob announces, 'but we met years back,
when I was a model. I'm Poppy, Poppy Brasch,
in deportment now and seeing you there,
standing how every Australian man should stand,
with rough-hewn roguish class,
I thought it was disgraceful, you getting booed
by mean old stockbrokers…but you never flinched
and now I'm writing you, Lew Johnson and your ALP
a big, big cheque.'
                So off Lew heads to
the *Poppy Brasch Temple of Elegance*,
and with that cheque finds dippy-hippy sweet romance.
        'Poppy love,' groaned Kurt.
                        '*This one*,' sneered Cath.
        In coming times Dad would often ask:
'How many couples collapsed that stupid year?'
Meaning, although he'd never say it,
being kicked out, with Cath to do the kicking,

if wishing all to understand
'She deserved a break…'
      And sure Cath did until,
there he was back again on the news, Lew at his best,
believing in himself at last, up on some dumb Ute,
giving stick to the corporate bodgies;
though what she hoped he was believing
(or what she needed to believe) was
'No matter how stupid I'll look for some,
I'm not doing this for them, I'm doing this
for us, Cath.'
     Lew Johnson, the man she married,
hero as fool as hero.
      And more than anyone she knew
that fool, that hero.
     A bit late though.
   'It wasn't his philandering,' Mum rationalised
however briefly, 'it's who he has philandered with.
He'll be taken where she wants him taken,
though this Poppy-thing won't last and she will
never get it. If politicians need a-woman-by-your-side
Lew's trouble is he needs half a dozen; and it's not
just sex, spend your days with bloated,
arch-important men, each with their silly world to run,
then wouldn't you be screaming:
Bring on the girls! But this one?'
      This one,
this Poppy, for her wedding snared some villa from
the National Trust and with a week to go
Lew, Kurt and I surveyed the ballroom.
'I'm crashing through…' came the look on my father's big,
Whitlam Government face, 'crashing through right through
with this…'
   Or crash.

With the Homemakers or Cath Goes to a Bunfight

   During those days of tragi-comic desperation
who gave Lew the go ahead? No one,
he simply did it, which bewildered Cath.
For if that lunch hour made him Lew the Legend

it also made him Lew the Fool,
with her elation more than matched by
her annoyance. And there I'd be receiving calls:
how what the decent Party man had done
wasn't done at all for Lew; or else
how he had wasted all: his life, her life, their life, our life,
which later combining with the wretched Poppy
more than sapped her patience.
        Years later I'd be informed how: 'No,
I never kicked your father out per se
(he would've stayed, though stayed for what?)
except I had to tell him: Lew,
this is a marriage, let's do something together
for once and quit it, we've seen each other twice,
in as many months.'
        Hyperbole? I never asked.
Poor man though, sacked twice within a year,
then sinking into that parody of all big-hearted
loser politicians as Cath rose slowly
into her reinvention.
        Meanwhile in outer Brisbane,
someone knowing enough to stir asked Rod:
'Say, wasn't that madman on the news your dad?'
And my brother, hardly due to anything familial,
just loving the perversity defended him, that madman.
        'Yes, these times are wedded to perversity,'
thought Cath and acting so, sought out, it seemed to us
all she couldn't stand.
        There was a breed of constantly concurring women,
ladies who in staffrooms, during seminars, over dinner,
seemed to have their all-in-one response
to any sorry or not-so-sorry lot.
'As you do…' they would sigh, mutter, natter or proclaim
to suit the situation, 'Oh…as you do…'
        And were you Cath you'd itemise a few:
'I hear the government's been sacked…as you do;
I better join a book club…as you do;
I recommend my therapist he's very…as you do.'
Then detesting it yet loving it enough
Cath was ignited and improvised on our behalf:
'My son works for a Queensland property developer…
as you do; my daughter lives in Vermont South yes…

as you do; my former husband's current wife runs
a deportment school...as you do *not*!'
        Was Lew forgiven? One day Cath would judge him
quite forgivable, if only after a few years' solitary sulking
she knew she'd have to quit, allowing the feistier of
her friends to offer this support:
might Cath still be the politician?
                        'What now,'
she quizzed, 'at my age?'
                        'Who says,' they urged,
'you're too old for pre-selection?'
                        Oh yes and have her ex
vacate his seat, with Cath to do the taking-over,
as somehow they'll be reconciled:
the latest feelgood, Aussie comedy, an As-you-do Production...
for whatever women are they need to be
so much more than *this*.
                        'I've done with,'
she informed me, 'that side of the political.
It's more than the political. Anyone can say
"The other team is wrong, they'll never get it..."
There's much more than that needing to be said;
I trust one day I'll be the one to say it.
I know of much that even my Aunt Jean
never allowed herself to utter,
and she was known to utter plenty.
Wouldn't I love to be the bane of those
who think that women speaking-out
remained part of some Marxist plot,
who'll never forgive their traitor forebears
giving us the vote, what a thrill to taunt 'em,
copping all of their attendant rage
if one day I were able.'
        Though canny enough not to let it show
my mother rarely deferred to anyone except
her aunt (my great aunt) Jean. As an adolescent
and beyond I got to know Aunt Jean, this tiny,
one-time Ladies College resident bluestocking,
tolerated, she maintained, as any ratbag's tolerated.
        'In those days were you,'
I'd to ask, 'one of that emerging species
a 'professional woman'? She surely was no amateur,

160

and as for being anybody's maiden aunt,
much less a maiden, she would want it known,
though somewhat of an aunt.
      'I'm not one for dotage,' Jean admitted,
'but as my body turns to relic the mind
continues to sharpen. And if these never can
be reconciled, here's my tragedy:
I still believe the worst that anyone can say is:
It's too late now…'
                  Enjoying Lew,
and what the public Lew had done, Jean thought
the private Lew an amiable mess.
We're glad she saw him make the Labor Ministry
those few months before she died,
gladder still she never got to view
his other wives.
               Yet Jean still lived of course,
those words and phrases she'd employ
had taken root in Cath's vocabulary:
hoop-dee-doo and turnout, bunfight and beaux.
      Once when visiting her Beau Mark One,
an English suitor she had met before the Great War,
we heard how Jean was much the paragon
of what he was attracted to:
a radical if independent woman, whom he once
had courted, briefly, and then remained
as friend and correspondent: 'It was delightful
not needing to agree with her, for though she entertained,
Jean was more than entertainment.
How that woman challenged!'
               'Which is why,'
Kurt some years later posited, 'Jean is everything
that Ingrid thinks she is…and isn't.'
      Here's the one time Cath encountered Ingrid,
and when, what she had often wanted to believe in,
some form of new career, commenced.
      A friend at work, she with the fired-up faith
in Cath as politician, was adamant: 'The hunt,'
this friend insisted, 'the hunt, *our* hunt is on!'
      And the hunt for what?
               'For backers,
they're wanting to find backers for

this all-purpose, consultative committee and,
here comes the killer…it's women only!'
     Killer? Cath bet it was.
But a flier was produced and the flier read
Victoria Is in Need of Women Such as You!
at some evening conflab, some place.
And fearing another bout of *As you do…*
Cath declined, yet still the friend persisted:
'Please attend, men at last are asking for advice
and the topic's…us!'
            Us? Cath bet it was.
     Some friends do not relent:
'More than merely taking minutes we'll be needing notes,
your kind of notes, for aren't you excellent at jotting notes?'
     'I trust,' mused Cath, 'notes aren't my only forté'
Though of course were Jean alive there would be notes,
they'd been the greatest pair at similar, well-meaning
turnouts, ones where you would murmur loud-enough
asides, jot-and-pass these inevitable notes.
     What might be on that evening (any evening)?
Plenty to be avoided; though for Cath this conflab seemed
the least avoidable.
     She saw no charade at first, and if
there would be certain tensions
Cath would be disappointed if there weren't.
Being a gathering more than beyond *well meant*
still this was understood: even when we disagree
aren't we in this together?
          She itemised those present:
numerous professionals; the heads of certain
charitable trusts; businesswomen staring askance
at activists, who returned the stare;
students yes there had to be students;
journalists of course; academics of course of course;
the fussy types (possibly librarians) checking
the agenda and the protocols;
and yes yes, a few murmuring 'As you do…
as you do…' as well (alas for some)
a tribe of nurturers-and-carers,
ten self-proclaimed Homemakers letting it be known
someone had to be the irritant, terming themselves
Real Women, representing those still wishing

to remain both real and women.

     'We can't quite give you everything you want,
but yet…but yet…' On behalf of whoever
sponsored this event an appropriate man
welcomed all and removed himself,
well understanding he would not be needed.

     'Never will be.' Cath overheard.
'Hold us up to the light, there's not a bloke
in sight.'

     And with so much seeming obvious,
under a heading 'Motherhood Statements',
Cath's jottings were commenced.

     The evening seemed made to bounce along,
so much goodwill was evident as 'Fine…fine…fine…'
soon was replaced by 'We are agreed…agreed?'
But no. Certain parties never would agree,
for then a grand unravelling commenced.

     The Homemakers had, pouncing early,
commandeered the front two rows; having little need
of actual opinions, why should they when
they possessed unadorned belief?

                 'Please,' Cath wished to ask,
'why are you attending?' Of course she'd hardly dare,
but sat bemused to view a dozen of these
meek yet furious matrons, some much younger
than herself, lowering their heads in near-to-prayer
muttering 'No no no no' to birth control, abortion
and divorce.

         And it seemed of little use
for Cath or anyone to offer:
'Let's at least agree to disagree…'
since lacking a charity, even for themselves,
these Homemakers were hardly made for that.
Perversity once more reigned, and how she loved it:
to see this kind of legend being born,
not nurturers-and-carers but martyrs, even saints,
hoping to be acclaimed for their good fight
and how they fought it; for then the topic of
their evening turned to children:
those they as mothers raised. 'As if,' thought Cath,
'you are the only ones who've given birth.'

     'This stand we take,' the chief Homemaker offered,

'is for our daughters' sake…' and you tried explaining how,
yes, termination, contraception and divorce
should never be imposed, excepting worse was
still imposed on us, on ours and everybody's daughters.

      But then their leader had to mention God
and there was little use suggesting
'Now hardly is the time for God…'
since they already had, and tonight to talk with *them*
you had to talk of *him*, or whoever he was,
which in the interests of civility many,
Cath included, wouldn't; and the meeting stalled
to finger drumming; until a very strident woman,
Ingrid, Ingrid Curnow (that's what the name announced)
demanded: 'Who told you to do this,
who told you to do this? Come on come on,
I bet I bet I know!'

             And the Homemakers may have had
an answer, but it never came.

      'I too speak,' Ingrid told them, 'as a mother…'
and since the game, their game, her game was on
the meeting skidded to a halt.

      With some motions passed, though more delayed,
the evening finished just a certain side of shambles,
a few like Cath admitting they'd been entertained.

      'Well,' posed one of Ingrid's allies
when some of them adjourned for drinks,
'Real Women, eh? Won't be seeing them again
and you had to laugh, the way they sat there
oh-so-housewife-earnest with their knitting…'

      Though only one was knitting. Fair game?
In a sense most excellent fair game,
since that's how martyrs want it.

                Except,
still considering: 'Who told you to do this?'
Cath tried imagining what exactly they'd been told,
still were being told and who would do the telling.
It hadn't been so long before
(a decade, a decade-and-a-half no more)
she'd seen this photograph:
of six, parched, purse-lipped men-in-black
staring at a camera and all beyond the camera.

      'The hour belongs to us,' they had announced,

and how 'this oral birth control,
like all birth control is henceforth banned…'
trusting that their sullen ignorance would pass
for truth, and how through the Almighty's grace
all that they proclaimed might yet be seen
as nothing less than a Father's holy love.
      Who had told the Homemakers?
Only two thousand years or more of men-in-black.
      Cath went home and wrote; wrote, revised and wrote
till four, slept till nine, phoned in ill, wrote again
and phoned a friend, phoned two, three, me,
and read us what she'd written.
      That was hardly the first occasion
Cath had jotted notes, not the only time she had decided
when to be passionate, when to be dispassionate,
and how to disguise them both.
'You can view this how you like.'
she thought a readership might understand
'but given my evidence you'll gather where
my engagement lies.'
      'If much of this comes from life with Lew,'
she had explained, 'it's more than likely
what I taught myself: when to step forward,
when to pause, when to retreat; making certain
all know where you stand.'
                In-house with friends,
that's where the article remained,
an amusing way to spend an amount of hours.
      Who then passed it onto Jeremy and Jake,
two young men running
'One of our foremost literary journals…' who,
so intrigued by Cath, a meeting was assembled.
      'Do you,' she asked, 'sincerely think
my efforts qualify as literary?'
      'Oh yes they may as well you see,'
she was advised, 'many out there write what they consider
literary…and we do not. Furthermore we like the way
you're bearing witness, as we believe in bearing witness.'
      'Yes,' Cath supposed, 'if that evening's scrap
required a witness.'
          Oh yes it did,
and they too enjoyed the name she'd given her account

'A Bunfight.'

       She ran with their ideas but then demanded:
'Though I've no desire for any pseudonym
we are returning to my maiden name, correct?'
       She liked that word and imagined how
even a passing nurturer-and-carer, never doubting
where Cath stood, might admit she'd certain things 'correct'
and thus deserved some prayers, which may have happened.
       Even more 'correct' what followed
had to happen. I've no idea how Ingrid found
this or any literary journal, no matter
the slightly compromising way she'd been portrayed
the result enchanted her: 'Who is this Cath,
who is this Cath? She's mentioned me,
she's mentioned me…woo-hoo!'

Swinging

       So we asked Lew the dirt on Bland:
'When his colleagues term him Gib the Glib
(and who are we to question colleagues?)
he just grins on. When I call him
Gilbert the Filbert the Knut with a K
he continues grinning, says a master called him that
at Grammar. He knows *men* you see,
that's why he was decorated Blahblahblah and Bar,
men served under him and *women* too I bet.
When all his grinning stops you'll know Bland is terrified.'
       He'd never enemies only an opponent
who alas was Ewan.
            As conference delegates
Kurt and I sat either side of Ewan,
catching the strangled moans of his quiet,
bank official's groans as over-over-over
these slogans unfolded: the bosses-bosses-bosses,
the depression-depression-depression, and how
the workers-workers-workers would never-never-never…
but yes, yes and yes they would in Vermont South,
where Ewan was our candidate and each time lost
to Bland.
       Politics? Like Uncle Will

the man seemed far too good for it
(not even Lew had such innocence, whilst Ingrid
never would) and somehow out of weird respect
for him we caught groan fever,
to wander through our house groaning:
at oven mitt, shower tiles and clothes dryer,
at the ANT-RID, the Duck and, groaning into
our garden, the Blood and Bone. 'You're…'
we'd catch each other out, 'you're doin' a Ewan!'

       Des Curnow meanwhile, needing a straight man,
foil and mate adopted him, Ewan hardly seeing
the double-act. There they were though:
Ewan and Des on school working bees;
Ewan and Des planting, weeding and harvesting at
the Community Garden; Ewan sober, with Des (less so)
saying: 'Can't you see him, I can, Gib the Glib staggering-
up, to turn over his fourth Mantovani LP
for the evening…' and Ewan barely getting the gag;
Ewan, Des and Kurt doing their right, gratis thing
helping to shift furniture into a women's refuge;
Ewan and Ingrid tolerating the other, though never much
enjoying the toleration; Des making Marlene giggle
and Marlene making Des snigger; and Des making Kurt
arrive home with that kind of stunned look you knew
had a story behind it, saying: 'Somethings I reckon
need to be reassessed. Somethings I believe
are going down.'

       You rarely dream
like dreams that truly happen.
No need to imagine this for here's Kurt, on a train,
and here's Des, pissed and beaming, sweaty and shameless,
perving his way through *Searchlight* or some other of
the Adult Press.

       'Oh Kurt,'
he looks up, not at all surprised,
'take a peek at these…' as he flips through:
'My wife loves to watch and I love to watch my wife…'
or what about these combos:
Both of us love watching or better being watched…
and in twenty-five words or less tell us what makes for you
a very raunchy couple…first prize…Us!'

       Too drunk to drive Des left his car and,

as Kurt drove him from the station,
was sounding very purged and pleased:
'Reckon you might be guessing something, right?'
merely to increase his trademark sniggers.
            Now with all available data
this verdict was delivered: 'This isn't just any
open marriage, those two are swingers!'
And we'd been picked out for their game: not to swing,
merely to suspect; who with our loyalty
precluding any gossip were too discreet to ask.
And if we had, who could be told?
Swinging? Ewan wouldn't want to understand
and we doubted if the subject had been covered yet
in *Cleo*.
            Might Labor then pursue the swinger vote?
Non question. Mind you, if it's not Winmallee Drive,
even less Yarralea Close, it's sure to be home in
Karinya Crescent where you can fantasise how
in Vermont South another couple too are fantasising
'I wonder what those Curnows are up to…right now?'
Though right now all this couple (us) can think is:
'They've work, they've kids and isn't there the ALP…
where would you find the time?'
                        And yet, yet, yet,
we knew we'd caught plenty of their incautious,
less-than-innocuous items, like that time the branch
is BBQing on her patio and Ingrid's asking:
'Some of us just have our darker sides, eh Des?'
Who sniggers 'Yeah, yeah you've said it dear.'
Hearing that and knowing we would never ask
were we being informed: 'Read it like this, kids:
it's just a way that certain adults love to pass
their time.'
            And yet again: if in Vermont South
something-or-things were 'going down' then what?
And even could we prove such 'what'
then what? We tried to guess their swinger protocols:
was Des in charge or Ingrid the one who leads with
'Hey hey hey babe, tonight we swing…?'
            So much for protocols,
next came euphemisms we would never know:
imagine it, every time the two of them

chatted with the two of us, was it in code,
some getting-them-oh-so-horny code that
when we left each cried to each:
'Ahh what young, young fools, they'll never get it!'
to finish ravishing the other on their much-too-big,
white alpaca rug.
           Perhaps, though we also guessed
what might be the Curnow consolation:
'You're safe from all those nasty swingers, darling.
We're in Vermont South, with Helen,
the much-too-sensible and Kurt there with his
patchy beard and boffin's beanie.'
              'Reckon,' said Kurt,
'when swingers see each other in the street
it's as if they'd once shared a dream,
so nothing's really happened. Might politics
be heading close to this and are we in effect
swinging then with Bland? Next branch meeting
why not bring it up?'
           Why not?
Sometimes it seemed we'd only be attending to,
if not solve then more simply to uncover,
the next bit of the Ingrid-Des enigma.
        Though how could we but guess
that the swinger-mistress of the friggin' friggin'
could show herself so friggin' formal?
         'Rory! Rollo!' Ingrid urged her little lads.
'Say hello to Ms Johnson and her husband
Mr Stead.' Or 'May I introduce my Mumsy, Mrs Frame.
Our boys will spend the weekend at their Nana's.'
     I told my mother.
               'Mumsy?' Cath paused.
'Mumsy?' She repeated. 'Mumsy?' She demanded.
'Pure Glen Iris, 1961.'
           With her generation,
my generation, any indeed to come, she knew that kind:
their all-show-and-no-go private school pretensions:
'And don't tell us *Has she got a mouth on her!*
I've heard her in action.'
     I'd never add the swinger element.

Yoo-hoo!

1980 had once again been Ewan's year,
when we could've, should've, would've won
except we didn't. By early '82
the start of next time had arrived and
Ingrid was our candidate.
          'My heart,' she told our branch,
'extends to Ewan, to Ewan and Marlene who've flown
our Labor flag these past elections.
Let history show that Ewan was the man
who brought the margin down to two per cent,
and due to your banking expertise, I'd love you
as my campaign treasurer.'
                    He nodded.
                              'As a woman,'
proclaimed our candidate, 'as a woman my heart
also extends to women: sisters I will never let you down;
yet just as much my heart goes out to men:
you know how the best of families work so brothers,
brothers, more than just together we will triumph:'
          And thus to the jobless and the recycling movement,
to land rights activism and day care centres,
to first home buyers and (like ourselves) current mortgagees,
out went Ingrid's heart, out, out, until it stopped,
as a poised, if just that touch impatient smile appeared,
one which knew her greatest lines (their spontaneity
so thoroughly rehearsed) were in the offing:
'My heart does not extend, and never will extend
to Gilbert Bland!'
                    Hour: a Saturday morning.
Scene: a shopping plaza, where Bland MP
is a-meeting and a-greeting his electorate.
          'Hi, I'm Ingrid Curnow, I'd like to say hello.'
          Gilbert glibbed: 'Things going good, damn good?'
          They were for Ingrid: 'Please meet your opponent,
Mr Bland.'
                    What was or wasn't she supposed to say?
          And what was he? Bland didn't,
but had his face adjust to that all-things-to-all-voters,
Liberal Party of Australia grin, barraged as he was
by a series of unanswerable questions: 'You know like *Labor*?

170

The other crowd that truly *matters?*'

      Still grinning Gilbert seemed as if he'd get the gag
if only he weren't part of it. 'And your name is…'

      Ingrid gave her card.

      Thereafter, on shopping strips, in malls and plazas
they so hailed each other: 'Yoo-hoo Gilbert!' 'Yoo-hoo Ingrid!'
that any passing psephologist might surmise:
'This is no election, it's sibling rivalry by some weird default.'

      She had a dart board made,
featuring his face, and once a day (twice on weekends)
she'd aim those darts straight into Gilbert Bland.

      Kurt though was set:
Labor, even in Vermont South, needn't mean ongoing *Woo-hoo!*
let alone *Yoo-hoo!* and so he sought some inter-factional
ginger group.

      We quit conference too. Now Ingrid and Phil
(Phil Baxter of the Bellbird Branch) joined Ewan and attended.

      Then there was that speech she made:
women (her) reaching out to men (men!) with
'I am a feminist, I am a mother, I am a wife and
I am a lover…' front page of *The Age*
then turn to their feature articles:
'The Very Human Nature of Ingrid Curnow'.
Indeed.

      She phoned me to confess:
'…after which I got so sloshed Phil, Phil Baxter
drove me home.'

      (His repertoire of Ewan-groans redundant,
Kurt would prowl the house: 'I am a lover,
I am a lover…')

      Next, our rising party welterweight met
my Dad, and all that hidden lineage unravelled.
'Your Lew Johnson's daughter!' And Ingrid's stare still betrayed
the entrancement and the disbelief which shuddered
through her. Why though hadn't she been told?
'That man's my hero! I was there that day,
saw him on his Ute, taking plenty yes,
yet dishing back more than plenty. And from then I knew:
You aren't just voting for this mob, Ingrid Curnow,
you are joining them.'

      Oh lucky them,
Oh lucky Lew! More than any Melbourne personality,

could my Dad be anything now than just another
Labor legend, clambering onto a Ute?
Who wasn't there that day, or wished they were,
or knew someone who said they were?
The total Melbourne dream.
          'And do you know Pet,' Ingrid asked,
'that my CD, Phil, was there that very lunch hour.
How he admires your father. "If you've to lose,"
says Phil "you better lose with style."
And Phil loves style.'
                    Whilst very soon
'Comrades,' Phil would be announcing, 'comrades,
I bring greetings from the Bellbird Branch,
for up there by the Blacky Lake we sure admire
your powerhouse crew that's Vermont South.
And as CD (Campaign Director, what?)
I'm feeling humbled just visiting your branch.
With Helen there for secretary, Evan as treasurer
and someone very dear to all of us as candidate
this'll be one zinger poll…Bland beware!'
           What a way to end! He didn't end.
         'My wife,' continued Phil, stocky, balding,
with a certain fringe of curls, though not enough
to form an Afro, 'my wife wishes she were here,
one day though you're sure to meet my Gwen,
my fab Gwen, what?'
                Was he going to coin-a-phrase?
indeed he was for though
'…a housewife's lot is not a happy one,
she is our party's secret weapon:
spouse, mother and mate, comrade and candidate
Ingrid Curnow thanks, what?'
          Though what of Mrs Baxter, what?
Some place off-stage in Blackburn, a briskest jog between
the Lake and Furness Park, there's this nursing mother
(Gwen) whom I imagine after each migraine eased,
sweeping up some soft, damp Autumn leaves,
her dynamo-husband's better-half since
he'd said so, hadn't he? 'Just wait until you try
my better-half's new carrot cake yum yum,
just wait until you meet my Gwen and don't forget
our Nipper One, Nipper Two and the Nipperene,

oh boy the Nippers, what?'
If never small
Phil still seemed that half-inch shorter than
the rest of us.
'How are you employed?'
asked Des.
'The question?' Phil replied.
Did Des mean Baxter Enterprises? Well every day like
everyone he got into his car…
'Imagine this,'
I'd fly past Kurt, for my antennae seemed to be cataloguing
something, though I didn't know the what-exactly,
'there they are, coming home from Conference and,
as he parks the car, she's hearing "You know how much
I love you Ingrid Curnow what?"'
How could or couldn't I be saying that?
Was I, Marlene style, on the case?
But then what was *the case*?
Phil Baxter,
if I, my better-half and the ALP did not invent you,
we may as well have, silly, silly man.

'Perspective'

They tracked her down:
Cath: Deputy Head of a prominent girls school,
whom friends had sensed, indeed now knew
required changes, big enough changes.
Melbourne identities Godfrey and Gail,
the broadsheet's 'power couple': Chief-of-Staff
and Literary Editor had tracked Cath down,
having for all their mutual repartee
a somewhat hip intelligence, well it was hoped.
They started with an aside:
both their daughters were Old Girls now,
but had Cath taught them?
Which was no aside
but code: 'Please understand you're one of us,
well aren't you? Set to agree on near to everything,
well aren't we?'
Requiring something different,

173

the Literary Editor explained, they'd read
(at least had heard about) 'A Bunfight',
Cath's very well-regarded 'Bunfight'.
            'Thanks,' the husband added,
'to those young and rising literary men…
one of whom, you might be amused,
dates our eldest, they near live together!'
            And really…imagine that!
Cath recalled a half-remembered phrase of Jean's
something like 'Melbourne as a gigantic living room.'
So yes, wasn't it easy being tracked down,
with this for their plan that, were she amenable,
over the next month, might there be composed
something like that 'Bunfight', if less in length
and less vexatious, for the moment.
            'Since we believe,' it sounded like a chorus,
'that certain colleagues, though they didn't know it yet,
are sure to find it's what the town requires,
once a week at least, a woman's perspective,
well-read but more than that, much more,
our times are demanding it.'
            To which my mother played them:
'Not like those Women's Pages: patterns and recipes,
hairdos, debs and above all gossip?'
            'No,' she was assured,
'things now are improving, we're shedding all
that seems remotely tabloid.'
                        Then, if she wrote,
surely it mustn't be merely some 'perspective'
but one where certain folk who'd considered Cath
a colleague, might be surprised at some ideas
being entertained. For she'd joined
('I supposed I've joined…') this all-purpose
Women's Movement, trusting it was worth her effort,
trusting the result would be much more than yet
another natter-session.
                        'Though,' my mother often told me,
'I am divorced, I find there's nothing less desired
than *as you do* nattering with chums,
where'd that turnout ever get you?'
            And she thought of those Homemakers
with all their God-endorsed 'Real Women' Issues

and how, when the *Boomboomboom*
of that entertaining show pony Ingrid Curnow
blitzing the Homemakers was analysed,
it would prove hardly more than natter.
      Now *that* was a way Cath hoped
never to be her way, and she would want it,
love it, that yes even certain men
might sympathise with her 'perspective'
(though at times they'd little else to do but that).
      She recalled Lew, not just one night but often,
telling her over dinner:
'Met some right ones today, Cath…
but I guess that's how it is with Groupers,
let alone their priests and wives,
pleasant enough when one-to-one
but with some pretty weird ideas.'
      'Yes,' mused Cath, 'I bet.'
      Pre-, during and post-divorce, Lew had been
as ever 'No-fuss Lew', and you'd never wish to put
the hex on him, but getting snapped up cheap
by that ex-model Poppy, Cath almost felt
she wanted to.
      Poor man, what a parody.
For Cath still had some sympathy for parodies,
even if they were those Homemakers,
the night they took on the Women's Movement
to achieve…nothing at all.
      Who'd ever wish to be a parody?
Since Cath was aware of a certain divorcée
ploughing her past seven years into little
but career, one she knew would have to end.
Yes she might retire, if she knew how,
and knowing got around to it.
      It even amused her, this novelty of indecision.
Should she, this woman then, be allowed to take
her overdue long service leave, seeing where
this talent, as they proclaimed, would land?
      After her brief taste of some literary life
Cath had jotted down:
- Quit now or near-to-now
- Turn 'fabulously freelance'?
- (Whatever <u>that</u> means)

- Anything else might happen
- Men?
- And yet of course…

     Now with this Gail and Godfrey,
who just might supply 'anything else'
she sought to add a rider:
'As I informed your Jeremy and Jake
I won't be hiding under any pseudonym,
and haven't any need to be Anon;
I'll just regain that name I never lost.'
     The couple paused, then both proclaimed 'That's right!'
For wasn't Cath the wife no sorry no,
hadn't she been married once to him, Lew,
'The man on that mythic Ute…'
     And if, that moment, Cath had a message
for Australia and Australian men, it would be
'Go on, grab yourself a myth, any myth'll do
and flog it senseless!' Wouldn't it be great
to end a piece like that!
     Her reverie over she saw the couple staring.
'Please,' said the stares, 'don't tell us Cath
is unconvinced.'
     But Godfrey stepping back,
girl-to-girl Gail commenced to natter, asking:
'As an example, would you like to interview,
you must've heard of her, Ingrid, Labor's latest bombshell?'
     Hadn't this Gail even read 'A Bunfight'?
     'Why not,' asked Cath 'a certain Gilbert Bland?'
     'Who?' came the reply.
     And if Cath almost verged on quitting,
she'd get back to them on Tuesday,
after that winter's long weekend,
when, not quite a public figure (yet)
she walked out in parks and gardens
with girlfriends or alone, her decision evolving
one day at a time: 'I just couldn't…' soon replaced by
'Yet if I could…' then erasing 'yet' and 'if'
she paused at 'could' which soon transformed to 'Might,
I might indeed…' till it became by Monday night
'Yes, and make that *must*.'
     'I hear,' said Lew, 'that Cath your mother…'
(as if we'd any other form of Cath)

'that she that she…' And he couldn't exactly say
what Cath was doing except 'Well done,
tell her please well done, she has my full support,
and if there's anything that I can do…'
        If there was time. There wasn't. Enter Dee.

Dee

        Poppy with her Poppy strut had strutted off.
        'I'm very fond of Lew,' she bleated,
'my lovable rogue-and-all; his politics but are wi-erd!'
        Though little seemed more wi-erd
than his stalled career.
                They asked:
'Why don't you nail the Minister then?'
        He asked: 'So what's to nail?
Shadowing the least most major member of the Government
I look at him and see myself. The end.'
                    Not quite.
Here's how he met the ultimate Lew-spouse.
All he needed were the words:
'Hi, I'm Dee Glover of the *SMH*…'
and the Shadow Minister for Lurks, Perks and Jerks
was rubbing his hands and letting forth:
'Wacko, wacko, wacko!'
             Now try this for courtship:
'How's the idea of Melbourne sounding?'
                    'With you Lew,
pretty grand.'
        'And Labor?'
                'I'd give anything a try.'
        'Look, look,' Marlene was enchanted, 'a *Cleo* profile.
In Sydney they call her The Go-to Girl.
How can I meet her?'
             Ingrid quizzed me:
'What's she really like, this love-ly Dee?'
        But I deferred to *Cleo*:
slim, coiffured and to divert him looks a man
right into his eyes.
           Cath acted with charitable bemusement.
'The last one was a fraud. Very fond of Lew?

The world is very fond of Lew. This one?
I was in Sydney and read her column once.
The Go-to Girl indeed.'
                         'Woo-hoo, the love-ly Dee!'
Was Ingrid sneering? Hardly. Not yet to meet her,
still, she was growing quite proprietorial,
as if she saw a-woman-like-myself,
since didn't the earnest and the vapid somehow meet
in Dee: elegant, straight-talking, a true celeb's celeb!
          One jetted into Sydney and, if one were famous enough,
with a *Heh-heh-heh* and a *Ring-a-ding-ding*
there Dee was, all set to pen a profile.
Seductive yet with a common touch,
no one in Melbourne could remotely sponsor
an Easy-listening LP titled *Dee Trax*:
'These are some of my favourite songs,
I know you'll love them.'
                         And Ingrid loved them.
          But even Go-to Girls get older,
for though there was so much Dee was giving up
(her *Herald* column, her drive-time guest spot,
all those panel shows) now she required
that kind of loving time-out Lew kept promising
(besides there lay that novel, deep within her).
          'But who's she marrying now?' asked *Sydney*.
          A kind of Melbourne politician, though the girl
was making her move once more for love.
          'Sometimes,' sang Kurt,
'it's hard to be a woman...'
                         Not for Dee it seemed,
she'd made herself property, first Marlene,
then Ingrid, Cath (and all Melbourne were Dee
that lucky) wanted an encounter.
          Cath got in first, daughter as facilitator
and Lew was none the wiser.
                         Was this 'done'?
'Til now no it wasn't, but nothing my mother ever did
was 'done'.
               'Have you,' Dee was asked, 'lived with a politician?'
          Well she'd dated heaps.
                         'Heaps,' said Cath.
'Ever lived with one to become that rare and not quite

interesting specimen, the political spouse?
I won't presume in saying *don't* but consider these:
so where's he off to this time: an upcoming wassail,
the next Labor turnout, one more Canberra bunfight?
And whose skirt is he chasing now? He's not?
Then what skirt's chasing him?
Whatever you are giving up you are giving up
for a man plenty in this town love far more
than they know you. Here's my line Dee,
can you share him?'
                      Sharing? She knew the score
and certainly knew men, well Dee-men like her husbands:
a Rugby star we had never heard of,
and some aging Fairfax; though not quite any politician yet.
But she liked our town and she liked Lew.
      'Very fond?' asked Mum.
                            'Yes, very fond…'
and when the government changed, since change it would,
Lew was set to be those few, tiny steps from power,
real power, right?
           Dee thanked Cath and later she thanked me:
'I haven't quite met anyone like your mother.
I must read those articles of hers,
has she read mine?'
                And Cath?
'Dee doesn't *get* and will never *get*
what we all *get* but she's getting something…
unlike that bleating Poppy!'
          Next in line came Ingrid who, at a candidate-
and-spouses afternoon, was so won over,
over and over by the love-ly Dee:
'Just as they said in *Cleo*: "All Dee Yet More".
Pet's father is a lucky, lucky man.'
         So would she tell Marlene? And
'Am I that much of a bitch?'
we copped the brunt of Ingrid's mock affront.
        Bitch? That Pet would ever think she was,
but yes, she'd hardly keep this from Marlene,
from anyone, how Lew had promised her that he
and Dee and Bob, Bob Hawke, would be heading out
not just to Vermont South but her place,
23 Karinya Crescent, as by the very hour

arrangements firmed.
                              Except,
immune to all that self-deceiving rush
of Ingrid's latest calls, we'd stopped our listening
months before, allowing Madam's sweep of nouns
and verbs to float us where we wished to float,
so that this time I commenced to conjure Ingrid's latest
as her ultimate in masquerades:
a Come as Your Favourite Personality fancy dress:
politicians, politician's wives, media and sporting stars.
        'Let's hire the friggin' Burvale,' Kurt was primed,
'cast Ewan against type as Hawkey
and bags I go as Bland!'
        And our truth may have been the truth except
'Haven't you two been listening?'
and it was Dad, first apologizing, now confirming
how yes! he had arranged that Hawkey,
the nation's foremost politician was, repeat it, was
heading to the Curnows, from where we almost heard
one woman's catalogue of pure revenge:
'Shove that school captains, corporate bum-patters,
multinational root-rats, Gib the Glib and you,
Glen Iris Young Liberals you…
Woo-hoo Bob Hawke, woo-hoo!'

Sydney

        Dee's wedding, oh and Lew was part of it:
his third, her third, so this had to work,
and there we were, in early summer Sydney,
on one of her dear, dear friend's Harbourside back lawns,
swamped by the town's identities:
this one the judge, this one the being judged and this one
making sure all knew he or she approved the judging,
three interchangeable roles.
                              And, if Kurt was muttering
'This sure ain't Vermont South…'
such sardonic understatements ceased,
as the bride came punting up, on some form of gondola;
and at a cute landing doubtless built for the day,
Lew took a hand, leading his Dee to shore,

180

then kissed that hand: 'Oh you wag wag wag!'
        Just to be best man
Uncle Will had flown from London,
he loved Lew, thought Dee worth the effort,
and knew too well 'This kind of thing...'
surrounding us that day:
'...seven years ago (or fourteen, twenty-one)
some of these-these-and-these were set to lynch
the likes of Lew. Correct? Now though,
in the name of love, booze and a free feed
see them flocking in.'
              He'd become a widower
and always would be. 'Helen,' he confided,
'when the great one's over, yet still lives on,
why should she be replaced?'
                  Will tried hard
not to be, but was the most romantic man
Dad would, we all would, ever know.
The least romantic man, my brother Rod
was present too, straight from Karana Downs:
'Keeping the Red Flag flying, Helen, Kurt?'
        Kurt knew even better: 'Our candidate,
the local Farrah Fawcett-Whosits, is up against
some remnant from a Brylcreem ad,
so Hawkey's heading out to her place, oh
and we're invited.'
              Rod produced a stare,
one which intimated
'Let's trust you aren't that dumb enough to put one
over me, eh Kurt...' Then 'Okay, okay...'
he lapsed into his land-developer's smile
'Well isn't that the truth!'
          Did he want to prove a menace?
If it amused him to amuse us, menace on,
for here came the truth:
as Kurt, Rod and Will looked on,
one arm around his daughter, another round his bride,
Lew gave that truth: 'Why did I tell her
"Hawkey at your place Ingrid, all things are possible..."
and why was I believed?'
              And now we entered on
that kind of politics Ingrid, for all her local-level chutzpah

was never going to get: bemused attrition:
'Bob gets me off his back so I get her off mine.
He knows I know that when we win by the upcoming
seismic shift, Lew here will be offered nix.
Lew may not be knifed but he'll be owed:
you can reward me once, twice, as you can sack me
once, twice, but each time it's to that old refrain:
first as tragedy, second as farce. So bring on the farce
and one night soon, for he knows how much I'm owed,
Bob will be coming out for drinks in Vermont South.
And I'll add this:
when your opponent's that kind of quietly sexist sleaze
some ladies are known indeed to love
(but just how sexist, just how sleazy, truly sleazy
blokes only are allowed to know)
and you're to make one choice, either beating Bland
or hosting Hawkey, that Ingrid will be hosting.

Rumpus

So when did I first suspect, fear and maybe know
she might never make it?
Let's be innocuous, let's start with Ingrid on the phone:
'Marlene's Book Club wants to meet me. Please?
I mean, help me to believe it Pet? What have I
been reading? What have you? Oh please?'
        I arrived, knocked, and thinking I heard
Karinya Crescent's neighbourly 'Let yourself in, just
let yourself in...' I let myself in, right in
to marital dysfunction.
                        Repressing sniggers
soon to merge with mumbles, Des waved dismissals
at his spouse, who returned them with a snarl:
'Get fucked, Des!' Which didn't work, for his snigger-
mumbles went into repeat mode as, snarling-on
she reiterated: 'Get fucked, Des...'
        And I was there. But even worse
they knew that I was there and,
as if I'd never heard such dull and tiny words before,
I filed all three for Kurt's despair,
imagining how Lew might sing

182

'Three little words/Oh what I'd give for those/
Three little words…' But Tin Pan Alley had been
long displaced by hi-octane punk:
'I said get fucked, Des!'
      And knowing I'd arrived
was this Ingrid's revenge on my being half of some
'normal' couple, on Vermont South itself,
with Madam asking: 'So you're our friend?
Okay, have we a test for you, Pet.
Just treat yourself to a peek-a-boo
at just how phoney we can be.
As in *family* restaurants, behold our *family* values!'
    But if Kurt had stumbled on
some kinky liberation, Des had conjured
that night on the train, Ingrid the prefect
now reset the fishwife balance:
'Wanna separation? Pussy bring it on,
but you have *not* the balls!'
    'How's the sexlife, Helen?' my friend
may as well continued. 'Ours is fucked
and ain't it great.'
      She didn't ask;
instead with 'Fatso, you've a good idea
what our marriage is and always was…'
exit fishwife into their corridor,
hubby sneering in pursuit:
'Not only is she losing this one,
our dildo queen needs to know she's lost it,
Vermont South, her total it!'
     Their sons were where? Mumsy's?
Wherever, it seemed better they remained
Glen Iris bound for life.
       Their parents' boundaries?
There weren't any: both knowing I was there,
then acting like I wasn't, was Ingrid ever more
the politician?
      In my car,
heading to the book club, Ingrid talked of rooms:
the women's one, the one with a view,
the one of one's own.
       Kurt was asleep
when I got home, though I stayed awake 'til Four,

my brain a-thump with all that Curnow rumpus,
that or the prefect's Pettity-pet-pet-pet
nipping after me.

     I thought of phoning Marlene
but desisted, and sparing Kurt's despair he'd not
be told: soon I sensed it had to be his turn.

   Just a week until the poll
would be our Hawke night, and soon after lunch
Kurt brought liquor from the Burvale to the Curnows,
only to dump and scuttle. There came a rumpus from
the rumpus room, the missus screeching hard:
'Look at me Des, look at what you'll miss.
After I've won I'm fucking whom I like!'

    And yes we could imagine Des
sneering and sniggering, sniggering and sneering,
rolling his rope-a-dope roll throughout
these fishwife punches, lapping her contempt
that brilliant way I'd seen him.

     'I'd say all swinging has been put on hold,'
said Kurt, 'unless of course that's the way it starts.
Where were their boys? And who could sit through *that*?
Let's get out of Vermont South if Vermont South does *that*.
For, when we have kids will we end up like *that*,
will they? Helen we'll have one more week like *that*
(or something like *that*) and I've little doubt
all Karinya Crescent heard. Well votes all round
for Bland I say, for whatever Bland is doing now
I'm certain it's not *that*. So let's tell him, Ewan,
Marlene, Lew and beyond them all, Bob Hawke,
these comrade-friends of ours are very stupid people.'

    And I wanted to say:
'Have you forgotten, Kurt: "Serenity ain't my middle name..."'
but the phone rang, it was Ingrid,
upbeat, chatty, pushing (she'd love to think) serene:
'Tell Kurt thanks, the booze looks grrreat! What news?'

    Weren't *they* the news? Well they would be but
Dad had phoned and the love-ly Dee would not be coming.

    'No,' and Ingrid gave some form of
empathetic sob, 'Marlene will be so gutted.'

    At Christmas Kurt's hippy brother Greg
gave both of us a bag of weed. Taa Greg.
We'd hardly touched that stuff since Dad was sacked

when, if we weren't distracted as required,
we simply raved about The Dismissal, stoned.
What better way to see Dad on his Ute?
    Now a pact was being made:
never again to enter Karinya Crescent unless we'd used the stuff;
whilst sharing an ale or two with Hawke and truly out of it
might prove quite instructive.
                  Kurt was certain:
'Those two are finished, they don't deserve us straight,
well Des perhaps…' and a hand got waved
in *mezzo-mezzo* mode. Then came an ominous
'After she's won (and she is going to win)
perhaps we don't go back? I know I won't.'
    Not quite Stand Off in Vermont South
but distances were to be established,
friends transformed to slight acquaintances.
And Ewan felt the same? Sure did.
    And not just Ewan, Dad.
                      'Darling,' he'd said,
'I'm being blunt if homely blunt. I'm not doing this for her,
you've the wrong lady, waste of a candidate,
everything your mother isn't…' which didn't surprise.
'No, I'm bringing Hawkey out *for you*.'
    With the Greg-weed setting up our evening
we enjoyed our stroll through Vermont South
and, under a rising full moon,
one block until Winmallee Drive intersects with
Karinya Crescent, see us glancing down
an already sleepy Yarralea Close where,
for all of Marlene's open marriage fantasies,
the Adcocks, just as we did, never remotely swung.
    Which had me saying: 'Remember Kurt,
when swingers were those rumoured distant friends
of distant friends, or else these nicknamed Sydney
merchant bankers, and dental nurses who remained anon,
saying things like 'Has swinging helped?
Well it hasn't hindered!' And how, for a time,
the Curnows seemed to fit this mould,
if you could imagine some Ooo-baby,
finger-snappin' Eastern Suburbs Rat Pack. Now though
something sure is screwing Karinya Crescent,
and I doubt if we could term it *sex*.'

'Oh yes they've swung,' mused Kurt,
'or something like it. Are you sensing,'
he started thinking through,' that if in pragmatic,
let's-be-realistic Vermont South a swing is on
and his name is Phil?
Since all trends are heading towards swing
I'd say it's mighty likely.'

     Barring proof,
though most mighty likely, we had arrived at 23.

  'Wait,' I offered, 'and let's see
if Marlene our pollster-on-the-case
has heard and processed chatter-on-the-ground,
for now there seems a far more pressing poll.'

  'Sure is.' Kurt pressed the buzzer muttering:
'I'll never vote for Ingrid Curnow any more than
I will vote for Bland.'

Moonlight

  'Friends,' Lew bustled through his leader,
'I'd like you all to meet Bob…
(who knew what trajectory might follow?)
'Hawker…Hawkins…Hawken…Hawke!'

   And with my father's drunken dotage
arriving earlier by the hour
Phil took charge.

     'Bob,' he puffed,
'welcome to Vermont South (and you must be Lew).
Well here's the gal, our candidate, her hubby Des
and Helen, Kurt, Evan and Marlene.
I'm the CD, Phil, and I'm married too,
but you know how it is, Bob,
there she goes whippin' up a kedgeree,
my wife that is, when in the middle of it what?
Migraine! Had to drop a Valium. Mind you
our sons apart Gwen's your biggest fan,
for the nippers love their Bob.'

      'Processed that?"
Kurt asked.

   'Sure did,' said Bob.
Grinning more than even Bland

our hostess didn't need to hurry.
It was enough her leader had arrived and,
given one week more, wouldn't she,
in a small yet solid sense,
be working with him, woo-hooing from the backbench,
sure, but if not cabinet per se
(too too much a pipe-dream for the moment)
one day, sooner than she'd dare, a Ministry,
a certain, seemingly minor Ministry where,
due to some crisis, yep some crisis *not*
of her bidding but which she solves,
everywhere Australia goes there's Ingrid Curnow:
front page/lead item face-of-the-day,
not just the face of some woo-hoo-hoo
feminist/mother/wife (oh why had she said *lover?*)
but this woman, this crisis-solving woman,
not merely one-to-watch but the one you're watching
now!

      Well not this evening's now, but a future now,
and, as she adjusted in her kitchen,
'Pet,' she suggested, 'out on the patio check please,
who is speaking with whom?'

      I brought results: Phil button-holing Bob,
Lew dumped with Ewan, Marlene entertaining Des,
Kurt tending the bar.

              ' Yes. Yes. Good. Good.
And if Bob requires another *evian,*
he shall have another *evian.*'

      We didn't hate her, though she could be tiresome,
be mistrusted, there'd be no revenge (revenge for what?)
and if it would be Ingrid's doing, making her friends
fair-weather friends, factor that accordingly.

      So blame Vermont South,
blame our curiosity for these enigmatic Curnows,
blame it on some drug she'd never know I'd smoked,
the one giving me the courage to consider
'Since you're near elected, let's tempt you with
a tiny crisis, Question Time if you like…'
so that 'Ingrid,' the Member for Winmallee Drive
asked the Minister for Woo-hoo!
'Ingrid, have you and Des had anything like affairs?"

      (On her patio, into his fourth *evian,*

Bob was telling gags which Phil was trying hard
to trump, except that telling further gags and
better gags Bob was making Phil's redundant.)
        'Not merely just affairs,' asked Ingrid,
'but…anything like affairs?' Then sighs arrived:
'Mmm-h-yes…mmm-h-yes…' although she steadied.
'That? Oh *that*! Think Pet think of all the options
marriages contain, as if Pet cannot guess.'
Thinking-on-her feet these measured words continued.
'But when one turns a public figure,
a public figure heading to Canberra,
one rather puts the lid on many things.
Helen, why must I be asked tonight?
Forgive us if we've misheard each other.
Maybe I'll inform you on some future day?
So please, the savouries?'
        Bringing out our savouries, 'Bob,'
I heard Phil say (meaning: Bob let's keep your attention,
Bob) 'yours is a great campaign, it would be churlish
to apportion any faults, not with a week to go.
But Bob since yours must be an overview,
an overview indeed of overviews,
let me inform you of our local front what?
We have some motto some place, I've forgotten it.
Mine was Bland Beware! which got voted down.
But Bob isn't that democracy?'
        Someone got up to put a record on.
Someone else got up to turn that record over.
Someone else again got up to put another
record on, whilst through *Hot August Night*
and one side of The Bushwackers
Phil zoned further into his Hawke-trance,
primed for that magic phrase
'I could do with a fella like you…'
        '…and mind you Bob, given that whammo migraine
her kedgeree was stuffed, what?'
        Tight-lipped yet still polite
Ewan had been very poised since Bob's arrival.
        'Philip, please?' Ingrid the serene was firm.
'Comrade Hawke doesn't need to exercise
more patience, tolerance and tact,
share the poor man round.'

It took thirty seconds?
It took less for where had Philip gone?
'Miffed or for a slash,' Kurt guessed.
'But he'll be back, Bob can hardly wait.'
By now it may have been some dream,
since that's how I'd be telling Mum (and even Rod):
'...we are on some patio and Bob Hawke's here,
it's a party celebrating just how truly stuffed
the Curnow marriage is, though Des still sniggers
for Marlene's telling him what her Book Club's reading;
Ewan's trying hard to ask Bob something,
Bob though isn't interested; Phil's off to the toilet
for Ingrid's pointing him the way;
and I am doing all of my dreaming stoned,
whilst Dad is here, he's drunk and wants to sing.'
'Listen all,' cried Kurt,
the only man sensing he'd the powers to say it,
'Lew would love to sing a few brief words.'
And as my dreaming stopped,
my father spoke. 'With...' Lew was expounding,
'this combination: full moon, place and leader,
I've never felt more tempted.'
Though candidate and her director had gone missing
Lew cared for neither: he'd been the silky-voiced star
of many a post-war Town Hall hop, those two
would hardly make a garage band.
Bob had felt that he owed Lew and Lew had felt that
he owed me and so tonight had been arranged for me,
for Kurt and me and by extension Des, Ewan and Marlene,
who received not quite his penance,
more his apologia.
'Politics,' said Dad,
'mightn't be a total racket, but sure has
racket elements, I didn't so much play around
as played: two wives thought me an adolescent,
my third is heading that way fast; whilst my son
just knows me for a goose. I've been an erratic dad,
an in-law to be bemused by or disposed of.
Can you guess,' he asked, 'what it was like,
trying a decade to enter into this game
and knowing when you did you'd never be as good
or feel as great as that moment you strode out of court

winning your famous Kickback Case?
And after that the next best thing I did?
Climb on the back of that Ute, laughing at those bosses
and all their dickhead stooges, like your pathetic Gilbert Bland,
the one I know for sure is worse than me.'

      Lew shook his head my way and here it came,
his meaning, meaning, meaning imagined:
'He is the worst but are we going to replace that worst
with her, your Ingrid Curnow?'

                        And if that lunchtime crowd
of merchant bankers and their ilk mobbing his Ute
hadn't been so set to lynch him
(well that's how the myth now played)
Lew might've serenaded them.

      'Yes, that's how I cope,
keeping my crooner options open, pretending still
I'm your featured vocalist…'
and motioning to an invisible pianist: 'Maestro…

Back yards neatly mowed
washing hanging on the line
moonlight in Vermont South…

Next week to the polls
electors making up their minds
spotlight on Vermont South…

Holdens and Falcons
they cruise Burwood Highway
and travel each bend in the road,
people who vote in this sub-urban setting
are so hypnotised by your charm, Bob…

Just a week to go
Hawkey's heading for The Lodge
Moonlight in Vermont South…

You and I and Bob in Vermont South.'

      The night's applauding since it must:
would Karinya Crescent ever catch
such a chance again, would anywhere,

since this might be that last if ludicrous time
Lew Johnson sang like anything in public?
On the patio such seems certain,
elsewhere (though we didn't know it yet)
somethings far more ludicrous were jelling,
at the Curnows and beyond; and given one more week
of Ingrid's overreaching, jelling rapid.
Though to look at Des, plodding to their LP collection
you'd never guess it. Whilst there's Lew,
trusting that the night has just commenced,
getting Kurt to pour a further beer, with beer chaser,
with his leader doubtless praying there'll be found
(and soon) a way to close this fool event.
Whilst here I am putting into words
whatever's going through your head, Bob Hawke:
'That Phil, this Ewan, have I come to whatever suburb
just to get lectured on migraines, on kedgeree?
Or to catch echoes of my own inanities:
'Labor Unity? Both in the same faction are we Ewan?
Well you little beauty!' What do such dickheads really want?
I mean with women it's assumed all they require
is just to meet Old Hawkey, stare right into his eyes
and snatch their slice of fantasy…isn't that enough?'

       But as Bob turns to smile at Ewan's wife
Marlene doesn't see him, for the woman's urgent,
urgent with something she can only talk about
with girlfriends: 'You know,' she whispers,
'women's issues, Helen'

                      I took her to the kitchen.
      Somewhere at the Curnows there were two toilets
and she, Marlene confesses, chose the wrong one.
Of course she knocks, she knocks: 'Hello?'
      But Ingrid's in there snapping back:
'Stay out Marlene, stay out and read a friggin' *Cleo*!'
      And someone else is in there and that man
isn't Des.
       'They wanted to have it, Helen, not just plain sex
or even sex during your Dad's song,
but sex whilst Bob Hawke's in the house!'
      And as the night, the Curnow marriage, all our campaign
seemed turning kedgeree, 'Stress,' I had to float
(the only word in my state that I could)

'yes stress yes, yes, it must be stress.'
            For Marlene it was: 'First no Dee now this.
Ewan must never know, how would he understand?
No one must, Kurt would not believe it,
and as for Bob…'
                        Oh yes they would,
and I thought of the leader's vanity on very high alert:
'Sex whilst Hawkey's in your house? That's what I call charisma!'
            Now Marlene's horrors multiplied:
'How many campaign quickies have they had?
How is Des to be protected?'
                              Or, I considered,
has Des set it up, was this some kind of sexual-politics
apex to their *Searchlight* lives? Then I thought of Phil,
yapping through the act what? Though such speculations,
fantasy or truth or both, had to cease for Marlene
needed guidance.
                        We'd another week of our fool friend:
were she elected she would be too busy,
if not elected surely disappear. *Surely* though was
not enough. For Marlene stalled: 'But Des,' her voice was hoarse,
'I've always had a silly crush on Des…'
            A few tears came, so I conceded Des was a fine, funny
and very loyal man, and if they had some open marriage
Phil was not included.
            'Marlene,' I soothed, 'Marlene.
We must rise above all this, think Bob, think Bob.
Make sure that when he remembers Vermont South
it won't be our mad-woman candidate,
it won't be her hyper-boring Campaign Director,
but you, the quietly considerate, most attractive
Marlene Adcock. Let this be our revenge.'
            And if such were counselling, I knew
I never would again. Meanwhile Marlene,
just find another toilet whilst I find Des
a-moochin' on the patio.
                  'Helen,' he muttered, 'none of these pricks…'
commencing with that mutter his voice continued rising,
'these I won't excuse my language fuckin' pricks
of Vermont South will never comprehend full moonlight,
make that any moonlight. Why do we ever bother with
this country and its Fascist sunshine?

Doubtless because anywhere else is just as stuffed.
I've told Ewan, I've told Kurt and now I'm telling you.
Reckon I'll pass on Bob.'
                    'Big day Des?'
                                        'Too bloody big,'
he puffed.
                    Part patting down/part flouncing up her hair,
his wife had left the toilet. No Phil? No Phil.
Des saw her and thought, I knew he thought,
of Phil.
            'You know what this Baxter does?
Any idea who he is and his invisible spouse?
Some plant of Bland's? Treats Ewan as disposable,
treats us all. Campaign *director*? That man's an *auteur*:
you matter, you and you might matter, you, you, you
and you certainly do not! Look at the way he's spent
the last hour, auteuring Bob. Poor Bob. Poor Marlene too,
doesn't she look deflated, the lamb deserves a cuddle,
bet Ingrid's ruffled her, Ingrid loves a ruffle.'
            I rather loved a ruffle too,
and we enter the final hour of Pet's campaign,
the freeing up of her desire to spill it, spill it total.
Maybe in that legalistic free-for-all which is
the United States, the personal was the political;
our land though seemed one where like tonight
the political turned out far more the personal,
and having a husband canny to appreciate
both personal and political I headed to
our tally-room.
                    'Though,' Kurt said,
'the candidate has returned, her campaign director still seems
unavailable.'
                    'Marlene,' I replied, 'informs the swing
is on.'
        'Right now?'
                    'Right now.'
                                'Tonight?'
                                            'This very one.'
        'The leader is aware?'
                                'The leader I am sure is unaware.'
    'Will the swing then unseat the incumbent?'
    'Difficult to say. My knowledge of the local factors

leads me to believe that in seats as marginal as this
it'll be down to preferences.'
                                   'Marlene has toured the booths?'
         'She's been on the case.'
                           'And at ground level,
what has been the chatter?'
                           'More up against the dunny wall than
on the ground.'
                   'Mm. How then will this effect not just Marlene
but the overall campaign?'
                           'In a race this tight (I've told her)
you do your best to insulate yet cultivate the leader.
Bob has more to contend with than factional disputes in...
where are we?'
                   'Vermont South.'
                                   'Indeed.
Why there she is. Thumbs up, Marlene!'
         'Thumbs up!' she beamed. 'Up and on the case!'
awaiting her charismatic rendezvous.
         'That Lew sure is a songbird! You both...' and it was Bob,
'look like the proudest parents.'
                           Like *that*?
I must have been, for even in my stoned dream-state
there couldn't be much better:
polls heading six percent our way,
only a week remaining of the Curnows,
and right now being drenched in moonlight, moonlight and
Bob Hawke!
                   Then I saw how you became PM:
ignore the Ingrids, suffer the Ewans, extricate yourself
from every Phil and work the patio.
                           'Now Kurt,' Bob asked,
'we're told this is a swinging seat.'
         'Plenty of swinging here,' said Kurt.
         'And please, don't mind me saying,'
asked our comrade, 'you're married yet have different surnames.'
         'Yes!' we chorused whilst he said 'Interesting...'
with such conviction, we felt it would turn
party policy.
                   And it would except Dad, post-primed,
was trying to sing again, and this time fully clunked.
So it fell to Marlene *Fully on the case* to grab her moment,

to close the night with a way Bob would remember:
'He's tired, he wants to go, he wants to be Prime Minister.'

    'Correct on all accounts.'
Up on his toes then down, up on his toes then down,
he beamed at her and she beamed back.

    Ewan sulked. Phil had taken near-to-all Bob's time,
now Marlene was hogging his farewell.

    'But Bob, but Bob,' for Phil was back and butting back,
'Monday being our candidates' debate,
give us please certain thoughts on Bland.'

    'My Liberal friends,' confided Hawke, 'inform me Bland's
a double-dealing, wife-cheating, cliché-spouting,
featherweight boozer. I'd never take him lightly.'

    But Ingrid did and did we all.

Woo-hoo!

    On Monday evening, as the candidates assembled,
it was tragic in its way, Ingrid itemising
her opponents, set on entertaining me with
such a focused monologue;
if only she could view herself as she viewed others,
a certain kind of friendship might, just might,
have been maintained.

    'See that one, Pet, with her hennaed crew-cut:
a Trotskyite she's boycotting the stage,
rather be embedded with the masses,
though given near-to-half this crowd
are Liberal stooges I rather doubt it;
and speaking of Liberal stooges, there he is…
Yoo-hoo Gilbert! I do believe the poor man's blushing;
guess that arty Independent must be on some drugs,
you mightn't understand it Pet but I know my druggies,
it's in their eyes; I can't imagine how
(all earnestness herself) our young Democrat
would share her favours round, not like me at twenty-one;
and her! yes her! arriving with a hubby and a priest
for bodyguards, do we detect a Homemaker?
Indeed we do, have you ever seen one?
There was that famous night I battled with a dozen,
until now my finest hour; and lastly moi,

on the cusp and heading into overdrive…'

Her finest hour? There'd never be another.

All his opponents being women
this brought forth the elemental Bland:
'Who was it said a-pretty-girl-is-like-a-candidate?'
(Gasp!) 'Well let me say that when it comes to ladies
and to ladies' issues…' (gasp-gasp!) 'my wife (darling!)
assures me I am anything but bland!'
Then to assuage any evolving uproar be blathered into
a supposed retraction: 'Bad pun, bad pun…'

Out of the crowd the Trot arose and snarled:
'Who brought this sexist fool?'

'Who brought,' Bland replied, 'all of us my dear?
Democracy! But seriously folks…'

And as that sage young Democrat seemed nodding
in concurrence (though with what I doubt we'll ever know)
and the eyes of that arty Independent were ever more
the glazed, and Ingrid sat back silent, smirking,
I glanced towards the Homemaker, slumped I guessed
in what were prayers for Bland.

He knew we'd got him, knew yet floundered on:
'Bob Hawke?' he asked. 'Bob Hawke?
I wish I could have *his* charisma, but if I did
I doubt if I would be your damn good local member.
I'd spend my time just being charismatic,
and *you* would suffer. Oh yes oh yes you would…'

Ingrid's campaign got to *Woo-hoo!* smirk no higher,
since see her ninety minutes later with Phil, at the Burvale,
shouting the bar to loud 'n' louder skolling,
then getting asked, both asked to leave.

'Okay let's friggin' leave!'
The ignition's on, the engine revs, the cops descend.
Burvalegate! Or to be objective
LABOR CANDIDATE IN DRUNKEN PUB FRACAS.

Then Bland launches a Women's Refuge Trust Fund,
in honour of his late mum.

Once hadn't Ingrid been proclaimed the media's
favourite *human nature* gal? Okay, okay,
but the Burvale, cops and above all, Bland,
had spiked her drinks, correction drink,
just one, you heard her one.

Yes everybody heard but who would listen?

Not when it was so fab, turned gruesome, turned
so-fab-again, imagining her and Phil trudging sloshed
through Vermont South to Karinya Crescent,
and Des with his sniggers.

                       Hawke won, Bland won.
And through all that Grand Australian Seismic Shift,
Vermont South was stuck, under its unalterable moonlight.

       Recall those words when her bravado
was at full tide: 'After I've won I'm fucking whom I like!'

       One half of these proves true.

       She strides en route through their rumpus room,
and by the time she's out the spouse is ex:
Des, one more chubby chump dumped in the middle of
Vermont South, bug-eyed at her cold-press passion:
'You're being dumped for Phil, Phil Baxter, right?'

       If only Bland had copped such pure and frigid passion:
'Oh Bland oh Bland, you wowser lush, you simpering
blowhard, you womanising poofter…'
that seat would be ours! Instead the nation
(if it bothered) saw, heard, read and knew
BLAND BUCKS THE TREND
and there we remained, losers in a winning team,
a footnote's footnote to ALP folklore.

       Not the way Phil and Ingrid saw it,
Marlene was certain:
'Everywhere you go they're wishin' and hopin' and
thinkin' and prayin' they'll be sighted.'

                     Which they were:
lunch trysts in some mellow nook of the friggin' Burvale;
nuzzling between inferior Eastland lattés,
whilst Ingrid shows her man their latest lingerie;
picnics by the Blackburn Lake, the Ringwood Lake,
just name the lake and they'd be spreading the rug,
our electorate turned into their lovers' boudoir;
whilst Des sat smoking in his Box Hill unit.

          'Ewan brings him videos and pizza,
but he eats badly if he ever eats and what…'
on the case Marlene kept up her babble,
'what of this Gwen?' (The invisible Mrs Baxter,
Valium addict and/or nursing mum par excellence?)
'Bet he's made her up, those kids too.
Since every second sentence seems to include *my wife*

who'd say such things unless there wasn't one,
or one you were about to dump?
I read in *Cleo*…'
                              Someone is moving out, someone else is
moving out, someone and someone else are moving in,
and please don't start on the tragedy of Rory and Rollo,
doubtless spending weeks of it with Mumsy…
since that's where we recoiled.
                              'Domestic flow-charts?'
pleaded Kurt. 'Forget 'em.'
            Their branch attendances were over,
though when it came to the Party's party-life
the couple still could play the comrades.
                                      Until,
stage two of a progressive dinner and, outside the Adcocks
Des has arrived to ambush Phil: bugger moonlight,
he's left the engine running and in a blast of
high beam in Vermont South he flails his rival with
some roly-poly pummel.
            And I would continue watching but but
men don't hit each other, not today, not
in the ALP!
                  'I'm not *in* the ALP!' Des wails.
'I've gone Commo: hear me Ingrid, hear me Fascist Phil?
Commo!'
                  Then Ewan grabs Des,
pushes him into the passenger seat, drives to the unit
and when he returns just Kurt and I remain
with Marlene whimpering how stupid Ingrid spoils all,
all she ever gets her eyes on and how,
because of her, we were left with Bland,
years of unending Bland.
                                    Soon stupid Ingrid phoned me.
I wasn't to come around, tears were flowing,
they'd been for days, making her look:
'Some kind of cut-price nun halfway through
her penance.'
                  The nun-talk ceased
and girl-to-girl talk started:
'You must know by now I cannot stand this hole
this Vermont South. Most men (not Kurt not Kurt)
are pigs are dogs, think of any animal well each

is it. And as for those women with their
yippity-yip 'n' yappity-yap…
Know who respected me? Bland, friggin' Bland.
After I lost we swapped notes, his said I fought
a damn good clean campaign,
wishing me the best. Who else did that?
Not my comrades only my opponent.
And when it comes to Vermont South, Pet,
you have been my best, my closest and
my only. But you know that…'
       And in my perverse sorrow
for those bossy, big-noting prefect types
who'll never make School Captain, tears were
surging my way too.
           '…we're going round the coast,'
I heard, 'to Pambula, we've shares in this motel…'
       My tears checked.
Hearing of his weird hots for Ingrid,
that was Bland's affair, but shares in some
Pambula motel and *she* had been our candidate?
       'Don't lose touch, visit one day, please Pet please?
And give our best to Lew and Dee?'
       Lew and Dee indeed.

Nothing of the Natter

       Vocalist/barrister/politician:
mightn't there be some pattern present
as Dad lounged back in their South Yarra penthouse,
taping himself for Dee to transcribe, prune
and polish?
         Come off it Lew, sure,
give us *The Decline and Fall of the Ding Dong Daddies*
but what kind of memoirs were they when
the 'Kickback Case' seemed swamped by sportsmen's nights
and Telethons?
         So for the moment this becomes
the marriage: Lew reminisces, Dee edits,
except when he returns to Canberra:
joining the Honourable Members for Carringbush,
Sarsaparilla, Snake Gully and Woop-woop

passing to the right and/or left of the Speaker's chair,
hear bloody hear. Then, for Lew loved all and
all loved Lew yes all, spending evenings getting sloshed
with Bland and his attendant *damn good* grin:
'C'mon Lew, which Commo mates supplied that Ute,
the Wharfies? The Missos?'
                          'We stole it, Gib.'
            'That Ute!' was Mum's bemused despair.
'There was his singing, there was his profession,
his career; there was friendship, love and,
in case it's been forgotten a family.
But all we ever hear about is Ute,
these men and their legendary Utes:
defending liberty, Eureka encircled by Utes,
and Utes storming ashore at Gallipoli;
Want to take on the Kelly Gang? Simple:
· drive up to Glenrowan, in your Ute,
but watch out, Ned also has a Ute;
Phar Lap never won the Cup,
that was a Ute; and since it's time for the Depression,
facing-up to Bodyline, here's Bradman…
yep, in his Ute; and as for the Kokoda Trail…
forget any Dee, let alone any Poppy,
your Dad left me for a Ute.'
                          Was this for effect,
the Debating Captain's hyperbole in the rebuttal stage?
Maybe, for Cath, now Cath the columnist-identity,
had decided to smile, since she was '…juggling
fifty thousand beaux and counting,
something I should've attempted decades back.'
            And seeing no need to cheer her up,
still I cheered her up: my bunfight news from
Vermont South.
                  She'd viewed it all before:
'Will or this Phil and the wife nobody saw,
Margot or this Ingrid and the husband
everyone knew? What a pattern:
Exhibit A: near tragic in its tight-lipped,
modish style; Exhibit B: outer-suburbs slapstick.
            Then Mum who liked to say things
because she liked to say things,
veered back again to Lew and how, only now,

she knew what had been missed:
'Were we born when you were born
I would've been the politician.'
                                        She sure would.
            Cath didn't want her column named *Perspective*
so that's what they named it.
                                    She'd prefer
Nothing of the Natter, 'Which,' Gail advised,
'sounds more like a headline, of a review,
one that's heralding your first of many books.'
            The Power Couple certainly were supportive.
almost too supportive.
                            'A memoir?' Godfrey asked.
'Maybe? One day?'
                        Oh please, she'd just commenced
her current life. Why should she contemplate
her former ones?
            The National Broadsheet tried to poach her,
it didn't work. Instead, syndicated to the SMH
she interviewed those who Dee just wouldn't.
            'Can you,' I was asked, 'envisage Dee
with Germaine Greer? Can you imagine me with
Peter Allen? Certain things are never as-you-do.'
            'There might be worse,' I posited.
'We could approach the love-ly Dee and suggest
a *Cleo* profile: you, me, Kurt, Rod, all of us, no?'
            How serious did my mother think I was?
She must've known Dee had taken leave to aid
in Lew's memoir, then to embark upon
that novel.
                (We saw her as the Dinner wife,
Mum lasting until well after Lunchtime,
with Poppy for a very vapid High Tea.)
            'I'm not that kind of Dee-professional,'
Cath would insist. 'I'm too old to be professional
per se, which I assume is why they've chosen me.
I'm hardly a writer, no not yet...'
            One day though she would commence that memoir,
or something like a memoir;
and to a manila folder, stored with four, five/
nine, ten years of notes, hand-written notes
she gave the name *A History of My Times*.

Shame and Scandal

One Sunday afternoon
(knowing he couldn't hack her) we let slip to Lew
all the Ingrid, Des and Phil debacle.
        Lew lounged further back:
'That's one less motel I'll visit.'
Yes he recalled her men, the sniggler and that
little big-noter, correct? And that was where
he'd made himself a fool in front of Hawkey
(even more correct) but not as much a fool as her:
being beaten by Bland, then shooting through
with that ultimate in small-business blabbermouths.
'How'd Labor ever let him in, Kurt?'
        'What other party would have him, Lew?'
        Which got Dad turning Caribbean:
calypso, reggae, mento, ska…having heard something,
someplace, soon he was improvising…

'In Vermont South there lived a candidate,
whom Labor had chosen thinking she was first rate.
An activist mum for our in-coming tide,
rewarding herself with a bit-on-the-side.
And who was the object of this peccadillo?
Her Campaign Director and her hubby don't know!

Woe is me,
shame and scandal in the ALP,
woe is me,
shame and scandal in the ALP.

She lost the election yet still showed her face,
though losing to Bland seems a mighty disgrace.
Then to have sex with some small-business dork,
and all this occurs whilst she's hosting Bob Hawke.
We're making a sitcom, the name of our show:
'Her Campaign Director and Her Hubby Don't Know!'

Woe is me,
blame and stuff-ups in the ALP,
woe is me,
blame and stuff-ups in the ALP.

"I'm quite liberated," she said to her chums,
"There's much more to women than our tits and our bums.
Since the victor I am in my marital wars,
and though it's a secret I'll tell you the cause
of my heart palpitating and my face all aglow,
he's my Campaign Director and my hubby don't know!"

Woe is me,
why was this couple in the ALP?
Woe is me,
why was this couple in the ALP?

Well they're livin' the dream, this twosome from Hell,
who have gone interstate now to start a motel.
And if you have intimate things on your mind,
be it conjugal bliss or the dalliance kind,
and you're after some action, please trust our mott-o:
'Her Campaign Director and Her Hubby Don't Know.'

Woe is me' (Kurt sang it)
'shame and scandal in the ALP.
Woe is me' (I sang it)
'shame and scandal in the ALP.'

I phoned Marlene, the Adcocks came around,
we all sang it, even Ewan sang it.
But then Des died.

I can't say perving at the contact press,
yet with one enormous howl he toppled over,
a very flushed and flustered man on a late-night train.
She returned from Pambula (Phil at first
hanging back, right back with the kids)
Ingrid on this dull Spring day,
in her Jackie Onassis sunglasses, knowing and us knowing
how heroic they had to make her look:
failed candidate, failed wife, failed widow.
Marlene dodged her, Marlene couldn't dodge her,
and like it was some playground two schoolgirls
were at it, saying their not-so-soft
and very nasty words.
Now glasses more than ever on high-beam
Ingrid turned and strode my way:

'You saw Marlene? You saw Marlene?
Bitch says I killed him. You'd never say that
would you Pet?' (And Pet had to hug
the most unhuggable woman she would ever know.)
'The man was weird, well he was weird enough,
and I was supposed to act *the candidate*?'
      Then as Kurt and I sat beside her and Phil
and the sons, Ewan in his stolid Ewan mode
gave some eulogy how 'That man was our mate…'
meaning 'Don't blame him if stupid Ingrid
couldn't get herself elected.'
                  In the carpark
she took off her glasses and I would never see
sadder, more ridiculous eyes.
      'Going to the wake Chez Adcock?'
Her joke was barely working and once more
we were to give their best to Lew and Dee.
'Please?' Then came a gulp, silence, more silence and
another gulp: 'For fuck's sake Helen, I only wanted love!'

That Fool, That Hero

      Did Dee's third marriage work? Did Dad's?
The best we understood would be *it didn't not.*
      'Kurt,' I asked, 'is our marriage working?'
      'Search me,' he answered, meaning, I assumed,
it worked.
          Whether you could call it 'marriage'
the Curnow freakshow had in its way worked
too friggin' well.
          Mr and Mrs Vermont South?
Well a DIY *Cleo* quiz gave Marlene a rating:
eight point five, pretty good she thought.
      (One more election came and Ewan Adcock,
giving his greatest ever groan defeated Gilbert Bland.)
      Rod? His Rochelle was very Queensland,
very dinky-di, but their 'Conjugal'?
(He never called it 'marriage' hahaha.)
'Listen,' we knew he'd say, 'you will never know.'
(Resorting to guesses we felt it doubtless worked.)
      Until the time arrived to stop

Mum made that marriage work, for everyone but her.
Now each beau would have to work for Cath.
        Poppy's wedding worked and that was it.
        As for the Baxters: the carrot cake worked,
the kedgeree didn't.
                (Phil and Ingrid?
You'd hardly even guess the guesswork.)
        But Dee and Dad? It seemed to work,
better than the end of his career:
no chance with caucus, no chance with Hawke,
and if he remained Lew the ever-popular,
ever-popular rarely means ever-reliable, ever-competent,
ever-subtle. But these, comrades, are hard-nosed times,
want to get fooled again, brothers?
But let's be generous and through
sources close to the incoming government
make this known: 'Lew? Hasn't any enemies bar Lew.'
Who didn't know that? Perhaps he should have
got some: union enemies, boss enemies, inter-factional,
intra-factional and why not spout something still apt
against those Stalinist stooges from two decades back,
to reignite their indignation?
Well too late, mate, and Lew would rather sing,
though who would know or want to know
Dad's *K-Tel Big Band Hits*? Unfashionable?
Sure he was unfashionable, though it hardly meant
that he was work-shy. Give him anything:
Speaker, Deputy Speaker, Chairman of Committees,
Whip? Nah, nix, nope and no!
        'Tell you what we'll do, Lew...'
and they would ask around. 'Let's set up a fund
and you can get a stipend, shepherding through
our latest members, skills coach if you like.
Then after this coming term, a diplomatic posting!'
        Costaguana: which junta had
'Strangely quite progressive views...'
that's what he'd read and 'Wow,' he penned upon
an early postcard, 'couldn't one retire here!'
        After which the envelopes arrived, Dee-snaps:
Dad presenting credentials to El Presidente;
Dad squinting at Pre-Columbian artefacts;
Dad surrounded by nuns and orphans; in poncho,

in sombrero, the Ambassador in cha-cha-cha olé! mode;
though what he was doing, what he was *really* doing
in Costaguana was acting-out the late-middle-aged man,
fooling himself over females and the mighty female form,
starting at the Diplomatic Corps then ever-ever outwards.

Just before one of his señoras wouldn't leave her señor
Dee quit Dad, who took a month's leave at some spa-resort,
dying in the second week.

Rod, I, Mum, Dee and Uncle Will
knew no one wished to say anything too original,
leaving it to anecdotes, just anecdotes.

'Great front man for a rally, Lew,
especially if we're about to lose, though with his help
not by that much…'

Some Labor Unity heavies
considered sponsoring a Lew Johnson Memorial Oration,
and there it remained, an ever-affable afterthought.

And while we're on the thought of afterthoughts,
how about it's ten pm,
Saturday February 26, 1983 again,
with nine of us lined-up on the Curnow's patio,
looking out over backyard upon backyard ablaze
under Vermont South moonlight:
with Ingrid so very, very likely to defeat Gib the Glib,
her marriage let alone her husband to survive,
Marlene to remain her friend, the Baxters
to be reconciled in some Pambula motel,
and big-hearted Lew Johnson still hoping to be made
someone memorable in the forthcoming Hawke Government.

Plenty can occur, though never these afterthoughts,
for now, as if to place some hex upon the future
Dad thinks *It's Time* to continue serenading:

'Swing of six percent
jobs are heading for the boys
how about one, Bob?'

'Don't be fuckin' silly Lew,' snaps Hawke.
Woo-hoo!

VI Mixed Businessmen

The speaker is a former teacher now on an Invalid Pension.

       Reliable as anyone I've known,
Bob Arnold is the kind of man for whom life works
because (please excuse my sentimental aphorisms)
he loves life's work; he's lucky too, since he makes
his luck: wife, two girls, an extended back/
extended up weatherboard, the briskest walk
from Dennis station, a mum and dad further up
the Hurstbridge Line.
                  He's never said so
but unlike me he's never let his parents down.
Can't you hear mine? 'Why turn out yet another teacher
for the state and why then did you quit?
Why'd you marry whom you did then let
your marriage rot?' Or 'Why,' in my own phrase,
'that lack of any focus?'
                    Not that I would mention it,
but when you respect their aptitude, their nous
and clearly their results, when a man does plenty
and it's all success, a friend like Bob will focus
for you: which dictum, Bob need never know,
also applied to Beetle.
                Let's say someone walks by,
walks into any spot that's yours along the strip
at three or four or five pm and 'Yes,' you get it
'today I'll score!' Let's further say that this is how
the world of Beetle starts, as one windy, warm
late August afternoon I was at his place and
this girl was there: just past attractive,
just starting to age.
              Sure, with a few days left
of hanging back I felt detached,
though with my growing edge which told me:
'Take what's offered. If that girl dies
(and she may die) your man won't even care...'
       I had, I have my still and centred love
of self-respect (rules which even now may rescue me).
Where though lay self-respect in the ever present *that*?
Where it was to be regained of course, that swiftest,

207

simplest way, the Beetle way.
Those days it seemed
like every second staffroom (that's where I'd been
a year before) let alone every spot along the strip
had one of us at least: happy-go-usey, slightly sad,
making and remaking ourselves ever so slightly
sadder.
My wife had never cared for me-and-sadder,
so she quit. I'll always hate her.
She and the boyfriend though, I bought them out,
aiming to live alone, which dispensing with the lot
our lot (furnishings, white goods) I did,
enjoying all that propped my pride in minimal living.
Next-to-last off the carpets came, paring me to floorboards
(with a front room facing Lygon Street opposite the cemetery)
and my Invalid Pension. So I shrugged,
put my place on the market and finished each few days
with silent wails to some distant god,
hating it, hating her for that little twerp I was,
so that I would catch, I *had* to catch the bus
to Clifton Hill and then wait for the Beetle tram.
Until that summer's day I saw the man who sent me there,
Big Mike on the strip announcing 'Beetle's? Don't exist now.'
And I'd be best advised it never had.
Except it had.
And I thought of us: retailers, clientele, those stickybeaks-for-now,
as kids jostling in line with Skunk, Keno, Des 'n' St-st-stu
at Mother Beetle's tuckshop, big-noting sure,
though most days more big-noter wacky than big-noter paranoid:
like Skunk announcing 'Wanna join the army so I can give
the officers head!'
'Well,' Big Mike sneers, 'somewhat possible
isn't it? If he can get away from Beetle. How can he but?'
Not with the quiz-master himself
(our one with all questions, answers, prizes) reminding both how
hadn't he been Cap'n Midnight's Two-I-C? and how
'...for a year whilst we were flogging his little bags o' joy,
the ol' Midnight wasn't he the Pope!'
Well, Beetle taunted,
weren't our wishes always jelling, jelling,
to be part of such a pedigree? But in some Reservoir back street?
Never for our Cap'n! Which made me wonder

why indeed for our Beetle? Not that I need ask,
since this is what Beetle ultimately does:
forces you to imagine. I know I had to.

*

This sure is useless-bastard weather…and near Midnight,
stone-bored with these past two days of Northerlies,
Des 'n' Stu watch Wogs on Elwood Beach wrap up their soccer.
And even if tomorrow's Sunday, Sunday can be work for some
like Des 'n' Stu: sitting it out, staring at videos, listening yet again
to Beetle and agreeing with him how Dæmon's been
a very stupid boy. Tonight but, they've credit enough with which
to hit the Crystal Palace, to choose and pay (which gets as innocent
as they shall ever be).
                              Welcome to Beetle's,
this useless-bastard Summer Sunday.
It's some place which, though boarded-up,
may have passed for a milk bar, where
through all the rich, twenty minute glug
of video trailer voice-overs, he's been phoning.
          Then when he's finished and the order's 'Kill it!'
his boys understand their choice. Beetle or the feature? What choice?
Not when he's chosen how this afternoon they're getting Dæmon round
just so these very stupid, very stoned and very minor dealers
(Beetle, Big Mike, Skunk, Keno, Des 'n' Stu) propped by Beetle-rules
can kill him, correct kill him, Dæmon a thirteen-year-old
user-dobber-thief. Well that's the Beetle option and if his boys
are out, right out of it enough, this will be done.
                                        The kid's brought in
and all is prime for Beetle versus Dæmon time, how:
'It was you wasn't it sent those fuckers round to bust us?'
          'Shit Beetle-mate, that wasn't me!'
                              Which might be answered
'Who then but?' Except everyone's got so distracted by some boy,
some boy who's hardly entered high school
calling their mate Beetle…Beetle-mate? Go on, try believing it!
          'Hey Beetle-mate,' Stu asks in nervy spite,
'c-c-can't we start the feature now?'
                              Dumb beyond useless-bastard useless,
you never had the energy to fast-forward anything.

You've been superseded by this grand stoned silence, Beetle as thinker,
who pauses, once, twice and then orates.

'He gets tied up.' Beetle stands.
'And gets put there...'

And where is there? 'There there there!
Underneath! Underneath!' Underneath where Beetle's jumping!

'Feed him dog meat, feed him dog shit, anyone of you
know any better?' Of course they don't. 'And let it be way-out,
right Des? Right Stu? And by right I mean
so real-real way-out, beyond mere real way-out, this'll be
Return to Way-out City and St-st-stu that's not some video.
Correct Keno?' Who always keeps on nodding 'Correct, Skunk?
The day has now commenced and we are made for it!'

Not quite Big Mike. Earlier that arvo,
once he saw this Dæmon thing unfolding (as if he'd stay
around for *that?*) he left. They were mental. And, either on it
or not, today's product sure was. 'Yep, on yer bike Big Mike,'
he told himself, shuffling like he was in some folk dance,
sideways to the door. 'On yer bike, we're relocating.'
And he had to since with all of his dealer's skills and effort,
the product and the risks, obedience was the only other option.

'I've taken risks,' Beetle would announce, 'such risks
none will understand.'

Who then murders some prepubescent user so that him and
his Beetle gang of pro-dealers, amateur killers get caught,
and for a few days' worth of Summer's news they hog it.
('Off the record,' a spokesman said, 'the underworld is shamed.')

And I knew them. But also knew myself:
that if it had been necessary I might have been there
that summer afternoon in Reservoir, it might've been me
shuffling an exit with Big Mike, or else with Des 'n' Stu
giggling whilst we tried to dump the corpse
(sure hadn't done that sort of thing before had they,
the things ol' Beetz got you to do!).

For even through
that slow mania of the Beetle toll, people got to know each other,
cooperate. ('J-j-jeez Beetz,' Stu who thought he was funny
once gagged, 'don't give them ambos t-t-too much work.'
Wherever he's been sent there's plenty imitations starting.)

And truly he unites folk does our Beetle, so that when guilt,
actual proven guilt strides in, presenting itself to sighs of joy,
with the Bench contributing each decent, hard-working Aussie's

two bob's worth, oh Beetle just listen, even the very bludging,
the outright indecent are falling one-over-the-other, just to ensure
how banal you truly were.
                    And, excepting that we had to survive
there was little like it.

                          *

         Me, I was fortunate. I could still promenade North Carlton
beaming to and marvelling at the Moreton Bay Figs.
Beetle couldn't own me *that* much, though he still required it known:
'Your thoughts are my thoughts and my thoughts are your thoughts which are:
you'll be forever Beetz, the best there is.'
                              And it fits doesn't it,
how when I heard that him and his losers were set for judgement
I knew that I'd be seeing him this final time.
And though I liked and trusted that idea, a witness seemed required:
this friend to whom I could announce: 'Now you get it, don't you?
he's the dealer I've been dealing with.'
         The trial occurred in school vacation time so I asked Bob,
who as he had been painting rooms Ange permitted one day off,
gatekeeper Ange, the wife who took me for 'My husband's pin-eyed
user friend, him on his Invalid Pension.' Let her,
she wasn't to know that for all the headaches, all the heartaches
(why bother mentioning withdrawals?) R v. Beetle was the primest
vengeance show in town, my year's grandest attraction.
         We caught the train to Flagstaff which got me questioning:
'Just how many users train it to their dealers?'
Unfair asking Bob of course, his problem if he wasn't in our
Beetle club, though come, come Mr Arnold haven't you gone teaching
spaced on your very own drug of choice? Most probably not.
Who on any 'drug' could ever be each student's matey-favourite
yard duty martinet as you are?
                          One lunch hour then,
Bob is motioning to me: 'See him grinning there in his long black coat
and big thick boots? Today's E.T. I'll stand any bet is stoned…'
After which we commenced those Friday evenings when my wife and I,
Bob and Ange fronted bistros, though even then the Arnolds
must've guessed the bit, that little bit I'd be using Saturday
to get me through a day a night, another day and night of married life.
(I've seen her with the boyfriend once: at the Vic Market where

we gave each other a tiny nod: *Go on darling guess who that was…*
my useless user ex!)
                                   And at the next bistro or the next,
just to annoy the spouse Big Mike got referenced in passing.
And *that* Big Mike? Bob knew him from La Trobe. On Bob 'n' Mike terms?
'Near enough. A Maoist once…a teacher once…' hoping to be a junkie once;
any fad taking him to an edge, though hardly so *edge* you couldn't *Oops…*
easy-does-it and adjust.
                             Anyone's capable, just be nice if a touch desperate
and ask about in any suburb, any town (in any staffroom!)
'Know where I can find myself a Beetle?'
Well now's our final chance to find you a Beetle, Bob,
my chance to get my final taste of Beetle, him to cop
his final shot of me.
                         And as if I'd conjured it here came his look
that slightest pause part way between 'Well, wadda ya know…'
and 'Who is that prick, I think I know that prick, who is that prick?'
Though when the judge, who doubtless knew less than one per cent of it
mentioned him by the name Ma and Pa Beetle gave their baby
'Who?' I briefly found myself asking. 'Who? Oh yes yes yes
I used to buy from that deadshit once except that now
since anyone can deal he's not being done for dealing and Beetz…'
I kept staring back, a prick enough to taunt him, 'Beetz,
not anyone can kill and weren't you at very base-camp-base
all death?
              'So that was him?'
                                     'Was him once.'
                                                        'Nice word *once*,'
said Bob.
              Look Beetle, look Bob, at what I was back then:
twenty-nine, bound for divorce, a head-and-heartache prone
high school teacher who, one Thursday after work
approached a man I knew, that same Big Mike, who sent me out
to him, this charismatic squirt (squirtier than even me,
who'd hardly make Bob's shoulders).
                                         'Yeah we're Beetle.
What are we doing you for?'
                                I told him what. Who sent me then?
And as I answered, don't say we 'bonded' though we did,
over Big Mike's snigger-producing, ever-ripening moustache,
there on a Reservoir back street where Beetle worked out of his shop front.
     '…so,' I asked my dealer, 'this was a milk bar once?'

'Mixed business,' he replied, 'just like any day.'
And who was there that any day? Taster girl, another woman too,
one I later took for Dæmon's mother, found within a year
wailing in some park.

Though by now I had a little bag inside
my jacket pocket and having survived that afternoon
I knew that I'd survive this little bag, this anything.
And I have.

For look at what's evolved:
an even more prone, divorced, ex high school teacher of thirty-two
trying his embarrassed 'Thanks for coming.'

'My pleasure,' Bob replies.

Except for headaches I think I'd like to think I'm clean.
Lying down though, which is often, my mind remains on her: my wife,
whose secrets forced me into mine. And I could blame that woman plenty,
who though would listen to the blame?
Even Bob, a friend who's always heard me out would walk away.
I've seen him, down the other end of a park, playing with his kids,
and as we waved I knew his feeling in return:
'There he goes, someone from *then* I'd rather wasn't *now*.'

And never say you've never felt that way…
driving through this heritage town who's that limping relocated man?
Big Mike, one Interferon day to the next. That girl must be dead;
but for each Des, Stu, Keno, Skunk, who wants to make some
living-or-dead effort? Hardly me. And Dæmon?
He was a kid on the news whose parents two, two and a half decades ago
gave idiot name upon idiot name to their disposable offspring,
as if their Dæmon would grow into his generation's Beetle.

Who just degenerated. For I've heard this,
someone's required to wheelchair him, King Beetle-mate with Aussie flag
round and around the Z Division yard, this someone being recompensed
with product.

So it continues, my tick-off list of
them, them and them, those, those and those 'til it will have happened
much too many years ago, and even these memories, our sour
and blighted memories, must surely need to cease.

VII Yarraville Confidential or The Boyfriend Experience

The speaker is Hailey, the elder daughter of Angela, Labor member for Fairfield and Victorian Deputy Premier. Bob, the father and Bianca, the sister complete the family.

Politics is the art of looking for trouble, finding it everywhere, diagnosing it incorrectly and applying the wrong remedies.

Groucho Marx

Prologue

Once in my days serving behind some bar
I met a poet, a certain Mr Wearne
who, avoiding 'Have a nice day blah…'
proposed some questions, for he desired to learn
whom I admired and why. 'Why? Hahaha
chicks,' I replied, 'with attitude to burn.
Talented, strong-willed, don't you get me, Al?
Like Julia Gillard and Diana Krall.

Nina Simone, Elizabeth the First,
that Danish PM, you know the one in *Borgen.*
Those who don't in any way feel cursed
by lacking a male reproductive organ.
From tacklers of sleazebags at their worst,
to Third World women reaping rice or sorghum
(an excellent example of the Other)
and above all these, Angela my mother.

In olden times, when girls would Women's Lib-it,
she learned a lot consorting with those Reds.
And ever since Ange isn't one to squib it,
with deftest hands she'll quietly crack heads.
A Labor zealot no one can inhibit
she aims her sights on Liberal re-treads,
though copping a bout of sexist repartee
when she became Victoria's Two-I-C.

The Premier says her loyalty's: "Unbelievable!
And in the front row of your many talents!
Achieving more than might be thought achievable
with a husband and two daughters for the balance…"

All Angelas conceive her most conceivable,
and since I've heard you represent the Alans
how might you rate her in your world of men?'
He nodded his approval, smiled, and then

holding a note pad like an old-time journo,
with furrowed brow he chewed a pencil stub.
His act succeeding he deserved a Pernod,
yet I would quiz him to the very nub.
'Why do you seek such information Wearno?
It rarely goes with working in a pub.
Seeming an oblique way to have viewed me,
When you write your next book, please include me.'

A few years on: the ultimate igniter:
I met Lewie and by love was shook.
He felt the same, this made it even brighter
and as a result, to Yarraville we took,
where he was asked: 'If I could be a writer
would our adventures make it in a book?'
And an answer came, in this case redirected,
for it was in an email unexpected:

Dear Hailey, you once asked 'to be included'
and your request I still think simply stellar,
firing imagination as very few did
(please never ask, I'm just that kind of fella).
So knowing what you've viewed and how you've viewed it,
with tales to tell believe me, you're the teller,
a canny dame who'll sort out what the fuss is,
with a fairness that's a paragon of justice.

You're often present when the action landed
watching these stories somewhat from the side,
which attribute I'd never class as 'standard',
and here is more to supplement your pride:
when to be discreet and when be candid.
With gifts like these (how can they be denied?)
our narrative won't find a better choice
than making sure it's written in your voice.

I won't portray you as some fairground barker,
who'd put a well-read readership to flight.
Our art demands it, and no choice is starker,
avoiding both banal and erudite
(which stunts are for the whiteboard and its marker)
with folks we quote, from left-wing through to right,
the gamut of democracy's dominions
(the best of course shall mirror our opinions).

I've followed your career and your romancing,
so please forgive such literary stalking
but that's a risk I am forever chancing:
to capture modes of thinking and of talking,
the poet's art which, if it works, enhancing.
We've different minds to, let's say, Stephen Hawking,
a Galileo, Newton or an Einstein;
plus better morals than a Harvey Weinstein.

With our nation ripe for every con,
from the 'free speech' quasi-fascist gentry
onto each mock-Mafiosi Don
Australia's crop we're harvesting a-plenty,
no matter what the stimulant they're on.
From year 2000 well past 2020,
with base essentials, ever changing vogues,
candidates for our gallery of rogues.

Which won't include your mother, never fear,
her qualities I won't remotely ration,
seeing in Angela's public-life career
a loadstar of integrity and passion.
A woman whose worth increases by the year,
a throwback of wonder! Not of this current fashion:
in hock to each conspiracy they're told:
going once, twice, three, four times…then sold!

Can we assume our task is worth the viewing?
I'm sure this poem won't be overpriced.
Although I've found there's criticism brewing:
those hauntings of the philistine zeitgeist
with 'Who is he and what the fuck's he doing?'
Like I was set to mastermind a heist.

And if on arvos see me a trifle dreamy
I'm staying put, though some might love to see me

put out to grass, down in a distant paddock
(the race being run there shall be no reprise).
I've still a focus, if a touch sporadic,
cognisant of my propensities.
So will admit that I've turned out an addict,
with, for my drugs, outlandish similes
and trying to capture how Australians yap,
with use of rhyme to give that extra snap.

This music's potent echoes, beats and chimes
(it bugs me, man; can you dig it, baby?)
whose outline comes from far more structured times,
devoid of an equivocating 'maybe',
with this the pattern of the first six lines:
A.B.A.B and then another A.B.
The final two unfolding fairly easy,
think of Saint Francis ending in a C.C.

I learnt such early as a versifier:
they're like the crescendo, rondo, scherzo, tutti;
like putting all those damp clothes in the dryer;
which metaphors I trust enrage the snooty.
How I adore my ramping up their ire,
so even better let's resort to footy:
to rise above the pack and take a screamer,
now that's the beauty of ottava rima.

Could never pen a haiku in a fit,
to haul through three lines their syllabic curse,
there's grander options in a poet's kit.
So all your puzzled doubts I'll now disperse:
daggy rhymes combined with half-baked wit
shall make a novel, albeit in verse,
and this approach no more shall be a mystery
for we've the backing from the bards of history.

These tales of you, your mother, father, sister,
are what I'd term 'reality unbounded'.
Not 'fantasy' unravelling like some twister

but narratives humane and very grounded,
the artful bedrock of that mighty vista
on which all epics, prose or verse are founded;
each with their quirks; so here's my variation:
combining gossip with imagination.

Since weren't embellished facts the best of fiction
which Homer through to πO poets prized?
The voice shall be yours, the vocab and the diction,
for emphasis they'll be italicised.
But please allow collaborative friction,
with such results to be uncompromised.
In Yarraville you've nothing to repress,
learning to love this stanza form, I guess.

Its pedigree's distinctive rhyme and metre
giving ottava rima quite a smart beat,
were it a tonic I'd flog it by the litre
to give a pleasing increase to the heartbeat.
Little in verse seems remotely neater
for our collaboration, so we can't beat
calling each other 'cobber', 'comrade', 'matey';
we should complete it by the time I'm eighty.

All life-tides surging ever to their ebb
much remains towards my master plan.
(Though hardly as some 'blogger' on the 'web'
with a Tarantino film script in the can.)
Opting perhaps for novelist-as-celeb
announcing what it's like to be a Man?
But let's leave such to Flanagan and Winton,
although you'd stand a better chance with Tintin.

Throughout my brain spot-fires were alighting,
heartbeats surged and knees commenced to buckle.
I couldn't conceive of anything more exciting
unless I were a babe about to suckle.
'To be dead-centre of a poet's writing!'
Lewie proclaimed, if ending in a chuckle.
'Pour forth the Champagne, Chardonnay and Moselle!
How could a girl not fall for this proposal!'

Fairfield Confidential

Before we disembark at Yarraville
there's time to spare with Angela and Bob,
my Mum and Dad, two activists who fill
these pages with their first romantic throb,
and soon us kids, whose sounds familial,
that full parade from giggle through to sob,
would institute reactions most parental:
though sometimes critical, nothing detrimental.

To grasp my mother let's first sketch her father,
though rich, he was a somewhat wettish Tory,
whose second home lay nestled at Mount Martha,
(except this house won't enter in our story).
He had a jaundiced view of that palaver
from those who worshipped Menzies in his glory;
applauding each time 'would' defeated 'wouldn't',
he'd love to be a rebel but he couldn't.

This was the role which landed on his daughter,
he, in reflection, quite satisfied would bask,
as often in a kidding way he fought her.
So Ange replied by taking him to task,
like when our war of Indo-Chinese slaughter
had reaffirmed her faith in mainstream Marx,
the man exhaled, relaxing with a 'Wow!
At least you have avoided Chairman Mao!'

This power of tolerance she understood,
embarrassment though, drove her to excesses.
The time was ripe to join the Sisterhood,
if draw the line at other girls' caresses.
'A few less youthful antics than I should…'
are what she, in private now confesses.
Though for the moment see us close that door,
time to present the future son-in-law.

Bob liked to drink both pilsner and lager.
Good looking? Yes. And all the girls they dug it.
His motorbike will feature in this saga,
whilst to the mordant sigh of 'I'll be buggered…'

right-wingers he would itemise as 'gaga'.
Rough-hewn if not ridiculously rugged,
folks at times mistook him for Jeff Bridges.
His repartee kept everyone in stitches.

High-grade bemused, anything but solemn,
all forms of 'Liberation' as his guide,
with beers to toast the Third World see him skol 'em,
applaud the ebbing of th' imperial tide.
The student rag would run his racy column,
polemical, with an irreverent side.
Bob was mighty proud of his opinions
so didn't need girl-groupies or boy-minions.

When they first met both were doing Honours.
Angela's learning showed she was no shirker,
though politics would prove a two-way bonus
and Bob recoiled, ferocious as a Gurkha:
'What kind of hyper-zealot is upon us,
this would be mouthpiece for the average worker?'
She'd done her BA at another Uni,
whose intellect she rated pretty puny.

Working-out lean, complete with ponytail
(she's been unaltered these intervening years)
Angela's word-power makes opponents quail
or gets the full endorsement of her peers:
'If necessary I would go to jail…'
Bob bit his lip: 'We can't resort to jeers,
but please Ange please, your reasoning's delirious,
sometimes we Lefties take ourselves too serious.

Far removed from any hoi-poloi
there lies your heritage, one you refuse to utter.
Let's take your father, those in his employ
know how their labour earns *him* bread and butter.'
Her background being outed by this boy!
To rescue something all she could do was stutter:
'And if my old man sits on many Boards…
he never speaks of womankind as broads.'

Yes Angela was not exactly deft
so such riposte could never quite un-man him.
But believing Bob lacked academic heft
'Featherweight!' the term with which she'd brand him.
'For if like me ostensibly *on the left*
he is no comrade and I cannot stand him.
Since sixteen I've turned my eyes on men,
but if I marry…it won't be one of *them*!'

A former outer suburbs high school lad
Bob as judge and jury made this ruling:
'Her commitment seems the merest fad,
who does this silly woman think she's fooling?
I've rarely met this form of undergrad,
complete with Ladies College style of schooling.
She sounds like Pravda, well I guess that figures…'
It took no time to activate more triggers.

Always primed to ambush Angela,
as grin turns smirk he's going into bat,
confronting unsubstantiated blah
like 'bourgeoisie' and 'proletariat'.
These will continue in each seminar:
'Don't tell me, Angie, you believe in *that*!'
And every time she snaps back at His Lordship.
(How'd they to know this commenced their courtship?)

Hardliner she, he slightly more the supple,
neither displays a modicum of prudence,
nor even know they're acting 'like a couple',
so obvious to all the staff and students.
But the man is froth, she'll prick every bubble:
'I've news for you, oh supercilious nuisance,
unlike some I'm grounded in essentials.
I've been arrested, *that* heads my credentials.

We know your type who occupy the fringes,
fantasy-radicals of the insipid kind,
all 'let's pretend' to prop your ego-binges,
the first of volunteers to be side-lined,
forever missing when The State impinges:
straight to the copshop, into court then fined.

Whilst those like you keep penning endless memos,
the rest of us are out there having demos.'

Yet after another city demonstration
he sees her crossing south on Princes Bridge,
with all that stride of hardline calculation
(doubtless you'd find more warmth inside a fridge).
But something flares in Bob's imagination
(a little bit this side of ridgey-didge):
what if, behind such sombre, gritty cover,
he senses, she desires to take a lover?

With all that chilled, self-satisfied containment
(her clothes if plain are no way 'dressing down')
as each encounter turns to an arraignment,
both set to run the other out of town,
from which is born a certain entertainment,
(though who's to play the straight man, who the clown?)
Bob's brain is fogged, and yet this fogging jells:
'I'd fall for her…if she were someone else…'

He'll seize the chance! Bob's scooting on his Honda
through inner-urban Melbourne as he hums
a Beach Boys hit, no doubt 'Help Me Rhonda',
but this tune's over-ridden, for there comes
a hefty, vibrant sound from over yonder
(less than a K when adding up your sums)
down the road there's demonstrators chanting,
disgusted at the order they're supplanting.

A women-only protest is arising,
for men to join such action would betray 'em,
plus they've this leader set on evangelising,
much in the style, alas, of Billy Graham.
Then Bob's bemusement stops and needs revising,
since conflict's brewing in this demo-mayhem,
which turns to horror as he's getting nearer
for a group of neo-fascists (from that era)

are ramming home their counter-demonstration
(it helps there seems no presence from the cops).
Some decades hence they're bound to join One Nation,

and when that happens let's sluice out the slops.
As Bob stares down this sewerage of creation,
a-swagger with their boots and riding crops,
around the women see the thugs amassing,
with Angela the one they're most harassing.

Bob has one aim, and revving at the melee
screams 'Get on!' which in a trance she does;
her arms are holding tight around his belly
and clearing out associated fuzz,
with a mind of steel that never turns to jelly
she makes expletives; he thinks 'What a buzz!'
Through some back streets who knows where they're headed?
(How's Ange to know they'll end up being wedded?)

Such was their first, if accidental date,
some place between commitment and a hobby.
'We're fools,' she said 'to mutually berate,
let's learn instead, first up how to lobby.
With this in mind I'll term you 'comrade', 'mate',
please never think I'll stoop to call you 'Bobby'.
Sure you can play the ruckman to my rover,
but call me 'Angie'…all of this is over!'

Next year their fellow students would unfetter:
one opting for a life of meditation,
another in the aid-work world of Quetta,
two buy a Kombi and leave to tour the nation,
for one a few years smoking dope sounds better;
and after her prize-winning graduation,
with sights now aiming at female improvement
Ange is snapped up by the Union Movement.

With such potential see how the boyfriend backed her,
proud of viewing Angela's other side,
love of course turns out a solid factor
as he admired her being (how she tried!)
much more initiator than reactor;
and if she asked for guidance he would guide.
Meanwhile to prove he's not some overreacher
Bob did Dip. Ed. and became a teacher.

He told all: 'I once sought to believe
like Penny Wong she'd end up in the Senate,
for even then with plenty to achieve
this was no case of 'if it comes' but 'when it'.
Maybe my heart pounds often on my sleeve?
I've read Jane Austen, know my Lizzie Bennet,
and heard Ange reckon I'm her Mr Darcy,
though nowhere near as stuck-up nor as classy.'

All the above transformed to family myth,
which we four won't ever swap for quids.
Now let's head to a much more racy riff,
with items as the wowser world forbids:
their nights with friends passing round a spliff,
or somethings hidden, rightly, from the kids:
though we supposed that often they had sex,
there were no signs of love bites on their necks.

Ange taught us much from where she'd done her schooling,
dating boys from Grammar, Wesley, Scotch.
'And,' she would delight us with, 'no fooling,
sexism was *verboten!* on my watch:
as when he slobbers with excessive drooling
boy gropes girl to carve an extra notch,
the titillating envy of his peers…'
(Welcome to the world of Ange the Fierce.)

My sister, though she's nigh on five years younger,
vaulted this age gap with her mother's zest,
that assailed cheat, coward, rumour-monger,
thug and snob, for the kid possessed
the impact of a well-placed double-bunger,
demanding anytime she was assessed
a full five stars, if you had cause to rank her…
or else you'd cop the fury of Bianca.

And though each year her canniness increased
some things there were that she barely dug.
On BoganFM they'd this rap-artiste
extolling virtues of some date-rape drug.
Ange intervened: 'Who is this gruesome beast?
If face-to-face he'd cop one mighty slug.'

On the alert nocturnal and diurnal,
though feminist still very much maternal.

An all-girl school, that was the Ange intention,
my pragmatism showing her I'd cope.
(Those many friends I made there we might mention
had this narration given me the scope.)
Bianca though inspired Bob's intervention:
'With our youngest this is my fervent hope:
when clambering through her adolescent rubble
she won't live in a private girl's school bubble.

Co-education where the system's State,
in teenage years I reckon she will crave.'
And though we see her losing the debate
Mum, who's giving good as what he gave,
no matter what the auguries indicate
launches a fifteen-minute counter-rave,
certain there's something extra she can teach us,
since Ange is always great at making speeches.

Thus politics became the trek she tracked,
and who would have the gall to question 'Why?'
Familial support she never lacked
possessing this potent weapon on the sly,
a husband well-attuned to the double act,
his straight-faced prompt, her straighter-faced reply:
'Really Ange, you see this as your mission?'
'Well someone has to be the politician.'

The kind of suburbs to elect our mum
were moderate in drinking and in gaming.
No freakshow like some latter-day R Crumb
but honest folk, quietly proclaiming
'We work, we're proud, we're nothing like a slum…'
and to a voter most, it seems, were aiming
with lots of leftish arrows in their quiver
at leafy bourgeois Kew, across the river.

But come the night we're itemising fears,
forever on a lookout for the Greens.
Though joining in a brace of hear-hears

I'm never one adept at causing scenes.
By nine pm though see me verge on tears,
for some things hit when being in your teens:
a swing was on and yet we were rejected,
so Labor lost, though Angela was elected.

And gave a speech of stunning affirmation.
'Yes,' she proclaimed, 'to all my campaign workers,
devoted to our party, state and nation.
Yes, to unions belting scabs 'n' shirkers.
To yoga? *Yes*, my mode of relaxation.
To Islam? *Yes*, even with your burqas.
And to our queers an all-empowering *yes*,
who without shame now publicly caress.

'Yes, to single Mums and their pre-schoolers,
sisters you do your gender very proud.
Yes, to our Greek friends, all those Cons and Toulas,
proclaiming your ethnicity out loud.
But no! to Old Boy Grammar born-to-rulers,
ever seen a more insipid crowd?
And no! to One Nation, that latter day Falange!'
With which a cry erupted 'Bewdy Ange!'

'Though I'm elected ours is the team which lost,
that's where arrives the bitter-sweetest crunch,
since in the game of bosses v the bossed
I'm set to play a Judy to their Punch
and take it on, for we well know the cost
of propping those who eat the free-est lunch.
Leadership is *not* some rich man's hobby
with Gold Pass to intimidate and lobby.

Name us a mindset, well beyond repair,
so out-of-touch it verges on the alien.
With our beliefs both rational and fair
I for one can't wait to start regaling them,
and if we're tagged as 'Lefties' for a dare
'No,' let's reply, 'unabashed Australian!'
Were Ange an actress grappling with *that* bogey
then she'd deserve an Oscar or a Logie.

Give but two years Angela had impacted,
blogs and websites chronicled her assent,
the Government beyond the point of fractured
most obvious when Ange was on their scent.
With horse-sense, guile, and all polling factored,
plus rounds of handshakes, as rituals which meant
she's now proclaimed, with caucus's permission
Deputy Leader of the Opposition.

The former one, most pliable and loyal
just gave way (though why nobody mentions).
The Leader spoke: 'She's brought us to the boil
delivering all her highest-grade intentions.
You should see the Government recoil!
With old style vigour clothed in new dimensions
here is a woman certainly fast-trackable
since female voters find her very backable.

Where she's from she's known as Fairfield's finest,
and now in sharing Angela with the State
I see all plus, cannot detect a minus,
in equal parts a mother and a mate.'
'I'm not,' she blushed, 'like some Royal Highness…
let's hold a barbeque to celebrate.
It's open house at Bob's, the girls' and mine
near Dennis station on the Hurstbridge Line.'

Her opponents were of nuances bereft
and had but sneering phrases for their fuel
like 'Union heavy…darling of the Left…
who sends her daughters to some private school…
and owns a home when *property is theft*…'
day in and out, news-cycling on a spool,
their prejudice and ignorance parading,
for three weeks straight the clichés kept cascading.

Angela's girls were known throughout the area
(dead centre of our post-pubescent forge):
both placid Labrador and yapping Terrier;
and as a dragon well primed for a St. George
my sister, I am proud to say, was scarier,
with countless males on humble pie to gorge,

they had to for, if she said 'Eat!' you ate it,
though more bewildered than humiliated.

Scene: the parents' BBQ fundraiser,
all polls are up, a fine time to rejoice.
The Leader's present, beaming like a quasar,
when a sound comes powering through the party noise.
It's human speech, relentless as a taser,
a lecture's on, it's in Bianca's voice:
'My observations tell there's no iota
you're resonating with the younger voter.'

The action's freeze-framed. Could this be the Truth?
A question pounding every adult head.
Ange just smiles and in her smile's the proof:
'This girl's her mother's daughter, born and bred.
We haven't raised a bimbo or a goof,
she's just the kid from Generation Z.'
'Time to pause,' the oldies know, 'our drinking,
and listen to what younger folk are thinking.'

The Leader's bailed-up copping her backhander,
this teenage girl who doesn't even vote
hectoring full force on the back veranda.
He's not the first who she's got on their goat.
Were he litigious he might sue for slander,
were he a knight-in-armour he might smote.
But being who he was responded 'Ouch!
This girl Bianca's certainly no slouch.'

I like there's not a morsel of the flirty,
since such behaviour's merely built on fibs.
I like she's upfront to the point of shirty
with metaphoric elbows to my ribs.
She'll make a Cabinet by the time she's thirty
(God help us if she ends up with the Libs).
And if her prospects I have over-puffed
next I'm sure she'll tell me to get stuffed.'

And is my sister praised or is she damned?
How he loves such ambiguity!
It feels like the encounter has been planned,

a masterpiece of seamless continuity.
Clasping a crisis firmly in his hand,
and like a wine that's reaching its maturity
held to the light he pondering, inspects it
and then, to his advantage, just deflects it.

He has a multifarious persona
to court both tabloid- and the ABC-folk.
Italian grannies he'll greet with 'G'day Nonna!'
The Irish cop dumb gags about the wee folk.
With Kate his wife, his children Jack and Shona
appealing to those just-like-you-and-me folk
he is a somewhat Centre-Left Prince Charming,
whose quirks are in the best sense quite disarming.

It helps when leading any opposition
if you possess head-kicking as an art
to add a sly self-deprecating frisson:
'I'm a clean-living Catholic lad at heart.
Watch out though when winning is my mission.
Mess with me, mate? Who'd ever want to start?
It won't take much to mix it with you nerds.'
And the game was won in just four simple words.

The Leader was being quizzed about his faction:
'Right? Centre? Left? And are there any others?'
Hoping to give the Government some traction.
To which he muttered 'What a pack of mothers…'
But recovering threw this into the action:
'A tiny something from the Marist Brothers:
as a Mass resounds to an almighty Gloria
so let's sing out *My Faction Is Victoria!*'

Behold the birth of our prize-winning slogan,
what think-tank thinkers could have done it better?
Appealing to both bourgeoisie and bogan
it helped to all our confidence unfetter.
He even got a thumbs-up from Paul Hogan,
Seventies-colloquial to the very letter.
(My sister though, thought this quite a shocker,
to be endorsed by *that* brand of ocker.)

The Government in its dying days had weaved
a mindset that the voters would acquit 'em.
Wrong of course, why should they be believed?
Though there were some most certain what would hit 'em,
who played for time, and that's all they achieved.
A footy parallel I'm sure will fit 'em.
(I like it when the metaphors are sporting,
in poems yes, though never in reporting.)

Those free kicks they were forever staging
made us appear less and less the novice.
And though most options narrow as you're aging
this bigger shame remains, nobody bothers.
'So sorry it's the other bloke we're paging…'
As someone's in as someone's out of office
the future's taking over from the past.
After eight years they knew they wouldn't last.

If their Premier was this under-average Joe
devoid of logic, nous and intuition,
with sympathy you'd appreciate the woe
when voters say 'We're closing your commission.'
A few hours back he was thought our foe,
a footnote now, the losing politician,
though none possessed a braver front than he did
who, putting an arm around his wife, conceded.

Concession over now bounced up our Leader,
with votes of thanks, I counted ninety-nine,
concluding thus: 'Let's give a mighty *Viva!*
to that keystone in the ALP design:
Angela our sterling workhorse diva,
my Deputy who sees I toe the line…
and whilst we're in the mood for seizing moments
let's give a certain thanks to our opponents.

Adieu! Adieu! O legislative vandals!
Breakfast, lunch and dinner we awaited
your ever evolving, latest batch of scandals,
I for one feel quite satiated.
You spluttered for a while like Roman Candles.
But now post-fireworks, set to be mandated

see Labor cross the parliamentary isthmus,
a heart-warming saga, just in time for Christmas.'

As feminist and one time union heavy
Ange knew power at its most berserk-est.
Knew also fame imposed this for a levy:
the rule of PR dominates all purpose.
So see them as battalion or as bevy
the media with its four, five, six ring circus
into our parent's lounge room soon descending;
here follow extracts, no need for amending.

'...according to reports on BoganFM
there's rumours of a time that you were jailed.'
Sounding embarrassed a throat was cleared. 'Ahem.
From fiction out of facts they haven't failed,
trusting to hint, *Is she one of* them?
And hoping your career will get derailed.
Surely such tactics couldn't get much worse if
you were charged with being a subversive?'

'Though,' Mum replied, 'we've mighty vistas vast,
women-in-power for some remain mere novel.
Still they persist in digging up our past
with half-baked innuendo as their shovel,
I shall not bend to BoganFM's blast,
that source alone has never made me grovel.
Subversively credentialled as attested,
since as a student I was once arrested.'

She reminisced: 'It started as a melee
and ended as a few hours in the clink.
There was an issue, it became a rally.
Supporting gays, we all were wearing pink.
A fire was in my head, heart, loins and belly
and so ablaze there seemed no time to think.
Finding a car I clambered to the bonnet,
then knocked a cop's hat off and jumped upon it.

Who hasn't proved excessive at nineteen?
Please don't promote my actions as iconic
(I hate to think who'd play me on the screen)

231

though the combative still remains my tonic.
Shock-jocks in your never-ending preen
who cultivate the bigot and moronic,
here is the news to suit your dead-head hunger:
I've no regrets for what I did when younger.'

Ange rounded off (and who could be surprised):
'I reckon I can gladly bear that yoke.'
But a voice arose, the kind well-recognised
with quasi-snort and imitation choke.
'Don't play me for some mug…' he emphasised,
attempting to evoke the average bloke,
the sneering sort, brash and uninhibited
(we reckoned his employer was News Limited):

'A right-wing thinktank says you're a Marxist stooge,
joining a line of Labor antecedents,
believing that you'll tax like Mr Scrooge
for a nanny state in excess of Sweden's.
Given these allegations rate as huge
don't you think they should be given credence?'
She stared him down without one spot of blinking:
'What right-wing thinktank ever did much thinking?'

Message received, Mum stood up. But wait!
'Angela could you introduce your girls?'
She sighed but knew of little to debate
when the human-interest flag unfurls.
So with a media pack to cultivate:
'Okay you swine, may I present my pearls…
and since our family won't do things by half
line-up women for your photograph.'

As subjects of some pretty snazzy snaps
they'd Hailey beaming and the Bianca glower;
who'd great occasion playing them for saps
and utilise all airtime they'd allow her,
straight-talking stuff, no maybe or perhaps.
Our interview seemed heading to an hour
when, after fifty minutes quizzing daughters
a certain frisson surged through the reporters:

'Behind this woman, it's reckoned, there's a man…
having two girls most surely means a spouse.'
And one there was responding with élan:
'Now that you've asked, my role proves extra grouse.
Call me advisor to her master plan,
supplying what I trust you'll deem as nous.'
With such support, ticked off as expected,
on 'current issues' here's how he deflected:

'Better ask Ange, she's much more the left-winger…
persistent-to-stubborn, certainly a Taurus.
Nabs a fascist, puts him through the wringer.
Though when tears arrive proves mighty porous.
She writes the songs, I'm just another singer
obeying orders in her backup chorus.
We've had our problems but will stay the course,
for no way could we contemplate divorce.'

How Bob enjoyed adapting to this quiz,
when in demand his mode would switch to charming;
and loving to hear reporters go 'Gee whiz…'
felt safe to make an offer quite disarming:
'You can give my resumé a squiz,
a bland summation not the least alarming,
though in my way I'm feeling quite invincible,
since late last year I've been a high school principal.

Any more data you have cause to seek?'
(Such 'innocence' we knew was shot with guile.)
'I've drinking habits very much boutique,
enjoying Wheat Beer in the Belgian style.'
His folksiness ascending to its peak
caused Angela to shake her head and smile.
Mock gormlessness and mocking hahaha,
she'd known these since that Honours Seminar.

A Girlfriend Experience

Sundays at Noon we used to raid the fridge,
you must know the stuff: teenager food.
'It's ages,' Mum sighed, 'since I climbed that ridge.

233

I look at you both to feel quite deja vu'd.
Bianca's diet I will not abridge
even though she terms it *rager food.*'
Dad raised a hand, intoning like mine host:
'It's Sunday Dinner, father shall carve the roast.'

We stared at him who seeing us announced:
'A while back when, around the twelfth of never,
men wouldn't big-note, women rarely flounced,
the Nineteen Fifties, Sixties, err whatever…
imagine…' he paused, found the right words and pounced,
'this blue chip, nuclear family endeavour
(some things are sacred, not to be done by halves)
that meat which mother roasts and father carves.

Not from an ashram with unending oms,
nor from the Champs Elysées nor the Ginza,
this was an inheritance from the Poms,
about as useful as the House of Windsor.
At least our mums wouldn't be turning moms…
but *Sunday roast*? How does one begin sir?'
We agreed and thought that meal a right no-brainer.
Our old man is a pretty smart explainer.

Explain this then: how very soon Bianca,
our muscle-toned, sharp-tongued, worker-outer,
with much more charm than any merchant banker
(though when she'd pout there'd be no greater pouter)
had in her soul a curmudgeon's canker,
for there was something undisclosed about her,
but which would solve (leading to *of course!*)
the who, where, when and why my sister was.

I often know where other folk seem headed
and try to counsel (since I have the gall)
for grumpy Bianca, hardly level-headed,
had hit some teenage quasi-spinster wall.
If there's experience, why not start to spread it
seeing that, I too have done it all:
'I need no help to make it through the night,
nor any boring clichéd Mr Right.'

234

Time would give the kid its healing traction,
she'd find her Monsieur Priceless, what a pearl,
with extra-special, soulmate style attraction.
And out of my mind's well-intentioned swirl
arrived the apex of our interaction.
'It's known,' I urged her, 'you're that kind of girl
can get a fella any time you like…'
'Y'speakin' bullshit Hailey, I'm a dyke!'

'But you're my sister…' 'I'm your sister…*and*?'
Bianca giggled, dispersing any gloom.
'Who's to decide how anything is planned,
once history gets traced back past the womb?
Love's not just licensed to the hetero-bland.
When her head goes *snap*! and her heart goes *boom*!
and she mopes about, foiled by her latest crush,
we Lezzos too can tumble into mush.'

Within ten seconds it had all made sense,
with full blown signals pulsing through the static.
I'd always loved her comic innocence:
'In the closet? I was in the attic!
Do you think my life lies in the future tense?
Your thoughts?' 'My thoughts: quit being enigmatic.
It's time to give all reticence a rout,
take three deep breaths and then just blurt it out.'

Her name was Gemma (for my plan succeeded)
a twenty-year-old checkout girl at Coles,
and she felt just as our other she did
on love and body shape and gender roles.
They held a party knowing one was needed,
and both turned out dressed as gangster molls.
Our folks informed, assumptions weren't corrected,
'Thanks,' said Dad, 'it's what we both suspected.'

Bob also said, and this a few years later
(on superannuation he'd retired):
'At my age I know nothing that is greater
than full support for children we have sired.
Bianca beamed with joy: 'Oh thank you, pater,
my comrades are ecstatic and you're hired!

Father and daughter both have wrongs to right
campaigning for the Marriage Plebiscite.

Welcome, Dad, to Gay-and-Lezzo-Power,
all fine additions to Australiana.
With your support diversity shall flower
like the Banksia, Wattle and Lantana.
And yet each hour on the wretched hour
we're hearing Pentecostals do their na-na.
They won't give up, it's giving me the shivers
that certain 'Christians' never will forgive us.'

'That's factored in,' said Bob, and Ange agreed,
'why not reverse the roles and plain forgive 'em?'
And when the vote was over and decreed,
with so much of the straight world siding with 'em,
'Next stop,' cried Gemma, 'legalizing weed!
There is no greater war cry than *We did 'em!*
Although that was a clumsy way to win laws
I'm proud to say I reckon you're my in-laws.'

Both plebiscite and, better, legislation
saw opponents, at the most, half-arsed,
for what beats such a re-evaluation
as when the rainbow spectrum die was cast
and Queer nuptials sprouted through the nation,
to ask that question whilst our breaths held fast:
would *they* be next? But nobody reckoned
when, for Gemma rural Queensland beckoned

and, for what her reason, brought on board
a wildest card to disrupt any plan,
this strange romance that had Bianca floored
(her girlfriend hadn't run off with a man!).
But something struck a hefty Outback chord,
and I'd be adept as anybody can
to portray such Sapphic squeal-and-squawking,
but that's unfair. Let Gemma do the talking:

'Nothing can come between our you-and-me,
but there's this upcoming rendezvous with fate.
Although I've never been to QLD

my heart seems tethered to the Sunshine State.
Of all my passions it's the co-Grand Prix
that only my love for you could replicate,
a love which through this crisis we will weather,
in hoping that up-North we'll hang together.

Sorry to have kept you none-the-wiser,
since I was scared, fearing you would laugh.
For Queensland's big (I'm just the Big Surpriser)
there's heaps of 'Bigs', though some are pretty daft,
along the highway heading to Mount Isa
I've heard one town has got the Big Giraffe.
Hipsterville might think it the utter scream
but Outback living's an unending dream:

the stock and station agent and the pub,
the burnouts down some main drag in y' Ute,
the endless gibber and the saltbush scrub,
there's little doubt these qualify as beaut.
I'm sure if tended as an exotic shrub
our interlude apart will bear some fruit.'
With just one way to further her narration
Gemma filed an online application

and was accepted as a jillaroo.
Anyone present surely must recall
their multi-revved, tongue-kissing toodle-oo,
one part farewell to ten almighty gall
which, when over, caused a collective *Phew!*
resonating through the departure hall.
Some were supportive (we saw how they tried).
Some called it smartarse. Bianca called it Pride

as off flew Gemma on her Northbound jet
brimming with Southern, *Lezzo* anti-matter,
which might've lasted, that is till she met
'This sweet old bloke…I think his name is Katter.'
Reckon that's weird? Just wait 'til you get
her selfie with elaborating chatter:
'Excuse me if I look a trifle skimpy,
but I've this bar work, somewhere west of Gympie.'

Which fashion statement merely posed: what next?
The Drover's Wife meets inner-urban glam?'
Such outback missives mightily perplexed
and Melbourne girded for an upcoming *Wham!*
From back o' back o' Bourke arrived this text
(which in old times would come by telegram):
'The Southern Cross is added to my tatts
and better still this dyke has joined the Nats!'

Humanity had to wish this great kid well
(hoping her ideology might adjust).
And though Bianca went through a lover's hell
this, I'm sure, can be as good as sussed:
raised as a singular, independent gel
she hardly cared for shape of bum or bust
with all that hetero-centric fol-de-rol
aimed at some white, picket-fencing goal.

What e'er the crisis I turn Pollyanna:
to find the plus-est end of a gradation,
to see the works and throw away the spanner.
Spin-doctor-wise I sought an apt quotation
(if such quacks possess a bedside manner):
'It isn't like she's gone and joined One Nation.'
But sibling sighs are snappin' at my psyche,
for a new dilemma's revvin' like a bikie…

Camped out once more at my parent's digs,
I'd broken up with my most recent latest,
and never caring any amount of figs
give me a fortnight I'll soon feel the greatest,
this girl whom fate soon enough re-jigs,
if you can tell me what this thing called fate is.
Or when indeed shall fate roll forth its dices
since here emerged another family crisis.

Bianca sighed (home that Sunday arvo)
'…your great support when I broke up with Gemma
…or taking us through the intricacies of Mabo
…those books you gave, *The Second Sex* and *Emma*.
To all of these I'll yell a mighty Bravo!
But now I'm wracked with filial dilemma.

I love you all, don't want to cause a scene,
but Labor's stuffed, folks I'm turning Green!'

This melodrama transformed into hugs
which re-transformed to highest voltage sobs.
'You never wished to play us three for mugs
Bianca,' I could only urge, 'No probs.'
To catch our tears we'd be requiring jugs.
Leadership needed it turned out as Bob's.
So faced with wife and daughters turning mopey
Father howled 'Stop acting like a soapie!'

'Ever-ready' Eddie Moon

Young Eddie was his father's son-and-heir
(if with a sister for a fellow scion)
who loved the spotlight, if couldn't hack the glare,
and there'd be more since adulthood was nigh on,
responding with, he had that certain flare,
some apt quotations from *The Life of Brian*,
for all this 'growing up' it kind of bugged him.
No matter what his Old Girl always loved him.

The boy's persona showed how little daunted,
with strands of hair he'd snap-back in a flick
to compliment the toothy grin he flaunted,
this charming both each mother and her chick.
Blissed and blessed with these Good Eddie sauntered.
Bad Eddie though was this annoying prick,
holding one constant through his adolescence:
'I aim to treat the bulk of you like peasants.'

His Dad 'developed', developments made wealth,
whilst clout with those in power verged unbelievable,
and balancing both in-your-face and stealth
he achieved far more than the mere 'achievable',
with failure proving toxic to one's health
and all compromise quite inconceivable
he thundered forth, via his PR mouthpiece,
to all and sundry through the Melbourne South East:

'We won't be ranked with arsonists and killers
whilst we update your Inner Urban Eden.
And if our wrecking balls demolish villas
let's equate that with a spot of weeding,
my credo when I started as it still is,
for what we're building plus the ones we're breeding.
And I believe this shows no way of ending
at that well-known school my son's attending.'

Except his fine example of a progeny
each month, week, day came close to being branded
A menace to our Upper Bourgeoisie
as in detention constantly he landed,
crime-sheet reduced to plain ratbaggery
in which young Eddie topped each golden standard.
But now we'll wheel in for a hahaha
the Moon and son double *coup de grace*.

Scooting through chapel on his roller blades,
which seemed to some kids verging on the spiffy,
inspired in teachers' multiple tirades
that Old Man Moon, grandmaster of the iffy,
quashed with his sweetest talking of charades:
'New pool and gym? Erected in a jiffy!
I swear my workforce rivals jet propulsion.'
And that's how Eddie missed out on expulsion.

For a wild-man/rich-boy set on causing scenes,
like bras a-flutter on the chapel steeple,
perhaps these kinks were buried in his genes.
(If not, then this excuse sounds fairly feeble.)
Played in a rock group sometime in his teens
named Bob Menzies and the Forgotten People.
And when the Old Libs granted extreme unctions
the Young Libs used to hire them for their functions.

'Wither the future of our son the loony?'
So asked his parents Annabelle and Ian.
Sheer uselessness in sending him to Uni,
with TAFE of course considered most plebeian.
Whilst FIFO work would rate him extra puny
for life in Mount Tom Price (or even Zeehan).

Mum though was psychic, and saw in Eddie's stars:
'He'll carve a great career in selling cars.'

Heading their local Liberal Party branch
there ruled a mighty stalwart nicknamed Digger,
who treated all like peons on his ranch.
And Eddie idolised this father figure
without the slightest sign of blush or blanch,
which was returned with good-hearted snigger;
you coped with this, his bluster and his hector
since Digger was a Managing Director.

Real Livin' Motors was this man's domain
(they'd started with Toyotas from the Japs).
So Eddie told him 'With my kind of brain
reckon I'll sell to multitudes of chaps.'
Which went somehow against this Digger's grain,
Moon junior's eager momentary lapse
in sucking up. Yet still the man enjoyed him
to the point of smitten and, henceforth, employed him.

With only Rolls and Bentleys more upmarket
Eddie sought to itemise *tout de suite*
when to do the smooth talk, when to bark it,
how to be both upfront yet discreet.
'Love this work, I'll stay here 'til I cark it.
Eddie,' he reckoned, 'your life is near replete.'
Except those weekends he'd put out the feeler
for any passing chick, dame, broad or sheila.

At the Cup she looked mega-trendy,
as Eddie watched her peek from a silly hat.
Then post their first date (something at the Dendy):
'Sex I suppose is where we both are at…
but afterwards…' he asked himself, '*Comprende?*
Of course she's spoilt but what a hot-hot brat!
With bum and tits all of the finest fettle,
Eddie knew he'd found his bride in Petal.

On this romance her folks would dine and sup,
her father was a sentimental guy
rating his child beyond the up-and-up.

There's a cliché for the guessing, go on, try.
One big, red, round and juicy apple? Nup.
But the total orchard of her father's eye;
who fearing it wasn't quite what he had planned
still granted Eddie his Princess's hand.

Dazzling the upper, social firmament
a plutocrat is lowering the boom
insisting on a media event,
and *The News at Six* has to find the room
although omitting (who knows where it went)
that footage where her Old Man whacks the groom.
Take a backseat famine, plague and slaughter,
when a rich man's son weds a rich man's daughter.

Her bridesmaids musing: 'How long will it last?'
a bookie's offspring catalogued the bids,
this highlight of the nuptial repast
that satisfied their egos and their ids.
And they wouldn't have been particularly aghast
when after those two obligatory kids
and fears this marriage game just wasn't working
Eddie resorted to a spot of jerking.

Getting so far without the pox or herpes
for a reward this fantasy was cued,
the benchmark kind for men in their early thirties:
with a full parade of girls to be reviewed,
from S&M queens to the giggling Gerties
all arrayed in near enough the nude;
and thinking he knew those hormones that possessed them
in his imagination thus addressed them:

'My favourite boob size? Acres upon acres!
My favourite possie? Not quite mission-ary.
Come on ladies are there any takers?'
But there were none, and it was a trifle scary
with feminists and similar ball-breakers
who'd turn you into some limp-wristed fairy.
Since Adam perved wasn't it the norm
to be captivated by the female form

and stride our plazas, shopping strips and malls
to connoisseur the backside and the bust?
So after weighing up the all-in-alls
Man As Victim! that's what Eddie sussed,
and his heart went out to anyone with balls,
from first arousal to the final thrust
these normal blokes he'd certainly vouchsafe 'em,
calling himself 'The Thinking Man's Mark Latham.'

He'd quit all reading with Young Adult Fiction,
then tuned to BoganFM, for a laugh.
Enamoured with their cackle-fuelled depiction
of fairest dinkum (anything else was chaff)
full compliment of vocab, syntax, diction
A-grade bogan, nothing done by half,
rewarded with the audience they mined:
Aussies like Eddie, of the average kind.

Hard to the Grunge-Right spectrum of the media
BoganFM lived up to its name,
for daggy turmoil increasingly the greedier:
'If the fuel lies out there we'll supply the flame,
and if your self-esteem is getting weedier
there's always an extra somebody to blame.
You know what types: so start with those élites,
good Aussies all let's get 'em off the streets!'

Never had our hero felt so heady
since Digger had in passing off-the-cuffed:
'You'll need a nickname, why not 'Ever-ready'?'
The heart rate bounced as out his cheeks he puffed.
Now schemes aplenty surged the brain of Eddie:
'If BoganFM says the place is stuffed
reckon I might make my contribution…'
and conjured forth this following solution:

what with the Liberal Party and his looks
behold the next South Yarra MLA!
And only a bunch of envy-ridden sooks
would dare impugn, through rumour, to betray,
how Digger, wishing Eddie off his books,
lobbied all branches in that hard-nosed way,

stacking when necessary, got him pre-selected.
(Now guess the assistance any passing cheque did.)

Though Eddie at times possessed a certain deft
he specialised from now on in detractions.
'I'm here,' he quipped, 'to horrify the Left,
my side has mates, that mob has only factions.'
But this attempt at parliamentary heft
only copped a slew of these reactions:
howl and giggles, moan, guffaw and screech.
Here's further extracts from his maiden speech.

'…learnt this from Digger at Real Livin' Motors:
I'm Free Market to the very letter,
choosing words that resonate with voters,
caught my motto? *Good times just got better!*
Saying it straight, dispensing with iotas
(your wife's a cutie, must be glad you met her!).
And though some road rules hardly suit my traffic
you're most welcome to my demographic.

I've based my life round total self-reliance,
a big supporter of the little chap.
For that's the backbone of our Oz Alliance,
be he Pom, Wog, Abo, Towelhead, Jap.
I crusade to balance Faith with Science,
I believe all climate change is crap…
With your response I'd say I've won Tattslotto
so for your pains let's give another motto:

All unionists deserve to end in Hades…
fair go Comrades, can't you take a joke?
I'm a great respecter of all ladies,
a pal to every Holden owning bloke…'
Interjection: 'You drive a Mercedes!'
'I pity such class envy, okey-doke?
For love's my proven creed and never hate,
so you're forgiven, mind if I call you *mate*?

Let's hear the tale of my Great Uncle Maurie,
a halfback flanker for the mighty Bloods
he played it hard, shirt fronting like a lorry.

Some mealy-mouthing pack of Elmer Fudds
rubbed him out for life with ne'er a sorry
(their prissiness would rival Kevin Rudd's)
and taking to booze then onto metho, kero,
poor Maurie Moon became this kind of derro.

Yet still he never wailed and never whinged
but shrugged away "I reckon that's their loss."
Seeing how certain workers carped and cringed
he, with respect, could stand up to the boss.
Sure there were occasions that he binged
but few were finer under the Southern Cross,
and features in my maiden speech because he
had all it takes to make a dinkum Aussie…'

Shut up Eddie, since you're getting teary,
let's put a stop to blubber-on-the-page
and view once more your stronger points (in theory)
for few toil harder on an MP's wage,
and few on Brekky talkbacks sound as cheery,
if not the World all Melbourne is your stage!
And though some foes might think it slightly sinister
within a year see you a Shadow Minister.

Throughout all this Angela stayed bemused:
'Just one more Old Boy Grammar Alpha Male.
Factor that in, some small things get excused,
though plenty more rate well beyond the pale.'
For if with mates his plusses were enthused
with women though commenced a truer tale:
this other Eddie seemed to be emerging
with certain traits that might require purging.

One Melbourne Writers Festival Q & A
my sister and I went to see our mother
as panellist on some chat show roundelay.
'I read of course as much as any other
but don't exactly *write*,' she chose to say.
The Moderator sought with charm to smother:
'The writing outlook's bright and getting brighter
since everyone is nowadays a writer.

Our topic for discussion is The Genders.
We've come a long way (panellists agree?)
from days of girdles, stockings and suspenders.
But here we've one whose potent recipe
ignites his most virulent defenders
with back-to-basics wit and repartee.
Eddie Moon requires no introduction.'
And how we booed this archpriest of destruction.

'I most respect,' he mused, 'the girl next door,
the apex of Australian womanhood.
Who wouldn't hold her purity in awe?
Does Feminism do her any good?
Quadrant says it's Marxist to the core.'
But Mum barged in, as we knew she would:
'Pardon Eddie, here's some important info,
this girl next door might be some raging nympho.

For we have more than mere maternal urges,
there's a damn sight more to female/male encounters.'
He felt such comments 'Worse than Stalin's purges.
Angela, beloved leader, paramount is.'
'Stop these,' she parried 'chauvinistic dirges.
When the heat's applied see the way he flounders.
So please accept Michaela knows not Michael
when she's subjected to the menstrual cycle.'

The Moderator smiled, 'We get the gist…
but look, there's other people on this panel,
a male midwife, a female (men's) urologist,
a footy mate, straight from the Mateship Channel,
and someone transitioning, there's an extra twist,
dressing in both taffeta and flannel;
all hoping they can reach some form of nexus
if not *in* sex at least between the sexes.'

As theories and schemes were now promoted
some objections raised were being met.
With 'midwife' dumped, 'midpartner' now got floated,
how non-sexist will we ever get?
Though mainly all was banter, sugarcoated,
with remarks that rarely raised a sweat.

The footy mate soon caught on pretty quick:
'I reckon it's a bit like kick-to-kick.'

Eddie of course with everybody scuffled
and (metaphor continued) soon was decked.
Though one could sense Bianca getting ruffled:
'Is this *art*? You call it *intellect*?'
Muttering as exit-wards we shuffled
'Gimme a beer, all tolerance lies wrecked.
How can we get that 'moderator' pensioned?
Writers they said and not a book was mentioned!'

A reception next, occurring in the foyer
saw high-priced wines set to make you swoon,
rice-paper rolls being dipped in soya,
a young guitarist with her songs to croon.
This five-star hubbub, worthy of a Goya
all backdrop to our meeting Eddie Moon.
'Hide,' said Mum, 'your hash-pipes and your roaches,
the Member for South Yarra now approaches.

Women, meet our resident Alpha male,
unless of course he finishes as Omega.'
He rode the slight, decorum would prevail,
for our acquaintance seeming very eager:
just say the word, he'd be on our trail,
and hinted at some motel south of Bega.
Bianca growled whilst he went 'Joking…joking…'
then headed out to do a spot of smoking.

Kat Namow and Raen Bo

Among the tribes of Melbourne's inner-urbans,
where every second body seems tattooed,
a woman takes to multi-coloured turbans,
rope sandals are the way she's being shoed
(and if at times there's hauteur of the Bourbons,
with down-and-outs her heart becomes imbued)
plus granny glasses, through which she will peer.
Thus the portrait; we give you the career

of Kat, the greyist eminence of the Greens,
possessed of her correct-line, to a fault,
who also had a knack of counting beans.
Though never mention 'upper class revolt',
for legacies kept Kat within her means
(and Grandma had been chums with Zara Holt).
Though these were hidden, much more wouldn't last
when certain foibles bobbed up from her past.

'Katherine' she was on her B.A.(Honours)
'Katherine' she was on the electoral roll.
But say that name…an apocalypse was upon us,
which tortured Katherine to her very soul.
'Down with Primo Dons and Prima Donnas,
androgyny forever!' was her goal.
Katherine? Don't ever call her that!
'No, no, no! I am Kat! I am Kat!'

Her surname vanished (she adopted Namow)
a patriarchal dragon which she slew.
Threats being both her weapon and its ammo
with every issue more were produced on cue:
'The Bourgeoisie let's ram 'n' wham 'n' slam, oh
our commitment's of the deepest hue.
Any shade lighter I consider heinous.'
Of all the Greens Kat doubtless proved the Greenest.

Sound-tracked by the folksongs of her youth
came such tenacity she never lacked.
Even the hardest-liners muttered 'Strewth!
Can't she allow a modicum of tact?'
They had a metaphor, verging on the truth:
like apparatchiks from the Warsaw Pact
extricating finger nails with pliers,
all the while accompanied by Joan Baez.

Kat wrote a poem, indigenous was the speaker,
a teenage girl addicted and abused,
who after being flashed at by a streaker
headed bush, mightily confused.
The best of us sobbed: what life could be bleaker?
The worst of us were thoroughly bemused

248

when, most empathetic with her plight
this parrot spoke some lines of Judith Wright.

With gasps erupting at Kat's recitation,
some even thought it verged on touchy-feely.
For she played well that end of the gradation,
in private though would ratchet up the steely:
'I'm wary of all victim consternation,
our Blacks,' she sighed, 'are just like kiddies really…'
No time to spare though blubbing into tissues
since now her sites were aimed on Gender Issues.

For she saw the best minds of her demographic
starving hysterical naked as in 'Howl':
bi-sex, tri-sex, men-loving-men and Sapphic,
that acronym with hardly any vowel.
Whate'er the direction of your sex-role traffic
from high camp squeal to unremitting growl,
passive/active/none of the above,
Kat would support with unconditioned love.

To challenge such commitment you'd be mad to,
for red tape slicing Kat was near to fabled.
With those indebted proving mighty glad, too:
women, Kooris, gays and the disabled.
Then stepping back (Kat sensing when she had to)
for surer ways to get her work enabled:
'I'm no Big Fish: Hammerhead or Marlin,
the backroom life's for me…' err yeah, like Stalin.

Kat's vision's size was crater, no mere dent:
spine was required of party bureaucrats
and limits placed where activism went,
for what can top the flow-charts and the stats?
Though this adjusted when proved evident
celebrities required their welcome mats
and a younger crowd would keep the party buoyed.
So very soon Bianca was employed.

Her job was in recruitment, she recruited
mid-morning TV's expert in Pilates;
the ruckman drag queen (vetoed though when mooted);

the former model, well known for her nighties,
whose career was recently rebooted
with charms (enhanced) that outdid Aphrodite's;
her ace barista she'd met on a tryst;
and best of all the talkback therapist.

This was Raen Bo, her other name was shredded
(being the maiden one it must be noted)
but due to karma 'Bo' was now embedded:
swathed in saris she forever floated.
Yet something in her verged on the hard-headed,
for few would see the main chance as Ms Bo did,
emerging from her stately home in Brighton
this seemed her task: to counsel and enlighten.

Out of ten my sister gave her eight,
complexion-wise she rivalled Julie Christie.
And what were Raen's essentials in a mate?
He-men? No, but neither the limp-wristy.
On married life she would elaborate
(though talking of divorce might turn her misty):
the who he was and where she'd met her spouse.
Bianca urged: 'That would be extra-grouse.'

'…some place in Asia…' Raen waved a hand '…you know…'
Big place Asia but we get the gist.
'Where I met and married Mr Bo…'
a Malay-Chinese computer analyst,
attentive, committed, bringing in the dough
until arrived an extra-extra twist,
for though to him marriage was no fad,
two kiddies later Mr Bo, the dad,

was captured most flagrante in a sauna
committing carnal congress with a male.
And having no idea he'd turned *that* corner
Raen's initial instinct was to wail.
But more a celebrator than a mourner,
the world soon heard her with delight regale:
'We've readjusted, are now best of friends…'
Well that's her version how the story ends.

With *sex* for years residing in her head,
though it's approved to say it still resided,
her choice was made: abstinence instead,
that long term plus, if you've the time to bide it.
A virtue too, though which it's often said
depends upon the celibate who's tried it.
And how to pass on this celibacy baton?
Let's write a book, that surely is the pattern.

Annabelle (guess what, she's Eddie's mum)
read the tome, no better still devoured
like her poodle gobbling up its Chum.
'I've an idea!' she screamed. Her husband cowered.
'Let's track her down, I hear this psychic thrum:
with talkback therapy everyone's empowered!'
The Raen Bo Hour went on without a blip,
Real Livin' Motors did the sponsorship.

If what they saw was somehow what they got
some were bewildered and one day might confess:
'A therapist but in exactly *what*?'
Raen answered with a coy 'You'll have to guess.'
Her show was like some pizza with the lot,
as reprimand was balanced by caress
her theme tunes alternated between two:
electro Pan-pipes or else 'Love is Blue'.

More a homely substitute for reason
with her advice to all souls tempest-tossed,
Raen's *savoir faire* seemed that of a Parisienne.
The sponsors were delighted damn the cost!
For ratings peaked during the footy season:
just dial-up Raen Bo after your team has lost.
For few possessed such empathy that she did:
uncanny skills to counsel the defeated.

Over her bosom a flowing sari spills
to downplay that with which she's been endowed.
Supplying so much grist to New Age mills
most think that Raen's descended from a cloud
(though a few might opt for some place in the hills).
Giving a nod to the Om-and-incense crowd,

all questions of her origins unsolved
they deduce Raen Bo just evolved.

But *Sixty Minutes* came with an exposure,
how Daddy wrote and Mummy was a writer.
And to both little seemed as rosier
than knowing endless daytime would delight her,
then onto nights devoid of any closure.
If only those years had unfolded brighter,
but being one more victim of home-schooling
teenage time had proven a trifle gruelling.

Though now the parents loved her turnabout
to see in Raen their ultimate win-win.
Having been so adept at dropping-out
how proud both were that somehow she dropped-in.
They'd nurtured a celebrity with clout!
Let Part Two of this narrative begin:
with damaged Melbourne lining up to thank her
she's snapped up by the Greens, great work Bianca!

The MLA for Yarraville goes and dies.
It must be fate with its excessive cunning
(all of which mortality implies:
you cast your vote and you vote for…nothing?)
which hits the Premier, hear how he hardly tries:
'We've just those Greens, since the Libs aren't running
I'm like some gigolo lacking his erection,
oh yeah ho hum a safe seat by election.'

Our candidate was chosen without fervour
(maybe three on a scale of one-to-ten).
All parties have that ultimate time-server,
some ongoing Who? that finally finds his When!
Always male (at least to this Minerva)
that's been around the traps then back again,
logging up credits, near measured by the ton.
In Public Life what beats 'You owe me one'?

Our rivals meantime formed themselves a posse.
If a hunt was on we didn't exactly dig it,
they were the ones you swatted like some mozzie,

an ultimate in household pests, we sniggered.
With data sourced from each right-thinking Aussie
our backroom bunch reckoned they'd it figured:
a Labor swing near-verging on the dozens,
always the way it was. Until it wasn't.

For with a cry of 'Voters, all aboard!'
Raen Bo enters, to represent the Greens.
How we muttered one almighty 'Gawd!'
at this Brighton princess, snug in tailored jeans,
who hoped to strike an empathetic chord
that stretched from geriatrics to the teens.
As leading New Age radio personality
(with Yarraville her hoped for principality)

and therapist (we pondered on what therapy)
blossoming into bourgeois middle age,
she was a top shelf, talkback rarity
this counselling, consoling lady mage.
All Melbourne knew her, Pakenham to Werribee,
high-life mega-rich, battlers on their wage,
considered her part prefect and part genie.
'Raen Bo's the name…I'm proud to be a Greenie!'

Democracy needs an occasional corrective.
Yet must such realignment mean a coup?
This candidate most viewed a good deal suspect. (If
voted-in imagine the day to rue!)
Both Right and Left possessing one objective:
to give the ALP its toodle-oo,
and Raen-Bo-mania increasing all the speedier
she opened up to the assembled media:

'My partner's psyche hurtling on a bender
(there's many an acronym for this condition)
his body-love required another gender,
whilst mine alas has gone into remission.
But name his preference, I'll be its first defender,
and bring our spirit-love unto fruition,
since he-and-I are much more sister-brother,
if still and all I am a single mother…'

So well beyond politically correct
this kind of spiel could never be white-anted.
We stared, guffawed and, shrugging, what-the-heck'd,
dismissing all she'd rant and how she ranted.
Our crime? Viewed in a fatuous retrospect
the biggest one: taking her for granted.
Some Green (anon.) didn't mind confessing:
'Name any button, Madam does the pressing.'

For Raen opined: '…an onslaught of the giddies,
to these unending emails, texts and faxes.
But never think I'm one of your precious biddies,
put on the pan pipes, how this girl relaxes!
You asked about co-parenting our kiddies?
Windchime and Greenpeace truly love the access,
for from their penthouse on St Kilda Road
Daddy and Daddy-Partner share the load.'

And see how next a Raen Bo portrait draped
full front page of the Yarraville Gazette.
As Liberals cackled and Labor merely gaped
the beaming Greens thought their campaign was set,
not knowing that her interview was taped
which somehow landed on the Internet,
leaving her colleagues both bemused yet flustered
and here's some extracts, rather unadjusted.

To 'How do you find us locals?' Raen replied:
'My (former) Brighton life was rather sheltered.
This therefore adds to self-esteem and pride
your Western Suburbs love, I've truly felt it,
as house-upon-house is getting gentrified
all prejudice I'm pleased to say just melted.
Whilst for your lower socio-economic,
saints I've discovered, nothing at all demonic.'

If honesty (of sorts) must be admitted
yet a pause occurred, then a mumbled 'Thanks…
we see you are the paragon of quick-witted
so this one's easy, we never go in for pranks.
Footy?' They asked. Caught off guard she tittered,
'With all those ruckmen on their halfback flanks

I feel I've landed right in the Eagle's Nest!'
'The Eagles, Raen, are somewhat further West.'

And yet this interloper grabs *our* seat.
Embarrassed by the leeway that we gave her
the Premier with contrition was complete.
Put on a brave face? Sure, no face was braver.
For when you less-than-willingly compete
you grant both Greens and Yarraville their saviour.
Bianca texts me with a 'Ho ho ho!
Have I a job! I'm workin' for The Bo!'

When cabinet met, that Monday in late Autumn,
consensus deemed: 'Let's not discuss the vote.
Each have views but attempting to report them
might further slit our collective throat.'
Yet this turned out the Yarraville Post-mortem
for an 'unnamed source' with their 'ready quote'
was set to chart each bruising and abrasion
and here is what was gleaned from this occasion.

When Angela entered, all in a white-lipped quiver,
fearing she hadn't slept her colleagues stared.
Was there something dodgy with her liver?
But the Body Politic and how it fared,
that cadaver down to the merest sliver
seemed the one item that she wanted aired.
With those to blame being brought to book
she catalogued the reasons why she shook.

'Please understand what propels my shaking.
Ever see a campaign more insipid,
an edifice to multi-level faking?
A prize on offer, all we did was squib it.
With Women's Rights a long time in the making
how could we think this Raen Bo we'd inhibit?
And given her talkback therapeutic touch
I can't blame the voters over much.'

Angela's colleagues stared and shuffled papers
(or their latest e-equivalent)
with muffled prayers transformed to silent vapers

(off past the ether is where such drivel went).
Having her fill of pussy-footing capers
she launched a broadside, unambivalent,
the fine-tuned kind, full of well-wrought clout:
'Comrade Premier…pull your digit out!'

He murmured, nodded. Then the man rebounded
with rhetoric to rival any speaker:
'I swear by those who saw our party founded…'
(which itemised extended past Eureka)
'Yarraville spoke, and boy have they resounded,
and yes the outcome couldn't get much bleaker.
There's no excuse, I campaigned like a mutt.'
And yet he smiled, to swing in with a 'But…

if Angela you're our conscience and my foil,
with ratings showing you most highly rated,
as Deputy beyond the merely loyal
not for once have you ingratiated.
But when occasions bring you to the boil
I'm begging please, get decaffeinated!
Good cop and bad within you interfold,
you're like a strict mistress with a heart of gold.

Whilst we endorsed some factional time-server,
that Green-celeb certainly was able
to have the voters think they might deserve her
(though history will prove this utter fable).
I promise you I will regain my fervour
(but when required promote myself as stable)
becoming the most dogged of our terriers
in Melbourne, regions and all country areas!'

Commencing with a homespun talkback blitz,
then sweeping through a splurge in public works,
next, schools received their anti-bully kits,
with one day on, the shattering of perks.
It's hardly most were dining at the Ritz,
but the Opposition looked a pack o' jerks,
falling on the wrong side of the schism
to slightly Left-of-centre populism.

A Boyfriend Experience

My drugs were lightweight, no hitting up or snorting.
The booze, the weed, the hash? Not over much.
Hardly are they in any way worth reporting,
unless in psychobabble double-Dutch.
My passion? Blokes. And there I'd be consorting
with young blades who I'd, in the clinches, clutch.
Or older, balding, slightly shorter men
(like Carlo Ponti with Sophia Loren).

For a dare I dated with a tradie,
his name was Marko and about my age,
straight-down-the-line, ambitions hardly shady,
just wife and kids upon a decent wage.
Whilst I enjoyed my treatment as a lady
for hard-word antics never were his rage.
Glad we met, I'd have been the poorer
to miss his very basic kind of aura,

right from the time he gave my cheek a peck,
entrancing me with proletarian glamour,
and telling why his urges were in check:
'When you respect them, chicks commence to clamour.'
His school had been a Western Suburbs tech,
(whilst I'd been sent to Ivanhoe Girls Grammar).
What kind of gods over our roost were ruling?
For Dad had taught where he had done his schooling.

'Mister Bob! Fuck, I remember him!
Who messed with that guy? Only the ultra-thick.
When one-in-five verged on apprentice crim
he stared you down 'til you obeyed his schtick.
Though for a bleak hardliner-to-the-brim
your old man was one amusing prick,
cutting Year Nine dickheads down to size
with drumming fingers and piercing laser eyes.'

That was Dad? My psyche heaved a jolt.
Classroom commandant, schoolyard martinet?
I feared more info from this retro-vault
(if what you don't see is what you'll never get).

Patient, supportive, laidback to a fault,
on Bob I knew my sun could hardly set.
'Wow,' I replied, 'since I commenced to toddle,
you couldn't name a decenter role model.'

'Babe,' he urged, 'thanks to your old man
the time arrived when I'd to choose a team.
And there's just two: the can't do and the can…'
informing Babe how his Golden Mean
was Estate Living, gated, off-the-plan.
Something more gentrified, alas, is this Babe's dream,
knowing through Marko's visionary hubbub
her ambitions won't remotely scrub up.

'I'm into land development, on the side,
more than a hobby really,' he confessed.
'A cousin 'n' me will bring to you with pride
the Holy Grail of every Aussie's quest…'
(I shuddered at assumptions this implied.)
'We've these paddocks some place in the West,
with bitumen and curbing both laid down,
having a mind to call it Tradie Town.

Yes,' he believed, 'there's such a thing as fate,
a bumper's snicked to slips and mate, y'caught.'
(Why be a Babe when you could be his mate?)
'Hailey,' he sighed, 'y'selling yourself short.'
Since here propelled this evening's tête à tête:
'I've seen the future (all else comes to naught):
my missus, kiddies and our big back yard!
No hard feelings Babe, and here's my card!'

Poor chaps who'd never hack my Hailey pace
(you'll get the ironic import that it sounds,
since this woman's hardly in-your-face)
for upon hearing that she too had bounds
they looked as if they'd copped a spray of mace
or had been savaged by some pack of hounds.
Though I'm a girl quite easy to be blissed
I've caveats and here present my list.

No career in two or triple timing,
timing once seems difficult enough;
no mystic arts in male-libido-priming,
the wink? the nod? dismiss that kind of stuff;
no 'come hither' exercise in miming;
no prancing round some penthouse in the buff;
no sugar daddy's long-long term annuity;
my life was hardly one of promiscuity.

Inscribe it via the keyboard or the pen,
underlined, italicised and bold,
that A-One Rule for getting your way with men:
Let's see if this here boy can break that mould:
'Dump or be dumped and once more start again,
from those who cling like they're some three-year-old
to those who blame-and-ditch you come their crisis.'
(Marko, though, was amongst the nicest.)

I dated blokes from Trotskyites to Sikhs
(well one was fine, a certain Mr Singh)
but having them grope your bum and squeeze its cheeks
there seemed no loving joy that they might bring.
(Maybe the breath that from your boyfriend reeks,
if that approximates your kind of thing?)
For sex with men by now was quite a turn-off,
unless I'd extra calories to burn off.

Name me, if you dare, the shortest odds
by eight pm I'm putting on a nightie,
having my fill of all those XY bods
who just deserve the flirty and the flighty.
Then, at an assemblage of the Gods,
'Let's change Hailey's luck,' urged Aphrodite.
And all of Mount Olympus cried 'Hear-hear!'
So, one evening, at a wood-fired pizzeria

behold the moment that you least expect...
a paragon of inter-gender civics
who spoke of lands and cities he had trekked
(London he'd seen, its Tottenhams and Chiswicks)
but holding in reserve his intellect,
with a PhD in Speculative Physics

his thesis title seemed, like him, light hearted:
Daily Life Before the Big Bang Started.

One hundred and eighty centimetres tall
he'd crafted an unpretentious ginger beard.
My inner self was having quite a ball,
'Has love,' she urged, 'this moment reappeared?
Behold your prospects, since this latest haul
seems nothing like the bozo that you feared!
Your physicist most surely has impacted,
all's going well, I think you've interacted!'

Friends introduced us yes, those kinds of friends
on-a-mission-plus to get you mated,
for whom true worth on coupledom depends.
Yet underwhelmed and over-satiated
I understood the message which it sends:
your catalogue of dickheads whom you've dated.
Such would be past, all consigned to *Phooey!*
Named Lewis I would call him Lew or Lewie.

First-date-time what info never ceases?
(Our wine was red, our pastas were al dente.)
Macquarie U was where he'd done his thesis,
Sydney he knew from Rooty Hill to Bronte.
A movie buff not sold on new releases
he preferred Fellini to Visconti.
'All through *La Strada* it's obvious I cried…
over to you,' he motioned. I replied:

'I went to Uni just to please the folks,
and Honours was my academic booty.
If bar work found me mothering old soaks
I'm also quite a high powered arty-cutie,
a sucker for musician gals 'n' blokes,
craving each cadenza, riff and tutti.
And though I dread you'll think me a meany
I prefer Visconti to Fellini.'

Fearing the best we blurted out 'Aw shucks!'
The Lew one overlapping with the Hailey.
Then after a dozen pretty awesome fucks

which made this girl feel very much female-y:
'You sir are the buckest of young bucks,
but could I face you over breakfast, daily?'
Lew tried looking not a wee bit flat.
'Guess what,' he mused, 'I hadn't thought of that!'

Too late, for each day saw a new unfolding
accompanied by varieties of tone,
like 'What's this female body part you're holding?'
and then responding with the sweetest moan;
or murmurs of 'Aren't you the dearest old thing…'
(which phrase is best kept for some twilight home).
Yet I was guarded, still had to come to grips
with legacies of ex-relationships.

My analyst had well prepared this thesis:
hadn't I an inner urge to scupper?
Beyond reproach like any wife of Caesar's
for gentlemen with whom I played the sucker
how could I iron-out certain kinks and creases
being too stiff-upper-lipped and pukka
to issue even a low-key ultimatum…
so expectations dived each time I'd date 'em.

But under my latest circumstance, as if
there'd be the time such nostrums I'd unravel.
You name the journey Lew would prove terrif
from freeway-smooth to pot-holed tracks of gravel.
Yet he'd this dress sense verging on skewwhiff,
and trusting he'd accept the way I'd cavil,
with such examples that through my mind were roving
I homed-in on a certain choice of clothing.

'Footballers in guernseys, painters in their smocks,
 such garb is necessary to the trade
(some drag queens even go for Fifties' frocks)
but certain fashions should go un-displayed,
thongs might pass muster, never though with socks,
the line is drawn, attend to this parade:
tuxedo, three-piece, track suit, kilt or hi-vis,
your dress sense (got the message?) sure is my biz.'

He understood, shoes replacing thongs.
(Strange I can't recall what else he wore.
I'd notice if his wardrobe held sarongs.)
So I explained: 'Don't want to be a bore,
nor am I righting non-existent wrongs...
though with Bob and Ange I must be sure,
since up 'til now you'd see me run for cover
before I'd have the parents meet the lover.'

I paused for Lewie to return my service.
'Just wait,' he volleyed, 'till you're meeting mine.
In theatre terms I see you're first night nervous,
but Bob sounds great with which to drink and dine.
Angela? Though some might think this perverse
with clear conscience I believe it's fine
my heart goes thump each time she's on the news.
Share them around...' So how could I refuse?

Bob, Angela and Bianca meet Lewie

Time to present the parents' double act,
neither of whom proved remotely coy,
and if subject to a certain clumsy tact
their excess warmth I knew they would employ.
To separate the rumour from the fact
Bob had a repertoire Lewie might enjoy,
with his approving and disapproving serves
(not quite a lecture more a case of nerves).

His paterfamilias 'Welcome to the tribe!'
was so enthused I feared he'd do his durst
and ask the intended, 'I trust sir, you imbibe?'
like in the Eighteen-Fifties, at their worst.
Luckily there's a less archaic vibe
when your century is Twenty-First
and interpersonal cool seems all the rage.
Though Bob commenced with 'When I was your age...

in Melbourne of those times (this might amaze ya)
discoveries blossomed in their wide array:
how indeed we were now part of Asia

and yes there was no sin in being Gay.
As poker players ramp-up with *I'll raise ya*
grand visions every week went on display,
with dads like mine building their extensions
which granted family living new dimensions.

But let's side-track to the shared household,
ever know one under a siege of crabs…
complete with any boy whose hair is tousled
being pursued by latter day Queen Mabs,
all prancing round the maypole of arousal
where so much of the self is up for grabs.
Though like the Prince of Wales and his ex-mistress
one more partner needn't cause much distress.

Name a couple most will find their niche.
We knew this pair who dropped out very briefly,
convinced there was a fortune making quiche.
Cuisine a motivation? Yes…though chiefly
a way to hook-up with the nouveau riche.
Fast forward decades, this sums them up completely:
I've lately dreamt how every twilight year
they'll spend whole weekends shuffling round IKEA.'

Through all these targets Lewie stayed bemused.
Bob entertains, no matter what the cause.
My boyfriend's face both pondered and perused,
and seemed to say 'Within this Dad of yours
the passion and the intellect are fused.'
Drinks were served. Followed by a pause.
A minor one, for taking up the slack
Bob headed to this far more global tack:

'Consider mankind in its current chapter
and where these personnel are set to drag it:
the populist with protest votes to capture,
all screaming child inside the strutting braggart;
that Pentecostal waiting for The Rapture,
still hoping to eliminate the faggot;
those snarlings of the BoganFM rapper;
can you conceive of any things more crapper?

But par-for-the-course amongst us quickly aging
are rants like these and since you're on a visit
it's hardly fair to bombard with such raging
item-upon-red-hot-item, is it?
Call this an act my wife and I are staging,
politically of course she's still the wizard!
The daughters rarely think this as surprising
so often parody our itemising.

Tell us Angela, what's on your agenda?'
'Silence,' she answered, 'but that's been revised,
with heaps piled into *your* opinion blender
(flick the switch *Voila!* they're vitamised)
remaining on our motor-mouthing bender
here's a selection I have lately prized...'
(Shudders through veins and arteries were coursing
for I feared continued hobby-horsing.)

'...let's take you back to that not distant time
when Abbott was the Minister for Ladies,
and some out there proposed this as a crime:
the overt public nourishment of babies.
We copped the gamut, sermons through to slime,
I for one a blast of moral scabies
as when this would-be Liberal Party leader
called me once a pretty lousy breeder.

Well that made him the vilest fertiliser,
I've great pride in that retort and gag.
He'll never get it, so is none the wiser,
on BoganFM now piles up the slag.
You know surely what these kinds of guys are:
straight out aggro, not some game of tag.
Sorry if I'm getting rather wound-up
but in such knots some women do get bound-up...'

'*That* wasn't too bad,' urged my supportive lover
after we had left the home parental.
'Though mums and dads over their daughters hover
trusting her chosen combines strong with gentle,
there's no need now to keep me undercover
(which verged at times upon the temperamental).

Let's to our place, first to stoke some chillums
then choose a highlight from our batch of fillums.'

For we'd added to our life this extra girder,
a fifties/early sixties movie binge:
I'm All Right Jack, *Anatomy of a Murder*,
La Dolce Vita with its risqué tinge,
and Jeanne Moreau, though in French we heard her,
produced in us an existential twinge.
(If Joanne Woodward knew indeed what's what
the young Paul Newman made me extra hot.)

When told I was as gorgeous as Lee Remick
I hardly saw the need for extra 'dating'.
Instead our interactions turned alchemic
with hormones that kept up their escalating.
My folks for their part went most academic
assessing Lewie with an HD rating.
There was no better man with which to tether,
courtship's over, now let's live together.

Said Bianca, offering her blessing:
'I trust you have, sir, watertight intentions.
Do her wrong with me you will be messing,
I know you straight men with your endless wenchings.
You'll live where?' His answer near-confessing:
'Though certain streets rate honourable mentions
of inner-urban life I've had my fill,
I've saved some cash…let's live in Yarraville!

For I crave that land some pundits love to curse,
dumped in the SkyNews/BoganFM tip:
diversity that's way beyond diverse.
So when you take your Western Suburbs trip,
in Yarraville guess what, it's even worse
with Cultural Marxists, vanguard of the hip,
cottages with extensions and sun decks,
a bookshop and a cinema complex.'

Kurt and Helen meet Hailey

But first let's have a Hurstbridge expedition
to meet his folks, each other's Ace of Hearts.
Though getting there might border on perdition
through roundabouts with all their stops and starts.
But if a pilgrim's worthy of their mission,
and if you have an interest in the Arts,
the area verges on the creative side,
with Kurt the father acting as your guide:

'Five decades back it's said they held *Don's Party*
some place between Kinglake and Lower Plenty.
Today? Life drawing, more restrained than tarty,
and silkscreen workers, I could name you twenty,
and haiku scribes aetherial yet arty
who think that they approximate our gentry.
Walk out your door and hail a passing potter,
and no use asking *Must I?* for ya gotta!

In retrospect little could be dafter
than those few years we spent in Vermont South.
Please feel free *not* to suppress your laughter…
did I say *that*? I did and hush mah mouth!
Whilst in these days 'twixt now and the hereafter
nothing can move me, blizzard, flood or drought.
So whether you've brought the sunscreen or the brolly
welcome to Hurstbridge and our mudbrick folly.'

The mother, Helen, had been out a-jogging
and looked most fit, whatever age she is,
'So what's,' she asked, 'the saga he's been flogging
this CEO of the crusading biz?
His war against red-tape and pettifogging
sure gets the local council in a tiz.
But Hailey's not arrived to hear him burble.
Like some tea? The normal or the herbal?

I hear your Mum's Victoria's Two-I-C
it's obvious she has my admiration.
With options they've to choose remaining dicey
for women leading any state or nation:

to play it full-on-bitch or nicey-nicey.
Though life's unfair *that* is a fair summation.
Meanwhile I sympathise with your position
having had a parent-politician.

Singular and bemusing Lew, my father
who, for a government sinking in its trough
plus scandals which kept pouring down like lava,
still remained a competent one-off.
No glamour job (even if he'd rather)
just a grab-bag Ministry under Gough.
And though I shouldn't run this for a spoiler
perhaps the old boy should've stayed a lawyer.

After the Sacking this tremor through him rang:
'No hope remains, our fortunes won't revive.'
Though to exit with some tragi-comic bang
on this, maybe his finest day alive,
he climbed on a Ute to give one last harangue,
you did such things in 1975
when reputations rose and then came crashing;
Dad was a mini-legend, in his fashion.'

'Helen and I had this grand concurring
we'd name your boyfriend after Lew-the-Great.'
Kurt was set, his ardour was un-erring:
'About the man there shall be no debate,
he deserves more than just mere raconteuring...'
'Then write your book before it turns too late,'
Lewie urged to redirect proceedings,
'I'm sure to put an order in at Readings.

But tell us about the time you met Bob Hawke...
and didn't you both take acid trips together?'
'Well not with Bob,' amended Kurt's retort,
'In PMs that seems somewhat less than clever.
Hallucinations nowadays I baulk,
though parts of our past I'm not inclined to sever:
well before the world was mobile-phoned
you sprawled on beanbags, watching the News quite stoned.

In that condition we saw Lew's performance,
thinking him foolish, thinking him heroic,
the dividends for any nonconformance.
But bravado turns increasing claustrophobic,
door-knocking we almost felt like Mormons:
confused, abused, patronised if stoic.
For us it was *Democracy or Bust*.
Old Lew kept his seat, but only just.'

'If there was,' Helen added, 'missed potential
in that cluttered public life of Lew's,
and few 'great heights', at its most essential
more than once or twice he'd make the News.
So to combine pedigree with credential
gathering snapshots, footage, interviews,
our eldest son has made this documentary,
let's watch it for a decent point of entry.'

Old Lew and Cath: an interlude

His hair was thick, and puffed-up like a doona
(this was the time when sideburns were the rage)
with smiles like any well-pleased honeymooner,
a politician at home on the stage
in earlier days he'd been a dance band crooner,
still holding a decent *timbre* for his age.
(When some float parallels with Peter Garrett
I'd say you'd find more 'music' in a parrot.)

Okay, his demonstration was impromptu,
but why the western end of Collins Street?
To give those Big End fogeys the old one-two?
For fogeys though, who'd take on any heat,
they'd been around and guessed what he was up to,
knowing how farce equated with defeat.
He'd little chance with bankers and stockbrokers,
grand masters of the corporate hocus-pocus.

Since the War through every boom and slump
he'd honed his craft around the word *persuasion*.
But for that day's speech-upon-the-stump

hoping to be a showcase for abrasion
far exceeding any parish pump,
and all set for his Collins Street oration,
knowing well to make his claims as ambit
onto the Ute the politician clambered.

And if this rally ever came to blows
he'd union mates as bodyguard or claque.
'Let's keep,' he urged, 'these bastards on their toes…'
then a batch of QCs waved and he waved back.
Few in the crowd were hardly CEOs,
such gentlemen had sought a different tack:
by sending forth their office boys to heckle
they deemed his cause was hardly worth a shekel.

For he'd turned into some inefficient hater,
just one who waved his arms around and shouted,
another well-intentioned bloviator,
sincere of course, that was never doubted,
yet once he'd been this furious debater
whose logic had this ruthlessness about it:
first to plunge in his metaphoric dagger
then carve away with forensic swagger.

The QCs pondered: 'Isn't this a rally
against an act which saw our nation riven?'
Their lunchtime gave them half an hour to dally
and sympathise with Lew, since they were driven
by the fraternal more than the merely pally
(that I believe would make a fair 'as given')
for if these gentlemen were hardly Labor
he still remained a well-liked legal neighbour.

Alas they saw him floundering and flailing
as he sought to issue just desserts.
Then laughter rose, essentially derailing
attempts to castigate the Big End squirts,
which motley mob deserved a spot of jailing
for flared lapels, wide ties and body shirts,
plus demeanour, hollering delirious:
'This old goat surely can't be serious!'

That's the way with orators as fighters,
competing with the deadhead and the pesky.
His voice by now verged on laryngitis,
or ockers downing tubes around an esky.
To replicate such sound would stump most writers
unless they had the skill of Dostoevsky.
Upon the Ute, stuck with his croaky muse
he, five or six hours later makes the news.

Now Kurt came in, the mordant-eyed perceiver:
'Old Lew was done for, never to recover.
Strange how politics' special form of fever
destroys the father, truly makes the mother.
"It's time," says Cath, "for me to pull my lever
and write a book, no not like *any other*.
Wedding my life to latterday alarms,
a fifty-fifty memoir/call-to-arms."

She'd read, heard, seen, met, even known the mob
who ran the place, Cath believed unfettered.
And needing now the Woman for the Job
through journo friends who aided and abetted,
with fair ideas of how and what she'd lob
a column's put on offer, so she's netted.
The book's a hit, folk read it, even quote it.
'But why'd you think,' Kurt asks his wife, 'she wrote it?'

'Your future's made by learning from the past,'
and Helen laughed, 'that's what mother taught.
Dad's in her tale (though hardly heads the cast)
part cameo, part co-star in support.
Loyal in his way, almost to the last,
foe of the hypocrite, the backbite and the rort,
though if a hero Cath might be anointing
he comes across as somewhat disappointing.

A sign hung by her study some years later:
"I'm working on my memoir, don't disturb.
And like a seasoned Ladies School debater
my outer bitch I'm trying hard to curb,
for inner I'm a lover not a hater…"
With a quote from Germaine Greer as the blurb

270

it wasn't gossip, Cath found gossip sordid.
Book clubs and festivals heard her and applauded:

articulate, thriving on upheaval,
the strident kind your panel show invites,
the moral drives her, not the merely legal,
who's known the condescension and the slights.
That Mod Con Era now sounds medieval,
unequal pay, no reproductive rights.
It's Cath who should've been the politician,
reincarnated that'll be her mission.'

All of which inspired my interjection
recalling how *A History of My Times*
had reinforced in Angela her direction
there was none better since she saw the signs:
in making her life so open to inspection
Cath jettisoned so many paradigms.
Scrawling on margins, underlining pages
my mother thought it witty and outrageous.

'When,' Helen added, 'you're activist and young
it helps there's no concession to the trite.
Here was a score demanding to be sung
which women her age weren't supposed to write.
"Those pleasures when hypocrisies are sprung
that's my reward…" her preface says. Well quite.
Crash landing readers in the discomfort zone
of two terminations, one of them her own.

Plenty were annoyed but worse frustrated,
fearing Cath's age would mark her as immune.
They pitied her? Mock-pity born of hatred,
you must know their mealy-mouthing tune
not then, not now, not ever has it dated,
that hallmark of the educated hoon.
But steeling all nerves Cath rode-out their crescendo
of allegations fuelled by innuendo.

After my parent's marriage had collapsed
(as politics provides the parallel)
with spousal time once built around *perhaps*,

Mum's independence started to propel.
Life with Lew through heaps of minor scraps
a feisty side was there she'd never quell.
Her lowkey wrath could always rise with Cath
(or had she been American, her wrath).

From this memoir here's the way she said it:
"I'm much bemused what constitutes renown.
To Lew on his Ute most archetypes seem wedded,
some as a hero, mine alas a clown."
Knowing the mess we've made and where it's headed,
as arch-opponent of the dumbing down,
and life exceeding all attempts in fiction
I'm sure her words present the best depiction:

"When Lew was sacked and everyone was sacked,
which act demolished all I took for granted,
watching the News I knew his deck was stacked
the evening of that afternoon he ranted.
A man with whom I'd shared my marriage pact
reduced to this! All self-respect white-anted:
not jeered just laughed at by that Big End mob.
I was sobbing and I'm not a girl to sob…"

A queue of would-be boyfriends lining up,
soft-centred ones and those as tough as gristle,
all being set to lunch or dine or sup
she asked where they had stood with The Dismissal.
If they approved she shook her head with 'Nup!'
Whilst her libido took a mighty fizzle.
Aiming to be the mistress *and* the master?
Although a guess, I wouldn't put it past her.

A decade's fun, we'll not even ask,
saw Cath performing without intermission.
Under her gaze the gentlemen would bask;
one marries her, a Mornington physician.
And though today she's plodding task-to-task
at ninety-two remains quite self-sufficient.
If I'd advice it's *no* to underrating
Cath's middle class divorcée's style of dating.

On the high dive over the mating pool
Old Lew chose for his next bout of marriage
this ex-model with a deportment school.
All mayhem-plus, and yes I will disparage
she as vamp and he as vapid fool.
But toning down this step-daughter's barrage
just to accept both were highly sexed…
unless they weren't…we move onto the next.

Dad in desires wished to be well fed
(if this depends of course upon the feast).
And in the kitchen, plus we reckon bed,
his third wife nourished well, to say the least;
that kind of lady journo, Sydney bred,
who had appeared on *Beauty and the Beast*.
A shrewd appraiser, supportive and unruffled,
when off the parliamentary stage he shuffled.

Being outdated, all lobbying ignored
and since *that* life was over…' Helen sighed,
'Sprawled on the backbench Old Lew often snored,
awaiting the next surge of the Labor tide,
obtaining a few years later this reward:
a diplomatic posting…but he died.
The fullest gamut had put him out to grass
tragic, tragi-comic, comic, farce.'

Yet Helen loved Old Lew's greatest fling:
'Midway between a call-to-arms and prank
(if you've a mind to catch such reckoning).
We know of course it could hardly rank
with any dream of Martin Luther King
or Boris Yeltsin climbing on that tank.
But as of now we still feel pretty beaut
to see my Dad haranguing from his Ute!'

> *"Man's love is of man's life a thing apart,*
> *Tis woman's whole existence…"*

Bianca one arvo issued forth this text:
'You never will believe our lack o' luck.

Each day commencing with *Whatever next?*
The answer lands with one resounding *Yuck!*
To somehow prove the office must be hexed
by a Twenty-First Century Oberon and Puck,
all sense and order having had the gong
The Bo has found her total Mister Wrong.

Although a Dyke I get it well enough:
with men, for some, there must be more adventure.
But like a tee-shot landing in the rough
it's chaos here, and I'm not one to censure
but nought's prepared, all seems off-the-cuff.
Beaming more smiles than any passing denture
Raen's lost it, Hailey, coming in at Noon,
after she's spent all night with…Eddie Moon!'

Raen thought the Speaker yelling 'Order! Order!'
was not the reason she had been elected.
Debates, if you could call them that, they bored her,
one side sulked whilst the other hectored.
Unlike talkback everyone ignored her,
and even smiles were glared at and rejected.
Except for Eddie, who made her feel quite sane
and took the time to utter 'G'day Raen.'

Late one evening found her in his office.
Like a mewing kitten or some lapdog pooch
'I'm still,' she sighed, 'a parliamentary novice…'
'You need,' he offered, 'a shot of A-grade hooch.
Or this,' he posed, 'tax free from my coffers…'
approaching her mouth to give the softest smooch.
But slightly recoiling (you somewhat bet your life!)
she posed the question 'Haven't you a wife?'

and raised a hand. Which hardly caused much slowing.
Clutching, he applied it to his lips.
'We've sorta this trial separation going…'
Why did she place her hands upon his hips?
Because little in her soul had seemed so glowing
since those few, mid-twenties acid trips;
plus, what man had touched her since that day
her partner sought to tell her he was gay?

274

How long was it since she's been in the clinches,
with flesh aflame and with conscience numbing?
Now, Eddie's ardour, growing by the inches,
certain phrases through her brain were drumming.
Some 'Mad as hell!' outburst like Peter Finch's?
Though for an MP that was unbecoming.
And well aware of his condition (spousal)
but also well aware of her arousal,

consider all such questions if she gave in.
Would Raen emerge the creditor or debtor?
And other options that in her mind were ravin'...
I'd love to follow through unto the letter.
But these exceed my talents so I cave in,
quoting Byron, since Byron does it better:
A little still she strove and much repented
And whispering, "I shall ne'er consent"- consented.

Eddie though 'bad' no way was the worst,
seeming deep down a somewhat decent fella.
And her ardour throbbed a passionate full burst
like an A-one track from Sarah Vaughan or Ella.
Unfortunately, Raen was not his first.
(To those who know I beg please never tell her.
With more than a few parts prime-cut paranoia
romance can prove one mighty harsh employer.)

Their deep-end plunge maximised and total
caused her to sing 'We've only just begun...'
as they left their assignation hotel
whilst Eddie urged 'I've a fine diversion, hon.
Let's scoot to this Great Ocean Road motel,
discreet enough for couples-on-the-run.'
Staying two nights they quarrelled a bit, returned,
frazzle-shagged with certain lessons learned

or so was hoped. But somebody knows
and, betting on it, somebody always does.
Uncovering carnal highs and carnal lows
is how the hyper-prurient get their buzz.
And no use shrugging 'That's the way it goes...'

Sure makes a girl wanna call the fuzz.
Small matter that calm care with which you scoot,
there's always wowsers ringside at a root.

Neither being the grooviest of groovies
they hardly sussed any alert was red.
And all this minor fault is set to prove is
Love conquers *Reason*, it smites from toe to head.
And, like phrases we've all heard at the movies,
this I believe is what was surely said:
'Can't keep my hands away from you.' 'Me neither.'
With words like this lust rarely takes a breather.

They bought lingerie, some place in the city,
though such diversions never have time to wait.
Too bad they served on the same committee
both turning up more than an hour late.
Which cancels out all modicum of pity
for this extended, undercover date.
All veering, tacking, now arrived at naught
and ripe for tabloid fodder they were caught.

To folks who can't grasp why Raen took such action
let's make it plain: you'll never catch the bus.
There's such a thing as female/male attraction,
in this case though behold that extra fuss,
for politics revved up the gossip traction.
Labor smirked: 'Nothing to do with us!'
Kat meantime morphed, to high-tone drama queen:
'How could you, both as Woman and as Green?'

Yet softly to disguise her inner screech
Raen replied: 'I for once was noticed.
I saw him smiling through my maiden speech
as I view now your suffering tight-lipped protest.
We were soul mates, very each-to-each,
of men I've met he never was the grossest;
for though at times Eddie might be sexist
here's where he gets me: right in the solar plexus!'

This didn't work. It went against their charter
and so was sought some fine-tuned Green solution:

'You're still persona, let's adjust non-grata…
no service wash just a quick ablution…
it helps us to possess our minor martyr…'
Like something out of the Cultural Revolution
Raen was urged: 'You'll have to face the press,
get rid of him and publicly confess.'

She wrote 'Dear Eddie,' hoping he might thank her
'our fling is over, they've put in the knife.
Yet after our past I'm not one to hanker,
for if estranged we know you've still a wife.
Let's quote instead my P.A. Bianca:
"I wish those fuckhead prudes would getta life!"
Whilst in the House you were the only bloke
who wouldn't treat me as some kind of joke.

Is love then like Lord Byron's famed quotation
women's whole existence? Well not quite.
Females have led both our state and nation,
and for a male you surely saw the light,
nodding through my maiden speech oration
as if to say "This chick's pretty bright!"
Seeing in me both a soul and brain,
and so I thank you XXXX Raen.'

She got a profile in The Good Weekend.
Her colleagues knew it wasn't 'good' enough.
'I too,' crowed Raen, 'have plenty of rules to bend.'
Certain and pleased she had called their bluff.
'Quitting the Party I will not pretend
ditching my lover sure sounds pretty rough.
But when Greens shake they well 'n' truly shakedown.'
Eddie meanwhile scored a nervous breakdown.

More than an exercise in hubba-hubba
she'd been all goddess, not some passing treat.
'For it was love!' his mates could hear him blubber.
So they consoled with words thought pretty neat:
'Well you hardly rooted with some scrubber!'
Eddie resigned. Labor snatched the seat.
Right now he flogs (a way to make amends)
Lamborghinis and Mercedes Benz.

Tradie Town Confidential

A card and doco arriving via my folks
'Hailey you knew I'd always make it! M'
consider the bewilderment this evokes:
'M's I'd known? Grandstands full of them!
'Given,' said Lew 'your variety of blokes
could it be porn?' he posited. 'Ahem.'
Hardly, for through its slick production sheen
someone I recognized burst upon the screen.

You must remember Marko whom I dated
(only once and then we never kissed)
well here he was thoroughly fixated
at his mobile scrolling down some list,
when up he beams and speaks beyond elated,
few I've seen and heard this close to blissed
by every verb and adjective and noun
throughout his promo-doco *Tradie Town.*

'My friends,' he urged, 'at Marko Enterprises
we offer homes to which I know you'll flock.
Unit-to-townhouse in all shapes and sizes
on Aussie's good old quarter acre block.
And I've this message from our advertisers:
Outer Suburbia? We say let it rock!
Boyfriend, girlfriend, fiancé, husband, wife,
you couldn't find a better way of life!

If he was the star, yet the show was hosted
by a graduate in all required studies;
with smile and bosom both she proudly boasted,
transforming most men into instant buddies.
Onto an easy to-and-fro she coasted
skilled in appropriate, spicy repartees.
If innocent enough she up and caught him
when asking what this kind of work had brought him.

'Well bringing home a pretty decent screw…
err not that other kind…' his blush announced.
Seeing him wipe his forehead with a *Phew!*
her smile continued, she knew he was trounced.

'And…exactly…you are Marko…who?'
There was a gag approaching so he pounced,
moreover bounced since he was mighty bouncable:
'Forgive me Babe, my surname's unpronounceable!

So what's *your* name again…Felicity?'
She nodded yes. He took her on a tour.
With the main chance on and not a one to miss it, he
commenced in his own chastest way to woo her,
explaining 'I'm a big fan of ethnicity,
it may be Bombay, Shanghai or the Ruhr,
in Tradie Town we welcome all the races.'
And the camera spanned a multitude of faces

hailing 'G'day' to their benefactor
at school, church, sportsground, retail park and mall.
Lacking the guile and artifice of an actor
he'd charm at first and very soon enthral
even the most belligerent detractor,
a finely-tuned performance all-in-all:
'Every fast-food outlet has its Wi-Fi,
we've Bunnings, Officeworks and JB Hi-Fi;

we've crèches, preschools and a drop-in centre.
Plus two bookshops: a Readings and a Dymocks;
with mentors nearby if you need a mentor
at all our medical and dental clinics;
and offer to both homeowner and renter
(that only the most detestable of cynics
would dare to fault) the moment you move in,
free of charge an extra wheelie-bin.'

If suburbs were a drug then he was drugged:
'I'm just another Western Suburbs techie…'
Coyness enveloped Marko and he shrugged:
'Some rove the packs whilst others take a speccie.
Tech-savvy? Yes, yet very much unplugged.
Never one for a Heavymetal Brekky,
I'm out a-joggin' when the dew's still glistening,
and much prefer a dose of Easy Listening.'

Pausing the doco Lew and Hailey stared,
she stammering: 'To think my father taught him!'
Lew recovered (being unprepared):
'No country's freer, so we can't deport him.
But I see villagers, bowing to their laird,
with tributes by the cartload that they've brought him.
I doubt if Bob and Ange could bear the weight,
this man's a future Liberal candidate!'

For Marko spoke both the style and jargon:
concerned, polite, who'd never tell a fib.
If spiced with salesman-speak like 'What a bargain!'
his pragmatism equalled any Lib.
Felicity just floated on the margin
fashion-plate demure, which verged on glib.
Press fast-forward, let's see where it's heading.
The doco ends with footage of their wedding.

Then some months on a further happy ending:
with Angela and Bob chez mine and Lew's
a pleasant Sunday afternoon are spending,
and here's the Premier headlining the news
with '…Labor's message to the state we're sending
it is my humble privilege to enthuse
that the icy grip on Yarraville is unfrozen,
someone of substance has today been chosen.'

Continuing on high beam with his coup,
though trying not to morph this into gloat:
'He's Western Suburbs, Labor through 'n' through,
a businessman I gladly will promote.
With a wife and one son, soon they'll make it two,
and an ethnic background ripe for the ethnic vote,
neither an ocker nor an Old Etonian
Marko's his name, his surnames…Macedonian!'

None of us four had ever seen this comin'
and fury now dislodged my even temper:
'We've hit all depths as down and down we're dumbin',
The Light on the Hill is but a tiny ember.
Yarraville,' I cried, 'deserves a woman!'
Forgetting one was still the local member.

It turned the tragi-comic side of torrid
as Lewie kept on pummelling his forehead.

Through the announcement Angela kept nodding,
this candidate she knew ticked many boxes:
'His seeming both mercurial yet plodding
now *that's* a trait opponents might find noxious.'
These words she spoke dispensed with any prodding:
'Our leader sure out-generals and out-foxes.
Call me a martyr, the grin-and-bear-it kind,
but Marko's hardly what I had in mind.'

It's Saturday and I am hearing 'Babe!'
In Yarraville it's Marko out campaigning
and so meets Lewie. You need no astrolabe
to sense directions each of them were aiming.
With honesty exceeding Honest Abe
Marko's bonhomie certainly was draining.
I phoned Bianca, my sanity she'd save
with her strident, younger sister form of rave.

Down Ballarat Street the two men strode
heading surely for some form of showdown.
(And such remains the essence of this ode:
how all human interactions go down.)
So I carried as we women do their load,
awaiting my man with his Marko lowdown:
both the lessons taught and lessons learned,
when after thirty minutes he returned.

'I've met few greater men,' the boyfriend gushed,
'we've been invited to inspect his shed!'
If I wail inward, outward I am hushed
for something must be skewed inside his head.
Then onto ideologies he rushed:
'As mateship leaves all faiths and creeds for dead
I proudly affirm Marko as my mate.'
'It sounds like, Lewie, you've been on a date,

have your senses left you?' I implored.
'Once the main course of our left wing feast
mateship nourished Australia's groaning board,

281

today it's tethered to the corporate beast,
a concept sullied to the point of fraud.'
'True,' he replied, 'at the very least
we now see "mateship" housed in inverted commas…
but *not* when you are barracking for the Bombers!

Isn't it great, through footy we have bonded,
as brains (as souls!) and not as a pair of jocks.
Just now through Bomber trivia we wandered,
as the past was golden, so the future rocks.
Whilst deals for naming rights are being pondered
Tradie Town will get a superbox.
I've no desire a Bomber fan to make you
but, next season, I resolve to take you.'

Thus we enlisted in the Marko Mob,
pledging full commitment, to the wire.
Powerbrokers with whom he might hobnob
were great of course but few could quite inspire
like my dad, and his teacher, Mister Bob.
None Marko knew were ever rated higher.
I volunteered to institute a meeting,
for comedy it wouldn't take much beating.

As kiddies clambered over swings and slides
the scene that day seemed total by-the-book.
Bob's psyche though had found where gloom resides,
'Don't,' he implored, 'take me for a sook,
some victim of the generational tides…'
But with a startled interjection: 'Look!'
Throughout the park that Sunday afternoon,
with snoring derros sleeping off their goon

and separated fathers on their access,
curmudgeon Bob became increasing bolder:
'…see how each social moré wanes and waxes,
at least to the mordant eye of this beholder.
All ends as dust, y'Facebooks and y'faxes.
Are these a further sign I'm getting older?
Is my fate destined to be skewed
between retirement and decrepitude?'

When all success looks like it's been hexed
(each specky marked and every goal I've punted)
should I care what train's arriving next
when into the final siding we'll be shunted?
Sorry if you've to take this for my text
but any cutting edge has long been blunted,
the reflex *snap!* which verged on mega-clever
has morphed into a shrugging *err whatever*...

I'd this friend, let's call him John the Junkie,
though up the laidback end of that gradation.
Teachers we were. Though some kids thought him 'funky',
he O'D'd in the Gents at Richmond Station.
John's back being clawed by any amount of monkey
call it an addict's form of graduation
this quiet end, for plenty more were seedier,
you need *that* kind of clout to make the media.'

From where arrived such post-midlife stupor?
My parents' lives both looked exceeding grouse:
few health care costs (see Medicare and Bupa)
no mental state disorders to de-louse;
they'd two mil plus invested in each Super
whilst decades back had paid off the house;
no hip-replacement, bypass, stroke or cancer...
'What ails ye, Dad?' And here drove up his answer:

'It comes to this: Marko as candidate!
His Year Nine bullshit quotient was sensational:
a line was spun, you knew you'd take the bait.
He better not rave in Dude-speak International...'
(Hardly, since every second word was *mate*.)
'I figured out, once it seemed quite rational
he'd finish up as drug squad or as narco...
let's see what we can do for your boy Marko.'

A charm offensive? It was a charm hi-jacking:
as if in class a hand shot up 'Sir! Sir!
Now's the time for straight talk not chiacking:
you're still my hero as you always were.
Sorry for all this motor-mouthy yacking,
please Mister Bob don't stand there saying *Err*...

that's hardly the most quotable of quotes.
Glad you're on deck to hand out how-to-votes!'

Gemma, Kat and Old Lew: an Interlude

And now from a postcode starting with a four
Gemma sends a spirited up-dating.
'Out here,' she writes, 'with men on the gender score
if some we meet can be ingratiating
most sense we're worth as much as iron ore,
whilst meanwhile we give each of them a rating.
Yet though their risings often exceed their falls,
to be a woman certainly takes balls.

Don't be surprised, there's action in The Sticks,
we've got a movement, Outback Females First.
Whilst major parties play with each other's dicks
small wonder Real Australia's feeling cursed.
This nation needs a few more bright, young chicks,
there's plenty who have fought 'n' taught 'n' nursed.
Won't be a case of 'if it' comes but 'when it',
give a few years you'll find us in the Senate.

We lobby hard for girl-enhancing skills
from shearing shed to nuclear reactor.
Be on the lookout Jacks, here come the Jills,
we too can drive a forklift or a tractor.
And to alleviate any clash of wills
every month let's slap-on the Max Factor
and have a bonding dinner with some Pad Thai,
though quite a few would rather eat some Camp Pie.

I'm singing now, it's great for an activist
to belt out songs, completely do your block.
And there they are the sober, stoned or pissed
craving my music, you should see 'em flock
to all my gigs and stare back ultra-blissed.
Who says the Outback doesn't truly rock?
Playing for FIFOs, shearers, truckies, miners,
with my all-girl group The Pantyliners.

284

But heading Thirty am I growing old?
With kids on drugs of which I've never heard,
who still persist, no matter what they're told;
'It's just a pill,' they mutter, undeterred;
or do a U-turn sure to break the mould,
finding Jesus, walloped by The Word;
I shrug them off with "If you say so…fine…"
Reckon that generation isn't mine.

I miss Gay wit with all its *Blahblahblah*,
I miss our *Is she? Isn't she?* intrigue,
the Derby, Cup and Oaks Days la-di-da,
the all-night rave, the all-next-day fatigue.
I catch the Footy in some corner bar,
the front one having screens 'n' screens of League.
I miss organic shops, their choice of herbs.
So what's life like in Melbourne and its 'burbs?'

Two streets away with her mate Simone
my sister moved in with accustomed *whoosh!*
And seeking admittance to the Bianca-zone
the door gave way when Ange served it a push.
(Meanwhile Lewie, devoid of mobile phone
was helping his brother, some place in the bush
with physical and intellectual backing
to make a documentary on fracking.)

Mum, Dad and I having been invited,
of family living Bianca knew its worth,
throughout the hours there Simone wasn't sighted,
a midwife she was present at a birth.
Gemma's report though everyone delighted,
with admiration leavened by much mirth.
What a missive! What a powerhouse friend!
A reply was ready and, to such an end

Bianca reciting, performed her e-response:
'I work for Raen Bo, she's a legislator,
whose affair with Eddie, what a ponce,
caused Kat, Green Party-president to hate her.
Since hatred's centre of that person's wants
we've quit her orbit, for planets so much greater.

In life and work I'm now a Yarravillian
regarding which employment let me fill you in.

Here's some demographic I'm decoding
using the right and left sides of my brain:
with smart young poets Yarraville's exploding
(though some I know have moved to Castlemaine)
buskers a-plenty, their soulful blues unloading,
whilst giving a complimentary refrain
opera singers, baritones and mezzos,
whilst you'll love this, some of them are Lezzos!

But all such influx wasn't even planned,
and be they clothed in evening wear or grunge
their cafes are well-womanned and well-manned.
Yet if towards hyperbole I lunge
here's an example I think you'll understand
Kat's moved to Yarraville, property values plunge!
Rumour announces this is the time and place
she's meaning to consolidate her base.

Then without a modicum of transcendence
for it gets worse, Kat's the candidate.
We've known for months she's schooled herself for vengeance
and stares Raen down the barrel of her hate.
I've lost desire for revving-up search engines,
my office hours are spent just to berate:
a pox on this malignant so-and-so,
her word is out: she must destroy The Bo!'

Ange, listening to this discussion warmed:
'Kat's ambitions grow much more the vaster.
Though given all those citadels she's stormed
is it fair as villainess to cast her?
Still here's a role that's constantly performed:
Kat as hyperventilating pastor.
I see you nodding as you get my gist,
whatever the cause, she's the evangelist.

Leading that demo where I was arrested
and later the one with Bob on his motor bike,
this emerged: whatever Kat contested

name any issue, first to grab the mike,
all with an ego zealously invested.
I've seen, I've known these surely are the type
that start in preschool, end in graduation,
throughout a private girl's school education.

Of this career tell me, what's it taught her?
tries out the backroom, still the limelight beckons.
And then her fervour turns most Greens to water,
though I agree with Bob each time he reckons,
applying it to you our younger daughter:
If Kat's the main course few return for seconds.
Horse laughter is the ultimate reality
when Aussies face the cult of personality.

I've finer foes set to disturb my sleep
than this Czarina of her self-collective,
on the lookout primed with her *beepbeepbeep*
for any issue needing her corrective.
I see Kat being played by Meryl Streep
combining both obsessive and invective
with poutings of a grumpy kindergartener
and never-ending emphasis on *partner*.

So why do I cringe when *partner* is employed?
For it was Kat who had the term imported.
With 'husband', 'wife' now words you must avoid
(oh how she'd love to institute an audit!)
making her shudder far beyond annoyed,
culprits I feared would be hung, drawn and quartered.
For all those high-flown theories she proffered
it was her practice truly put me off it.

Kat heard The Word, with its desired ovation,
some conference in America's Midwest.
So she returned, crusading through the nation
casting forth the sinners from the blest.
Seared in my mind how's this for a quotation,
issued more as order than request:
"Our heritage has arrived please don't abuse it.
The word is Partner and we all must use it!"

Entwined in my naivety and wisdom
I challenged with rejoinders over-clever.
If strictures are demanded I resist 'em,
which frequently turns out a lost endeavour
when language is locked into any system.
Who gives a stuff now? *Partner* rules forever!
We're nurtured by such lessons in futility
like Lewie's grand-dad up on his Utility.'

Then finding that doco on the internet
we watched those scenes where Old Lew made his mark,
in which the wailing and the railing met,
from minor prophet or Labor patriarch.
Knowing the past could never be reset
he stopped all biting, that day was just bark.
I sensed a croaking voice that verged on tremors
needing perhaps a backing group like Gemma's.

'Old Lew and his Collins Street debacle,
if here,' said Bob, 'is an aging reference point,
it still possesses some nostalgic sparkle,
a legend you'd, when in the mood, anoint.
This footage shows him hardly patriarchal
(though he might be if we smoked a joint).
Near enough five decades on his story
in black and white retains its grainy glory.'

Said Angela: 'With nothing of the fake,
and that's not just the smoothing out of time,
call him naïve he'd not remotely make
those ultimates in public figure crime:
hypocrisy and being on-the-take
all smothered heel-to-head in tabloid grime.
Trusting ourselves not to be thought like that…
so please don't mention Eddie Moon or Kat.'

As the hours unfolded no way would it weary us
this family confab, raising every bar,
the power of which headed near-delirious,
a brain-fest overwhelming to our Pa.
'Tonight I've never felt so super-serious
since,' said Bob, 'our Honours Seminar,'

Seeing in all this intellectual surge
questions like the following emerge:

wither rebellion when the rebel rules?
How far can actions complement belief?
And when you suffer, as when you suffer fools,
what price must you pay for gritted teeth?
All hottest problems; but the story cools
for reader, don't you need some light relief?
So better than Monty Python or The Goon Show
it's time that we reprised the Eddie Moon Show.

In the Village

Yes cantos back we seemed to farewell Eddie,
devoid of wife and lover, plus embittered,
his former nickname morphed to 'Never-ready',
in mainstream nine-to-five he hardly fitted.
With self-esteem increasingly unsteady
days, weeks, months and onto years he frittered.
But the Fates spoke up as they rolled their dices
confronted by his latest midlife crisis:

'You've a special gift, we wish to see you work it,
go seek an outlet for your comic talents!'
So he tried a foothold on the stand-up circuit,
but the crowds were Commos, lacking any balance,
and knowing that a lesser man would shirk it,
'With decent Aussie humour by the gallons
there's little,' Eddie mused, 'I'd rather do
than join the BoganFM Brekky Crew.'

Fee-Bee and Dropkick these BoganFM dags
weekdays at breakfast paraded their berserking,
propping up, like all those tabloid rags
Voiceless Australia, white male and hardworking.
Dropkick's comments (some considered gags)
were of a kind where prejudice lay lurking.
This gormless chap who seemed a trifle weedy
when put beside the very ample Fee-Bee.

A mistress of the low-rent quasi-serious,
who'd tried a course in something at a TAFE,
she found a way to deal with her inferiors:
'You alternate the suck-up with the strafe.'
Which credo now seemed verging on delirious
with loaded hints most thought pretty naïf:
'Is Cancer in each vaccination shot?
Perhaps Autism's some Islamic plot?'

Offsider to this airwaves Mother Hen,
chirpy and bland, her rightwing Mr Squiggle,
ghosted author of *The Rights of Men*,
grandmaster of the backbite and the niggle,
Dropkick's morning reached its climax when
he, to the tune of her unending giggle,
at Eight-Fifteen put Asians in their places
with loser comments many thought quite racist.

Or live-on-air he'd stalk down the élite,
Cultural Marxists soaked in their Chardonnay;
spring them on (why not!) Lygon Street,
delivering this cliché-ridden spray:
'Listen to the Voiceless! Cop it sweet!
Time's up exploiter! The hour's arrived to pay!'
Then rounding out, to give that extra jolt,
the latest quotes from Credlin and/or Bolt.

In all bar one Dropkick surely had 'em,
a winner each time, few encounters fluffed.
But came a cropper with Vanessa Badham
who in delight turned him extra-huffed:
'If you're the pimp then Fee-Bee is the madam.'
With that rejoinder weren't they truly stuffed!
Seeking revenge with *Free Speech* for their slogan
they put out feelers for an extra Bogan.

Eddie applied, but come audition day
with bone-dry mouth, intestines all a-splatter,
sure any nay would outweigh any yay…
Yet after all their pleased-to-meet-you chatter:
'Suppose you'd like to see my resumé…'
which resumé performed in stand-up patter,

Fee-Bee squealed: 'Your cylinders are firing!
Darling Eddie, BoganFM's hiring!'

Such were the crew that Eddie went to join,
the Bogan Brekky Bridegroom and his Bride,
a.k.a the Mammary and her Groin.
Now view the couple grinning either side
in photos of the threesome newly coined,
with Eddie's eyes and mouth stretched open wide.
Bus shelters, tram stops felt the proper place
to see him pull a rather puerile face.

Blokey 'n' jokey adding to his fame
'Set yourselves for a Bogan Brekky stalk…
as nanny-staters shower you with blame
now's your chance to have 'em squeal 'n' squawk…
the higher the target makes the fairest game,
the smug litist transformed to a dork…
want the answers, I'll get all questions asked…'
under a blaze of ratings how he basked.

Yet inner Eddie turmoiled to the max:
that woman lay behind his worst decisions.
Raen it was who made him drop his daks,
have grunts and screams and finally emissions.
(Though nights he found the best way to relax
was cataloguing all their sex positions.)
With BoganFM now his single solace,
his pent-up fury gushing holas-bolas:

'I didn't start the war between the sexes!'
Whole streets away it's certain you could hear him.
'Her name's Raen Bo, one of my former exes!'
And after *that*, what woman would go near him?
'She wouldn't get away with this in Texas!'
Well go there please, they'll find you most endearing.
'I was a victim of their man-slave-culture,
the hour's arrived to feed it to the mulcher!'

Fee-Bee sniggered; Dropkick howled 'Go to it!
A Femmo-Nazi ex? You lucky sod!'
Though others asked, and in-the-know they knew it:

'Can we be sure if Fate won't give the nod?
Imagine the sponsor backlash if he blew it?'
But the Brekky Crew were rating next to God.
Ten to one on weren't *they* the total shoe-in.
Oh how they ruled from Bacchus Marsh to Drouin!

Yet here arrives the fulcrum and the pivot,
that moment where the narrative finetunes.
And if our saga needs a shove let's give it,
with gods out there laying forth these runes:
the might of Tradie Town few can inhibit
colliding with the BoganFM hoons.
So just six weeks before the state election
time for a Marko-Eddie intersection.

The day lies perfect, very much sun-decky
wide is the sky, streaked by a passing jet.
We hail our neighbours Pedro, Ling and Becky
(near to a threesome as you'll ever get).
Giving a miss to any Bogan Brekky
we view, online, the *Yarraville Gazette*.
'This morning,' it proclaims, 'we're giving notice
that candidates are out to meet the voters.'

We shut down breakfast, go on a backstreet ramble.
'I'm much bemused to view these candidates
and hear,' says Lew, 'that democratic scramble
of wild harangues and earnest tête à têtes.
Politically of course it's quite a gamble,
with those endorsed and certainly their mates
to partisan excesses mighty prone.
Reckon I should film some on my phone.'

Down in The Village most of them assembled:
meeting supporters Raen sipped herbal tea;
Marko's beverage Diet Coke resembled;
whatever Kat drank it was gluten free.
(For on this question dictators have trembled:
That you could agree or disagree.)
In campaign mode the babies all a-kissing.
(Though Liberal and Trotskyite were missing.)

And then this sound came screeching down the street:
'I know this sheila, boy she's looking grrreat!
Bogans all I'd love to have you meet
the über-nanny of the nanny-state!'
Raen stared at Eddie, hardly though to greet,
nor in much condition to berate.
With head/heart/lungs going through contractions
slicing up her psyche into fractions.

His rave by now increasingly the ravier
('Let's talk about some great times in the cot!')
with, from the outer-reaches of behaviour,
such loaded questions which, in code, she got.
Raen prayed to Krishna he'd supply a saviour
but smirking Eddie knew indeed what's what:
in give-and-take his take outweighs her give.
Then a voice arrived, this one booming with…

'Please show this little lady some respect!'
as ambit to commence their interaction.
So who's this bozo bogans must reject
and worse still who demands a swift retraction?
Eddie's frozen, all bonhomie's wrecked,
his voice by now approximates a claxon.
'What kind of bludger do you think you are, mate?'
'Marko's my moniker, Labor candidate.'

A standoff's on, it's High Noon in The Village,
except this noon's arriving four hours early.
The Bogan Brekky turns to brainstorm spillage
with Raen Bo being itemised as 'Girly'.
And though a few rungs less than rape and pillage,
enough to turn the sisterhood most surly.
As this gets filmed I see it turning viral
poor Eddie's tragi-comic downward spiral.

Out went his chest which into Marko bumped.
In America he'd use a Smith and Wesson,
like when a country's Morrisoned or Trumped
what better way for ramping up aggression.
His rival though preferred their meeting dumped,
with mediation rounding out the session.

When a fight is on Marko seeks to linger
invariably he never lifts a finger.

Eddie's fingers though became a fist
which peace-and-order (put on hold) invaded.
Lucky for both gentlemen he missed
and Western Suburbs air was where he laid it.
More aggro's found, it's said, in Crazy Whist,
which I believe, although I've never played it.
But gird yourselves when stalkers come a-hunting
and undeterred turn mightily confronting.

Those targets for their Bogan Brekky jabs
are well selected and with no restraint.
'This one deserves it!" Dropkick up and blabs.
And yet there are occasions when it ain't,
like when milady's honour's up for grabs.
Though Marko hardly saw himself a saint,
believing that he acted with impunity
he also saw a photo opportunity.

Into a grapple-dance the two men wrestled
and in slow motion toppled to the gutter
where, some might even say, they nestled
in heavy breaths, part-broken with a splutter.
As Eddie's moans reached their wheezy threshold
Marko, panting, was overheard to utter:
'Like a side of beef gets roasted on a grill,
you're history, sport, get out of Yarraville!'

Lew on his mobile caught the whole proceeding.
We flogged it straight off, fifty thousand smackers.
A slapstick brawl, no bruisings and no bleedings,
no headbutts and no kneeing to the knackers.
'I'm not,' said Marko, 'after special pleadings
for taking on these Bogan Brekky whackers.'
He'd confidence and proof to spare…because
our footage showed the gentleman he was.

'You'll pay! You'll pay!' Whole suburbs heard the roaring
of Eddie fuming East on the Westgate Bridge.
As exile beckons, once ego cops a clawing,

so 'Broome?' he pondered, 'Birdsville? Lightning Ridge?'
Except the Bogan ratings now were soaring
and a case of Brut went straight into their fridge.
Kat meantime thought she'd win unto infinity
after this bout of toxic masculinity.

'Why didn't they wait and see a counsellor?'
This blithe worldview she floated to the press.
'But playground antics proving an utter bore
the ways of boys aren't ours to second guess.
Though I'm certain, as in the days of yore,
one person (female) added to this mess.'
Inferring Raen Bo as some scarlet woman?
Dumb move, Kat, a most deadheaded omen.

For Raen just blushed. 'My hero!' spake the blushing.
The brawl once seen enhanced her reputation,
Eddie's demise the apogee of crushing,
especially on a tabloid style gradation.
All open slather, not a bit hush-hushing
our winner footage carpeted the nation
as Raen announced, applause beyond applause:
'Marko, all my preferences are yours!'

The Premier dropping by was most ecstatic:
'Getting it filmed certainly showed smarts.
Like a stallion in his agistment paddock
with women voters Marko tops the charts.
I know this gym whose offer's most emphatic:
freebee lessons in the martial arts.
And if perchance you're sued (obiter dicta)
we're hiring you a Burnside or a Richter.'

A self-described if un-named 'old school chum'
when interviewed well recognised the scene:
'...that one where smartarse tumbles down to dumb...
and then we find he's smitten by a Green!
It'd be no worse had Eddie bared his bum,
looks like he was a dreadful child to wean.
Masters at Grammar knew each dickhead defect,
no wonder Eddie never was a prefect.'

Though some there were who surged to his defence,
and Liberal HQ, not pausing for reflection
chose a tactic they thought would commence
a rush of swinging voters their direction.
If the rules of risk outweigh the rules of sense
it's understood when running for election
there's capital out there and you must make it,
unless like Trump you'd much prefer to fake it.

With the obligatory reference to Voltaire
and vague illusions to the Fall of Saigon,
their press release was headed *Freedom! Yeah!*
insisting that '…a BoganFM icon,
with snide-filled sneers they're hoping to ensnare.
So be assured bygones will *not* be bygone
whilst Labor cowards bleat their hateful tune
we reaffirm our faith in Eddie Moon!'

Down the fake news drain their spin was sluiced;
here's more examples from that dreary bevy:
'This incident gave two campaigns their boost,
both Mrs Rainbow's and her Labor heavy,
who hoping to rule some failing minor roost
drove up, we gather, in his vintage Chevy.
Voters are asked to put things in perspective,
since *Freedom of Speech* remains our top objective.'

Now Pentecostals overran that party
with all their trademark photos of the foetus.
They'd castigate you for your morning latté
as being both despotic and élitist.
At prayer they came on extra loud and hearty.
The still, small voice? A sign you're just defeatist.
Free Speech for them was who can say and what:
'We'll slag whom we like and you cannot!'

'I thought,' said the Premier, trying to keep track,
'that mob's *raison d'*être was making money.'
And some there were who sought that former tack,
for as a hive keeps pumping out the honey,
in deal-making they'd once the utmost knack.
And you'd scream in pain were it not so funny

that they asked Angela (better not say 'summoned')
to meet for Morning Tea with 'Buster' Drummond.

He was that long-time Liberal Party grandee
who disarmed with many a rough-house greeting:
'Whilst not a thug I'm no Mahatma Gandhi,
and neither be it known was your mate Keating.
But the best of power's when the cheque book's handy,
believe that and you won't regret our meeting.
For Angie, this'll make you maxi-glad:
you've heard of Eddie's ex-wife? I'm her Dad!

What he did and still does to my Princess,
Angie, the family's blighted, and for good.
Just say his name, see how our Petal winces.
This stand I'm taking's where I've always stood:
to see him ground, just as a mincer minces,
and Angie loves this as I knew she would…'
(But within she wailed like any hyper-banshee,
for few possessed the gall to call her 'Angie'.)

'…we've great respect though for your Marko Whosits.
The heaps I've pumped into his Tradie Town.
That's one investment too good to refuse. It's
sure to bring the rolled-est gold renown.
Though for my favourite item on the news…it's
Marko booting-out that Eddie clown.
And better yet, behold the Boardroom chatter:
that he's Labor doesn't seem to matter.

Ask any collective noun of wheeler-dealers,
the treatment Eddie dished out is deplored.
Most blokes were riled and certainly all sheilas,
we've this stunner sitting on our Board
who'll savage Eddie with her twelve Blue Heelers,
revenging every chick that dickhead's pawed…'
Onward he raved, sure flipside of the subtle,
who brokered no retreat and no rebuttal.

With jawbone grinding molar upon molar,
as some thoroughbred chomps upon its chaff,
'J'accuse!' he howled, just like Émile Zola,

which finished heaving into a spluttered laugh.
Not merely bi- this man was multi-polar,
though with a rostered paramedic staff.
All show was *his* (or would be if you let him).
'...for Angie you 'n' I are gonna get him!

I'd soon trust a funnel-web or dingo,
that cocksucker's sucked his final cock!
Ladies present...oops...excuse the lingo...'
Though he continued ramping-up the shlock:
'Just flash some tits then *this way big boy*...bingo!
Into the kitchen whack him with y' wok.
It's months again before he'll use his dick.
I'll pay all lawyers so let's sue the prick!'

Hardly warming to the sado-sexual
Angela sought a refuge in distractions,
making all context very much contextual:
'I must consult before we take such actions
(sorry if these details may perplex you) all
our committees, caucuses and factions
(we're quite restrained, adverse to taking chances)
and last, but never least of all, the branches.'

'My God, you do it *that* way?' Buster stared.
Democracy like this he'd not encountered.
The prizes went to those who always dared,
a credo which since birth he never doubted:
risk upon risk. Now though he hardly cared.
This race he knew was over, so dismounted
and offered 'Good luck...' (muttering compactly).
Though for what we never knew exactly.

But then the once proud Liberal Party split,
for a branch-stacked putsch brought in the Free-Speech-Corps.
Whither plurality? Never in a fit:
you fell in line or else were shown the door.
And though a few souls had been up for it,
the destruction of the one-time son-in-law,
all that remains: just mealy-mouthing bluster.
Divide-and-survive is now the way with 'Buster'.

The Yarraville Experience or The V'room V'room Job

Gone were the poll improvements they'd enjoyed,
that ruthless craft to resonate with voters.
And well-timed gags the Premier employed
just emphasised the way they'd lost their locus.
All Oppositions this one should avoid:
if you as rabble stay in daily focus
you'll cop one message, that only one which went:
'For all their faults we have a government.'

It fell to Labor now to re-engage
and finetune glitches (few and mostly minor).
The game was on! And taking to the stage
with clothing by the ALP designer,
and Angela nodding as his inhouse sage,
the Premier delivered this two-liner:
'The Governor is issuing the writs.
The Liberals think they'll win…they're off their tits!'

My Yarraville with its three-way tussle,
on what occasion had it seen such action:
around a time women wore the bustle
and voters were all male and Anglo-Saxon?
If spared the blight of neofascist muscle
I know that little beats today's attraction
of giving even a thuggish, racist jerk
the chance to glimpse democracy at work.

The curtain rises and behold the workings,
in Yarraville tonight they're on display,
devoid we trust of narcissist berzerkings
and smartarse gags ending in *touché*!
and all those self-satisfaction-smirkings
(bland and beyond, if we had our way)
that gall it takes to be a candidate,
as seven such assembled to debate.

In what was once a Mechanics Institute
packed with every Miss, Ms, Mrs, Mr,
our film footage seemed to be bearing fruit
for a lady stumbled forth to Raen and kissed her.

Those present cheered, acclaiming it as cute.
'Watch out,' Lew indicated, 'here's your sister.'
I sensed a night of most outlandish trouble
as bounded-up Bianca all a-bubble:

'According to some Green girlfriends (woo-hoo!)
I've information sure to be intriguin'.
Within her party Kat's just staged a coup
and I've been told by Fatima and Megan
that dietary constraints are in the brew,
her word is law, you *have* to be a Vegan!
Imagine a lifetime living this manifesto.
I might, for one day, with a little pesto.

Kat's in the kitchen playing to her base,
the organisers seem extremely piqued.'
Like coppers with their tasers and their mace
we tiptoed up (but still a floorboard squeaked).
I never will forget the time and place
as hearts a-thumping round the door we peeked.
There Kat sat, halting all proceedings,
oblivious to democratic pleadings.

'*I* need,' she recoiled, 'my sustenance…'
and kept a-spooning through her Vegan sludge,
leading all on a mighty torpid dance,
for half an hour they tried to make her budge.
And name what progress might you see advance?
A dudgeon of the utmost highest dudge,
embellished with asides like 'patriarchy'
and other phrases verging on malarkey.

In Karma-mode Raen Bo wore a sari.
'Evening Ma'am, and don't you look bewitchin',
charming the Globe from Bogota to Bari…'
Primed to impress Marko sure was itchin'.
'Where's Kat Namow? Boy that one's a harpy.'
But she was elsewhere, sulking in the kitchen.
Which, things delayed, this saga now relates
some visions of the other candidates:

a merchant banking whiz-kid circa twenty
possessed with all that Liberal Party swagger;
whilst guzzling from the bigot's horn-of-plenty
and slagging-off, One Nation's über-slagger;
the Trotskyite, bemused if argument-y,
a cheeky soul this latter-day red-ragger;
also a less-than-subtle 'Libertarian',
who had the gall to call himself an Aryan.

Foiled by the absence of the vegan diva
we stepped outside, that's where I remarked:
'Someone else is here to grab a breather,
next to where his upscale Ute is parked.
Its owner though seems in a sort of fever…'
We stared at him. He stared back and barked:
'Call me Darko,' a throaty voice came buzzin',
'I warn you, never mess with Marko's cousin.'

Wraparound his shades were, and reflective,
on his Toyota Hilux he reclined.
'Listen friends, think I'm some defective,
that madman front 'n' centre of y'mind?
Well check us out, send round a detective,
I know plenty, the bodybuilding kind.
We do weights like most do dental flossing,
you'll find us working out at Hopper's Crossing.'

My intuition heaved a mighty *click*:
'Please Darko please, we don't mean any harm.
This man is Lewie, I'm his partner-chick,
with countless ways to minimise alarm.
Since Tradie Town's a marvel brick-by-brick
the storm is over, now here comes the calm.
We see your psyche's somewhat overtaxed…'
Slowly he smiled and, on his terms, relaxed.

The better side of Darko coming out,
though there behind his shades we sensed a frown,
to have us leave with not a shred of doubt
his words were apt, every verb and noun:
'Come polling day I'll cart the prick about,
yes, you can call him Mr Tradie Town.

Marko as front man? Can't say that I mind it.
But just remember…I'm the brains behind it!'

Kat being fed, now came the debate,
its chairman was this happy-clappy pastor,
more than adept at passing round his plate,
of fellowship-bonhomie was the master;
except in crowd-control he wasn't great,
under his wing we headed to disaster,
conflict-ridden it stretched wall-to-wall.
Though Raen just beamed throughout the free-for-all.

In rushed One Nation (all were drawn by lot)
given this chance he couldn't wait to spoil it,
his narcissism running extra hot
we were hoping circumstance would foil it.
Combining who, when, where, why, how and what
we heard him scrape the bottom of the toilet:
'There's lawyers, Marko, on the case because
it's treasonous, this Tradie Town of yours.

I've been out there, seen the crap you've brought in,
some Muslim bitch was chauffeured in her Fiat.'
With outrage mixing boos 'n' howls 'n' snorting
the most the Chairman muttered was 'So be it.'
Marko glared: 'What are you purporting?
If there's a problem here I cannot see it.
Whether you're from Bangladesh or Serbia
you'll find a place in Tradie Town suburbia.

Three cheers for our Multi-Aussie-Culture!
Not good enough? Okay let's make it ten!'
So this opponent, like some wounded vulture,
slunk away. Yes we allowed it, when
he seemed no better than a seeping ulcer.
All knew of course they'd view his like again,
but thought his exit might see out the night.
Then one more blaze erupted on The Right.

Aimed in the Libertarian's direction
many gave sneers and this provoked his storm.
Demands were made for police protection,

302

since he'd this Aryan mortgage on 'the norm':
'I, a white man, hereby take exception
and thus present speech in its free-est form,
whose power shall wipe off sneers from every dial.'
The Trotskyite replied 'Sieg fuckin' heil.'

As natural as when a baby dribbles
Raen beamed in her beafitic fug.
VOTE ONE for this most serene of sybils
would be her message were she on a drug.
Meanwhile whilst Kat was munching vegan nibbles
that Trotskyite had truly pulled the rug.
Sneer-afflicted this Aryan hightailed.
As if in sympathy the Young Lib wailed:

'He's not to blame for these imbroglios!'
So Marko sought to bring this chap some joy.
'My cousin Darko's Uncle Solly knows
how smart investments are your latest toy.
Add shares in Tradie Town to your portfolios…'
Advice which was perplexing to the boy:
'But I've been told you are on The Left!'
(Two decades on he may have found his depth.)

Once each had seemed allergic to the other
(as with hayfever's multiple atishoos)
now Marko slapped the Liberal's back: 'Yo brother!'
Whilst Raen's repose reminded one of Vishnu's.
But a howl erupted, all love set to smother:
'Why aren't we discussing Vegan issues?'
Because we weren't. And having had enough,
shaking her head Kat strode off in a huff.

In a world of victor v her victim
the Trot proposed this fine form of redress:
'If he had any balls I would've kicked 'em!'
Marko and Raen came grinning through the mess.
That was an evening worthy of a dictum,
ignored of course throughout the Murdoch press.
With any front page sure to be exquisite
see us upstaged by some Royal Visit.

Four days later, Saturday in fact,
with leaders staring down each other's eyeballs,
Bianca and I resolve to make a pact:
we'll hit our polling booth as sibling rivals.
So knowing how opinion polls have tracked
political demises and survivals,
barring a cyclone, Typhoid or the Pox
all that remains is just the ballot box.

Bob driving up sees journos jotting notes
for headlines that their bosses love to choose.
*Angela's Hubby Hands Out How-to-votes
Beside Their Daughters* aren't his to refuse
yet still he asks 'Are these mind-numbing quotes
approximating *anything* like the news?'
'Oh yes they are,' reporters now declare.
'In Yarraville it's a family affair.'

With cameras aimed Bianca played the hostess:
'Now here's a busker with her ukulele;
and here's a wall, which all the campaign posters
are decorating (in the old sense) gaily;
I see One Nation's missing with its grossness;
here's my old man and here's my sister Hailey,
who's Labor this straight-shooting heter-o,
she's for Marko, me, I'm with The Bo!'

Facing the choice of his opposing daughters,
with how-to-votes their father alternated.
A human interest gift to all reporters,
hour-upon-hour Bob was congratulated
for everything since birth he would've taught us.
To BoganFM though that surely grated,
plus this, which one day may well prove archival:
the Marko Fan Club, awaiting his arrival,

arrayed in multicultural peasant dresses
with 'Mar-ko-Mar-ko' as their form of chant.
'From Tradie Town,' Bianca said, 'my guess is,
I hardly think the evidence is scant:
behold the petticoats and braided tresses
and beaming smiles devoid of racist cant.'

Whilst in a deck chair sprawled this Liberal biddy,
since their performance made her rather giddy.

Where was One Nation? I don't wish to brag
but in Remand! (Doesn't that make you drool?)
Ice-dealing was the downfall of this dag
assisted by that Libertarian fool.
Our Trotskyite? Yes, there she was, the wag!
And thinking we required their brand of gruel
the Greens had a stall, like some Vegan grocer.
I heard a distant humming…which got closer

and, with a sound which shook to every bone
came revving-up one very stretchy limo.
Bianca nearby, with her friend Simone
could only gasp: 'Wadda ya reckon, Simmo?
The real deal Marko, not some kinda clone…'
whose Fan Club celebrated with 'It's him! Oh!'
Whilst in his shades Darko at the wheel
kept right on revving, all the scene to steal,

as if announcing 'I'm on the *v'room v'room* job,
this man has separated from the boys!'
For Darko knew where, when and what to lob,
combining all with menace yet with poise:
'You must remember me, eh Mr Bob?'
And then he grinned, bringing forth a noise.
A grunt? A snigger? Maybe half 'n' half?
Being generous let's approximate a laugh.

Some former teachers when their past invades
will suffer it, just never please remind them.
'In class,' told Bob, 'he always wore those shades,
we reckoned on some microchip behind them.
With sixteen-year-old Western Suburbs maids
he had this kind of radar that could find them.
And if some left him feeling more than haunted
the charm was there for females, when he wanted.

Imagine the obligatory red roses.
Tell us, has he hooked up with a lady?
Told me once of his self-diagnosis:

ADHD with an extra AD.
Buggered if I know what's his neurosis,
he thought he'd make it as some form of tradie,
but was warned off doing *any* welding.
Darko, eh? We near enough expelled him.'

Enter now the Raen Bo entourage
and her couture nobody could falter
'Marko!' she hailed. 'Babe!' boomed his hom-age.
(Some thought that they were heading to the altar.)
Though the import of their meeting let's enlarge,
like Churchill, Stalin, Roosevelt at Yalta
leaders they were who never self-effaced,
and rivals round a single foe, embraced.

'...and this man's Mr Bob, who was my teacher,
if it wasn't for him, I wouldn't be standing here...'
On display Marko as overreacher
(for drama though it wouldn't beat *King Lear*).
'Whatever kids were, with Bob wouldn't feature:
Lezzo, Straight or Poofter, sorry Queer...'
Our candidate, we knew, for all his faults
would be the Brownlow Medallist of schmaltz.

Then Raen exceeded, stopping short of stutter:
'Oh Mr Bob, I've heard so much about...'
'Well I've heard more...' I caught my father mutter
which soon unfolded to 'I'm wanting out
of Yarraville in its multi-party clutter...
err Marko mate, please have no cause to doubt
I loved the way you worked your pre-selection...
but gotta scoot to my wife's re-election!'

Our bad results arrived at half-past six
and I could almost sense Kat's chilling chuckles.
I truly heard 'Exterminate the pricks!'
Darko's verdict propped by cracking knuckles.
When Marko's not receiving Great Big Ticks
he's sensitive and something in him buckles.
This night required a therapeutic session
to blubber forth the following confession:

'Ever since that Eddie said "I'll bop ya"
this whole campaign has verged on smithereens.
Play a shocker then the coach'll drop ya,
I fear I've ventured far beyond my means.
Should've obeyed my Baba back in Skopje
each time she ordered 'Marko, eat your greens!'
It's days like these set my synapses snappin',
woke up this morning sensing this would happen.

I dreamt I walked down Bourke Street in the nuddy...'
Lewie though was keeping him afloat:
'According to a recent in-depth study
Kat will garner all the Vegan vote.
If current figures look a trifle cruddy
it's early days, a cliché you can quote.
There's no conspiracy, hit squad or a conclave,
for Yarraville has quite a Vegan enclave.

Outside of them my urging is get real,
we've exit polling promising delight,
since there's Raen Bo and her preference deal,
the Vegan vote will vanish with the night.
This election won't be Kat's to steal.
Trust Carnivores, the red meat and the white!'
We were enchanted, for that instant motto
possessed the power to send us extra blotto.

On by Seven over before Eight
the statewide swing is unlike any other.
And from the Murray, finishing at Bass Strait
Labor remains Victoria's live-in lover.
Whilst with a small cross-section of the state
the ABC hosts Angela, our mother.
No BoganFM bullshit can impede her.
We now pause for the Opposition Leader.

'A new day starts,' he said, 'tomorrow morning...'
as the poor chap tried to rise above the rout.
'Your heritage they better not start pawning,
keeping you happy...until the funds run out.'
Ange came on the screen, we caught her yawning.
She verged on stuffed. How could you even doubt

that this epitomises (ain't it so, Mum)
when politics transforms into the ho-hum.

The Premier spoke: 'We have been believed!
This greatest verdict I accept with candour.
Not once was the electorate deceived,
though pundits may pontificate and pander.
We've been re-endorsed and *not* reprieved.
On gender issues I urge, take a gander:
half the cabinet women now will grace.
But give us the news on Marko What's-his-face.'

If you need pundits to complete that quiz
who better than this evening's instant cult,
those Grand Poohbahs of the election biz
who then turned to the Yarraville result:
'It looks like Labor…not just *like*… it *is*,
Kat Namow has just shot her Vegan bolt!'
Then, through the hubbub smashing our status quo
we heard Bianca: 'Make way for The Bo!'

Raen's words were teary, cheers though poured upon her:
'My preferences have made your win a cinch.
For Marko saved my person and my honour
and is, well in Australian terms, a prince.
I saved him too, he thought he was a goner,
well now he's resolutely not and since
the baton's passed with democratic splendour
from Yarraville's current to its upcoming member,

I'll write my memoirs, please congratulate me,
we've signed this half-a-million-dollar deal.
(Strange, I thought, I might get tuppence ha'penny)
with cash like that you should've heard me squeal!
Yarraville', she pleaded, 'don't berate me,
I'll shout all present to a ten-course meal.
And though the contract options television
my show won't be *The Raen Bo Coalition*.'

As if on cue all turned to the current TV,
for we required more updates on the polling.
Raen gave a gasp, like in the worst of 3D

to the floor collapsed and started rolling.
We'd never seen her like it. But indeedy
Bianca's helping hand was there consoling,
to mop the Raen Bo forehead with a flannel...
for Eddie Moon was on the Sky News panel.

The room's erupting with a brace of boos
which power exceeds all decibelic stats.
The widest gamut howls: Saints, Bombers, Blues,
Lions, Tigers, Swans, the Bulldogs and the Cats,
Magpies, Demons, Hawks and Kangaroos...
for your support we're offering congrats.
(Although these teams are, or were, Victorian
to those elsewhere please don't be *too* censorian.)

Thinking the evening would be retrospective
the Marko Fan Club dressed as disco-divas.
They were forgiven, the mood was a collective
Democracy in Action. Please believe us.
Darko though suggested this corrective:
'After today we're pulling *all* the levers.
From Venezuela to Burkina Faso
votes'll pour in...yeah...not bad for a Masso.'

Not bad indeed, for one a few hours back
who'd been, to use that Freud term 'pretty poorly',
now saw a swing of one substantial whack
(though plenty would miss Raen Bo rather sorely).
With eyes and ears for archives down the track
our candidate must have the last word, surely.
'...and like that *beep* when you scan a barcode,
so Yarraville is well 'n' truly Marko'd!'

Epilogue

A few weeks on from winning the election
one evening out we're set on bookshop browsing,
then home for a spot of Nordic Noir detection,
but before we hit such Sunday night carousing
a voice and face is urging recollection
and when recalled the outcome is astounding,

opinionated if devoid of hauteur
here is the man I know to be our author.

'Lewie,' I cry, 'please stop him from absconding,
for we've been partners in his master plan!'
With pleasure though the poet is responding:
'Permit me when I say this man-to-man:
wasn't it great with Marko and your bonding?
So pleased to greet another Bomber fan.
You have a near-to-inner-urban scene here.
Yarraville eh? First time that I've been here!'

We took him home and for the next few hours
the existential crimes of Copenhagen
were put on hold. Such moments would allow us
to smoke some weed. We soon were pretty far gone
in boosting our imaginative powers.
For entertainment we had scored a bargain:
our guest was in his element I dare say
to improvise, if verging on an essay:

'Imagine you're a scandal-prone backbencher,
and Dickheadland is no one-party state.
As each week brings another misadventure
a few brain cells we need to lubricate.
I'm just advising haven't come to censure
but for your good you better hear me, mate:
your very being is tax-payer funded
so listen hard and I will play the pundit.

If you wail once more "That wasn't what I meant…"
or even better "Don't believe the hype…"
such special pleadings far exceed intent.
Ranging from the big-note to the gripe
they prove the speaker less-than-innocent
with further shots of hubris in his pipe,
ratcheting up, increasingly unsubtle,
permit me space to itemise a couple.

You're fair game, sure, but in unending oodles
your contributions verge on kamikaze:
those, by now, indiscreet canoodles

of you-with-escort snapped by the paparazzi,
or that online stash of pornographic doodles…
one's better off being outed as a Nazi.
When the profile's big the stakes get even bigger,
so sorry friend, you're now a Public Figure!

Which won't I'm sure apply in Marko's case
(Darko remains a somewhat different matter).
In power or out or playing-to-your-base,
from well before our age of online chatter,
what's politics? That's when the human race
combines the threat, the soft sell and the natter;
it is the child when gossip mates with data
and has been going since the Magna Carta.

But Hailey, Lewie, let's close this edition…'
A pause occurred. 'We shouldn't feel despondent…'
Another pause. 'I'm making this admission
confessing that the three of us have bonded
and trusting you agree to this petition:
and sign up each as special correspondent.
If you see deeds to fit in our portmanteau
inform me and I'll pen another canto…'

We told Bianca, who started up chiacking:
'What's it with these poets and their urges?
It's my love-life he has been hi-jacking.'
'Movies,' she's told, 'propel his arty splurges.
So thanks to screwball you and your wisecracking
he thinks you're someone out of Preston Sturges.
There are no stars in his ensemble cast,
and edifying you we'll run it past.

If Bob and Ange remain its moral centre
our Premier's of course the Big White Chief.
There's Eddie as the ultimate low-renter
whilst Kat and Buster play the light relief.'
Then thinking this a game which all might enter
Bianca joined in sceptical belief:
'DeNiro as Darko I reckon would be super,
and Marko could be played by Gary Cooper!'

'Raen Bo?' I ponder, to hear my sister saying:
'Some prima donna without many clues,
though when required a natural at sashaying…
but since The Bo has dropped off any news
Bianca needs a break from such P.Aing.
I'm going on a Mediterranean cruise.'
'You'll keep in touch?' I ask and she says 'Yes boss.'
Sending this postcard all the way from Lesbos.

'My Gemma virus heads towards remission
for I have found the wonderful Monique:
a slim 'n' tiny Philippines beautician-
manicurist. And, in our second week,
it's like some H-bomb's over-mighty fission
to stare into her eyes and barely speak.
She gives great facials and she does my nails.
Looks like Ms Right…wadda ya reckon, Hails?

G'day to Lewie in his Bomber beanie,
let's rate him Alpha, far beyond a Beta.
Who's well aware of our hormonal genie
and thus the countdown of our bio-metre.
You've met the right bloke, make a few bambini.
I've got some fine names, Billie, Andre, Peta.
Certain that these choices in androgyny
will be a mighty asset to your progeny.'

Thanks Bianca, the required personnel
are well prepared for such an undertaking.
You head the list of those they aim to tell
once you become an auntie-in-the-making.
Meanwhile there's lighter issues to propel,
in sensing that for news you must be aching
here's updates on the Yarraville action stations,
live from Marko's Christmas celebrations.

With Darko poised whilst everybody entered
behind his shades he scanned what's in the offing:
there's crims who'll deal, but cops who can prevent it,
good-humoured both, not one of them is scoffing;
there's footy legends, most teams represented;
and there's the media, Cab-Sav see 'em quaffing.

I sense their drugs are uppers more than downers;
there's Labor folk and there's the Tradie Towners.

And now the host is waving from his terrace,
'Greetings!' he broadcasts, quite beyond emphatic.
'From yours truly, Felicity my finest
and from, to make things much more democratic
Chad who's our heir and Chantelle who's our heiress!'
Given this cue his party turns ecstatic
knowing that they'd voted in the best
those citizens of Yarraville and the West.

More than local member he's your neighbour,
part man of grit, part charming interactor.
Midway between the mallet and the sabre
he's stymied every Right and Left detractor.
A ten per cent, that's the swing to Labor,
if much indebted to the Raen Bo factor.
First past the post? Give me preferential!
And thus concludes *Yarraville Confidential.*

The Cast

In Our Four Dominions

The Narrator	an English journalist
The Narrator's Uncle	his editor
Mayor Moriarty	a Melbourne seed merchant
Mrs Moriarty	his wife
Jean Moriarty	their second daughter, a bluestocking
Heléna	their first daughter, an Anglophile
Edward (Ted)	their son
Stella and Vera	their youngest, twins
Doreen	mother of Ted's child
Ida	the narrator's wife
Ed	Stella's son

The Gumsuckers

Jock	an Australian born composer
Enid	Jock's sister
Douglas	Enid's husband
Birgitta Hoff	Jock's fourth wife
Wendy	a reporteress
Kitty	Jock's first wife
Peter Warlock	a composer
Norma	Jock's second wife
Errol Flynn	an actor
Jock's third wife	
Noel	a pianist
The Dean of Music	
Tunesmith	a prominent music student
Jean Moriarty	a bluestocking
Teddy Moriarty	Jock's late friend, Jean's brother
Cath	Jean's niece
Aubrey	a journalist

Post War or My First Husband

Cath	the narrator
Lew	her husband, an industrial lawyer and one time dance band vocalist
Rod	their son

Helen	their daughter
Keith	Cath's brother
Ross	Cath's brother
Jean	Cath's aunt
Teddy (dec.)	Cath's uncle

Anna	a friend of Cath's
Will	Lew's friend, a Liberal MP
Dorothy	Will's first wife
Popinjay QC	Lew's legal mentor
Darky Nolan	a Communist, a friend of Lew's
Grace	a University student
Gladys	Lew's mother
The Boss	a High School Headmaster
Trixie	a friend of Cath's a fellow teacher
Magda	a fellow teacher
Monica	a fellow teacher
Alison	a fellow teacher
Mr B	a fellow teacher
Lightfoot	a Civic Leader
Margot	a model, Lightfoot's first wife, Will's second wife
Poppy	a fellow model
Annabelle	a fellow model
Cherry	a fellow model
Jock	a composer
An Abortionist	

Breakfast With Darky

The Narrator	
Kim	his daughter
Mick	a fellow teacher
Darky Nolan	a Communist
Marj	the narrator's ex-wife

Moonlight in Vermont South or Also Starring Bob Hawke as Himself

Ingrid Curnow	an ALP candidate
Des Curnow	her husband
Helen Johnson	Ingrid's campaign secretary, the narrator
Kurt Stead	Helen's husband
Lew Johnson	Helen's father, 'The Shadow Minister for Lurks,

	Perks and Jerks'
Ewan Adcock	a former ALP candidate, Ingrid's campaign treasurer
Marlene Adcock	Ewan's wife
Phil Baxter	Ingrid's campaign director
Bob Hawke	Leader of the Opposition, later Prime Minister
Cath Johnson	Helen's mother, Lew's first wife
Rod Johnson	Helen's brother, a Queensland property developer
Poppy Brasch	Lew's second wife
Dee Glover	Lew's third wife, 'The Go To Girl'
Gilbert Bland	the local Liberal member, 'Gib the Glib'
Gwen Baxter	Phil's wife
Greg Stead	Kurt's brother
Will Fairburn	Lew's oldest friend, 'Uncle Will'
Margot Fairburn	Will's second wife
Jean	Cath's aunt, deceased
Gail and Godfrey	Journalism's 'Power Couple'
Jeremy and Jake	Editors of a literary journal

Mixed Businessmen

The Narrator	
The Narrator's ex-wife	
Bob Arnold	a teacher, a friend of the narrator
Ange	Bob's wife
Big Mike	a user, a friend of the narrator
Beetle	a drug retailer
Skunk	member of Beetle's gang
Keno	member of Beetle's gang
Des	member of Beetle's gang
Stu	member of Beetle's gang
Dæmon	a thirteen year-old, murdered
Captain Midnight	Beetle's mentor

Yarraville Confidential or The Boyfriend Experience

The Author	
Angela	Labor Member for Fairfield, Deputy Premier of Victoria
Bob	her husband, a high school principal, now retired
Hailey	their elder daughter, the narrator

Bianca	their younger daughter, an activist
Raen Bo	Greens, later Independent, Member for Yarraville
Kat Namow	Greens State President, later Greens candidate for Yarraville
Eddy Moon	Liberal Member for South Yarra, later of the Bogan FM Brekky Crew
Digger	Eddie's one-time mentor
Lewie	Hailey's boyfriend
Helen	his mother
Kurt	his father
Marko	a tradie/property developer/Labor candidate for Yarraville
Darko	Marko's cousin, the brains behind Tradie Town
Felicity	a graduate in media, Marko's wife
Gemma	Bianca's first girlfriend, later a jillaroo and outback activist
Buster Drummond	old style Liberal Party powerbroker
Poppy	Eddie's ex-wife, Buster's daughter
Dropkick	of the BoganFM Brekky Crew
Fee-Bee	of the BoganFM Brekky Crew

The Premier

Old Lew (dec.)	Helen's father, a member of the Whitlam Government
Cath	Helen's mother, 'Old Lew's first wife, a columnist.
Maurie Moon (dec.)	Eddy's great uncle, a 1940s football legend

Notes

In Our Four Dominions

Messrs Deakin ('Affable Alf'), Fisher, Cook and Hughes were Australian politicians all of whom became Prime Minister.

Herbert Asquith was Liberal British PM 1908-1916.

Hearts of Oak and *Drake's Drum* were patriotic British songs.

Cliveden, the home of Nancy Astor, wife of the 2nd Viscount Astor, was the meeting place of the Cliveden Set of the 1920s and 1930s.

During the Suez crisis of 1956 a demonstration was held in Trafalgar Square where at the end of his incredible speech, Labour Politician Aneurin Bevan proclaimed 'Get out, get out, get out!'

The Gumsuckers

Song of Australia is a 19th Century patriotic song, mainly popular in South Australia. It still survives.

Peter Warlock was the name coined by Phillip Heseltine, minor British composer and strong aficionado of the occult.

Grainger, Korngold, Poulenc and Walton were all prominent 20th Century composers.

RCM is the Royal College of Music.

The Rite is of course The *Rite of Spring*.

Farrago was the University of Melbourne's student newspaper.

Quota Quickie was a typically low-cost, low-quality film commissioned to satisfy the quota requirements of Britain's Cinematograph Films Act 1927.

Post War or My First Husband

Deep Mid-on is a position on the cricket field.

CWA is the Country Women's Association.

The Shop was an old nickname for the University of Melbourne.

Groupers were Right-wing Roman Catholic based activists centred in the Union Movement and in politics through the Democratic Labor Party.

Blue Hills was the preeminent radio serial.

The Yarra Bank was a Sunday afternoon open air centre for a wide variety of mainly political public spruiking.

The Colombo Plan was an intergovernmental First and Third World organisation aimed at developing human resources in South and southeast Asia often through education.
Ealing Studios were leading British film-makers of the 40s, 50s and 60s.

Fred Daly was a leading Labor politician prized amongst many things for his often-ruthless wit.

Melbourne and Collingwood were the preeminent VFL rivals from the mid-to-late 50s into the 60s. Melbourne was more often the winner but on that day were trounced in the wet: 7. 13 [55] to 2.7.[19]

The Eureka Youth League was the Communist Party of Australia's youth wing.

Brief Encounter was a 1945 David Lean film to a script by Noel Coward. It was a romantic weepie centred on two married people on the edge of adultery.

Nellie Melba [Helen Mitchell] was both the world's leading soprano and the most famous Australian of her day. Renowned for both retiring and making comebacks she eventually returned to Australia to live a semi-rural life somewhat east of Melbourne.

Matric: Matriculation, old-fashioned for Form 6/Year 12 and graduating therefrom.

Sharpeville was the site of the infamous massacre of Black South Africans by White Police in March 1960.

Late 1960 and into 1961 saw an extraordinary visit to Australia by the West Indian Cricket team.

'The Winds of Change...' In February 1960 British PM Harold McMillan announced to the South African Parliament : 'The wind of change is blowing through this continent. Whether we like it or not, this growth of national consciousness is a political fact.' The term immediately entered political language.

Breakfast with Darky

This poem has previously appeared in my volumes *The Australian Popular Songbook* and *Near Believing: Selected Monologues and Narratives 1967-2021*

Samizdat were supposedly subversive underground Russian publications throughout the Soviet era.

Sunnyside Up was a Friday night Melbourne television variety show.

Frank Hardy, Judah Waten and John Morrison were leading Social-Realist writers of the Post War decades.

Moonlight in Vermont South or Also Starring Bob Hawke as Himself

An extract of this poem appeared in *Meanjin*.

There was never a more memorable nor infamous act in Australian political history than the sacking of the Whitlam Government by Governor General Kerr on November 11, 1975.

The Burvale is a beer barn hotel on the corner of *Bur*wood Highway and Spring*vale* Rd...get it?

Korowa is an Anglican Girls Grammar in Glen Iris.

Cleo was a prominent women's magazine, aiming to be a touch more up-market than most.

Searchlight was a prominent Melbourne new-sheet for swingers and others.

Johnny Dodds (clarinet) and his brother 'Baby' Dodds (drums) were members of Louis Armstrong's Hot Fives and Hot Sevens, benchmark jazz ensembles from the 1920s.

Messrs Peers and Lanza were popular vocalists in the 1940s and 50s. Very middle-of-the-road.

The Democrats were a middle-of-the-road at times radical, political party somewhat in the tradition of the Teals. They were supplanted by the Greens.

It's Time was Labor's 1972 campaign slogan. For many it still is.

Mixed Businessmen

This poem previously appeared in my volume *These Things Are Real* under the title 'Mixed Business'.

Cap'n Midnight is a minor character in my verse novel *The Lovemakers*, a member of the Joy Boys Drug Syndicate.

The Crystal Palace is a brothel first featured in my verse novel *The Nightmarkets*.

'Today's E.T. I'll stand any bet is stoned.' E.T. is a Victorian term for Emergency Teacher, as in relief or supply. This line comes from my poem 'A High School Staff Room, Melbourne's Northern Suburbs, Winter 1977'.

Yarraville Confidential or The Boyfriend Experience

An extract of this poem was published in *The Australian*.

Being a bit of a lair the Victorian Premier I've created is not Daniel Andrews, for whatever Daniel Andrews is, he's no lair.

Bob Menzies and the Forgotten People is named after the Liberal Party founder and his call to arms on behalf of decent, hard-working etc. etc. Australians.

Real Livin' Motors first appears in my verse novel *The Lovemakers*.

Maurie Moon first appears in my novel *Kicking In Danger*. He played football in the 40s for South Melbourne, then known as the Bloods, later the Swans, later the Sydney Swans.

Zara Holt was a prominent Melbourne socialite who was the wife and later the widow of PM Harold Holt.

'Mad as hell…' refers to the wonderfully excessive and even better prophetic rave by Peter Finch in the 1976 movie *Network*.

Don's Party is a benchmark play (later a film) centred on the night of the 1969 Federal Election.

Readings is Melbourne's preeminent book store chain. The author has had quite a few memorable launches at its Carlton headquarters. Even better *The New York Times* recently mentioned Readings Carlton as one of Melbourne's highlights.

Light on the Hill… refers to an iconic speech by Labor Party leader Ben Chifley, Prime Minister 1945-1949.

'Honest Abe' is of course Abraham Lincoln.

Credlin and Bolt are right-wing polemicists.

Mr Squiggle was a television puppet beloved by generations of children.

Vanessa 'Van' Badham, a friend of the author, is the kind of leftist/activist/polemicist that takes on the Fee-Bees and Dropkicks of this world and wins.

Julian Burnside and Robert Richter are leading Melbourne barristers.

www.ingramcontent.com/pod-product-compliance
Lightning Source LLC
Chambersburg PA
CBHW011650010726
47497CB00011B/3198